Elizabeth Gill
Doctor of the High Fells

Quercus

First published in Great Britain in 2015 by

Quercus Publishing Ltd
Carmelite House
50 Victoria Embankment
London EC4Y 0DZ

An Hachette UK company

A CIP catalogue record for this book is available
from the British Library

PB ISBN 978 1 78429 148 8
EBOOK ISBN 978 1 78429 147 1

10 9 8 7 6 5 4 3 2 1

Typeset by CC Book Production
Printed and Bound by Clays Ltd, St Ives plc

For my lovely friend Joan and in memory
of Malcolm and Barrie.

Author's note

Determined to write about the first women doctors, I started reading about doctors in Britain but the most interesting stories came from the first American female doctors. My book was inspired by *Pioneer Doctor, the Story of a Woman's Work*, which is written by Mari Grana about her grandmother Dr Mary Babcock, who was known as Dr Mollie. The part that really got me was that she went off to be a doctor in a mining camp, so I thought: why not send my doctor to a pit village? If it hadn't been for this book I wouldn't have been half as bold about my own woman doctor. Dr Molly's achievements must have been inspiring women ever since. To Molly and her granddaughter, my thanks.

One

It had been July and as hot as hell the day that they buried Silas's father. His mother, full-bosomed and sturdy in black, had not cried once. Silas spent the entire time looking down at his shoes.

The heat in the graveyard was unbearable, not helped by everybody wearing black.

Dr Stanhope had dropped down dead in his surgery – which Prue thought could not have impressed his patients much, seeing as he was only sixty. It was his heart apparently. Prue thought that could not be true, the man had no heart. He was so disliked that she was amazed anyone came to the funeral, but they did, out of respect for his profession.

She had dealt with the funeral directors. Mrs Stanhope, having taken to her bed, like some heroine of old, had been no help and Prue's husband, Silas, claiming he had too much to do, had retreated to his own surgery. It was Prue who ordered the coffin, decided on the wood, chose the hymns, booked the venue at a local hotel – she had wanted to include 'Now Thank We All Our God', but she didn't think it was appropriate – and let people know about the burial. She thought she would never forget all the black-edged letters. She had written until her fingers cramped.

She could not blame Silas entirely, because he had heard the noise from his surgery and gone through to find his father slumped on the floor. Prue had never known her own father, and was mystified as to how to comfort her husband when he turned from her in bed, and was silent when they sat at the dining table, no one eating anything. Prue found it all the harder because when her mother had died the year before, all he said was, 'Everybody has to die some time you know,' and it was never mentioned again.

Only having had one parent, Prue found the loss of her mother hard, and the fact that neither Silas nor his parents had any concern for her made it harder still. There was no such thing as mourning – not until now, of course.

But if one's father dying were as bad as one's mother, then Prue *was* inclined to feel sorry for Silas, even if his father was the kind of man who shouted and swore, was given to drink and often had to be sent away from evening surgery because he could not stand up. Silas said that his father was a disappointed man. He had wanted to be a surgeon but couldn't stand the sight of blood. It occurred to her that perhaps a different profession would have suited the man better.

He complained about the state of the house, the food, the patients. Prue could not help being glad that he was not there any more to complain about anything else. She had been very tired of him. Nobody acknowledged that her own father had died when she was a small child, or that her mother had had to cope and bring her up and manage alone. They seemed to think, if they thought at all, that if your father died when you were a child and hardly remembered him, then it didn't matter.

When the funeral came and went, and the mourners had finally gone, Silas's mother said that she was glad she had decided that alcohol should not be served at the funeral. Prue, whose mother had taught her to appreciate a Martini or two, couldn't agree.

'You'll have to move in,' Mrs Stanhope said. 'I cannot go on living in that big house all by myself.'

This was something Prue had not foreseen. She was happy in her little home, well away from Silas's parents' grand house in Upper Manhattan. It was a very successful practice and the house reflected that, with its huge gaping rooms that had always to her seemed full of the sound of Dr Stanhope's raised voice.

'You could sell it,' she said.

Silas's mother looked at her for the first time that day, but it was Silas who said, 'That's where the practice is, Prue, that's where the money is made, and you and I will have to carry on the practice by ourselves so living there would be much easier.'

'I don't see why we should leave our house,' Prue told Silas later, when he had said he would go back to their house for what they would need that night. They were outside his parents' house and it was as hot as ever. Prue felt as if she couldn't breathe. She had never wanted to go into a house less. In the darkness it now felt more alien than ever. She could remember the first time she had stepped inside, and Silas's father had looked her up and down as if she were a prize cow.

'I daresay she will breed. She's big enough.'

It was Silas who had made it all worthwhile. He had hated his father. But now it seemed everything had changed.

'It isn't practical to run two houses, and we could hardly ask my mother to live with us,' he said, and his face had such a strained look that she could only say,

'I love our house.'

He kissed her before he turned away, but off he went and Prue was left standing outside a house she had never liked. His mother had gone in so she took several deep breaths and followed her up the long, wide steps.

The hall was dark but mercifully cool, the house being old. The maid, Nelson, was there to take her outdoor things. Prue had no idea what Nelson's first name was, or even her origins. Her name could have been something else, should have been in fact – she was coloured, but only lightly, and had the look of someone whose ancestors had been Spaniards. Possibly she was Mexican, or from some place further south. She rarely spoke.

Prue followed her mother-in-law into the drawing room. Mrs Stanhope was standing looking out at the garden.

'Would you like some coffee?' Prue ventured to ask. She would rather have had lemonade herself, but Mrs Stanhope drank nothing but coffee.

'I've had quite sufficient coffee for one day,' she replied. 'What a ramshackle affair that was. He would have hated it.'

Prue stopped herself from saying that he had hated everything.

'We ought to have had people here, not at a hotel as though we had no class,' his mother said. 'I was ashamed.'

Prue did not point out that she had offered to have the mourners at the house, but that her mother-in-law had said she could not stand the idea. She had given Mrs Stanhope a choice of hotels, but Mrs Stanhope had gone to her bed and stayed there.

And then the only good thing about the day happened, because Mrs Stanhope went off to bed, leaving Prue sighing with relief.

When Silas came back, they had dinner. It was awful. The meals in that house always were because Mrs Stanhope objected to the tradesmen's bills and bought everything cheap. Meat full of gristle, smelly fish, soggy vegetables and not a dab of butter anywhere. Prue thought such things would send you to gin and vermouth. She understood now why her mother had liked to view the world through a mild alcoholic haze. Unfortunately there was nothing in the house except ginger wine from last Christmas.

She had coffee, which Silas told her would keep her up all night. It was only when she went to bed that she found that her suitcase was in one room, and his another.

'My mother doesn't approve of people sleeping in the same bed.'

'We are married,' Prue pointed out. He only smiled and said,

'She's old-fashioned. She comes from a time when each person had a room. Just bear with her, eh?'

Too tired to argue, Prue closed the door and undressed, and although she thought she would stay awake, the day had been so trying that she fell asleep almost instantly.

They went back to work the following day. Prue sat in the side room. This was how she thought of it. It was her surgery, something she had striven for, been proud of. Now she was bored. She listened to Silas's mother directing people toward his room, deliberately she thought.

The city in summer was stifling. The heat drove people mad, she knew. They had no means of getting away from it and she longed to be out there doing whatever she could to help. In such circumstances it was women who were heavily pregnant or giving birth and those who were dying who had it worst of all, and so many of them were poor and in need of just about everything, and here she was sitting, doing nothing. Silas's mother maintained that he had not gone through medical school for such reasons and when Prue had said to him, 'Is this true? Do you think only to treat the middle classes and not get out there where people need you?' he had said,

'People need me here,' and of course he was right. He did not hold with fanciful ideas about the poor. To him poor people were those who did not try hard enough, who sat idly by while the rest toiled. They did not deserve treatment that they could not pay for.

Each day people plodded to his surgery and told him their woes and their worries and their aches and pains, and many of them really *were* ill, but, as time went by, even from her side room she could see the motor cars, big and shiny, the chauffeurs and the elderly women, short and overweight, their bloated feet spilling over their expensive shoes, wearing huge white hats and easing themselves briefly into the heat of the sun, gaining the cool of Silas's surgery with its tiled floor, iced water and her husband's smooth manner.

Over dinner sometimes she would mention one or other of these women, and Silas would brush it aside, but she knew some of them and they were suffering from boredom. She knew they paid well, she did not know how Silas endured it. He did not need the money, his father had done the same for decades, they were well off. This house was their only extravagant purchase – they had no social life, his mother wore cheap dresses. No penny was spent that could be saved.

Day after day, Prue waited for patients without complaint, and since he was not given to talking about his patients over meals, or even later when the evening surgery was ended, it was not until he said to her, 'I have too much to do, you could help,' that Prue gazed at him in hope.

They had been sleeping apart for weeks now, and earlier that month when she had given up waiting for him to go into her bedroom and had crept into his, he had only said that it was too hot for such things.

She thought it had more to do with the fact that his mother was sleeping across the hall. Prue could hear her snoring.

She had offered to take some of his patients and he had refused, saying that she was such a very new doctor, that they knew him best and that they asked for him, believed in his ability. Prue could have argued that she had years of experience, working in hospitals. Often she wished she was back there.

'I need a nurse,' he said.

They had had a nurse before his father died, but his mother had somehow quarrelled with the woman, accused her of not working, said that she was idle, and the woman had been offended and left. Since then his mother had managed somehow. Silas had said too that there was not sufficient money to hire a replacement.

'Will you do it, Prue, until we find someone else?'

He asked her so politely that she did not know how to refuse. So as the summer turned into autumn and the leaves slowly died and crisped, she wore a nurse's uniform and contributed nothing to his diagnoses. She saw people in and out and took their temperatures and made notes and ensured they had the right medication. All that autumn and into Christmas she was his nurse. Every time she complained he agreed that they really must hire someone new, but he did not do anything about it.

As the festive season approached, she was dreading spending the day just the three of them. She began to long for the Christmases of her childhood when her father was still alive and they were happy and reasonably prosperous. Her father had been an artist of some repute. After her father died, Christmas was never as good again and she and her mother became poorer. She noticed as she grew older that the paintings her mother stored in the bedroom were fewer and there were big spaces on the walls.

The house in Greenwich Village was small, but her mother had friends there among the musicians, painters, writers and even circus performers who often came to eat, and she would take Prue to see them. Prue always felt loved and safe. Other than that she would sit with her mother over the kitchen fire and her mother would read to her. She longed to feel like that now.

Her mother's last Christmas had been spent at the Stanhopes' house. The house was decorated, the fire was lit and Silas's mother was offering her mother sweet sherry. Her mother detested sherry. She accepted the tiny glass with a smile.

Prue had looked objectively at her mother and was shocked at how thin and sparrow-like she had become. When they sat down at the table, Mrs Stanhope said, 'Don't you wish you could sit down to a dinner such as this every week?'

Prue's mother nodded. She did not say that she hated the smell and taste of turkey. Mrs Stanhope wondered at the smallness of her appetite. Prue could have told her that her mother would go home, sit over her own fire, read, drink gin, play records of her friends' music and eat cheese and apples and crusty bread thick with yellow butter and be much happier there.

That Christmas was as bad as it could possibly have been, Prue thought.

Silas's mother had by now dismissed Nelson. She thought the girl was insolent, though as far as Prue could tell Nelson was no such thing. The cleaning and the meals and the washing and ironing all had to be done, and Mrs Stanhope had such high standards that Prue appealed to them both again and again to hire another maid.

'I'm wasted doing such work,' she said.

His mother sniffed.

'Being a wife was good enough for some of us.'

'You were not qualified to do anything else,' Prue said.

'No, and I think these things worked better when women were content at home.'

'I will be content when we have a maid and a nurse. I am not fit to be either,' Prue said.

His mother tut-tutted and said that women ought be brought up to be good at such things, and then she added, 'I would have said that these things come naturally – except that obviously they do not.'

Prue was stung by this criticism both of herself and of her mother, who had been obliged to raise her daughter single-handedly – over the years selling everything she had in order to put her through her education and medical school – but she knew it wouldn't help so she said nothing.

The pretty house where Silas and Prue had started married life together had been sold and since his mother had enough furniture, he said, he had to sell theirs, and all Prue had left were her personal possessions, her books, her clothes, the little jewellery which she had – only her wedding ring had been from him. She owned an elegant string of black pearls, which had been her grandmother's, a cameo brooch which her mother had given her and a thin gold signet ring which had been her father's.

Soon after Christmas they hired another maid since Prue refused to go on doing the cooking and cleaning, and she thought that things would be easier, but still Silas's mother directed the household. She said what they would eat and when, she dealt with the maid and whether her son's collars were still dirty after they had supposedly been scrubbed and starched.

Silas took to going out in the evenings, not explaining himself except to say that he was seeing friends, men only, and Prue would sit over the fire with his mother, darning socks as she was shown how and being told that she really must learn to be more practical.

One night in February Silas came back late, she had waited up for him after his mother had gone to bed. He smelled of liquor and some sweet scent, but he said only that he had met a couple they knew in the street and how he had embraced his friend's wife.

'Are you never coming back to my bed?' She had long wanted to say this, but somehow his mother was always in the way.

'Well of course,' he said, 'it's been difficult, I know. I don't want my mother here any more than you do but I think we are used to her now and it is her house – and a fine place, you must acknowledge – and we will inherit it. Why don't you go upstairs and I'll be there shortly?'

She did so and he came to her very soon afterwards, taking her into his arms as he had when they were first married and calling her his dear love and she was so happy. From then on they slept together and if his mother was aware of it, she had too much sense to say anything,

He hired a nurse three mornings a week so that Prue could go back to being a doctor. It made her happy.

That summer she had symptoms so strange to her that she was not sure what was happening. Her bleeding stopped, her breasts were tender and she was tired. In the end she laughed because she had not realized that she was going to have a child.

When she told Silas's mother, Mrs Stanhope wept with joy and said that she must take good care of herself and that she hoped it would be a boy and look just like Silas's father, she missed him so much.

The nurse began to come in five days a week and do both surgeries and though Prue would have gone on seeing people, had there been anyone who wished to see her, there were times when she was so tired that all she wanted to do was sleep. She had not thought that pregnancy did such strange things to women.

Once again, when she felt better, about four months into her pregnancy, she would sit in her side room watching the people come to her husband, and listening to his mother's voice directing them into his room.

One hot night when Silas was out seeing someone – she was not quite sure who but he had not taken his doctor's bag so it could not be a patient – there was a banging on the door. When his mother opened it, she found a small girl begging for a doctor, for her mother was dying. Mrs Stanhope said it was not one of their patients and nothing to do with them, but Prue could not sit there while someone needed help.

His mother begged her not to intervene, but she was determined. She followed the child down street after street, half believing that she would be robbed and assaulted, but finally she came to the poor lodging where the child's mother lay. Her husband and several small children sat by the bed and they were poor, she could see. The woman held her stomach, and at first Prue thought that she was pregnant, and then she realized it was something quite different. The heat had been intense for weeks now and many people suffered from it. She questioned the woman and found that her body was not functioning, she was not passing urine. Until she did so, she would become worse and worse.

She sent the children and their father from the room with many reassurances and then she took a catheter from her bag and inserted it into the woman. It was a difficult process, especially in dim light, but it worked and it was one of those things where when you got it right it was like a miracle – the woman's body responded at once and the urine flowed. She could feel her patient sigh with relief as the pot Prue had found filled up and she had to employ the washing bowl.

It looked like a cheap trick once it was done, but many a doctor had ruptured something inside a patient trying to carry out such a procedure and Prue could not help smiling to herself that she had eased her patient with so little effort.

When it was over she was able to call in the oldest child, a girl, who went off with the bowl and then came back for the pot. After that Prue allowed the husband and the children in. She urged the woman to rest, but she thought there would be no problem from now on. She must drink plenty of water. She knew what the problem was – they were a big family and someone had to ensure that everybody was kept well hydrated in such weather. It must be easy for a woman to forget herself.

The husband came out of the bedroom and thanked her and asked how much it would be for her services, but Prue only shook her head and urged him to go back to his wife, she would see herself out. She was satisfied with what she had achieved.

As daylight broke, she picked up her black bag and made her way onto the shadowed landing and there she tripped upon the loose carpet, lost her balance and fell, step by bouncing step. She could have counted each one, it seemed that she was moving slowly and very quickly all at once. She did not remember reaching the bottom.

*

When she came to, she was lying in her bed at home and was aware only of pain and of dampness between her thighs. After that it was just a question of how soon she could be rid of the pain. When it stopped, Silas took what would have been his child from her body. Prue closed her eyes against the savage sun which beat through her window unopposed.

He did not speak to her again that day, as though the loss were all his. She longed to cry but couldn't. It was as though the well had run dry. She felt empty.

She stayed upstairs for a week, until she was strong enough to venture down. Her mother-in-law was silent and her husband too, as though it had been all her fault. Now she looked back on it and thought that they were right.

After a fortnight, when she was feeling much better, she wanted to go back into the side room to help with surgery, but his mother said he had turned that room into an office for the accountant who had lots of good ideas about the practice and was helping them make more money.

'Besides, you should rest,' his mother said.

The next time that Prue found herself alone with her husband she said to him, 'Can we not try again for a child? I'm sure you wish it so.'

He looked deep into her eyes and he said,

'You lost our child. You cared so little for it. You risked it when you should not have done.'

She was so upset that she couldn't argue. She went to bed and cried hard and then in the morning she remembered his words and cried again. She could not go to him and he did not come to her and the weeks went on. Her surgery had long since been cleared and her name was gone from the outside door. She gazed at the space where it had been for a long time.

He suggested to her that she should do as other women did. She could learn to sew and do charity work – she liked helping people, why not? She didn't know how to do such things; she was a doctor. She ached to help, but there was no opportunity afforded her. In the end, she could do nothing but go for long walks and take air and try not to think.

His mother wanted to go with her, much to Prue's horror, but she would insist on looking around the shops and would not stop for coffee or for lunch. 'We have plenty of food at home, thank goodness, I don't need new clothes and neither do you.'

Prue couldn't see why she bothered at all since she rarely bought anything.

Prue didn't know that she was going to walk out. She had not thought of such a thing. She had grown used to the guilt of losing the child and the everyday monotony, but gradually she wanted to be there less and less until she couldn't stand another week and then another day. There must have been some spark of ambition left, because something compelled her to pack a bag, take what little money she possessed and go. It was the only thing she could think of. She didn't know how she would get away but she found the strength. She left the house mid-morning – she did not even plan it, she could have left earlier in the day or late at night – but in the end she just left.

As she went, Prue had the feeling that Silas was at her heels like a large dog, snapping there, ready to march her back to Manhattan. She had sufficient money for the train to Boston, where her best friend, Alicia, lived. Alicia's parents were musicians and had been good friends with Prue's mother for as long as she could remember. The two girls were more like sisters, but Silas had come between them and then Alicia had married and moved away.

Prue argued with herself on the train, saying that she should not be there, that she must go back, that she could not just land on Alicia like this.

Alicia's husband, John Harvey, was a wealthy man and Prue did not know him very well, so when she found herself, weighed down with her bags full of medical books, without a penny to get herself beyond Alicia's house, she knew that she should not have come. This was the best part of town, the most lavish of Boston's streets. The Harvey banking family was among the richest in the city and the house was set so far away from the street that at first she could not bring herself to approach, so she stood on the sidewalk and wept.

At last she walked towards the house. Her first fear was that Alicia would not be home – her second was that she would be – but if Alicia was not there then Prue would have to go back to New York, would have to wire Silas for her train fare. She thought she would rather live on the streets.

The long drive was set in what looked to her like a park, the grounds were huge. Eventually the house rose before her and sat there in such splendid triumph that she thought she should go round to the back, like a tradesperson. Eventually there was nothing else to do, so she left her bags and climbed up the long narrow steps to the front door and rang the bell.

Almost instantly, a maid opened the door. Prue had not prepared for this. She said her name and half expected to be turned away, there was a slight delay and a rustle of silk from the hall, and then a young woman threw back the door as far as it would go and flung herself at Prue, kissing her and holding her face and laughing, and Prue thought for the first time that she had done the right thing.

Alicia called for Prue's bags to be taken in and she herself was just the same as she had always been, with her plump body and plain, kindly face. The whole of New York and Boston society had been astonished when John Harvey chose such a woman for his wife. He was the crème de la crème and could have had anybody.

Alicia wore a grey dress so plain that she could have been mistaken for the housekeeper, though its silver threads gave away its expense as the two women moved into the sunlight of the hall, but it was modest for all that and without ornament. She ushered her surprise guest into an opulent drawing room. It had high ceilings and huge furniture, two fireplaces, floor-to-ceiling windows. Outside were walled gardens stretching for as far as anyone could see.

Alicia had come from a humble background. Her father was a pianist and her mother a violinist. They had been taken aback when she wanted to marry a banker but made no protest. Her father had died just after she and John were married.

Alicia had been married now for three years. Although she had invited Prue and Silas to come and stay more than once, Silas was always too busy, so he said, and although Prue had badly wanted to see her dearest friend, she had not felt that she could go alone.

As they sat, Alicia tried to get information from Prue, and Prue tried to pretend that it was not important. They had tea from a silver teapot, although Prue's hands shook so much that she could barely sip the hot liquid. Alicia offered her cake and tiny diamond-shaped sandwiches, but she was not hungry. She just wanted to go on sitting there forever, basking in her friend's joy at her arrival, because she was starting to feel that even Alicia would censor her for what she had done once she found out what had happened.

She watched Alicia's mouth go into a line and then Alicia looked seriously at her and said, 'What has gone wrong?'

It sounded so small. All she could manage was, 'I've left Silas.'

Alicia stared and then her eyes filled with sympathy. 'Oh, Prue,' she said, 'how awful for you.'

After that it was easy to tell the whole tale, and by the time John Harvey came home to dinner at seven, Prue was ensconced in what had to be the very best bedroom. It was vast, with its own sitting room, and a maid had been to unpack Prue's bags, so now she was arranged in a newly ironed dress, although one which had been hastily packed and not suitable for such an occasion. She was ashamed that she had not a decent dress.

She wanted to stay hidden upstairs. All she could remember of her friend's husband was that he was tall and handsome. She did not want to face another man. Surely he would take Silas's part, and what could she say in her own defence? She was half convinced that Silas was seeing another woman, but she could not say such a thing before John Harvey. After all, many men did such things and their wives did not run away.

She went over and over the things she could say which had led to her escape but none of them sounded even remotely relevant. He would despise her. She walked up and down the room until the clock struck half an hour after she should have been in the dining room, so she rang for the maid and let her guide her to where they were apparently having drinks before dinner, feeling worse because they had been waiting for her, not able to go into the dining room until she appeared. She had hated the idea of other guests, but it was obvious there were none. Perhaps her friends had thought their evening would be just the two of them and she had spoiled it.

John Harvey was standing by the fire and his wife was with him. She had not changed her dress and he was still wearing the suit which no doubt he wore for business, so it was informal in that sense. They had not dressed up because she could not. She thought it the height of good manners.

John came forward straight away and kissed her.

'Prue,' he said, 'wonderful to see you.'

He was so tall that Prue couldn't see past him. He was also slender with bright-blue eyes and a shock of black hair, the handsomest man that Prue had ever met. She felt such envy of Alicia that she had to suppress the feeling.

He offered her a drink and made it himself, much to her astonishment. It was a very large Martini and it made Prue feel better than she had felt in months. The double doors opened into another room, and to Prue's relief there were still no servants. They sat at a small table before the fire and helped themselves as they chose to a variety of dishes which were already on the table. Nobody questioned her. John told funny stories and Alicia laughed and Prue could not remember the last time she had had such a pleasant evening.

When it was late Alicia saw her up the stairs to her room where a generous fire had been lit, the curtains closed against the night. Alicia promised her shopping and excursions if she liked, but Prue faltered. Alicia became serious.

'Money is not a problem,' she said.

Prue tried hard not to cry.

'I cannot go back,' she said.

'You don't have to go back.' Alicia sat down beside her on the bed. 'John and I will help you. We know that you have not left Silas lightly, you wouldn't do such a thing and you are so thin and distressed. You adored him. Go to bed and don't worry. We'll look after you. In the morning we will work out what to do, but we won't turn our backs on you, no matter what.'

The next day, Prue wrote to the professor who had helped her so much when she was a medical student. Professor Albert MacKinnon, known as Professor Mick, had been an inspiration to the women on the course when she went to medical school. When she became a doctor she had begun working with Silas, but Professor Mick, who was going back to Scotland, had said, half joking but his brown eyes were serious, that he thought she was a fine doctor and if she ever wanted more experience she should cross the Atlantic and he would find her work. He wanted to encourage British women and the sight of her there would help them. He was in Edinburgh now, his home.

She stayed with Alicia and John for over two weeks, hoping that she was not intruding and aware that she must leave.

John Harvey, being a straightforward kind of man, had told her gently that he did not want to make her anxious but, since he had to go to work every day but Sunday, he would not leave her unprotected and after that two burly men were ensconced in a small room off the hall, should Silas come for his wife.

At first she laughed and said that she was fine, Silas would never hurt her. John said, 'I don't know Silas very well, but he would not be a man if he didn't come here, knowing how close you and Alicia have always been, to try to make you go back to New York with him. You will not be going anywhere except as you choose.'

She went out with Alicia every day, to museums, concerts and shows, because although she was worried and anxious, she didn't want Alicia to have to put up with a tedious guest. And, besides, it was pleasant to hear music and to laugh at comedy, to go back to the lovely house every evening. She became good friends with John Harvey and was grateful for his support.

Professor Mick wrote back very soon, saying that she should come to Scotland, that he was certain he would find work for her there. She regarded his letter with a mixture of fear and excitement and showed it to her friends.

John said, 'I'm sorry, but from what I've seen of Silas he wasn't worthy of you.'

'You shouldn't say such things,' Alicia said. She frowned, though Prue could see she didn't quite mean it when she said to her husband, 'A good number of my mother's friends weren't impressed with you on our wedding day. As I recall, you drank like a fish.'

John pulled a face and looked apologetically at Prue.

'And her Aunt Willis told her that if she married me she'd never see any of her money.'

'And I didn't either,' Alicia said, 'she died and left it to Audrey.' Audrey was Alicia's unmarried sister, so she needed all the money she could get. 'Silas seemed a perfectly nice man – I'm sure he still is – but you just aren't suited and things change after people are married. His mother is a very difficult woman. You didn't know you were going to have to live with her.' Alicia shuddered. 'I wouldn't like to live with John's mother.'

This wasn't true, John's mother was a lovely woman. It occurred to Prue that in some ways John had married his mother, Alicia was so like her. His mother was independent, strong-minded, large, red-faced, funny and adored Alicia. Prue could remember John's mother saying to different people on their wedding day, 'I don't know why Alicia wants to take him on, he's so impossible.' They had all laughed because they knew that she admired and loved her son as much as Alicia did.

She did not interfere, Alicia had said so often. She lived just far enough away that everyone was able to stand everyone else. It was hard not to envy Alicia and John. They seemed to have everything.

That night, however, when it was late, Alicia knocked on the door of Prue's room. Prue couldn't help crying. She tried to pretend she wasn't.

'I lost our baby.'

'It wasn't your fault.'

Alicia sat down on the bed.

'I didn't behave as a mother, I behaved as a doctor.'

'It was your job to be there.'

'It cost me my child and my marriage.'

'No it didn't. It just highlighted the difficulties of your circumstances.'

Prue sat back, dried her tears, but shook her head.

'So what would you do now,' her friend said, 'if it happened again?'

Prue was silent only for a moment.

'The same thing.'

'Of course you would,' Alicia said, and kissed her. She would have got up, but Prue caught hold of her by the arm.

'You and John have no baby either.'

Alicia didn't look at her.

'I've miscarried twice.'

'You didn't say anything.'

'I was so disappointed. I don't know whether we'll ever have a child. John says it doesn't matter and so does his mother, but I feel as if I've failed.'

'You know there isn't much evidence to prove these things one way or another and it isn't necessarily anyone's fault, even the husband's,' Prue said as gently as she could.

'I've seen a specialist.'

'And has John?'

Alicia hesitated.

'Don't give up hope,' Prue said. 'Most doctors don't know what they're talking about.'

Alicia smiled.

'I shall keep that in mind,' she said.

It had been such a shock when Silas turned up without letting her know, as though she was a parcel he had mislaid. He was casual and confident, his eyes were clear and his smile was not warm. He was irritated with her, as he might have been with a small child who had tried to run away in a huff.

'What on earth are you doing here?' Silas asked.

'I needed help,' she said.

'What kind of help?'

'Financial.'

He didn't understand, she could tell by the way he looked so blankly at her.

'Why would you need such a thing? We live well. What do you have here that you don't have with me?'

His eyes showed desperation. She was surprised.

'I am a doctor.'

'You're my wife first.'

'No, I'm your wife second. That's the problem.'

'I don't understand what you mean.'

'You put me after your practice, but you expect me to put you before mine.'

'Isn't that natural?'

'Not for me.'

'But you're a woman. A husband and children must come first.'

'Not in medicine. I thought you understood that, but you have demonstrated very clearly that you don't.'

'I never thought that. I wouldn't have married you if I had thought that your role as wife and mother would not come first.'

Prue tried to think back to their first meetings. They had worked at the same hospital before he went into practice with his father. They had discussed their work, their ideas and she had learned to love him at the same time, and of course they would have children, but she did not remember a single instance where he had tried to make her into something she had not been until they were married and she had joined him in the practice. Perhaps she had been unfair to him. He had certainly been unfair to her. As far as she was concerned her marriage was over.

Nobody spoke for a few moments and Silas gazed around him at the Harveys' beautiful drawing room. It was like something out of a museum. It had been John's grandfather's house and his family had always been very wealthy. Had they begun in railroads? Prue was not sure; nobody said anything about it.

As Silas gazed around him, Prue realized what these things meant to him. It was not enough to live decently and help those who needed it, you had to take more than your share in order to impress other people. And there was something sad about that. Why did everything have to be the best for him? Yet here she was, staying with her rich friends, so she looked just as bad.

A house like this was what he wanted. His parents had brought him up to want it. They had been so proud of him. He had achieved as much as his father, but surely you were meant to do different things from your parents, or where was the point in it?

'I knew you would be here,' Silas said. 'You always preferred John Harvey to me.'

She wanted to say that this was not the case. Silas's comment was ridiculous, she had barely known John before this but she had grown to like him and the trouble was, she knew, that when a woman was seen to like a man, others saw it as something sexual, whereas she felt about John as she did about her woman friends. She loved him because he was warm, kind, trusting, sure. She could not imagine what it would be like to kiss John and she felt that it was the same for him. He liked and admired her, but he did not want her.

She knew that Silas now wanted John to be his friend rather than hers, because John was so important, so influential. She did not care for such things. Her mother had always known people with talent, with gifts, but no one prosperous, and Prue did not care. She had the feeling that Silas's parents had kept such friendships from him.

John was so successful that other men envied him. He could have had almost any woman he wanted, so it was all the better that he chose Alicia, who was short and round and had unruly brown hair and a smile which could have lit the world. Prue could see why he had chosen her, though. She was so kind and, besides that, she was like a firework with her dear friends, private but fun. She spoke ill of no one.

'You must come back to New York and I will forgive you,' Silas said. Silas flailed his hands in comic despair, and tried to smile at her. 'You cannot care for Boston so very much.'

'I want a divorce,' she said.

Silas stared at her as though she were a strange being who had just entered the room, and then he laughed. The laughter seemed to go on for a very long time. She kept waiting for it to end and when it did he went back to staring at her for a few moments as though he could not believe what he was hearing.

'You're ridiculous,' he said.

'John has found me a good lawyer.'

There was silence again and he glared at her.

'You're his mistress.'

'I'm nothing of the kind. I don't want to go on being married to you. You have demonstrated clearly how little I matter—'

'That isn't true!'

'I'm a doctor. I am not your housekeeper, your maid or your nurse; I'm not the person who will endure your mother, and I cannot stand it any longer. I am going away and I will do so no matter what you think or say or do, and I will have a divorce. You do not own me, Silas, and it's poor of you to think that you did.'

Silas laughed, but in a way that held no mirth and his eyes were full of anger.

'You could never practise medicine as a divorced woman,' he said.

'I'm not staying here,' she said, 'I will be gone as soon as we are legally separated.'

'I won't let you do it.'

'I think you will find that I can file for divorce and you cannot stop me.' John Harvey had sufficient influence to do anything, she thought, but she didn't say it. Silas made as if to come across the room to her.

'Don't make this worse than it is,' she said. Silas stopped where he was, looking down, as though very disappointed.

'I will try to forgive you now, but this must never happen again. Your behaviour is disgracing my family. You have to come back and remember that you are my wife first. So, if you will go and collect your belongings, my car is outside.'

'I would consider it only if I am to be your full partner in the business, and if we have a house of our own and I have my own money and you do not ask me to do nursing or housemaiding.'

Silas looked at her in astonishment.

'You are in no position to make conditions. You are my wife and you will come home.'

'No.'

'You cannot stay here indefinitely.'

'I don't intend to. John has offered me a loan.'

She had been embarrassed at first, but was too practical to refuse the offer. Having borrowed as little money as she thought she might manage on and swearing to pay it back with such quickness that John Harvey shook his head and smiled, she felt better. She did not want to be in debt, but her greatest feeling now was that she never wanted to see New York or Silas Stanhope or his mother ever again.

Silas's eyes widened.

'He has no right to do any such thing, and with you as a married woman I would doubt the legality of such a procedure.'

'Silas, this is not a game. I am a doctor and I will not give it up for you or anyone.'

Silas said very softly, 'I think you have lost your mind.'

'Do you know for how long men have been telling women that they have lost their minds because they don't agree with their husbands?'

'You must pack now. I shall wait in the hall.'

'I'm not going.'

'If you can't think of me, at least think of our responsibilities, think of our name, think of my mother and my family's good reputation in New York. Come on, be quick. I have left a long list of sick people waiting for me and I have to get back.'

'Then go.'

He made as if to lunge toward her and she cried out though she didn't mean to and, very soon afterwards, two large men appeared in the doorway. She cursed herself and then she cursed John for being right and leaving these people to look after her when she had told him proudly that they would not be needed, that Silas would never try to make her do anything which was so much against her will. Silas stayed where he was, aghast, white-faced and furious.

He stared at the two men. They said nothing but one of them held open the door. The other went and stood beside Prue.

'I will never divorce you,' Silas told her.

'The law is a very useful thing,' Prue said. 'I think you will.'

Silas left in a flurry of agitated movement. Had he had the chance she imagined he would have slammed the door. Prue couldn't see by then. Tears of failure blurred her eyes.

In the evening, when John had come home and they were sitting in the lovely little sitting room and when they had each had two large Martinis, he said, 'Why don't you stay in Boston and set up a practice here?'

'You should, Prue,' Alicia said. 'We could see so much of each another.'

'With me divorced? People would talk.'

'What does it matter?' John said.

Prue thought how wonderful it must be to be so rich and important that you knew people would always accept you.

Kind as he was, though, she knew that people would soon become aware that he was financing her, and they would think she was his mistress. Doctors did not gain good reputations from such rumours, and though she loved them both she did not want to cause them any more problems.

Two

Tow Law, County Durham

The train deposited her in a tiny station. There was no porter, and no one on the platform. The snow was forming in peaks all around, still hurling itself sideways. She hoisted up her luggage again, regretting having brought with her so many books, which were heavier than she could ever have imagined. She had just got everything out when a man appeared out of nowhere to close the train door.

He disappeared back into the whiteness, and Prue stood on the dark platform as the train chugged away, very soon disappearing out of sight. She felt like a neglected relative and worse. Her stomach churned, and she couldn't feel her toes or her fingers. She didn't know what to do. She had written to say she would be there, but she knew that the train was very late and it seemed nobody had come to meet her.

She dragged her suitcases beyond the platform, but there was nothing but snow and thick darkness.

Just as she was about to give up and go in search of somebody, she heard a noise – a shout of 'Whoa, lad!' – and a buggy coming to a halt. A shadowy figure came towards her until he was but a few feet away, and then he said, 'Hello, lass. Are you the only one?'

He was an older man, though it was difficult to tell but for his voice, he was so muffled up against the weather.

'It seems that way,' she said.

He gazed around him.

'Nobody else got off?'

'Nobody.'

His look returned to her. He stared.

'Have you come for me?' she asked hesitantly.

'I've come to collect the new doctor,' he said.

'That's me. I'm Doctor Prudence Stanhope.'

He stared for a few seconds longer and then, as though it were amusing, he began to smile.

'Well, by damn, it's you I've come for then. Welcome to the wilds, pet. They told me the train would be late.' He picked up her bags, one by one, and stowed them in the back of the buggy. Then he came back and helped her up, before getting up himself. At his urging the pony moved away.

The snow was settling on her shoulders, and on his, and on the pony's back – flakes got into the pony's black mane and shone there like stars. The driver said they had not far to go, and she was grateful. At first she couldn't see anything, but almost immediately there was the little town, the terraced houses, the wide street. They stopped about ten minutes afterwards.

He took her luggage to the door and knocked hard. She was astonished at the place. She had thought the house would be big and in its own grounds, or at least set back from the road, but this was an ordinary street, an end terrace, quite large but right on the roadside. It was just another house, windows up and down and a door in the middle. The road climbed away up a steep hill on the right with buildings at either side; she couldn't see what they were.

There was no bell on the door, no knocker, so Prue stood and waited while the man banged his fists on the door again. There was silence from the house beyond, but after a little while, when he tried even more loudly, Prue discerned a light from inside, and at last the door was opened.

The young woman who opened it, lamp in hand, was small, slight, and looked to Prue no more than eighteen. She stared out at them. Prue imagined she was the help, so plainly was she dressed. She didn't invite Prue in, just gazed at her and at her suitcases. As Prue stared back, she saw that the woman was pregnant, just a slight bump which would not have shown in a larger or more generous figure. It caused a slight pain in Prue, remembering how her life used to be. Guilt swept her like a cold wind. Would she feel like this every time she saw a pregnant woman?

'I'm Dr Stanhope,' Prue said, moving forward.

'I'm Dr Fleming's wife,' the girl said, and she opened the door wider.

Three

The bags were taken inside, and Prue was aware of the pony and trap going off. She was so tired. She didn't want any new experiences now: all she wanted was to go home, but she didn't know where home was any more; New York was Silas's home, Boston was only the place where Alicia and John had helped her and Edinburgh had been nothing but a temporary refuge while Professor Mick looked after her and assured her that he would find her a good practice to go to.

Mrs Fleming closed the door and said, 'There is a fire in your room, but I can give you something to eat before you go up. I would help you with your bags, but as you can see . . .' She stopped there, running her hands over her swelling middle. Prue followed her down the hall, past two surgeries, a tiny dispensary and a big waiting room at the front of the house. Beyond these were a dining room and a sitting room and the kitchen right at the back.

As Mrs Fleming opened the kitchen door, a wonderful smell wafted towards them. The kitchen was a lot bigger than Prue had imagined, running the full width of the house.

'It's just broth, but I kept it warm for you,' she said, bringing the pan to the front of the stove, gesturing to Prue to sit down. 'Take off your wet things and I'll hang them up.' There was a large drying device which sat near the ceiling, not far from the stove, which Mrs Fleming pulled up and down by the use of a thin rope held on a big hook on the wall. Prue took off her coat and gloves, hat and scarf. She longed to take off her boots too, but the floor was bare and would be no warmer for her frozen feet.

Mrs Fleming looked somewhat anxiously at Prue.

'We were expecting a man,' she said. 'This is a pit village, you know. I don't think many of these people will have been used to a woman doctor.'

Professor Mick had told her it was a mining town and that Dr Fleming needed an assistant urgently.

'I'm happy to be here and will do all I can to help.'

'You have a strange accent,' the girl said. 'Where are you from?'

'New York.'

Mrs Fleming stared and then laughed a little.

'You came all the way to *here* from New York?'

Prue had to smile. It did sound incongruous. She didn't like to say so, but this girl had a strange accent too. At first Prue had to listen hard to understand what she was saying, but she had become used to deciphering accents after her move to Scotland. The thick vowels were somehow easier for her than the voices of the few people she had met from the south of England; these were nearer to some accents she had heard in America. She grew used to it in minutes, she felt almost at home here. How odd.

Mrs Fleming poured the broth into a large dish and, urging Prue to eat, she prepared the biggest sandwich that Prue had ever seen.

'It's ham and pease pudding,' she said.

Prue wanted to be polite, but she needn't have worried. The food was very good and she was hungry. As soon as the bowl was empty, Mrs Fleming filled it again, and gave her another thick sandwich. Prue could not help being grateful for the hospitality.

'Is the doctor here?' Prue asked when he continued not to appear. Mrs Fleming faltered and didn't look at her.

'He hasn't been well lately, which is why we need the help, you see,' she said. 'He wouldn't want to be rude, but he was very tired, so I'm sure you will excuse him and you'll meet him in the morning.'

The hunger appeased, all Prue wanted was her bed, so Mrs Fleming carried the lamp up the stairs, and Prue followed behind with her suitcases. When Mrs Fleming opened the door of the bedroom, Prue was pleasantly surprised at how big it was.

'There is water for washing, though I fear it won't be very warm now,' Mrs Fleming said, putting the lamp down on a table which was octagonal and covered in a white linen and lace cloth. Beside the far wall was the marble-topped table which had on it the ewer and basin and, beside it, soap and a neatly folded towel.

She lit another lamp and put it by the bed so that Prue could see the room.

There were thick curtains, already pulled across the window to discourage draughts, and a big oblong rug which covered most of the linoleum, soft under her feet. The bed itself was a double and high, and there was a chest of drawers, a wardrobe and a small writing desk with a chair. It was a lovely room, she thought.

'If you need anything more I am just next door,' Mrs Fleming said, indicating with her hand and closing the door softly behind her

After Mrs Fleming had left, Prue used the pot under the bed, washed her hands and face in the tepid water, took off her boots and stockings and put her feet into the water. It was bliss, sitting there by her fire on an easy chair.

After a while the water cooled. Prue found her thick nightdress, which thankfully she had placed at the top of her suitcase, plus bedsocks and a woolly hat. She threw her clothes over a chair, gave her teeth a perfunctory clean, and then fell into bed. She sank gratefully into it. The pillow smelled of lavender.

*

When she awoke, Prue was warm and comfortable. She lay for a few minutes luxuriating in being half asleep and then remembered that she was in a new place where she hoped to become the doctor she had always wanted to be. She got out of bed, stumbled over to the window, threw back the curtains and the room blazed white.

She said, 'Oh!' in shock and surprise. The snow had lain thickly during the night and covered everything. It was a new world. She was at the back of the house and could see the roof of what looked like a henhouse and below it a yard and then the wall which went around the house. Beyond was a turning point for carriages in the old days, she thought, and there was a well with a small roofed building to protect it, and past that she could see a big field and then bare winter trees and a graveyard. To the right was another field which had sheep and a few cattle, and beyond that was a long line of terraced houses. To the far left was a pit heap, large and black.

Prue washed and dressed and went downstairs. No one was about and the kitchen stove had not been lit. Did Mrs Fleming not have help? Prue thanked her mother and her background for teaching her how to do such things – she cleaned it and then she placed nearby papers, sticks and just a little coal on top. She lit it and had the satisfaction of watching the flames catch, lick and burn and she closed the little door at the bottom and pulled down the two lids at the top which kept the heat inside. When the stove began to pull, she half-filled the kettle from the little room beyond the kitchen which bore a good big white sink, then lifted one of the lids, placed it on the heat and hoped it would not take too long to boil. She needed coffee.

She heard a slight noise at the door and Mrs Fleming arrived in the kitchen, flustered and red-faced.

'You shouldn't have to do that,' she said, 'my sister is meant to come in early and see to such things.' She looked even younger and smaller than she had the night before, and pale, as if she would faint. She clutched at her stomach.

'I feel so sick,' she said.

Prue got up instantly and drew her by the elbow to the table and sat her down.

'Have you any ginger?'

'In the pantry.'

Prue went in there and found a jar of ground ginger. She put a teaspoon of ginger in a big cup and, once the water was hot, poured it over the top. She found a dry biscuit in a barrel in the pantry, and gave it to Mrs Fleming along with the cup.

When she had eaten and drunk, a little colour came into her cheeks.

'When is the baby due, Mrs Fleming?'

'May, Robbie thinks. The doctor, I mean. I'm Lily.'

'Prue.'

Prue hadn't taken a good look at the doctor's wife the night before, she had been so tired and so worried about the future but, looking at her now, she thought that Lily was the most beautiful girl she had ever seen, no wonder the doctor had wanted her for his. She had hair as bright as the sun, and eyes so blue they were almost mauve. Her skin was almost see-through, she was so delicately built and her movements were neat. She looked, Prue thought enviously, like the perfect woman.

'Robbie has promised to come down to breakfast,' Lily said, and sure enough, not long afterwards there was a noise in the passageway and a young man came into the kitchen.

He was about thirty, and beautiful in his own way. What a pair they must have made on their wedding day, Prue thought. He had creamy skin and black hair and cool black eyes, but Prue could see pain in them too. The man was ill, thin, with shadows beneath his eyes. He smiled as he entered, and then his eyes lit up, and Prue thought that when Robbie Fleming smiled, the world was a better place.

'Dr Stanhope,' he said, reaching out his hand in greeting. 'How good to meet you. I'm so glad you came.'

She shook his hand, smiled back and wanted to urge him to sit down, but before she could form the words he had done so already, and Prue poured tea for him. Lily was standing at the stove making porridge, keeping her eyes fixed on her husband as if in fear that he would somehow vanish.

As they ate their porridge, glistening with brown sugar and awash with warm milk, Prue asked, 'Have you been married long?'

They looked into one another's eyes and smiled, and Lily squeezed her husband's hand.

'Two years,' he said. 'I came here to take on the practice when my uncle died, and I fell in love.'

Lily blushed.

'Do you have any help, besides your sister?' Prue asked.

Lily shook her head.

'I'm from the village, you see; they think I'm above myself anyhow, marrying the doctor, and my mother needs my sister at home sometimes and I have a brother who is a foundryman and has to be looked after.'

Robbie made a noise which in any less a man would have been a snort, but Lily looked at him and they smiled at one another.

'Shall I take the morning surgery?'

He looked at her with gratitude.

'I haven't been able to do much for some weeks. I hope you won't find it too arduous.'

'I'm sure I'll manage,' Prue said. Her heart beat hard with apprehension, yet there was a big part of her that couldn't wait to get there. She had given up everything for this, and would not let her nerves deny her the satisfaction now.

'Ernie Smith does the dispensing,' Dr Fleming said.

They directed her to the front of the house where the

surgery was. In the dispensary a thin, anxious-looking young man was waiting.

'I'm the new doctor, Prudence Stanhope,' she said. 'You are Ernie Smith? I'm pleased to meet you.' She offered her hand and smiled at him.

She saw him glance at her and then nod.

'Right, Ernie,' she said. 'Let them come through in some kind of order, and stop them when I tell you, and until then you and I will labour—'

'But, miss—'

'Doctor,' she said.

The first woman she saw was very obviously pregnant and, by the look of her, poor and tired with it. She halted just inside the door.

Prue wished that the room had been more welcoming. It smelled of disinfectant and, across from her, as well as the couch and curtains were various dreadful-looking implements which should have been kept out of sight. Somehow it stank of authority and not of somebody who would be keen to help.

'Is Dr Fleming not here?'

'I'm afraid not,' Prue said. 'I'm Dr Stanhope.'

The woman stared at her. Mrs Piper, her notes said.

'Do come in, Mrs Piper. How can I help?' Prue gave a welcoming smile.

She thought the woman must be forty, but then it was difficult to assess such things, they were dependent on the lives that people had led.

Mrs Piper said nothing. There were fine lines around her eyes and dark shadows beneath them and her figure had thickened with several pregnancies, spreading out in the middle beyond the rest of her body. She looked exhausted.

'What's the problem?' Prue said.

Mrs Piper gave in, sitting down in the chair across from the doctor and then got back up as if she could feel no ease.

'It's so heavy,' she said, 'as if it could come at any time, and I'm not due for weeks yet.'

Prue stood up.

'Can you get to the couch?'

Prue got up, went over and pushed back the curtain. Mrs Piper eyed it and then stood up and made her way slowly across the room. Prue helped her get up as far as she had to. Then Prue examined her and asked questions, but Mrs Piper didn't know anything other than that she had not been aware of being pregnant for that long. Prue thought it could be twins – she was not certain, but the woman was so big and from what she could feel she thought there was enough for it to be two.

'I've already got six,' Mrs Piper said.

'You should rest if you can.'

Mrs Piper laughed.

'I don't get much chance of that,' she said.

The next patient was Mr Batson. He was middle-aged, as far as she could tell. His cheeks were sunken and his face was grey. He was short and skinny and had little hair left upon his head. He looked around for Robbie Fleming.

'I'm Dr Stanhope,' Prue said. 'Dr Fleming cannot see you at present. Please come in and shut the door behind you.'

He shook his head.

'I thought he didn't look too well the last time I saw him. And you're a doctor?'

He seemed interested rather than offended, his tired eyes warm.

'Come and sit down,' she offered.

He did so. His breathing was heavy, noisy.

'I cannot breathe,' he said. 'At night it's really bad.'

'Do you smoke?'

He looked at her as though she was stupid.

'Aye,' he said.

'And what is your work?'

'I'm a hewer down the pit.'

Prue wasn't sure about the reference, but she took the point. This man was breathing coal dust every day as he worked. She took her stethoscope and said to him, 'If you could just lift your shirt above your waist.'

He stared for a second and then did so. She listened to his ragged breathing and then they both sat down again while he pushed his vest and shirt back into his waistband.

'You should stop smoking,' she said.

'Will that mend it?'

'It might make a difference to your lungs, I think. They need a break.'

'I've got a wife and four bairns, I don't have much to meself. I work hard and I like a drink and a few cigarettes.'

'The drink is all right, as long as it's not too much, but you should give up smoking.'

He looked helplessly at her.

'Well, at least cut down then.'

After he went out she watched him from the window. The first thing he did was light up. It was hardly surprising, there was no evidence that smoking hurt people, and yet she thought it must, drawing all that tobacco smoke into the lungs when it was something alien, and on top of that coal dust too, day after day, clogging things up.

A small boy came in.

'Me mam wants her usual,' he said.

Prue had no notes so she left the room, saying she wouldn't be a minute and asked Ernie what to do.

Ernie puffed out his chest at knowing more than the doctor did.

'The pink pills,' he said.

'Pink?'

'Aye, that's what Dr Fleming does. The lad's mam thinks they work and it makes her feel better.'

'I see. Thanks, Ernie,' she said, watching him fulfil the prescription.

Later, Prue saw a woman who worried her. Mrs Miles was all grey somehow, though Prue didn't think she was as old as she looked. She held her huge black handbag close to her chest, as if for comfort. She wore a hat which hid her face and an old coat, and she was so thin. Her legs were bare and her feet were covered in old brown boots.

When she looked at Prue she had colourless eyes, a pointed nose and bloodless lips. Her hat had no ornament, it was to keep out the wind and the rain; it said nothing of gaiety or the summer months. Prue could see nothing but wisps of hair. Mrs Miles sat forward in her chair.

'It's about my husband, my Jeremiah,' she said. 'I worry about him, but he won't come here.'

'I could always come to see him,' Prue offered.

The woman looked down.

'He won't have it. I just want to know what I can do.'

'Tell me,' Prue said.

Mrs Miles shook her head so slowly that it was several moments before Prue registered it, as though Mrs Miles had long since considered such extravagances and forgotten them.

'Always he got up before six and went outside. I would get the breakfast and I would call his name in the yard and he would come in.' She stopped, almost smiling and then remembering.

'Has something changed?' Prue prompted her at last.

Mrs Miles looked at her as a tiny bird might regard a hawk.

'I am his second wife. His first wife died having his son. And Jack was killed at the Somme.' She stopped there. 'Since that day he has been different and – we have no child.'

Prue saw again the guilt that she and Alicia had both felt.

'Just him and me,' Mrs Miles said and the hat, which was so unadorned and so grey, shook because of her tears.

All that day Prue saw people. Surgery was meant to end at noon, but, with Ernie's approval, she let it go on and on well into the afternoon, and then – after a tea break – the evening. At nine o'clock there were still people waiting, Ernie was pale with fatigue and Prue could barely speak, except to go into the room where they waited and say, 'I'm so sorry. Come back in the morning, please.'

There was no sign of Lily when Prue finally finished surgery, desperate for food. Lily had given them sandwiches and tea at midday, and more tea two hours earlier, but Prue was very hungry. She was therefore surprised to find a tall and thin young man waiting in the hall. If she had a type, Prue thought, he was not hers. He had a generous wet mouth, a wispy pale beard and calculating colourless eyes.

'Ah,' he said, getting up, 'you must be the new doctor. I am John Edwards, the vicar of St John and St James, our lovely church.'

'Good evening,' she said. 'Prudence Stanhope.'

Prue offered her hand. He regarded it with care for a few moments and then took it.

'I understand you are an American, Miss Stanhope.'

'Dr Stanhope.'

Mr Edwards smiled, but it went nowhere near his eyes. Prue didn't like it, she realized that he had already dismissed her. She was a silly woman to him, she could see by his closed expression.

'I came to offer my greetings, and to hope that we will see you in church on Sunday.'

'You do know that Dr Fleming is unwell and that is why I am here?'

'I had ascertained that much.'

He was like a talking dictionary, Prue thought. She was tired. She just wished he would go away.

'It would be good to introduce you to the members of the church. They usually come to the vicarage after matins for sherry or tea and coffee. You would be very welcome.'

'I do want to meet as many people as I can,' Prue said. 'I will come as soon as I am free.'

When he left she went into the kitchen and discovered a wonderful smell. Dr Fleming was not there, but Lily was putting up a tray for him.

'I won't be a moment,' she said. 'Robbie has gone to lie down and I'm insisting he has something to eat.'

Prue almost offered to take the tray to him, but that seemed intrusive and anyway she could hardly stand from tiredness, so she nodded and sat at the kitchen table which was set with two places. When Lily came back she ladled minced beef and dumplings, carrots and cabbage onto their plates. Prue could have cried with gratitude. It tasted like heaven.

'Do you go to the church?' she asked.

'Not since Robbie took ill. I was brought up Catholic. There was a terrible fuss when we got married and I can't go back to my church but I don't feel as if I can go to the Church of England either without him. The vicar comes to see Robbie, but he always makes me feel little and daft. You can practically see through his wife, she's always that tired. They have four bairns, all skinny, and the vicarage is colder than a hen hut. If he was nice to one of the pit owners he could probably get free coal, although they're all Methodists as far as I know, except Mr Gallagher, who doesn't seem to have anything to do with God.'

'Who's that?'

'Rory Gallagher. He owns half a dozen mines and hasn't been inside a church since his wife died more than a year ago. Apparently he blames God.' Lily lifted her eyes as she spoke.

'I suppose you have to blame somebody,' Prue said, 'and God can be so useful that way.'

Four

Rory Gallagher had never liked churches. He thought it was something to do with the fact that his mother had wanted him to be a vicar. Why she had taken on this notion, when her husband was a moulder in a steel foundry, he had no idea. Perhaps she hoped he would do better than she had, an up and down house in Sunniside, there on the fells, between Tow Law and Crook. It hadn't a lot to recommend it, and had he been the kind of boy who paid much attention to his mother's happiness, he might have seen that there was nothing for him here.

His mother longed for what they would never have: theatres and picture houses, art galleries and the kind of society which spoke of such things. But it was the nothingness that he liked, and that his father loved so much. You could look out of your bedroom window – because his bedroom was at the back of the house – and see so clearly and so far across the flat land which rose slightly up towards farms on the horizon that drew your eye.

The trouble was that her family had originally come from Durham, where presumably people had time and energy for the arts. His father had brought her to live in what in a temper she called 'this godforsaken hole'. Why she had agreed to marry him, Rory had no idea.

He was an only child. This might have been because his mother could have no more children. As he got older he thought it probably had more to do with the fact that from the bedroom where they slept together there was never anything but silence.

His mother wanted him to have piano lessons; she wanted a piano. She liked to read to him though he could not see the point of books. He much preferred to talk to his father about the foundry, and his work there. He wanted to go and see what it was like, but he was not invited and dared not ask.

He was clever enough at school for his mother to think he could go to the grammar school, but his father did not agree. The local school had been good enough for him, he said, and it would be good enough for his son, so although his mother wept Rory did not venture from the village. When he was old enough to leave school, since there were no jobs open at the steelworks, he went down the nearest pit.

His mother wept even more over that and told him that he would hate it – everybody hated it, it was nothing more than a cemetery-in-waiting, so many men died – and if he worked there she would not be able to hold up her head any more. She had promised her family that she would do better for him than the foundry, and now he had chosen worse. She did not blame him, she blamed his father – nightly, as far as he could tell.

The pit was strange, hard, but somehow he never doubted life there was better than being a vicar. The men cared about one another. He was part of something and he liked the physical work; he enjoyed being able to do it with ease. His mother no longer dragged him to church, and since his father did not go, neither did he, and he was glad of that. His father took him to the nearest pub instead, proudly. Since his father had ignored him up to now, he was glad of this.

He soon realized that part of the joy of work was the not doing it, the homecoming, his mother waiting with hot water for his aching blackened body, the smell of cooking from the kitchen, the hunger that he felt and the satisfying of it. He loved the way that she fussed over him, the way that his body developed into something muscular and fine with the hard work.

He loved the smell of the lavender-scented sheets which his mother provided and the very bliss of sleep. He loved the way that his father understood the difficulties he had and admired the work that he did and even spoke to him softly at home. They would compare their work until he grew to appreciate his father's work too. He came to know how proud his father was of him.

'My lad, the pitman,' became his father's mantra.

Rory loved the bitter cold days and nights when he was cosy beneath his parents' roof and the time off, the beer drinking and the way that he made such a good wage that his mother looked on it with awe. He was good at what he did and he liked that.

One evening, during the summer when he was fifteen, he went past the church and saw in the entrance a girl so lovely that it made him stop. Luckily he was alone, his workmates would have jeered and laughed. Churchy women were not generally for them. She was standing in the porch talking to somebody. She was not well dressed – nobody was rich around here – but he liked the way that she stood, the very presence of her, somehow. He lingered, and she must have sensed him because she turned, and he never forgot the sweetness of her face, her blushed cheeks, her creamy skin and the blue bonnet which framed her face.

The following Sunday he announced that he was going to church. His mother stared and then was pleased. She would go with him. The lovely girl was there with her parents and afterwards the vicar came out and spoke to everyone and she was still there, and his mother saw him looking and she knew the girl and her family and went over and introduced him.

After that his life changed. He could think of nothing but her. She had moved recently from Bishop Auckland, her parents had bought the grocer's shop, so he went there as often as he could, at last saying to her, 'Could I – would you go for a walk with me next Sunday?' and she blushed and said that she would.

Well away from village eyes he kissed her and the kisses were so blinding, so exquisite, that he thought he might die without her.

He knew no more than she did, but lads are keen and eager and he had enough clumsy ardour to persuade her that he must have her, and so he did every Sunday that arrived that summer. His life was so different, he cared for her so much, and so he was surprised one evening in the autumn to come home and find her father in the front room with a dark and angry countenance, and his parents serious-faced.

At first Rory did not understand, but after her father had explained the problem he said, 'But I care for her. I want to marry her.'

'You should have respected her.'

Rory knew what he meant and felt his face colouring.

'I'm sorry,' he said. 'I just love her so much, all I thought about was her.'

'And your own lusts?' her father said.

Rory listened to him, but he knew that it was only that her father was old and had forgotten what it was like to hold the woman of your dreams in your arms. He was glad that she was having their child, he would love them both, cherish them, he was happier than he had ever been in his life.

'I swear to you that I will look after her, that I will better myself to be the right person for her,' he said.

They were married as quickly as could be, for respectability's sake. How stupid it all was, he thought. Her parents insisted on them moving in but he wanted her to himself, he wanted a house for them, not to be told how to live and what to do because they were both so young. He discovered a cottage at the edge of the village, and then he went looking for what more he could do to make more money, and he found it.

Up on the tops of the fells there was coal and he was persuaded that he could sink pits there, small and profitable. With what money he had, because his parents had insisted that he save most of what he made, and a small loan from the bank, he bought the rights to the coal. It was a gamble but he took it, was pleased with his daring. He set up a shack at what he called the Anne, after his young wife, and he found pitmen who would work for him. The coal could be got easily which made it profitable. He paid the men well. He got the best workers and then set up the business, and when it made money he bought other small pits and flourished.

Anne never cared what he did as long as he came home to her. She would have followed him to China, to the end of the world, anywhere, he thought. She was his in a way in which nothing else in the whole world could ever have been. Her eyes shone over each idea he had, and so he kept having more and more good ideas so that he could astonish her and make money for her, and security.

He wanted to buy a house in one of the bigger towns, but when he suggested that they should move she simply laughed. She wouldn't let him buy her beautiful clothes or jewellery and every time they made money she gave it away, buying food and clothes for those who could not work whom she met helping out at the doctor's with the sick and the ill.

Once he could not help saying, 'What if they're taking advantage of you?'

'I'm sure some of them are, but I don't care. I'd rather do that than deny one person who was hungry.'

'You're turning into a saint,' he told her, and she laughed and kissed him in such a way that she was in his arms, and after that he remembered nothing but the sweetness of her body.

After she had given birth to their daughter, Helen, he swore that he would never let them down. She went through such pain but, by the end of it, his wife slick with sweat and his daughter newly born, he was awed that the circle of life was complete. After that he worked even harder to ensure that they would have a good life.

He tried once again to persuade Anne to move to a bigger house – only an end house, nothing special. She didn't care, she was happy that he came home to her at night, that whenever he did they lay in bed and talked softly so as not to disturb their sleeping child, but he was too proud not to display his growing wealth and so they moved into Tow Law, to a house on the corner which could have been a castle to Anne. Having said she didn't care, she loved it so much.

When they first went to see it she ran up and downstairs in her enthusiasm, exclaiming 'Oh!' at the entrance to each room. It had three bedrooms and a bathroom, and downstairs there was an entrance to the side with an inner door and an outer door, and above the inner door there was red and blue stained glass which threw coloured sunshine into the hall whenever there was light. Turning from there you could see the two generous rooms to the left, and down three steps there was a huge kitchen and a walk-in pantry beyond the sliding door.

Outside he was so pleased that it had at the front a tiny garden with a yard leading down to the wash house at the end, but the garden was big enough to boast a lawn and lilac trees at either side of the gate and wrought-iron fencing around it.

Anne was ecstatic. She had told him how clever he was, how wonderful he was, how happy they would be here, and indeed they were, but for the fact that after their daughter was on her feet and sleeping well, Anne did not become pregnant again, and they rued this.

When they had not been married, she had conceived so easily. Now it seemed she could not have another child. He told her it did not matter and it was true. Only the most stupid men demanded sons. Why would he want a son when he had so enchanting a daughter? As she grew and Anne conceived no more, she became more and more important to them and they lavished their affection upon her.

Helen was eighteen when her mother died. He had never imagined that their life together would end so soon nor that he would be left with just one child.

From now on he knew that his life would lack the thing which glued him to the earth. His wife was dead. She had not been long in the dying, nobody could accuse her of that. The cancer had ripped through her body like a high waterfall, taking with it so many organs that he could not keep pace, and she screamed as she had not screamed in childbirth and he had stayed with her and begged the doctors and nurses to do more and when they told him that they could not do any more he wished he could have put a pillow over her face and quieted her for ever.

Now he was standing in the sitting room in the house which she had loved so much, waiting for the coffin to arrive. It was the hardest thing that he had ever done.

Eventually, after what felt to him like many hours, Helen came into the sitting room.

'The motor is here,' she said.

Rory shuddered. Then he followed Helen outside, and they drove to the church. The church was not even the one where he had seen Anne so long ago. It felt alien, though he could hardly say so. Since they had moved to Tow Law they had gone to church for weddings, christenings, funerals, Easter and Christmas, as so many people did. He felt guilty now, that Anne might find it hard to get into heaven when they had lapsed so badly.

They had been so happy, so blessed and had neglected the church and all the things it held within it. He wondered idly whether if he had been more faithful to his religion, his wife would not have been taken from him or that they might have gone on to have more children. It was a ridiculous and fruitless pastime he knew, but it formed part of his guilt and he could not help himself. He would have done anything to get her back.

The church had never seemed so big and wide. The people watched as he came in and saw the coffin, my God, was she really in there? He wanted to run up to it and pluck her from it, but he knew that it was no good. She was gone. He had seen her dead and there was nothing left in that body to suggest that she was still on this earth, or that he could ever contact her or be with her again in any way.

He reminded himself of this. There was no way back, only forward, into the desert of his life without her. He must remember Helen and think how lucky he had been and try not to cling to her arm or in any way to lean upon her. She was his child, he was the parent and yet his face ached all through the service with the need to weep and have her comfort him. He didn't remember the people or the hymns; all he remembered was the coffin.

Five

When Helen Gallagher heard that Mr Edwards, the new vicar, and his family were moving to the village, she decided that she would offer to help them settle in. The previous vicar had moved on to higher things and there was a lot of talk in the village about what kind of man he would be. The ladies who cleaned the church knew the minute that the vicar moved in and so soon did everybody else.

She banged on the door of the vicarage early one morning. She was kept waiting for quite a long time and when the door opened, a diminutive woman of around forty stood there.

'Good morning,' Helen said. 'I do hope I'm not intruding.' She told the woman her name. 'I know you've just arrived, and I wanted to come and introduce myself and to welcome you to the village. I would love to be of assistance if I can.'

The woman stared and then she said in soft southern tones, 'How very kind. Do come in. I'm Mrs Edwards, the vicar's wife.'

When Mrs Edwards closed the outside door, the sound of their voices echoed throughout the house. It was a huge building, the staircase swept up to the first storey and the rooms were arranged all around it. Helen had been there before, she had played at the vicarage as a child.

Mrs Edwards saw her into the hall and several children ran in from the kitchen. Two boys and two girls. Teddy was the eldest, Mrs Edwards said, a lovely shiny-haired boy of seven or so. Then there were two smaller girls, Elisabeth and Mary, and a boy who was not much more than a toddler, Wilfrid. He came straight to Helen and put out his arms. Helen picked him up. He was warm and just gorgeous, she thought.

'We're sliding down the bannisters,' Teddy said. 'Do come and see.' She went, and since the bannisters were sturdy and round she followed Teddy all the way to the bottom in delight.

Mrs Edwards had carried Wilfrid into the kitchen. Helen followed. The kitchen was cold.

'I can't seem to work the stove,' Mrs Edwards said, and Helen, who had a similar stove at home, knew exactly what to do, and they soon had warmth coming into the room.

Helen offered to make biscuits as Mrs Edwards unpacked sugar and flour. Helen loved baking and set to. When she had put the biscuits into the oven, she helped with washing out cupboards and arranging foodstuffs and cutlery and crockery in the appropriate places. After the kettle boiled, they had tea and biscuits and the children came in to eat biscuits and drink milk.

They then began unpacking the rest of the Edwards' belongings and were in what was to be Mr Edwards' study when he came in. The first Helen heard of him was, 'Don't touch my books, they're in order!' as he came forward in a hurry. And then, 'You haven't got a fire on in here yet, I have my sermon to write. Don't let the children in!' And then he noticed Helen and she saw him.

He was so handsome: tall, slender and fair-haired with bright-blue eyes and clear skin. Helen had never been in love, but she felt a rush of feeling which made her blush, and he stopped, smiled and said, 'Oh, I didn't see you.'

They were introduced. Mrs Edwards went off with the children and came back carrying a huge bucket of coal. Her husband sat down at his desk and frowned at his papers. Helen took the bucket and also paper and sticks and soon had a fire going.

Then they left the new vicar to his sermon, Helen reluctantly. She had never wanted to be in a room with someone as much as she did with him this morning. He was abrupt, certainly, but he was obviously eager to make a good impression on his parishioners. She couldn't fault this.

She surmised that John Edwards was about the same age as her father, but then her father had been a complete fool and had to marry her mother when they were just fifteen so she could not think of them as being the same age, her father seemed so old. And then she was truthful with herself and knew that only since her mother had died had he grown old. Before then her parents had been happy and full of life, always laughing.

She didn't want to be by herself at the house when her father was at work. She was lonely there and she wanted to be among other people. So she stayed all that day at the vicarage. She showed off her cooking to Mrs Edwards, who admired the way she could turn cheap meat and vegetables into a huge and hearty meal. Her mother had taught her housekeeping and a certain amount of economy, not because they needed to economize, but because there was no need for extravagance every day, and cheap meals could be just as tasty as expensive fare.

Helen was aware that vicars were very badly paid and that they must make the best of everything. She made a treacle tart for the midday meal after putting the stew into the oven to cook slowly, and then she helped Mrs Edwards to clean the house. She was pleased when the heavy furniture the Edwards' had brought with them sparkled with her effort and smelled of lavender polish.

Mr Edwards had his meal at his desk. Helen suggested that the children and Mrs Edwards should eat in the kitchen where it was warm, as long as Mrs Edwards didn't mind that. The woman seemed grateful for the help, and so would anybody be with four children and an enormous house.

'The children are going to school for the first time tomorrow,' Mrs Edwards said.

'Have you someone to see to Wilf while you take them?'

'It's no problem, he will come with me. I'm very grateful to you, Miss Gallagher, I couldn't have done half as much without you.'

'I don't mean to intrude,' Helen said, 'so I won't come back and bother you. I will be at church on Sunday to hear Mr Edwards' first sermon.'

'He gives the most wonderful sermons,' Mrs Edwards said.

Helen left at four, aware that her father might be home at six and that he would have had nothing but the sandwiches she had made and packed for him that morning, and she had yet to conjure up something for dinner. Not that he would complain, he probably wouldn't even notice. If she couldn't get him to leave the office at home during the evening, he would work until bedtime.

She walked slowly across the village, down the long muddy lane which led from the church back to town, fields on either side, with the cattle market to the right as she came in, past the Cattle Mart Inn and up the slight incline. There she turned left into a street of terraced houses, past the blacksmith's shop to the far end of the street and there her house was on the corner with a small yard and garden to the back and at the other side the main door. She went in the back way.

Every time she entered was an act of courage, because she no longer expected to hear her mother's voice, but there was still a special quality which had not left. It was as though her mother was gently haunting them and it made Helen's heart hurt for how her mother's presence had not left them though she had been dead for over a year.

Inside Helen stood a moment, taking deep breaths which smelled very faintly of her mother's perfume, and she could almost hear her mother singing one of the old songs which she had loved. Helen could remember coming back from some school event or other, her father and mother dancing in the kitchen and laughing like only people in love did. They heard her and broke apart for a second and then her father lifted her up and she danced between them as her mother sang. Both her parents had beautiful voices and she did not. It had been a family joke.

Helen lit the fire in his office, but also she lit the sitting room fire too, in an attempt to pull him into some kind of family life.

He did not come home at six. In the beginning, after her mother had died, she panicked when he did not come home, trying to reassure herself that if there had been an accident at any of the six small pits which her father owned, she would have been told and there would have been activity, people hurrying and scurrying.

The pits were up on the fell so you couldn't always hear the pit siren if it was one of the furthest of them, or if the wind was blowing in the wrong direction, but he would send people to let her and the other families know. It had taken her months to work out that he too hated coming home.

He had been so very foolish in the early days after her mother died, saying to her that her Auntie Susan, her mother's sister, wanted her to go and stay in Durham and spend time with the rest of her family.

He went on about this for months in different ways. Finally, fed up with it, she had stared across the tea table at him.

'Are you mad?' she said.

He looked patiently at her. She regarded him scornfully, but tried to soften the blow by using his name, something she never did.

'Honestly, Rory Gallagher, have you completely lost your mind? Auntie Susan is a fool. She never thinks about anything—'

'She knows a lot of people there, she has friends—'

'And is that what you want for me, going to the Assembly Rooms and dancing with stupid young men who have nothing to say other than about themselves?'

'I thought it might be a start,' he said.

'Of what?'

She watched him flounder. And then he looked down at the food he was not eating and he said, 'It might do you good to get away.'

'From?'

'Me. And this.'

'And who's going to look after you?'

'Helen . . .'

'You and this are all I have.'

'That's why,' he said. 'You should have more.'

'I will not have more by you sending me to stay with my aunt. She never liked my mother and now she feels guilty and wants to make up for things. Are you going to eat anything? I made it especially for you because I know you like it. You're getting thinner and thinner.'

'If you don't want to go and stay with her you could go to university.'

'Whatever for? What on earth could I learn in such a place that I couldn't learn here?'

He said nothing. His saying nothing could go on and on for hours and she could hardly bear it. Her lovely, lovely stupid father.

'You are an idiot,' she concluded, barely able to speak for the foggy way that the room had turned. 'I love this place, don't you see?'

'How can you love it? It's a pit town in the middle of nowhere.'

'It's where I belong. I was born here and – and well *loved* here, by my parents. You are here and my mother is buried here. I will never leave.'

'There are other places which you could love and other people you could meet. This doesn't have to be your future,' he said. 'I would be happy to help you, to pay for you to see the rest of the world. Why not?'

She looked hard at him, and only said, 'If you eat your tea I promise not to sing when I wash up.'

He smiled and she got up and leaned over and kissed his cheek.

She wished she could ask him to come home earlier. He got later and later and she knew that each day he found it harder. That was the thing about grief. In the beginning it was something you thought you would get beyond, it was an obstacle to pass, but the more you tried to pass it the more it grabbed and held you and there was no way through. You were stuck with it.

She remembered him coming home one Friday to find piles of his wife's clothing in the hallway. He stared at them.

'I thought that there are people who could make use of these,' Helen said.

He nodded and said nothing, but when she had gone back to the kitchen she could just see him picking up one of his wife's dresses and closing his eyes and burying his face in it and then he put it down and went into the dining room.

When she heard the door at about quarter past seven, she shouted down the hall,

'It's almost ready.'

He came into the kitchen and kissed her cheek and said how good it smelled. He was such a liar, she thought, he couldn't taste or smell anything. He couldn't feel anything. He couldn't see beyond the next six seconds. When he ate, every mouthful was an achievement. He had lost so much weight in the past months that when he held her she could feel his bones.

Being young, she had long since regained her appetite, but she could remember, after her mother died, how the food tasted like cardboard, and the effort that was needed to get it chewed and down and how her clothes had so quickly become large and then huge, accompanying the loneliness she felt inside.

Her father was tall for a pitman, not as tall as John Edwards but tall enough to look very skinny now. He was thirty-three, but he looked fifty. She did not tell him that she had spent the day at the vicarage with the new vicar's wife and children; he would not want to know anything about the church and in any case he hardly ever listened to what she said or offered her information about his day.

She would wash up and he would go into his office and stay there. She sat by the fire and read. It was dark and cold and she was content to sit over the fire at such times. As it grew late, the streets were not safe, especially at weekends when the young men drank and thought nothing of flinging insults, even at women passing by on the other side of the road.

She knew that if she had wanted to go out he would have taken her wherever she wanted to go, and come for her too, but she did not like to ask him. She had refused to leave, she had said no to all his suggestions. She didn't feel that she could ask any more of him.

Six

Helen found herself spending more and more time at the vicarage. After all, her father would not complain, no matter how dirty the house was or how many nights they only had sandwiches. But Helen organized the house. She talked to Mrs Piper after church and Mrs Piper knew a woman called Mrs Saxony who had worked as a housekeeper at one of the big houses before she came home and married, but now she had no children, and when Helen approached her she found the woman was happy to clean and cook for her father, and do the washing and ironing too. Helen worked at the vicarage for nothing. Her father was liberal with money, so of course she paid Mrs Saxony. She didn't think he would mind, he wouldn't notice what happened.

Mrs Saxony made sure everything was done before Helen came home and since she was gone from the vicarage before six, she was always there when he arrived back. Mrs Saxony had always left a stew or something easy to cook like fish with all the vegetables ready and water in pans.

The first thing he always did was bathe, since he spent as much time as his men down the pits. Helen would make sure that the dinner was ready for when he came downstairs.

As the evenings lightened after the beginning of the year, he suggested to her that if she wanted to go out he was happy with soup for dinner and he could even come home early and take her any place she wished to be.

'I can walk most places.'

'I could come for you.'

Having thought she might want to do this, Helen realized that when it came down to it, she didn't. The gap left by her mother dying could only be filled by going to the vicarage where there was a family, or staying here by the fire. The vicarage drew her so much that it embarrassed her, and she tried to stay away.

Mr Edwards did not seem to notice her. In a way she wanted him to, and that made her warm-faced because he was married with children and he was the vicar, but then she did like Mrs Edwards so perhaps it was nothing to do with her attraction to the man, it was just the idea of children and some kind of continuity which she missed.

When the weather improved, she did begin to go out in the evenings, but since this was only ever to church functions, it was just a continuation from the day. She loved it when John Edwards was there, and during the day and in the evening she counted how many times she saw him. She was very ashamed of herself and was sure neither he nor his wife had any idea.

But there was so much to do in the vicarage. There were meetings for sales of work. Women knitted all kind of garments, and some of them were lace-makers and others embroidered tray cloths. She thought that was very clever. She and Mrs Edwards provided tea and cake which Helen had usually made. She liked putting the children to bed, reading them stories, she liked that she could hear the murmur of Mr and Mrs Edwards talking downstairs, just as she had lain in bed for years listening to her parents. Her own house was so silent now that often she couldn't bear it.

Her father took to coming for her in his car at about nine o'clock, when everything at the church finished. She would tell him about it and she would ask him whether Mrs Saxony had made a good dinner and he was always interested in what she had been doing, and Mrs Saxony apparently made wonderful dinners so how it was that Helen went to bed and cried she didn't know.

It was winter when the new doctor came to the village. Women doctors were rare and the only ones Helen knew of were married. Mrs Piper, who helped with the tea at the vicarage when it was the Mothers' Union or other events, knew all the gossip. She brought her children to play with the vicarage children. It suited everybody because they could keep an eye on them in such a big house and let them out in the garden. She told Helen that the doctor was from America, and that she was a big and real bonny lass, who sounded as if she cared. Helen heard admiration in Mrs Piper's voice.

'It seems a bit funny to have a woman there, but it's nicer for women, especially when you're increasing,' Mrs Piper said, and Helen thought, yes, it must be awful, having a male doctor attend you in such circumstances.

'Did you hear about the new doctor?' Helen said to her father when he picked her up from the vicarage that evening.

'Thank God for that. Robbie Fleming needs help.'

'She's a woman,' Helen said.

'Women do have brains, you know, Helen, contrary to popular opinion,' he said with a smile in his voice. And then added, 'She'll be a big help to Dr Fleming.'

'They say he's ill.'

'One doctor isn't enough in a place like this where men have dangerous jobs. There isn't a decent hospital for miles over the fell and the Wolsingham doctor can't always get up the banks when the weather is so bad.'

Seven

Prue could see that from somewhere the pit wives had learned cleanliness such as maybe other communities had not. Perhaps it was because the dirt from the coal mines tried to rule their lives and they weren't having any of that. They scrubbed their houses, they scrubbed their steps, they scrubbed their children, they scrubbed their husbands and, however they had gained this knowledge, she realized that it had saved them from so many illnesses and she thought also that the champagne air here saved a great many of them from infections.

They were always swilling and brooming their backyards with bleach and water, hanging out their washing while the wind howled across the fells, starching the nets which graced their windows and banging hell out of their mats on the line in the backyard. It was shameful here to be mucky, as they called it, though one or two didn't care.

By God, it was cold, but she was glad of the frost, it naturally took care of so many ailments; it must have killed every germ within miles. The wind screamed sideways over the fell and blew everything away from the little pit town.

Prue slept better when the frost came down upon the land like a hard blanket, because it eased so many of her problems. Bad weather made people less keen to call out the doctor for what often seemed to her to be trivial matters. She lay warm beneath the covers and had a hot water bottle every night. She was so exhausted that she could feel herself falling into sleep, breathing gently and regularly and often now that was all she heard.

Lily's sister, May, was supposed to come to see to the fires and the house, but often she did not turn up and Lily and Prue had to see to the house themselves. Prue grew used to getting up early and putting on the kitchen fire and the kettle above it to boil for the breakfast tea. It took her some weeks to get used to tea, but it was better for Lily's insides and she could remember hating the smell of coffee when she was pregnant so, rather than make both, she suffered tea, and grew to like it.

May was tiny and barely spoke. She couldn't have been more than fourteen, and was plain and wan-faced and in this way unlike Lily. She did not seem to want to be there and everything was done grudgingly and not necessarily very well, but Lily seemed reluctant to call her sister to task about such things. Prue had the feeling that if she had done so, May would have left and not come back, so instead, the two of them ended up washing floors late at night. Lily paid her sister generously, though May said nothing in thanks. Lily was growing thinner while her baby grew fatter. Prue was not happy with how Lily's weight was dropping, but it was hardly surprising.

Sometimes Robbie stayed in bed all day and Prue was aware of the struggle he had to take the stairs. Halfway down them, he could not breathe. Lily had become resigned to having a baby and no husband, Prue thought, and that was where her body weight had gone. She was already grieving.

Prue insisted on Lily lying down in the afternoons. May went at midday and after that they did what had to be done without the little figure sulking around them and skulking at doors. Prue was sure that May went home and told her mother exactly what was going on at the doctor's house and several things which weren't, just for her family's amusement.

Lily would fall asleep as soon as she lay down on the sitting room sofa. Prue would build up the fire in there and make sure it was giving out a good amount of heat and then she would leave Lily to sleep.

Prue had long days at first, but gradually the backlog of patients dwindled. She was now finishing the morning surgery by twelve and the evening surgery was from five until seven. Afternoons and later in the evenings she did visits and in between she tried to keep everything else going. Prue wished she could suggest they employ someone other than May, but she knew Lily couldn't have stood another person in her house at this time.

Remembering the visit of Mrs Miles, Prue went to the farm. It was a typical Dales longhouse, the barn attached to the house for warmth and ease, and it looked clear over the valley. When she got out of the car, she was greeted by an old sheepdog who ambled across to her. Prue caressed his head, breathed deeply of the clean air and went into the house to find Mrs Miles, who dried her hands on her pinny and told her that Mr Miles was in the barn.

'I had to tell him you were coming,' she said.

Prue promised she would be tactful and so she went off to the barn and there she found Mr Miles, nothing like she had thought he would be. He was talking to a carthorse as though it were a person and Prue managed to make enough noise so that he would not be embarrassed to be found doing such a thing, but he merely smiled at her and went on caressing the animal's long and beautiful head.

'Good afternoon, Mr Miles,' she said, 'I've come to introduce myself.'

'Aye, lass,' he said, 'I know who you are. You're a long way from home. Do you like horses?'

'I haven't met many. I'm a city girl.'

'This is Bella.' As he stopped his caress, the horse thrust her face against him. 'She's jealous.'

Prue touched the horse's head and gazed into her eyes and smelled the sweet smells of horse and hay.

'I hear the doctor's not well,' Mr Miles said. 'I'm sorry for that. He seemed a good lad. He's young to die but that's the way of things in this world. The good die and leave us grieving after them and, by God, it's hard. Do you know what it is, lass? You hunger and thirst for your bairns and when these things are not satisfied, it eats away at you. I lost my wife and then my son.'

Prue had by now realized that Mr Miles was ill in a way that few people would acknowledge. He had been grieving for years and it had become his whole life.

'Mrs Miles loves you very much.'

'She's a good woman,' he said, 'but I find the world a very cold place without my first wife and my only bairn. Have you ever lost anyone?'

Prue was astonished at herself when she said, 'I miscarried a baby.'

'Ah, people would say that doesn't count and doesn't matter, but the loss must be the same.'

Prue was astonished at his understanding, but she worried about a man who knew so much. He was not old, though his face was lined and haggard.

'I'd like to help.'

'There's nowt you can do. It's past help. Come in and have some tea with us,' he begged, and Prue went inside and sat by the kitchen fire. She could see then that Mrs Miles loved her husband, it was in her eyes, whereas he merely liked her. Sometimes that must be enough but Prue wasn't sure it would do here.

He was kind to his wife, his eyes were soft on her and Prue could see why she would love him. He spoke gently, but Prue thought that was guilt. His eyes kept roving the room as though he might see the ghosts of his child and his first wife, or as if he might turn back the clock and be young again and in love and a proud father.

This man was not religious, she could tell by the clearness of his face. He had decided that his loss was total and no religion would bring it back for him. He could have had education and gone away and led a different life, she thought, but as he talked about his father and his grandfather and those before him who were lead miners and farmers and lived a hard life, she saw that he could never have betrayed them by leaving. He was caught up here with the land and his sense of obligation and place, and it made her worry for him. Sometimes people were the better for moving away from the things that they knew.

Mrs Miles saw her out. 'I'm so grateful to you, Doctor Stanhope, for coming like this and caring. I don't think there's much you can do, but you're kind.'

It was three Sundays later when Prue first trod down the unmade road which led to the parish church. It seemed to her a strange place to build a church, set apart from the village. The chapels, the Presbyterian church and the Catholic church were all within the village itself. Also, the vicarage was enormous. It showed how important the vicar was deemed to be, or at least the Church thought he was, though with so much competition she wasn't sure he should have been able to maintain the charade.

Snow was falling and melting as she walked, because it was not cold enough to lie, but the countryside where it was less disturbed was prettily clothed in white because there had been showers all week. It reminded her of home. The seasons were not as pronounced here, but she thought of winters past and wished that she could be newly married and with Silas again. She tried not to think about him; she reminded herself how he had betrayed her and in the end had hurt her, but once you have loved someone it's like an old tune that goes round and round in your head and her regard for him would not be silenced.

She was almost late; the church door was closed and there were a great number of people inside. She had deliberately left it so that she would encounter no one on the way and she slipped in at the back so that nobody would have cause to watch the doctor come to church for the first time.

It was cold but people were well wrapped up and she liked the hymns, the swelling sound of the organ, the way that they lifted up their voices, hoping for better things. She wasn't sure she liked people kneeling, it played havoc with their knees and she felt sure that women spent enough time down there, scrubbing floors and dealing with children.

Arthritis was keen enough to cause folk pain without people encouraging it.

When the service was over she was the first out, but she did not want to rush to the vicarage, and so lots of people recognized her as she stood outside the church. Some of them came over, and a tiny woman with a clutch of children around her, came and introduced herself as Mrs Edwards. She and her flock were shabbily dressed, and her form was so birdlike that Prue thought she probably had difficulties when she was having children, but she was cheerful and happy to meet the doctor. She sounded almost well-to-do, as they said, Prue thought, with her flawless accent and polite manners. What a strange place for her to live.

Prue walked back to the vicarage across the narrow path which led from the church. The entrance hall was huge and a blast of cold air hit Prue as she walked in. She had rarely been in such a big house which was not well equipped with fires and she thought how impractical and thought-less that the vicar should be given this mausoleum while most people around him crowded into cottages; if they had large families their children slept head to foot. This building could have housed four families comfortably.

Cups, saucers and plates were laid out in the dining room, which was enormous, with a high ornate ceiling and full-length windows which looked out over the ragged garden that led down into the valley so far that Prue could not tell how big it was. Mrs Edwards and other women of the church began to make tea while Mr Edwards stood by the fire, keeping the warmth from other people and holding forth about the Bible. The women came through with large teapots. There were also small pink cakes dotted with coconut.

The ladies of the church wore a keen variety of hats and she amused herself watching them. It was a very middle-class congregation in the main, which she thought strange. She recognized a great many people. She was the only doctor in the village and by now many of them had been to consult her. They were too polite to do so here and she was glad of that, but also they did not accept her. Like the pit owner, the steelworks owner and the vicar, she was too important to be a friend.

Mrs Edwards, having braved the teacups, and seeing Prue alone, came across to her smiling. It was a forced smile, Prue thought, but then the vicar's wife was obliged to be on show. There was a heavy smell of furniture polish in the air and Prue thought this woman laboured hard to see to her husband and his parish and their children, who were now meekly lined up on the couch. It was by this time a clear day, and Prue thought they would have been much better playing outside in the fresh air.

As she went on looking, she could see that one of the children was pale and, looking harder, that he had some kind of rash.

'Mrs Edwards, how are your children?'

Their mother glanced anxiously at them.

'I thought Teddy ought to have stayed at home this morning, but my husband was adamant that they should all go to church.'

There was a very pretty young woman helping Mrs Edwards, but nobody offered to introduce them. She looked concerned, her face flushed, but she said nothing.

Prue went over to the child, looked at him, looked at the others, and then she said, 'This child should be in bed before he drops.'

Mr Edwards came over.

'Nonsense,' he said, 'there's nothing wrong with him.'

'I think he has measles,' Prue said, 'it's a serious illness, Mr Edwards, and since you insisted on him being at the morning service, a great many other people's children might possibly have been infected.'

Her voice carried so that other people overheard. The vicar looked angrily at her, while they decided they had to get back to their homes and left. Mr Edwards looked irritated.

'There was nothing wrong with him when he got up.'

Prue wasn't going to let him off that lightly.

'Measles can blind and it can kill,' she said, and promptly, as though he had been waiting for her, the boy slid to the floor in a faint.

Prue helped as Mrs Edwards and the other young woman put the children to bed. Mr Edwards had disappeared, but

Mrs Piper's husband, a very small man, picked up Teddy and carried him upstairs. Prue led the others. Mr Edwards did not appear even after Prue had examined the children and discovered that all four had measles.

'Where is your husband?' Prue asked, as they laboured.

'He'll be downstairs, writing his sermon for next Sunday,' Mrs Edwards said.

'An arduous task,' Prue said.

'He works very hard,' the younger woman said as though she needed to leap to his defence, and then she blushed.

Prue thought, Good God, the stupid girl's in love with the vicar.

The girl looked at Prue and said, 'What else can I do to help? I'm Helen Gallagher and I'm glad to meet you. We need a woman doctor here.'

Prue nodded, gave her instructions and was glad to see how swiftly she carried these out and how tenderly she treated the children.

Prue asked the district nurse, Nurse Falcon, to go to the vicarage and help Mrs Edwards. Nurse Falcon was always very busy so Prue didn't say more but she knew that Nurse Falcon would be there. She sniffed whenever she was asked to do anything, but then always did it.

Nurse Falcon was one of many people pretending that Dr Fleming would be back to work at any moment and that

Dr Stanhope was merely 'holding the fort'. Nurse Falcon had not come to the surgery to help, she had waited until Prue sent a note asking her if she could attend various people and had sent a brief note back saying that she always gave of her best to Dr Fleming.

Prue went to the vicarage the following morning to check on the children. Mrs Edwards was giving them vinegar baths and Helen Gallagher was washing up in the kitchen and attending to the stove. Prue wondered what the pit owner's daughter was doing here, but Mrs Edwards needed a lot of help and Miss Gallagher seemed a capable young woman.

When she finally came down the long vicarage staircase, she found Mr Edwards in the study, writing. He had obviously heard her but did not stop what he was doing.

'Are they any better?'

'Measles takes time and a great deal of care.'

'My wife is used to dealing with the children' he said. If there was a reply merited by this, Prue couldn't think of it.

Eight

Prue had been there six weeks when the pit siren went mid-morning and the surgery emptied. Lily rushed through and told her that it meant there was a problem down one of the pits. Prue took up her doctor's bag, making sure she had everything she might need because she was uncertain as to what she might find, and they both went out together. People were running in the direction of the nearest pit, the one just up on the fell outside the village.

It was a strange place to her with its wheel dark against a darker sky and the people gathered about, women with children in their arms, hoping and praying that their husbands, sons and brothers would come safely out of there. Prue had not thought much about the men's work, but she knew that it was one of the most difficult of such industries and that there were all kinds of reasons why accidents happened. It was not something you would ever grow used to, she thought, looking around her as the rain began to fall like pellets on the waiting crowd.

It was only a short while before the men were brought up and it seemed that they were almost all accounted for, but not quite. A man who carried with him some importance came to Lily and said, 'Can the doctor come, Mrs Fleming, we have a man hurt down there? We cannot move him.'

'My husband cannot attend,' Lily said. 'This is Dr Stanhope.'

The man looked sceptically at Prue, but he must have known who she was. In the past weeks she had been stared at more times than in the whole of the rest of her life and she knew that May gossiped and the little town listened.

Prue's heart beat hard because she had read a little about mining by now and had heard of the low seams of north-west Durham, that some of them were only eighteen inches high and she had always had a fear of being enclosed.

This was her job, she told herself, this was what she had wanted, she must do it, so she picked up her bag, breathed carefully and followed to the cage which carried the miners below ground, praying that the man did not die, was not badly hurt, that she need not produce some miracle which she knew little of.

They got into the cage. After a few moments it made its way down into the gloom to the bottom of the shaft – Prue's stomach stayed at the top and she wanted to be sick.

When they came out of the cage she could not see to begin with for the thick blackness, but there were lights and the man went ahead with his lamp and she followed. She soon felt better. It was big, it was high, it was not as she had thought it would be, but as they continued to walk her legs ached and her bag became and more and more heavy. The roof began to lower and she began to sweat and she found herself catching at her breath in a way in which she would never have done above ground.

His strides were longer than hers, because even though she was taller he was used to this place and surefooted. The walls grew narrow and the roof became low as they branched off into the depths of the pit. She had to bow her head, and then as they turned off into a side passage where the men must recently have been working, the thick blackness seemed to envelop her and she had to subdue the panic, because if she let it ride her she would turn around screaming and run, and after that all her credibility would be gone. By the time he eventually stopped, Prue was panting with exertion and fear.

There were several other men, more lights and Prue could see what the problem was; the roof had fallen in some way along and there was a huge heap of stone where they had moved the coal, but some of it remained, shining like jet against the lights.

The man she came in with was talking with someone, and a third man came to her. He was stooped over a long way as though he was used to not being able to straighten. He looked beyond her, not as if he expected Robbie to appear but as if all his hopes had just died, and then he spoke rapidly.

'I'm Gallagher. I own the pit. We cannot move the stone any further. I have a man caught beneath it and I am not leaving him here.'

He turned and she followed him. The light from the lamps was dim. She got down beside the injured man. His leg was caught beneath the stone. He looked unconscious but he wasn't, she could hear by his breathing and the way that he fought the pain.

She drew away, thinking that the injured man might hear her and said,

'You really can't get him out of there?'

'I daren't take the chance. If the roof comes down, we could all die down here. It could happen at any time.'

Prue hesitated at the idea of being down here when the roof fell in, a black and airless grave.

'Then his leg will have to come off.'

She heard him take in his breath with shock.

'Won't that kill him?' The man was hissing his words as though he too was afraid of what the injured man might hear.

'The alternative is to stand here and put him out of pain and watch him die that way. It's your choice of course.'

She tried to put all her confidence into the way that she looked at him, though she couldn't see him very well, only the whites of his eyes stood out from the blackness of his face and the darkness around him.

'Should you put him through it?'

'I cannot let him die without trying.'

Mr Gallagher let go of his breath, half in hope and half exasperation.

'What do you need?'

'As much light as you can and some space.'

'Have you done this before?'

'Not down a pit.'

Rory Gallagher was astonished. He had not met the new doctor but he had heard a lot about her. He had not been able to visualize her, though he had heard the men down his pits make lewd and admiring remarks about the doctor's breasts and ample bottom but somehow he had not thought she would be like she was, almost his own height with bright, fearless eyes, coming down here to a place where most people were afraid even to be, and meeting his gaze, telling him she would perform a difficult operation in impossible conditions. He thought she was magnificent.

He watched her hesitate, saw the slight panic in her face which she meant nobody to see. She covered it swiftly with an expression which gave nothing away as she had been taught, he had no doubt, but he was also sure that she had not performed such a thing before. Here the light was so dim and the darkness so close that it breathed on you and on the walls which, if you were afraid, came in to meet your fear until you could not breathe.

She gave her commands in clipped tones so that the men obeyed speechlessly, before standing back, well out of the light, as she demanded, and he waited in fear that the roof would fall in again and he and several men and the new doctor would suffocate under a mountain of coal and rock.

He was ashamed, as he always was when things went wrong, but it was a cruel game. You could not look after everything, and nature and the ground loved to trip you up so that you made mistakes you could not have foreseen. He wanted to keep his men safe, he tried hard to do so but the changing weather conditions, the narrow seams and the men themselves made it almost impossible. Each time you failed, somebody could lose a life – or at least a limb – and families were destroyed that way. Yet it was all he knew and with some twisted arrogance he loved it.

Prue shot Stan Wilkinson, the injured man, so full of pain-relieving drugs that she half thought he might die of an overdose before she got any further, but there was no point in worrying about that. She had never before felt so much like a butcher, but now she was glad of the strength that she had in her arms. Carrying all those damned coal buckets around the doctor's house was coming in useful.

This was where a man would have been better able, being stronger, but at least she knew what to do; she remembered Professor Mick's lectures and, even better than that, she knew how physically hard he had said it would be, and it was. The sweat dripped off her face and onto the man and everything around him. She thought she even swore several times. She heard somebody who sounded like her saying, 'Steady the bloody light!' as she never would have done, and she was aware of her own words disappearing into the blackness and of the circle of men around her. She had a feeling that they were trying to support her, willing her on, and she was grateful for this. If they had been negative at this point she might have been defeated or given in more easily.

She began to cry silently, blinking back the tears, in sheer exasperation at not being able to do this, no matter how hard she tried, and the pain, despite the drugs, left the man moaning. She thought she might never forget the sound of it. She controlled the tears again and again, swallowing hard – she couldn't afford blurred vision. When it was finally over and she could not be other than grateful to have got that far, they pulled him free. She thought she heard a faint, 'Brave lass,' muttered by someone around her and the other men all joined in, a ripple of voiced approval for what she had done and she was so glad to be there to try and help, to do the very best that she could.

At first it felt like a triumph but, moments later, she was shaking so much that she could not move. She was afraid. The lack of air meant that she felt faint. This would never do, she told herself, but the men either had seen such things before or experienced it themselves because they took her bag and her instruments and Mr Gallagher came to her and thanked her, but when she tried to move she found the ground pitching up to meet her. He steadied her. She was grateful. She hoped nobody had noticed. At one point, though she didn't think the others were aware, he even held her up until she regained the evenness of her breathing.

'It's all right, it's going to be all right,' he said very softly, and Prue wanted to nod but couldn't. He began to walk her towards the way out, she thought he even put an arm around her because her steps faltered.

She didn't remember exactly what happened after that, only she was aware that if he hadn't grabbed her she would have passed out.

'I'm so sorry,' she murmured.

'Don't worry, you just need some fresh air. You'll be fine.'

Somehow they got the patient into the cage, and Prue and Rory Gallagher went with him, Prue speaking softly to the injured man, reassurance automatically coming to her lips. She closed her eyes for a few moments and tried to think of something else, all the time worrying that the man might die, he had lost so much blood, though it was staunched and she was holding a tourniquet above his knee and even now his body could have found the operation too much and he might die of a heart attack.

The cage shot up, this time leaving her stomach below, and then she came out into the daylight, such as it was in these cold times, and blinked and didn't know how to get out of the cage into the glare though there were ambulance men to take the patient from her. She couldn't move for several seconds and hands came under her arms and legs and Mr Gallagher lifted her just a little way so that she was on her feet and then he handed back her bag.

'Thank you, Dr Stanhope,' he said.

She clambered into the back of the ambulance with her patient and went to Bishop Auckland hospital.

Rory Gallagher watched the ambulance until it went out of sight and then stood there for a long time. She had astonished him with her fervent work and her determination that a man she did not know would not die down there in the darkness. Somehow he felt he would always be in her debt for what she had done. But it was more than that. Close against her, as he lifted her even just for seconds, he had had new feelings. He had always wanted to protect Anne but this woman did not need protection. She took responsibility for herself and her life and, more than that, she was proving herself in a hard world and asking for nothing more than her pay. What courage.

She had felt so soft and so warm and there clung about her the sweet scent of a woman. It was mad. Her hands and clothes were bloody and her neck smelled of sweat, but for all that or perhaps because of it, he could not forget her.

She had endured to the end and then he had been able to help her, to lift her up just a little. As soon as she was above ground and breathing air which was not full of coal dust she had completely recovered and she was ready to go on, he could see by the set of her shoulders.

He remembered the first time he had come up in the cage after being underground and the air was heady, made him feel dizzy. People said the air up here was like champagne and, though champagne was alien to him, he understood the inference. Air never smelled so good again and she had experienced that. She had come back from the pit and she had brought Stan Wilkinson up alive, and it was one of the best and bravest things that he had ever seen.

It was late evening when Prue got home. She didn't think she had ever felt this weary. Lily had gone to bed and left a lamp burning in the hall. There was the smell of dinner, and she knew that Lily would have left something for her and that the stove in the kitchen would be on and the room would be warm, but she had never felt less like eating.

Another lamp burned upstairs on the landing. Lily was so thoughtful. Prue took the lamp out of the hall and made her way into the dining room. She was not quite crying, but she felt as though her throat had closed. She put the lamp down on the table and reached toward the court cupboard where Lily kept spirits which were never drunk, and there Prue discovered a bottle which said whisky. She also found a tiny glass and just as she was about to pour it, tears streaming down her face, she heard a gentle voice behind her say, 'Nay, nay, lassie, that's not the way.'

She turned and Robbie Fleming stood in the doorway, giving the illusion that he was fit and well. He was so tall and handsome and smiling that, for a few seconds, her heart caught and she believed he might be.

'I was just—'

He came to her and when she moved away he took the whisky bottle from her. She thought he was about to put it back into the cupboard, but instead he put it down on the table, opened one of the doors beneath and he said, 'You need bigger glasses for whisky.'

He put the two square, squat glasses down on the table, poured generously and handed her one.

'Come and sit down,' he said.

The fire was dead but the room still held the illusion of heat and she could bear it. They sat in chairs across the fire from one another as though they were married and about to talk over their day.

She wished he was hers. She wished that she had the right to sit here with him and tell him about what had happened and take comfort from his knowledge and his conversation. She wished that she could hear about his day and that everything was normal and he had been doctoring that day too, and that it was not all about pain and loss and how he was dying young and leaving his pregnant wife.

For a few seconds she thought they might be just beginning and stood a chance. And she liked this man more than she had ever liked Silas. It was everything she had wanted; it was what she had dreamed of.

Mrs Wilkinson had come to her in the hospital. She was beautiful, slight, fair-haired, very attractive but white-faced there in the corridor. They had both retreated to let the nurses do what they could to make Stan Wilkinson comfortable and she thought that maybe Mrs Wilkinson had come to thank her, but the woman's face was set and hard.

'What in hell were you doing, taking his leg off like that?'

Prue was so astonished that she couldn't say anything but she did recognize the lump in her throat which was constricting her breathing.

'Do you know what you've done to me?' Mrs Wilkinson said. 'You've condemned me to a life with a one-legged man, who'll be sitting over my fire like a babby for the next forty years. I have two bairns.'

'It was what I was supposed to do.'

'What are you then, a bloody butcher? Can you imagine me looking after him, wiping his arse, doing up his buttons? If he had died I could have married again. Did it not occur to you that me and my two bairns would spend the rest of our lives stuck with him? Did you not think that I would have to go out and work, if I can find summat to do in this shithole? My bairns are little, eighteen months and the other not three. Who's going to see to them and to him? You bitch,' she said and walked away.

'So,' Robbie said now, sitting back in his chair, the lamplight making him look even younger, hiding the thinness of his face and the lack of colour in his eyes. She couldn't see any pain and he didn't show it. 'Did Stan Wilkinson die?'

She shook her head and gulped at her whisky before she could reply.

'No,' she said, 'it was worse than that. He didn't.' And she told him about her meeting with Mrs Wilkinson.

He nodded in understanding.

'Aye,' he said, 'she wishes he was gone. She's an awkward sort.'

Both of them took another slug of whisky and he closed his eyes in appreciation because he rarely drank.

'He's in a lot of pain,' Prue said.

'Well, he wouldn't be in any pain if he was dead, not so far as I know, so be hopeful.'

'She says if he'd died she could have married again.'

Robbie laughed derisively.

'Who would have her?'

'She's very pretty.'

'She's a pain in the arse,' he said, and Prue choked and laughed. 'You did a damned fine job or he wouldn't still be with us. If you hadn't – and in the worst possible circumstances – he would have died down there. Nobody would have blamed you. I don't know how you did it, no light, no air, no help. It doesn't matter what she says, we're supposed to be preserving life the best way we can and it cost you dearly to do it. Was Gallagher impressed?'

'He didn't say much.' Prue's face warmed a little. She had been nearer to Mr Gallagher than anyone in a long time. She could smell the coal dust, the sweat and the way that he had let her lean upon him. She remembered how tenderly he had looked after her and somehow that made her feel worse. Tears blocked her throat.

'He never says much,' Robbie said. 'His wife's been dead a while and he's never looked at another woman as far as anybody knows. I want some more of this stuff. Would you get it?'

She was grateful to stand up, it took care of her emotions. She poured generously, he didn't even say 'enough' so each of them had a lovely, deep, reassuring pool of golden liquid, then she sat down again and she felt so much better, so relieved. She would remember this time, she knew. She had never sat in the evening with Silas like this and it had been so much a part of what she had wanted. Was it so very much to ask? And then she thought of Lily and the baby.

'Don't take any notice of what anybody else says about

what you do,' Robbie said, looking straighter at her than ever before. 'You're a damned good doctor. Professor Mick said you were the best.'

Prue's cheeks burned.

'Did he?'

'Of course he did. What did you think you were doing here?'

'He said nobody else would come.'

'They were lined up,' Robbie said, sweeping the room with one arm.

When she went to bed, she cried properly, for Robbie and for Lily but also for the man with his amputated leg and for his uncaring wife, and for herself: that she had not somehow been so lucky as to have deserved a man like Robbie Fleming. He was one of the best men she had ever known and he was dying. Was it always so? Did the good really die young? Did God want them so much more, need them so much more than the people who loved and relied on them, not just his wife and child but the whole village, and she would be left to cope with it. She didn't cry for long, the whisky had taken care of everything. She was soothed and very soon she fell asleep.

It was two days later that a message came from the hospital to say that Stan Wilkinson had died. She didn't know whether the pit owner had been told. She didn't want to tell him, but he lived just across the street from the surgery.

At first she had not been able to believe that the man lived so modestly when he had several pits, but she soon saw that the men who did well here did not set themselves aside from the people. She wasn't sure why; she assumed many of them could have afforded better houses. She liked the idea that they didn't. She liked less the thought that perhaps they were simply mean, but in any case they lived among the men who worked for them; the families lived close and the children went to school together and the wives shopped together in the little town.

Rory Gallagher's house was on the corner between Wesley Street and Cornsay Road. Being an end house, like the doctor's, it was a bigger house than the others; it even had a little garden to one side. It was the only house in the street with no net curtains and what curtains there were were drawn back such as would have been considered quite wrong in a place like this where people guarded their meagre privacy. It was a big house for one person and a daughter, but maybe he didn't think of it like this.

A bitter wind was howling up the road from the valley beneath the town and she didn't want to stand around any longer than she had to. The outside door was pulled open quicker than she had thought it might be and Mr Gallagher was in his shirtsleeves with a pen in his hand. He was a surprise. The last time she had seen him his face was covered in coal dust, now he was clean and reasonably presentable, but the way that he opened the door showed his impatience. His face was set as though his life had been hard and his eyes were guarded.

He peered out at her, looked surprised and then urged her to come in. She was glad to do so even just for the two minutes she had decided to give him, but he ushered her into what, to her surprise, was a warm hall. It was larger than she had imagined, with rugs hugging the floor, but then he was the coal owner, why wouldn't he have good fires in all the rooms?

The doors of the downstairs rooms were open and there was a lovely thick runner which stretched all the way from the front door to the back of the house before it went down several stairs into the kitchen.

The room he took her into was a sitting room, at least to most people it would have been, but he was using it as an office. There was a big roll-top desk with papers all over it. There was a dining table and chairs too, all pushed back against the wall, the table heavy with files. He asked her to sit down. Prue shook her head and didn't. She was mesmerized by all the photographs on every surface of a young woman, presumably his wife.

What had Robbie said, that he had never looked at another woman? To Prue's surprise she was not traditionally beautiful. Helen had her looks from her father, only softer; Rory Gallagher being too sharp-faced and broad-shouldered to be considered handsome. He was not tall and slender like John Edwards and his manner was abrupt. He also had a thick local accent, whereas the vicar was exquisitely spoken, as educated people often are.

The woman in the pictures had a long nose, a narrow forehead, small, close-set eyes. She was stout of figure and short of stature and for some reason Prue was astonished, though she could not have explained why. But then she stole a closer look at the photograph next to it and there was light in the woman's eyes and she was laughing and it was a look of devotion, of pure love and affection and also wit and readiness to go forward, and Prue saw the beauty in her then like an inner glow. Prue liked her very much and wished she could have met her.

Rory Gallagher looked quizzically at her.

'Stan Wilkinson has died, yes?'

'I just wanted you to know.'

'That's kind of you.' He didn't look at her, as though unused to such things. 'I didn't thank you properly at the time, but when the roof comes in like that it's my fault, it should have been better and to lose a good pitman – you were so practical, so clear-headed.'

Prue was confused. She said nothing.

'God, what nerve.' His dark eyes were so admiring, as one professional to another. Prue liked that. 'I should have told you how grateful I am. His prospects were bleak and that wife of his . . .'

'She harangued me for saving him.'

'He's a good wage lost to her.'

'Will you help them?'

He looked so straight at her that she had to make herself meet his eyes and there was just a little humour glinting in the back of them.

'The big bad pit owner, eh? I will, and other people will too and some poor man will end up marrying her because she looks warm, though I doubt she is.'

Prue doubted it too. At that moment the front door opened and then crashed shut and a youthful voice said, 'What a boring evening I've had. Mrs Edwards wouldn't let me sort out the jumble sale and I could have done so much.' The girl Prue had seen helping at the vicarage when the children had measles came into the room, taking the pins out of her hat and stopping short when she saw Prue.

She had her mother's smile and it lit up the room.

'Oh, Dr Stanhope,' she said. 'How lovely to see you! I've been hoping we would meet properly. I didn't have chance to say anything last time you came to the vicarage when the children were ill and you were so good. Has my father not offered you tea?'

'I must go,' Prue said. 'I still have a lot of work to do.'

'I was sorry to hear about Mr Wilkinson,' Helen said, 'when you tried so hard to save him.'

When Prue got up, Helen saw her to the door. Prue said a brief goodnight to Mr Gallagher.

For a few moments she regretted having to go out into the bitter wind, even if the house she lived in was just over the street. When she lay in bed she thought of Helen Gallagher, how bright, how intelligent she was. For such a girl to live in a pit village where she had no prospects but a hankering after a man who was married with four children was worrying, and it didn't look to her as though the vicar had any notion of this. Prue didn't envy Mr Gallagher's daughter or the man himself.

Nine

Prue was called out to Mrs Piper's house in the middle of the night. She had begun to long for things to go wrong during the day. Four o'clock in the morning was the worst hour of all somehow and it felt like it was still bitter night when one of Mrs Piper's children had appeared, banging on the front door.

Prue kept her clothes across a chair in her bedroom, ready for her to put on immediately. Her bag was packed in the hall, she pulled on boots, coat, scarf and gloves as fast as she could and tramped across the village on thick ice. It had snowed earlier, lambing storms Prue had discovered the local farmers called it, so the ice was more treacherous than it had been. She wanted to ask the boy to slow down because her bag was heavy, but he kept running ahead, then stopping and waiting for her. The Pipers' house was, of course, at the other end of the village, in one of the side streets near Wolsingham Road. It was the last house, the furthest away.

It smelled of damp and half-dry clothes. A lamp burned dimly in one room and the fire was only just alight. Mr Piper did not appear. Several children were about and from the stairs she could hear the moans of Mrs Piper in labour when she should not have been for some weeks yet, and this reinforced Prue's opinion that Mrs Piper was having twins.

Prue had worried about it. She took the steep stairs slowly, saving her breath for getting there. Upstairs were two tiny bedrooms. In the front of these a small fire burned and, there, Nurse Falcon was helping. She suited her name; she was a tall, thin woman with a prominent nose.

Mrs Piper looked exhausted, lying there huge on the bed and in obvious pain. The sweat was slick on her body. Every time Prue and Nurse Falcon met, the nurse would say, 'Couldn't Dr Fleming attend, then?' although she knew how ill Robbie was.

Prue ignored it as she always did.

Prue was there for the rest of the night, while Mrs Piper's contractions grew as much as they could, considering how early her baby – or babies – were going to be. By the time dawn arrived late, Prue was delivering two children, both of whom were alive. She felt a little frisson of excitement. She had not thought that the children would survive. She loved such things, it was a triumph. Both were boys.

Mrs Piper reacted as though they had been her first ones and clicked her tongue with joy when Prue settled the babies into her arms. Prue asked the nurse to go and make some tea. They had kept the fire built up in both up and downstairs rooms. Sometimes there were neighbours to do such things, but you couldn't always count on it so Prue and Nurse Falcon had come equipped. When the nurse went downstairs, Prue took the babies and put them, well wrapped and crying loudly, into the open drawer that was apparently to be their bed.

From their initial crying they quietened and Prue was satisfied with their progress. The nurse came back with tea and hot water and Prue washed Mrs Piper's weary body in soft, sweet-smelling soap that she had brought especially for this task. It was what she herself would have wanted – not an intimacy but an acknowledgement of how hard the day had been. That Mrs Piper should be celebrated now with tea and her body being tenderly looked after. Mrs Piper drank her tea and then lay with her eyes closed and her mouth smiling as Prue soaped and cleaned her in warm water with the hint of lavender all around them.

The nurse had claimed privately that she did not like children, but she kept an eye on them all night. They had not settled in the other bedroom but the smallest had fallen asleep next door. When Nurse Falcon took the water back downstairs, Prue could hear her talking to Mrs Piper's older children and no doubt giving them tea as well as the ginger biscuits she always carried on her. Prue thought that Nurse Falcon would have made a very good mother if any man had had the courage to ask her to marry him. No doubt she terrified them, as many sensible women did.

By the time the nurse came back, Prue had found Mrs Piper a clean nightdress, which she guessed the nurse must have brought with her. They put this on her dry and now fragrant body and she was comforted and sighed and thanked them. The nurse had made toast and Mrs Piper ate her toast and drank her second cup of tea.

Prue did not want to leave the woman alone and wondered if any neighbour might help. Sometimes the women in the pit rows were close, but nobody had put in an appearance this evening. The best she could do was to say that she would be back after morning surgery to see how Mrs Piper was getting on.

She and the nurse were packed and ready to leave by the time the door opened and Mr Piper appeared. Prue always thought such men would be large and drunk and fearsome, swearing and with foul breath, but these things could not be judged. Mr Piper, whom she had met before because the Pipers went to church, was tiny, shrunken almost, very respectable. His eyes were darting glints of light against the dawn. He stood just inside his own street door. He was filthy from the pit.

Nurse Falcon slipped past him. Prue felt obliged to stay.

'You have two little boys, Mr Piper.'

His face lit up.

'Do I really?' he said in a pleasant, softly spoken voice.

'That's grand.' His accent was not of this area; Prue placed it as Scottish, she couldn't get nearer than that. 'I was so worried when I went to work, but the nurse was here by then and you came, of course. Thank you so much, we do appreciate your help.'

Prue thought Mrs Piper was a lot better by mid-afternoon when she called back in. Three of the children had gone to school, of the others, two ran about the house until Prue arrived and then their mother ushered them into the back lane with a ball. The youngest was only just walking.

Prue privately thought that Mrs Piper should be in bed with her new babies, but she was nursing them easily and they seemed contented and, in any case, Prue knew that was a silly thought; the children would have to be fed. Her husband, of course, was in bed because he had been to work and Prue had learned by then that pitmen were the hardest workers of all.

'If you want no more children then I have a suggestion,' Prue said, when she and Mrs Piper were alone. 'When you and your husband are going to have relations, you should take a square of sponge, damp it and press it inside you.' Prue mimed it. Mrs Piper's eyes grew round. 'Then, you see, the chances of his sperm meeting an egg will be less likely with such a barrier in the way.'

Prue waited. She wasn't sure what Mrs Piper's reaction would be and she was surprised, as very often in her work she was.

'Does he have to know?' Mrs Piper said, looking eagerly at her.

'Not if you can arrange this to suit yourself.'

Mrs Piper nodded.

It was about a month later when the vicar, Mr Edwards, appeared at the surgery in the middle of the afternoon when Prue had finished doing her visits and was hoping to sit down and have a cup of tea before she began evening surgery.

He was sitting in the back room, and judging by Lily's wan face and the number of dirty teacups, had been there a while. Lily looked relieved to see her, offered to go and make more tea and disappeared into the kitchen so fast that Prue barely had time to take off her outdoor things. She retreated into the hall and took her time.

She had barely sat down before he launched into his subject.

'I have been very distressed to learn that you have been giving unpalatable advice to my parishioners.'

Prue understood exactly what he meant, but she was surprised that what she had told Mrs Piper had travelled that fast and she couldn't help being pleased that so many women had learned of such things. The vicar, recollecting the subject he had introduced, went scarlet from his neck right to the top of his head. It was not a good look for him.

He reminded Prue rather of a turkey before Thanksgiving. She was not about to argue with him.

'I cannot discuss my patients with you,' Prue said politely.

He got up and was tall. Prue, not wanting to look up at him, stood up too.

'You are new here,' he said, 'you don't understand how the people live and you cannot come in here and take from them the confidence which they have in themselves and their lifestyle.'

'How are the children?' Prue said.

He had never once thanked her for her care of his children, nor had he offered to pay her.

'You will find that people will shun you if you attempt such thinking here,' he said. 'You don't know what you are doing.'

'I'm about to have something to eat,' Prue said. 'I haven't had half an hour to myself all day so you must excuse me.' And she left the room, trying not to wish several ills upon the vicar.

Ten

'Must you go to the vicarage so often?' Rory Gallagher wished he hadn't had to say this but he had putting it off for weeks now and he was worried about his daughter.

'I don't know what you mean.'

'I just think it would be better for you to be with people your own age rather than with married people.'

'Oh yes, and who would they be?'

'I don't know, I just know that you are never here.'

'And did you want me here when you aren't?' She lifted her chin and challenged him just as her mother would have done and he couldn't think of what he was trying to say.

'Of course I don't.'

'Then what? You think I might socialize with the other young women of the town; the maids and the girls who work in the pubs and—'

'You're deliberately misunderstanding me.'

'Then what do you want me to do?'

They had been over and over this: he wanted her from

here even though he would miss her; she was caught up in a life which could not be hers. She could have had her freedom and gone to the city to spend her time dancing and in the theatre and at concerts or she could have learned more, joined some profession as women were beginning to do.

He did not know any longer what his daughter wished other than to spend time with Mrs Edwards and her brood of children as though she were a glorified governess. And yet his common sense told him that she was nothing of the sort and Mrs Edwards was too sensible a woman, the little he had noticed of her in the village, to wish such a thing upon a pit owner's daughter.

She was a lady, but he was more and more aware that John Edwards was not a gentleman. He might be educated and think he was and be tall and fair and handsome, but Rory Gallagher had lived there a good long time and he knew from pitmen's gossip that Edwards drank and that at least one woman in the village was keeping him warm in her bed.

He could, however, say none of this to his child: it would have seemed mean and, at worst, false. She would think that he was only trying to take her back to him and he could do no such thing. She was grown up. She knew very little, even though he had tried to teach her how to navigate the world.

But then again, whoever knew how to do such a

complicated thing? Everyone failed. You could not save your children from that. You taught them the wrong things, you did not see the way that they would slip and slide and perhaps even disappear from your influence. You might lose their affection if you told them what you thought. He was not prepared for that and so he said nothing.

Helen flounced off to bed and slammed the door behind her. He couldn't make his mind up after that whether to work or whether to go to bed and try to blot out the night; the dreams where his wife was still alive and didn't want him, where she had come back and he didn't want her, where she was beyond his grasp, only just out of sight and he could not even shout her name.

He awoke sweating in the darkness and yearning for her.

Eleven

Robbie's car was the bane of Prue's life. She neither knew nor cared what kind of car it was. All she knew was that it was a bastard of a car. She had not learned to drive. She had lived in the city and didn't see the need where there was public transport. She tried not to remember that she had had a husband who drove or she could take a bus or a cab, but now there was no husband, no cabs; the only alternative to the car was a horse which, as a city girl, she tended to think would be a lot less use and more of a problem than a car.

She had to learn to drive it. It was hopeless at first though Ernie, who was good at such things, encouraged her and showed her what to do and did not seem to be able to understand that it was difficult. She thought she would never get the hang of the three damned pedals and the gear stick and how she had to match the engine's revs, as he called it, with the way that she accelerated so that she could change gear without crunching the gears and be able to get up into a higher gear or down into a lower one. It seemed obvious. It was not.

The steering wheel kept the car lurching off in directions other than where she wished to go and the motor itself seemed huge and unwieldly. She wanted to drive it into a wall and forget all about it, but Ernie persisted and because he did she had to. She could not ask him to drive her to see her patients when he was looking after the dispensary.

The practice covered not just the village but also the adjoining villages at several sides and the plunge down not quite into Weardale so that the farms around the area belonged to the practice as well and Prue told herself that if there was an emergency she would not manage without the car. She was rather worried about what she would do alone at night beyond the village, but there was no point in thinking about it. She carried with her a small silver pistol which a circus friend of her mother's had given her and taught her to use when she was a small child and it had been a game.

Shortly after she had learned to get about by herself, there was a banging on the door in the middle of the night. She was used to it by now and hurried downstairs to find a young man at the front door. It was meant to be spring but a howling gale forced her backwards. Outside stood a policeman.

'Can you come, doctor? It's Hallgarth farm. Sergeant Tweddle's there.'

Hallgarth Farm was Mr and Mrs Miles' place. Prue had hoped very much that she would not be called out suddenly like this.

'Come inside,' she said, 'and sit there, I won't be long.'

Five minutes later they got into his car.

She wanted to ask why the police were there and what had happened, but she let him drive her through the freezing night and then thanked him. There were lights around the house and in the farm buildings and she discerned other policemen outside. She got out of the car and followed the lights and then she saw the policeman in charge. Sergeant Tweddle touched his hat to her.

'Evening, doctor,' he said, and then he went before her into the barn.

Mr Miles was hanging from one of the beams. Prue could believe it and not. Who understood what made people kill themselves? Sometimes she wondered why everyone did not do so. At other times, when the sunsets were pale mauve and streaked with pink, she didn't understand why anyone would not want to live forever.

She went across and reached up with the help of a ladder and two sturdy constables. The body was cold. He had been there for some time, Prue thought.

'His wife found him. She's in the house,' Sergeant Tweddle said and he signalled to the men to move the body. As they did so Mr Miles slid from their grasp to the floor.

Prue went into the farmhouse, through the back door. It smelled of cows and sheep, musty and cold. There was no light until she reached halfway inside and then she saw in the back room by the blackened fire one candle and, beside it, Mrs Miles was hunched.

She was wearing her nightclothes and should have been half frozen, her long nightie sweeping the floor, the sleeves concealing how thin her arms were. She was middle-aged, but her body had collapsed as though nothing could hold it together. She heard Prue come in and said, as though Prue had been an angel, 'Dr Stanhope, I knew that you would come. He couldn't have taken his own life, not my Jerry. We're good God-fearing people. He could never have done such a thing.'

'Of course not,' Prue said.

Three days later, John Edwards was again waiting when Prue got home from her rounds. Lily met her at the door, whispering frantically, 'The vicar's been here half an hour,' and she scuttled upstairs as if she were being chased.

When Prue went in, Mr Edwards got up, unsmiling. 'Dr Stanhope, good afternoon. I have come to see you on a parish matter. I gather you were called to Mr Miles' farm on Tuesday.'

Prue didn't say anything; this was not his business. She tried not to feel negative towards him. It wouldn't help.

Nor must she acknowledge that she really disliked the man. He was ungenerous, he was pompous, he was everything he should not have been as a vicar. How many vicars were kind and caring and down to earth? She wished that there were legions of them. They had so much power, so much influence over the people who believed in them. They deserved to be humble before the people they served.

'It has come to my ears that this man took it upon himself to end his life. Is it true?'

'I'm afraid I can't tell you.'

Sergeant Tweddle had taken care with the legal implications and the inquest, since these people were well thought of in the village and Prue had been hoping, vainly it seemed, that nobody had any idea of what had happened, though there was always talk when tragedy occurred. Perhaps the vicar was just guessing.

'Then I must assume that he did.'

'You can assume what you please,' Prue said. She had to stop herself from shouting at him, but she stood there and waited. It would not help if she became emotionally involved.

'I need to be certain – Mr Miles cannot be buried in consecrated ground.'

'I didn't know there were laws about such things.'

'Laws of God.'

'Mrs Miles told me that she and her husband had places in the churchyard, paid for.'

'Not for suicides.'

'Do you mean that you would not allow it?'

'It is within my discretion.'

Prue could not believe that he would have Mrs Miles more upset than she was.

'They intended to lie side by side.'

'Not in my churchyard.'

Prue didn't know what to say. She didn't want to offend John Edwards, she didn't want to alienate anyone; they were all her patients and, besides, you never knew when you needed men of influence, however much you disliked them. There was no point in trying to reason with him, or to threaten him.

'If a man in my parish is not brave enough to live, then he does not deserve to have the same burial as better people, those who have endured what the good Lord has seen fit to send them. They let God decide the hour of their passing. So I would like you to tell me what happened.'

'My profession will not allow it,' Prue said, in as stuffy a tone as she could manage. He was the only person she knew who made her talk as if her mouth were full of wet cardboard.

That evening, after surgery, Prue went to see Sergeant Tweddle, who lived down Ironworks Road. A wind was howling up from the valley and Sergeant Tweddle was obviously at home for the evening, out of uniform and peering out into the darkness when she banged on his door.

She apologized for intruding when he was not on duty and he gathered her inside and took her through into the sitting room where Mrs Tweddle was sitting over the fire. They had not been introduced and Mrs Tweddle, like many of the pitmen and their wives, was short of stature and broad-shouldered with a straight gaze, which Prue liked. She put down her knitting and got up saying,

'You talk to Mr Tweddle and I shall go and make some tea.' And out she trotted. Whatever would they have done without tea, Prue thought.

She sat down and explained the problem. He told her to think no more about it, he would sort it out. She did not doubt him.

The following evening, when surgery was finished, she was surprised to find the sergeant in the sitting room. She had already heard gales of laughter from Lily and Robbie, and when she got there all three of them were sitting over the fire, drinking whisky. They urged her to join them and she was happy to do so, cradling the whisky as it caught the light in her hands.

'I was just regaling the doctor here and his good lady wife with an account of Mr Edwards, who only the other day committed a felony, only you mustn't say so.' He put a finger to his lips. She hadn't thought of the sergeant as having a sense of humour.

'Are you allowed to tell me?'

'I'm sworn to secrecy so I cannot say that he did crumple his bicycle against a tree. It seemed that the tree came to him and did a great deal of damage and one of my constables was passing just at that time and the vicar could not stand. He said it was the shock, yes, said the constable, but he didn't take him and charge him with being drunk and disorderly, though Mr Edwards cursed the constable greatly. I have been to see him today and have told him about the other matter which had seemed to concern him: that Mr Miles fell and struck his head on the concrete floor and that you saw it yourself.'

Prue let the sergeant out and before he left she kissed him on his warm rosy cheek.

'Ah, doctor,' he said, 'I won't let my wife know what you did!'

On the day of the funeral, Prue didn't look at Sergeant Tweddle and he didn't look at her. Jeremiah Miles was buried not far from the church, in the plot he had paid for, and Mrs Miles, Prue could see, was imagining herself lying next to him. Through the sorrow on her face the only trace of satisfaction was that she had the plot near him waiting for her. His first wife was buried just a little way beyond. His son had a grave somewhere in France.

Prue called at Mrs Miles' home the following day. It was cold there, so far up the valley. The view was lovely down to the dale and up the other side, but she didn't think much of it that day. Prue called out the woman's name and, hearing no response, went into the kitchen. There was no fire and no evidence that Mrs Miles had eaten. She was sitting as Prue felt certain she had sat all night and into day and not moved. Prue got down beside her and when she had managed to draw the woman's attention she said, 'Come back with me and Mrs Fleming and I will look after you.'

There was no response, even after she had tried to talk to the woman three times. She went into the yard and gathered what she needed for a fire. This done, she put the kettle on and made tea and then she went back to the village and brought some of the stew which Lily had made earlier that day and presented it hot when it had been over the fire, but Mrs Miles couldn't eat it.

Prue gave her tea, white with milk and laced with rum as Lily had suggested, saw that she ate and drank a little and settled her down in her armchair with a rug and a cushion before the fire. Prue built up the fire before she left, putting a guard around it. She wished the woman had somebody to help, but Mrs Miles would have no one.

Lily and Prue took it in turns to visit Mrs Miles. Lily couldn't drive but Ernie seemed to enjoy taking her there. By the end of the first week, the woman was sleeping a good deal of the time.

Quite early on the Tuesday morning of the third week, the farm was different somehow, Prue could tell before she got out of the car. It was nothing to do with animals, these had long since been taken away, sold to various other people, but it was still as it should not have been. No sound rent the air. No birds inhabited the trees which kept the wind from the farmhouse and its buildings. Prue could hear her footsteps crunching where once there had been the barking of dogs and the bustle of the farm itself.

She tried the door though it was never locked. She called out Mrs Miles' name, but no one answered. The fire was out in the kitchen. She was used to this and she would put it on and make tea and by this time she was bringing butter and jam and bread and milk but she could see that she didn't need any of this today. She could tell that the woman was dead before she got into the room.

She was obliged to attend the inquest and there she received another blow, so that she wanted badly to cry. As she drove her way slowly home, her whole body ached because she would not give way.

Lily was making soup in the kitchen but came through into the hall when she heard her.

'I expect you could do with some tea,' she said.

Prue shook her head dumbly.

'What did they say?'

It took an effort for her to meet Lily's enquiring gaze.

'Officially it was malnutrition, cold, shock, that sort of thing.' Prue trudged into the kitchen, where the kettle was always boiling. She watched Lily pour water on to the tea leaves.

'It's very upsetting,' Lily said.

Prue felt tired in a way in which she thought she had not felt tired before. No, it was more than that, she felt defeated.

'Mrs Miles was pregnant,' she said, and that was when she started to cry.

There were not many people at the funeral, but Prue was glad to see the woman buried beside her husband in the churchyard as she had wanted to be. Lily had picked daffodils from the garden for their graves.

Twelve

The following night, Prue was called out to a man who was dying, way up on the fell. It was snowing. She had expected that it would always be snowing, no matter what the season. It must be late spring by now in other places, she thought, battling against the thick white flakes and her windscreen wipers, which weren't coping.

She had not been to the house before so she had to go up there and face the darkness and the fell and the scarcity of houses and hope to find the right one when there were no signs. It took her seemingly forever and she was admonishing herself when she came to a sign. The snow had finally stopped and it read, 'Westernhope', and that was where she was meant to be going so she urged the car forward, even though it was slipping all over the road and every time it did so she thought she would slide off the side, into the ditch, and be stuck there all night. There were no other vehicles so at least that didn't matter. She turned up the narrow track and the lights on the car guided her toward the house.

When she got there she had to pound on the door and it was opened by a small woman who looked askance and said, 'Oh, he's a lot better, doctor. I'm sorry you had to come all this way, but earlier on I thought he was on his last legs.' This was not something Prue heard often and so she was pleased. She went in and there he was, sitting up in bed and having hot milk with bread and sugar and he was smiling.

She sat with him awhile, basking in the joy of it and accepting a big cup of tea and a piece of fruitcake from his wife and then she got back into the car and started on the journey to the village. It wasn't far but it seemed so because the snow was blowing horizontally and though she was used to it, it didn't make driving any easier.

The snow stopped, the sky cleared and by the crescent moon that emerged, she could see something in the road. She thought that if it was alive it would move. She didn't think it was a person either dead or pretending to be dead, so she didn't worry and then she thought it might be a deer which had been run over. But there were no deer on the fell that she had seen, so perhaps the idea was stupid. It was too big to be a fox or even a fat cat; it was big enough to be an extremely large dog.

It didn't move, so she thought she might drive around it, but the trouble with being a doctor was that you could never leave anything which might have a breath inside it, so, cursing herself yet again for at least the tenth time, she stopped the car and got out.

She thought it was a wolf. It was furry and had a pointed nose. And then it growled faintly, just to let her know that it was alive and aware of her. It was a German shepherd.

She got down beside it. The moon unhelpfully disappeared behind a cloud. She ran a hand over the dog's back and couldn't discern anything broken. It whimpered.

'Can you walk?' she said.

It didn't answer. She tried to aid it, but the dog whimpered again.

'You can die here or I can try getting you back to the surgery and some light. I'm not a vet, but I could help.'

The dog refused to get up. Prue sat back in the road. It was cold and she was tired.

'I can try to carry you, but though I am quite big for a woman, you are an extremely large dog. If you bite me, I will leave you here. Do you understand?'

She tried to lift the dog and couldn't. It raised its head and stared at her. In the end, she got hold of it by its rear end on both sides and dragged it to the car and although it began to growl she said, 'It's the middle of the night. If you can't get up from there somebody will run you over in the morning before it gets light. Now come on.'

When she reached the car, she lifted the dog's shoulders and the dog tried to get up and in the end, somehow, Prue got the dog into the car without the dog biting her, but her whole body ached with the exertion.

She stuffed it into the well below the passenger seat, but the dog didn't lie down because there was not enough room. It put its chin on the seat. When she got home she couldn't ask for help because Lily was pregnant and Robbie was ill and there was nobody about, so she dragged the dog by its shoulders out of the car and into the house and along the hall and in by the kitchen fire. There it lay as inert as a sack. Lily stared.

Prue was instantly alarmed at the sight of her at this time of night.

'Are you all right?' she said.

'The baby's moving so much I couldn't sleep,' Lily said, and she got up and watched the animal as though it would bite her.

'What are you doing, bringing a wolf here?' she said.

'It's an Alsatian and you know it. Get it some milk and water, will you?'

Lily poured milk and water into a bowl and Prue got down on to the floor and she lifted the dog's head so that it could lap and when the mix was all gone she let the dog sleep. She examined it gently and found that it was not badly hurt, nothing appeared to be broken, just bruised. She could tell by how it growled in a low voice that there was nothing wrong with it that might cause them worry. It was neglected and skinny; she could feel all of its ribs. It was a female. It was worn out. Maybe the owner would turn up. Somebody might miss it. As she sat there, thinking of all this, the dog began to snore by the fire.

When it awoke in the morning she made it porridge. The dog lapped it up and then slept. For a week the dog didn't move except for struggling into the backyard where it 'did its business', as Lily called it – it was a very clean dog – then it went back to the rug and slept.

They discovered it had fleas and washed and disinfected it and the dog went on doing nothing but sleeping. After ten days it followed Prue into the surgery and slumped beneath her desk when she started to see people. She wasn't sure it was a good thing in a doctor's surgery, but the dog made no sound other than the occasional soft snoring and no one could see it, so she didn't think it mattered.

The dog followed her into the kitchen and back, into the dining room and back, into the sitting room and back. When she went out on calls on the first day that the dog was completely better, Prue tried to tell it that she would not be long, but it stood by the door as she left.

Lily came into the hall upon her return.

'Thank God you're home,' she said. 'That damned dog has howled the whole time you were out.'

'I've only been gone two hours.'

'You'll have to take it with you.'

'It's too big for the foot well.'

Lily put on her face the stubborn look which Prue was beginning to recognize, so after that Prue had to take the dog with her, wherever she went, and was even glad of it as early summer made its pale, tentative way into the little town.

Prue hadn't seen such a thing so obviously before, that huge contrast between day and night, and through a gap in the bedroom curtains the brightness of the mornings was beginning to waken her very early. The dog slept on the floor by her bed and didn't snore any more and she was the one who woke up first as rays of pale grey and cream crept beyond the curtains.

Lily's baby was due at the beginning of June, Prue thought. She had been big early and didn't put on much more weight until right at the end of her pregnancy, but Prue had ceased to worry about her. The sickness had gone, the baby grew slowly and Prue tried to make certain that Lily ate enough to ensure that the baby took no harm, though her concern over her husband would have prevented it had Prue not insisted. Robbie ate less and less.

Prue joked about spending all her time in Robbie's bedroom and at least that made them both smile, but the pain was increasing and she doubted that Robbie would be there, but for pure will, when his child was born. She was glad husband and wife had separate rooms. Lily was too big to endure in her bed a man who didn't sleep, was in constant pain and whom they know to be dying.

Nightly when she awoke, Lily would go in and pass cool hands over his sweaty face. Prue tried to make sure that Lily did not see him at the worst of his pain, but Lily was not the kind of woman who missed much so it wasn't easy for any of them, and Prue was tired all the time now because she was getting very little sleep.

Privately, Prue had tried to talk Robbie into going into hospital.

'I'm going nowhere except the graveyard from here,' he said, 'I'm not leaving my wife until our child is here. They can't do more than you are doing.'

'They can nurse you better.'

'No.'

'I can send for a nurse—'

'You will not. I know it's hard for you, Prue, and I'm sorry, but I don't want anybody else here. I want what peace I can have.'

'I can't imagine your pain.'

'You don't have to imagine it. Just keep the drugs coming without blotting me out completely.'

'You're a lovely man, Robbie Fleming. Bossy but nice.'

'Fancy me, do you?'

'Oh God, yes.'

'Well, if you get over here . . .'

Prue laughed, but the laughter was not far from tears and she had to stop herself. He was so thin, like a skeleton, and his looks were gone. His face was white and gaunt and his whole body was on the verge of collapse. He made her want to shake her fist at God, but so many young men had died in the Great War not that long ago, it seemed a mere echo that Robbie should die now when he was so talented and lovely and his wife was having their child and breaking her heart over him.

Often at night Prue would spend most of the darkness by his bed, watching over him as a nurse, giving him drugs then falling asleep so that she would awaken when Lily came in halfway through the night to see how things were. Towards the middle of the month she would find Lily curled up as small as she could be against him and he with one arm around her.

As the days lengthened and the nights shortened, they took with them snatches of Robbie's young life, his hopes, dreams and the future that he and his wife should have had together.

His parents did not come to visit. Prue had enquired of Lily if he had parents, and Lily had not looked at her. Then she said carefully, 'They live in Fife. I have written several times but they won't come. They didn't want him to be here and they certainly didn't want him to marry a common little lass like me with no schooling and a thick accent. I wasn't good enough for them.'

She would have turned away, but Prue went over and took Lily into her arms.

'You're exactly right for him and he knows it.'

'Whatever will I do without him?' Lily whispered into her shoulder.

That night, alone with Robbie, when he was half unconscious he said to Prue, 'Promise me you will take care of Lily and the baby.' He grasped her hand.

'Of course I will. You don't have to ask.'

'It will be so difficult. There are many things I haven't said to her or to you.'

Prue didn't think about it. She just went on telling him that everything would be all right.

Lily's baby was late, as so many first babies are. Lily said that she felt like a mountain and Prue was certain she was days overdue. She could hardly move and Prue estimated that the baby was so low it could arrive at any time. The weather was a lot warmer by then and the sun beat down.

Lily sweated her way through the hours and Prue had to change Robbie's sheets every day because he ran with perspiration. The dog panted constantly, looking for any cool spot it could find, but up here on the tops there were few trees and very little shelter and the town roasted.

One Friday night when Prue had opened the wide the window in her bedroom as she fell thankfully into bed, she slept instantly but was awoken soon afterwards, it seemed to her, by a stumbling, pale figure – Lily.

Prue was instantly awake, so fast that she almost fell out of bed. 'The baby?'

Lily clutched at the huge mound at her front.

'Either that or I'm bloody dying,' she said. 'My waters broke, as you told me they would. The bed is saturated.'

'You should lie down. Here.' Prue helped her into her own bed. 'How much pain are you in?'

Lily glared at her, clutching even harder at herself. 'Oh God,' she said.

'Breathe.'

'I *am* breathing, you stupid person.'

'Like we practised.'

'Prue, I will hit you in a minute.'

There was no sound from Robbie's room. Prue was glad to think that he was sleeping because she didn't think he would be able to sleep for long. Prue gave Lily what help she could, but she could see that the girl was in agony after the first two hours. The contractions went on and on, and though Lily was aware of her husband in the next room, she screamed.

After the second time that she screamed, Prue noticed Robbie in the doorway.

'What a lot of noise,' he said.

'You shut up,' she said, 'this is all your fault!'

'You lucky woman, you have two doctors to help you.'

'I wish at least one of you would, you bloody fools.'

Robbie sat down in the armchair, already exhausted. Prue wasn't surprised. He hadn't been out of his room in days.

Lily insisted on getting up and walking about and then hanging onto the bedpost and not letting anybody touch her and trying to breathe, and then came the contractions and screaming. The labour went on and on. Prue knew this was quite usual in first births, she only hoped there would be no complications. If this went on for too long and nothing happened, she might have to take Lily into hospital.

However, Lily's body began to respond and open, just a very little at a time. Robbie said nothing and let Prue lead, and Prue was grateful to him – since this was his child, she thought, this was his gift to her. He put his faith in her ability and let her talk to Lily and tell her what to do, when to breathe and when to try to relax, when to go with the contractions.

Come morning, Prue went down and told Ernie to let her know of any emergencies; other than that there would be no surgery that day.

'And look after the house,' she said.

Mid-afternoon, Lily and Robbie's baby was born and he was there to bring his child into the world. As he lifted the baby and Prue made certain the child could breathe and everything was all right, he said, 'Oh, Lily, we have a beautiful little girl.'

'I wanted a boy for you.'

'And I a girl for you. She's perfect, Lily.'

'She bloody should be after all that,' Lily said.

Prue cleaned up the baby and delivered the placenta and Robbie gave the baby into his wife's arms. Prue went downstairs and made up the fire as she had from time to time. She came back with tea and toast for the father and mother, and then she went back down and brought up hot water, and as the parents talked to one another and ate their toast and drank their tea, she cleaned up the mother and helped her into a nightdress.

'What shall we call her?' Robbie said.

'You should decide.'

'You did all the work.'

'Roberta.'

'Och, that's awful,' he said.

'What about Hope?'

'Dear Lord.'

'Well, I don't know.' She gave up.

He gazed down at the infant.

'She looks like you, Lily, she is so beautiful.'

His wife handed the baby back to him. 'Why don't we call her what you told me your grandma was called? It was so pretty. Isla.'

Prue changed the sheets on Robbie's bed and then put father, mother and baby into them. She fell asleep on the sofa downstairs and slept until evening surgery.

The birth of the baby changed the household. Even May seemed to like her and would gather the child into her arms at every opportunity, crooning and singing and neglecting the housework. Prue didn't say anything – she liked that May was there at this time for her sister. As long as Lily and Robbie and the child did not suffer, nothing mattered, and she went into her surgery each day with renewed energy. She felt as if she could do anything.

To their surprise the baby slept well. Prue had heard people say that babies did not know night from day – and how could they? – but the baby gave Lily a chance to revive herself and Robbie the space to rest. So it was that Prue found that she was often the one awake, rather than the baby, in the darkness of the night. She thought she could hear the church clock strike two and she lit her lamp and went through to check on Robbie and found him sweating so that the sheets were almost shiny.

She didn't have to ask if he was in pain; she just put him out of it. She knew it wasn't ethical, she knew she was giving him too much painkiller, but she didn't care. Who could watch anyone go through that much pain and not relieve it? She watched over him day and night when she was not at the surgery or out visiting. The workload seemed to grow larger. She was exhausted.

Then, after three or four weeks, the child realized that it was born and began to cry every hour that God sent and a few more that he didn't. Prue, who knew nothing about babies other than professionally, could not believe how much the baby screamed and how little there was to stop it.

She suspected that Lily did not have enough milk, but since the more she nursed the more milk she seemed to make, Prue let her persevere. Between looking after the baby and Robbie, both women were constantly fatigued and slept the second they sat down.

Prue felt as if her life were turning into a nightmare that might never finish. Worse, May began to be absent for longer and longer stretches of time, saying that her mam was poorly, but when Prue suggested she might visit, or that Mrs Bradley might come to see Lily and the baby, May was vague. Since Mrs Bradley did not come to the surgery, Prue did not think it could have been anything important. Perhaps she was jealous or didn't want her second daughter there, because although Prue sent Ernie to tell her when the baby was born, she did not come. Prue did not like to question Lily about her family; she considered it none of her business, but she never saw Lily's brother or her mother except at a distance.

Robbie's face had gone from pale to grey and he was losing weight at such a pace that Prue did not know how he stayed alive and yet he was awake and sitting up in the mornings and in the evenings to greet his wife and see his child.

Lily pretended to him that they would live to be old and he would watch his child grow and maybe even his grandchildren.

'Give me some more.'

'Robbie, I cannot.'

'Give it to me.'

'Robbie! I could kill you.'

'Give it to me.' The way that his body twisted as never before made her give him what he wanted, and when he ceased to ask her she sat down and cried. Yet he was still conscious and in pain. Prue went through and nudged Lily's shoulder.

Lily went to her husband. She didn't beg him not to die. She didn't say anything to him, she just got up onto the bed and placed her lips upon his lips so that he knew she was there and then she told him how much she loved him and that she would look after their child and she would always remember him, always care for him. She held him in her arms as he died, and Prue thought there was nothing better you could do for a man when you had loved him, lain with him and given him a child. Afterwards, Lily lay down there to sleep beside her dead husband.

Thirteen

Two days after Robbie died, Prue went to Lily's mother's house. She knew the street; several times lately she had been there to attend to people's needs. It was a back street beside the railway line. Lily's family lived in an end house and it was obvious to Prue that Lily's mother was as slovenly as gossip said she was. The nets at the windows were grey, there was no paint left on the door or the windows and down by the side of the house rubbish had accumulated; tins and pots and bits of vegetables were decaying there. It stank.

Prue banged on the door. At first nothing happened and then the door gradually opened and she saw May's wan face.

'Are you unwell?' Prue asked. 'We really need your help, May. I'm sure you know that—'

'Me mam says two lasses like you don't need help so I won't be coming no more,' May said, and shut the door.

Prue banged on it again, but nothing happened. However hard she rapped on the door, the only people who took any notice were several neighbours who opened their doors and greeted her with waves and cries of, 'Hello, doctor!'.

Lily had written to Robbie's parents and to other members of his family to tell them that Robbie had died and when the funeral was. Nobody answered. Prue and Lily went ahead with the arrangements and Prue wondered how many young women with a tiny child had to go through the matter of her husband's funeral with the local undertaker. There was the question of whether she would want the plot beside him. She had to think about the coffin, the wood, the place in the graveyard, or could it be that Robbie had wanted to be buried in Fife?

Afterwards, Prue and Lily sat over the fire and Prue took Robbie's favourite malt whisky from the court cupboard, the glasses he had chosen and they sat in the garden since the damned weather had chosen to be fine and drank a considerable amount of whisky before they came to the conclusion that Robbie did not want to be buried in Scotland.

'Do you really want the grave beside him?' Prue finally ventured to ask when neither of them could see straight.

'I'm not twenty. Do you think this is the end of my time as a person?'

'I think we should count on that not being true.'

'The answer then, in spite of how I loved him, must be no,' Lily said. Then she looked doubtfully at her friend and said, 'Don't you think?'

'Absolutely,' Prue said.

They staggered to bed after Lily had fed the baby, and that night the baby slept well; whatever whisky was in Lily's milk, they were both glad of it because they hadn't had a full night's sleep in so long that neither of them could remember it.

Robbie was buried four days later and it rained as though even the heavens could not believe it. It poured down.

The day before the funeral, Prue had not counted on the fact that she was opening the door to find people she did not recognize with Scottish accents coming inside and saying they had come for the funeral, trudging through the hall.

'Is there a hotel nearby?' one man enquired. Prue thought he could be Robbie's uncle but she wasn't sure and he didn't offer more conversation. He was about sixty.

'I'm afraid not.'

'Well then we must stay here.'

'That won't be possible.'

'This is a big house, is it not?'

'No, it isn't,' Prue said.

'Then where are we to stay? We're a long way from Fife.'

Lily had written and advised them to stay in Crook which was just a few miles down the road, outside of which there was a very good hotel which looked down across the valley towards Weardale, but either they hadn't listened or they didn't want to. Money, she suspected, was not to be spent.

Lily came to greet them with the baby in her arms, but all the uncle said was, 'So you're the lassie he left us for?' And he looked her up and down ('as though I was a brood mare,' Lily said later). 'We need rooms.'

'Oh, I'm sorry. I think the Black Bull halfway up the main street would accommodate you,' Lily said.

After they had gone Prue said, 'They don't have rooms at the Black Bull.'

'Don't they?' Lily said innocently.

The following morning when Prue answered the door she found a couple on her doorstep. A tall man dressed in black and a woman almost as tall also dressed in unrelieved black.

'Good morning,' the man said. 'I am Mr Fleming, Dr Fleming's father.'

'I am Dr Stanhope.'

He looked shocked, though Prue couldn't see why – there were more women doctors in Scotland than in England.

She led them into the sitting room and went to find Lily, but she was already on her way down the stairs.

'The baby's asleep,' Lily said.

She looked so tired – so dishevelled – and why would she not?

'His parents are here.'

'Oh God, I've only met them once and they didn't like

me,' she said, but she went on into the room and Prue made tea and followed as soon as she could with a tray and biscuits. Lily was seated opposite them. There was silence.

Prue put down the tray and offered tea.

'Would you like to see Isla?' Lily said. 'We called her that because Robbie said it was his grandmother's name and it's so pretty.'

Neither of them responded. Prue could hear them munching their biscuits and Mr Fleming slurping his tea, and she wondered how someone as lovely as Robbie could have had such parents.

'My brother set up the practice here,' Mr Fleming said.

'He was very respected,' Lily said.

'He did our son a great disservice. Robbie could have been a surgeon had he stayed in Edinburgh and studied further.'

'Perhaps he didn't want to study further,' Prue said. 'He helped a great many people here.'

Mr Fleming shook his head and finished his tea. His wife was crying into a tiny lace handkerchief. Mr Fleming said bitterly,

'He didn't want to be where we were, after everything we did for him and all the money it cost us. We thought he would look after us when we were old. He let us down, he could have married a local lass and practised in Fife, but he couldn't wait to get away to this awful place and – and these people.' He shuddered. 'How could he come to this godforsaken town, just because his uncle set up practice here? He knew what it would be like, he did it to spite us. My brother was a worthless sort of man, I didn't think Robbie would follow him.'

Lily got to her feet. She stood as tall and straight as she could at her five foot three inches and she said,

'You come here and insult me. You don't want to see our child. I think that perhaps you had better leave,' and she sailed out of the room like a yacht with the wind behind it.

Mr Fleming got up. He looked helplessly at Prue.

'I'm sorry,' he said, 'you must think we are awful people, but our son, our only child, has caused us such grief. We had high hopes for him, we were so proud, but once he was grown—' The man stopped there, trying to control his breath, his lips shaking. He helped his wife to her feet very gently and urged her back down the hall towards the door while she went on sobbing, the handkerchief held close against her face as though it was all her comfort.

Prue saw them out. When she went back inside Lily was standing looking out of the window.

'Don't answer the door to anybody else, Prue, I don't want these people in my house,' she said.

On the day of the funeral, Prue thought that the heavens themselves were crying. She liked how everybody was wet. She liked that the black hats drooped, the feet were sodden, that trouser legs stuck to the flesh beneath and that rain drummed on the coffin as it was lowered into the earth. The sky was leaden, and even as Mr Edwards uttered the words he should, there was thunder banging nearby and lightning cracking over the hill, going forward as Prue had never seen it before; a few feet and then it cracked light again and so it progressed, like a funeral march on and on, stabbing the landscape as if the end of the world were nigh.

The widow gazed straight ahead, the baby screamed all the way through the service, the organist had broken his wrist so that there was no accompaniment to the singing other than the enthusiasm of Mr Edwards, who – possibly for the first time, Prue thought – was doing his best though he was half a note out at least when he sang.

The whole area had turned out for Robbie's funeral and if his parents could not see from this the good he had done during the short time he had been here, then that was not right. The church was packed with the village people and the farmers and the pitmen and the foundrymen and their families.

Lily's mother and her brother and sister followed the coffin, though they had not been to see her, nor offered any help. Robbie's father and mother stayed at the back of the church, even though his coffin stood at the front.

Lily's family stuffed themselves into the front pew on the one side and the side opposite was empty. It reminded Prue of what she had read of border skirmishes; the Scots in one place and the English in another, both glowering, both upset, both horrified that Robbie had died so young, yet they could not make their peace with one another.

The hymns were drowned out with the noise of people crying. Neither Prue nor Lily was one of them, they kept handing the baby back and forth between them, but the child's instincts were accurate. Isla's father was dead, the future was uncertain – so she screamed.

Steam rose from people's coats. Umbrellas left in the hall produced a stream of water from the outside door to the sitting room. Shoes squelched. Coats gently warmed and gave off a mouldy scent as the mourners held up pale fingers to the fire. The chatter rose and Prue thought, yes, they were the lucky ones – they were not under the ground, they were not grieving as Lily was, they were not without a father and they were not so sorry that they could not drink tea and eat cake and talk.

Mrs Bradley, Lily's mother, was a short, stout woman with tiny black eyes that were enfolded into the flesh of her face like buttons. Prue could not believe that she could have mothered such an exquisite daughter. Lily was holding the baby who was still crying and her mother came to her and said, 'You're spoiling that bairn, picking her up all the time. If you had six you wouldn't notice. You can come and stay with us. What would a lass like you want with a great big house like this?'

'The practice is here,' Lily said.

Her mother stared at her, not comprehending.

'What, is that American lass going to run it? Who does she think she is?'

'It's what Robbie wanted.'

'The lad's dead. Isn't what you want more important now, and you with a babby?'

'It will be properly sorted out by a solicitor.'

'Oh,' Mrs Bradley rocked on her heels with mirth, 'a solicitor, is it? I think you've forgotten your place, missie. It's your family you should be thinking of now and not some foreigner.'

'I'm not going anywhere,' Lily said, 'and neither is she.'

'We'll see about that. This place would fetch a pretty penny and keep us all for a good long time,' her mother said.

Lily had gone white. She put her lips together, picked up the baby and left the room. Her mother straightened, thrust out her ample sagging breasts and went back to the table to consume the egg or ham sandwiches which the vicar's wife and the ladies of the church had supplied. They had also baked cakes and biscuits and were now making tea for what looked like the entire village; they had a word and a smile for everyone and they walked among the mourners with great plates of food.

Prue went after Lily, who was sitting on the upstairs landing, crying almost as hard as her child. Prue wanted to ask her why Lily let her mother speak to her like that, but she knew. When you had blood between you, things were complicated and could not be easily explained. Friends understood, they did not expect you to put up with them when they were being hateful to you.

'I want her out of my house.'

'She's just upset,' Prue said.

'She's upset? How the hell does she think I feel? I know my dad is dead but he was a drunken bastard. Why does she say things like that to me?'

'She doesn't know what to say. She was enjoying your status.'

'I think she blames me for Robbie dying,' Lily said. 'She was so proud of her daughter being the doctor's wife, in a daft sort of way, though she had never stepped over the threshold before today. She enjoyed pretending that she wasn't pleased, that she wouldn't lower herself since I had overstepped the mark and married somebody out of my class. I don't think there's much status in being the doctor's widow.'

Prue didn't think so either, but she didn't say it. At that point, perhaps because she didn't like the competition, the baby stopped crying and fell asleep. Lily stayed there in the quiet, and Prue went back to find May devouring chocolate cake and licking her fingers.

'I've been offered work up at the big house,' May said proudly.

The big house belonged to the family who owned the steelworks, the Dilstons. They had a solid house in grounds outside the village, looking down the valley toward Weardale, as if they were too good to belong.

Prue only wished that the doctor's house was big enough to accommodate help from outside the village. These people knew Lily as a pitman's daughter and Prue felt sure that anybody who came to help would talk about her or think of her as one of them or, worse, as an oddity which was what both of them were now.

Prue had not been surprised to see Helen Gallagher at the funeral, and with her was her father. They were sitting halfway back and he did not look like a man who was pleased to be there, but she thought he had cared sufficiently to come. Helen sat beside him with a comforting hand through his arm.

They even came back to the house after the service and Prue saw him go over to Lily and shake her hand and look her in the eyes sympathetically, Helen close beside him as though for support and comfort to both. Lily smiled and talked. Later, Mr Gallagher came to Prue and he said, 'Now you have to take the whole weight of the practice. Do you know what will happen?'

She hadn't thought of it; she hadn't had time.

'I have no idea what the legal position is,' she said.

'I'm sure the solicitor will be hard on the heels of the funeral – they always are,' he said. And then, to her surprise, he said, 'You've helped me. If you find there is anything you think I can do, I will be happy to help you.'

He went off before she could thank him. She was astonished and found also that she was pleased – but then he needed a doctor for his pitmen and there would not exactly be a rush to such a place as this for any new doctor.

There was sufficient to occupy her that day, but when she went bed, exhausted, she could not put from her mind that she had no idea how to go forward and Robbie had said nothing. Whether this had been because he was in such pain, she didn't know, but also she thought that it was unusual for a man who was leaving his wife and child not to make certain of their future. After all, she was not his partner, she worked for him and not with him. But she knew she had to have faith, so she did not doubt that when the solicitor arrived everything would be sorted out both to her satisfaction and, more importantly to Lily's, and that Robbie would have made sure that Prue would have adequate help, because he had not been able to run the practice alone and neither could she for any length of time.

Prue heard a banging mid-afternoon on the Saturday. She had made sure the outside doors were locked after discovering that people had a tendency to walk straight in. She thought it a strange custom. She told herself that she was a professional and a degree of privacy was important, but it had more to do with her ideas about people barging into the house than anything else.

The banging on the door had increased by the time she turned the key and slid back the bolts at top and bottom. Lily's mother barged straight in and walked past Prue, down the hall and into the dining room. Prue, astonished, followed her.

'I'm having my furniture delivered,' she said to Lily who was seated there, holding the baby. 'Tom will be coming on shortly, since the football match is over.'

'What?' Prue said.

'We're moving in.'

'I don't think so.'

Mrs Bradley tried to stare her down.

'Lily won't come to us so we're coming to her. Tom will bring all our belongings on a cart. In a few days it'll seem as if we were always here.'

Lily had gone very white and clutched the baby to her. She had been up all night and obviously didn't know what to say.

'No, it won't,' Prue said, 'because you aren't staying. You have a perfectly good house five minutes away and if Lily needs you, we can send a message. You have a great deal to do looking after your son. Why would you want to take on more?'

Mrs Bradley sniffed.

'A lass needs her mam at times like this.'

'No I don't,' Lily said, cheeks white and lips quivering.

Much more of this, Prue thought, and Lily would burst into tears and that mustn't happen.

At that moment the door burst open again and Tom, Lily's brother, appeared with various household items in his arms. She could see down the hall a big cart outside, loaded up with their belongings.

'Where do you want these, Ma?' he said.

Prue came forward.

'They're going back with the cart and so are you.'

He was not as tall as Prue but three times wider. His eyes were small and darting and his whole expression was lascivious. He let his eyes linger on her breasts.

'Oh aye and who says?' He looked insolently at her, opened his mouth slightly and then ran his tongue all around his lips. She was just a woman, what could she do? He was smirking.

With an armchair in his hands he tried to walk past her. She drew back slightly as though afraid and at that moment there was a very slow, deep growl and the dog came forward crouched, teeth bared, eyes black glints and gleaming in the light. As the growl grew, saliva slid from the dog's open mouth.

Tom looked at the dog, mesmerized, and, for the first time ever, Prue enjoyed smelling fear. They could not mistake the menace. The dog was huge, its black and tan coat was standing on end and it was poised to tear out his throat.

The dog rose a little more from where it was, its body lithe, crouched to spring with jaws that looked ready to drag flesh from bone. Mrs Bradley seemed nervous. She hadn't moved but she did now. She regarded the dog with awe.

'That animal isn't safe. You shouldn't keep him here where there's a small bairn.'

'Actually,' said Prue, 'it's a she. She's called Mabel.'

Fourteen

Prue was just glad that they had enough to do so that they could not think every moment that Robbie Fleming was now dead and buried. Lily had the baby and the house to see to and Prue had to get up for surgery the morning following the funeral. There was some comfort in that, she thought, until halfway through the morning when a woman of about twenty-five inched her way into the room. Prue encouraged her, said what she hoped were the right things to make her feel at ease. Mrs Watson sat in her chair, looking nervously around her.

'So,' Prue said, 'can you tell me what the problem is?'

The young woman's gaze searched the walls as though she were looking for a way out. Prue waited. There was no point in asking any more.

Mrs Watson got to her feet, the panic huge in her grey eyes. She had an apron on – a pinny as they called it here – under her now unfastened coat. Usually women were too proud to go out in such garments. Mrs Watson must have grabbed her courage and dashed off with it. Her hair was falling out of its bun around her face like cobwebs, it was so thin.

'Please don't go,' Prue said. 'Let me try and help you.'

The woman paused, her lips trembled. 'I shouldn't have come here.'

At that moment Mabel snored very loudly, followed by a great deal of snuffling and somehow that huge snore took the distress from the room. Mabel came out from under the desk, still asleep, and collapsed between the two women with a huge thump to the floor.

'She's an Alsatian,' Prue said.

'She's bonny,' Mrs Watson said, and sat down again, staring at Mabel.

There was a long silence. Prue waited.

'It's him,' Ada Watson said at last. She turned sideways so that she wasn't looking at the doctor and her hands worked together in her lap as though she were darning socks.

'We've been married nigh on three years. I'm not from here, you know. I come from Esh Winning, down the valley.'

People here were very parochial. A distance of a few miles altered everything. Just as every street in New York was a separate place, Esh Winning lay at the bottom of the Deerness valley , along with several other villages. Prue had patients just north of there on the fell tops.

'We're a big family, ten of us, and my mam and her friends are asking me why there's no babby.'

Prue nodded. 'Sometimes it takes a while. Is your bleeding regular?'

'It's not that. It'll take forever with us the way things are going.' She stopped, drew in her breath, and then she said, 'Erik doesn't come near me, you see, and as far as I can work out, we won't have a babby until he does.'

Prue was taken aback. She knew that pit people did not discuss such things and that Ada Watson must have been in a very bad way to come here and be brave enough to talk to the woman doctor, and in a way she was pleased to be a woman because she thought that Mrs Watson would never have spoken to a man like this, even if he was a doctor.

'It is quite common,' she said, trying to put the woman at her ease.

'Is it?' Mrs Watson looked eagerly at her. Also she looked relieved to have got the words out.

'Too much work, too tired.'

'He's never been able to,' she said.

Oh hell, Prue thought.

'Have you talked about it?'

Ada Watson looked at her as though she were mad. 'Nobody must know.'

'Does he drink?'

'Like a fish.'

'It could be that. Would you like me to speak to him?'

Mrs Watson's eyes were huge. 'Him talk to a lady doctor?'

'Leave it with me,' Prue said.

Mrs Watson's eyes shone. She thanked Prue over and over before she tied her headscarf tightly beneath her chin and left.

That afternoon Mr Connor, Robbie's solicitor, arrived, and Lily, chatting easily, showed him into the room at the back which they used for their sitting room. Prue wasn't sure she should be there, but Lily didn't want to receive him by herself.

Prue remembered seeing him briefly at the funeral and he had asked if he could call, so it shouldn't have been awkward, but somehow it was.

For a start, Mr Connor did not look a happy man. That might have been out of deference for Robbie's death, but Prue thought it was more than that.

Sun streamed in through the window. Despite Lily's care, the room was shabby and the furniture old. Prue went off to make tea, Lily sat him down. Isla was asleep upstairs for once, which made things easier. It didn't take long to make the tea, the kettle had been boiling for the exact time when he would arrive. She was back within minutes.

Mr Connor finished his tea and cleared his throat and put down his cup and saucer. He cleared his throat again as though he were nervous and opened his briefcase. He took out papers and what Prue assumed was the will and fussed for several moments before he put these down too and a helpless look came over his face.

'When Dr Robert Fleming took on the practice it was already in debt. His uncle was a good doctor but he did not charge his patients, mostly because they had no money and he wanted to treat everyone.

'There is, of course, an income from the pits because that is how these people pay for their medical problems but these have been going into a black hole and there is a great deal of money still owing. He borrowed heavily from the bank. Dr Fleming – Robert Fleming, I mean – thought he could remedy these matters.

'It was unfortunate that he did not live long enough to do so. Even then there were and are demands on his pocket that have to be met. The house has a mortgage which must be paid each month or the house will be repossessed by the bank. I would advise you to sell. The practice itself could be sold.'

He stopped there, presumably to give them enough time to take this in. Lily sat motionless as though she did not understand.

'But if the house was sold, the practice could not go on,' Prue said.

Mr Connor coughed and then he looked straight at her.

'That is not true. The practice can be carried on anywhere. The premises are a separate issue.'

Prue had not yet been paid. Robbie had promised he would pay her every six months, open a bank account and put the money into it. It had not occurred to her to doubt him. She had thought he just didn't mention it, such matters were not so very important to a dying man with a pregnant wife.

'How much debt is there?' Lily said.

'Just less than five hundred pounds.'

Lily didn't cry out, it was as though she were being strangled. She put up both hands to her mouth as if she could not bear to hear herself cry.

Prue could not believe that an hour ago she had thought things could not get worse. She had even begun to plan, to think that she could take over the practice and carry it on and that in time all three of them would have some kind of future.

She wanted to shout and shriek at Mr Connor. Could he not have told them? Could he not have talked to Robbie about it?

Mr Connor read her face.

'I did say to him many times that I thought he should tell his wife about his financial situation.'

'But of course you could not do so because of your wretched ethics,' Prue said. 'You protected him—'

'Dr Stanhope,' he began to protest.

'There's no point in this, Prue,' Lily said, and Prue had never heard her voice so clear and cold. 'Do you have anything else to say?' She thrust out her chin, tiny as it was, and looked at him so that Mr Connor got up.

'Indeed not,' he said.

She moved out of the room like a queen.

Prue retreated to evening surgery. When it was over and Ernie had gone home, she went in search of Lily, thinking she might be crying or she might be with her child, instead of which she found Lily by the backroom fire, gazing into it.

'Is Isla still asleep?'

Lily looked up. 'I think I will regret it later but I'm grateful for it now.'

'Would you like me to make you some tea?' Prue asked.

Lily looked up at her. She had obviously rehearsed what she said next.

'I can't afford to employ you here, Prue, this is not your problem. I will sell everything and in time you will be paid for what you have done since Robbie died. I'm so sorry for what has happened. Maybe if you go back to Edinburgh your old professor will find you another post. He sounds like a good man.'

'And what would you do, go back and live with your mother?'

Lily's mouth quivered.

'What else can I do?' she said.

'Well, other than going into Bishop Auckland and wringing Mr Connor's neck, I can't think of anything.'

'He couldn't help it.'

'That's what men always say. They can't help their appetites, they have to stand by their ethics. Strange how it's never for our benefit.'

Lily blew her nose.

'How could Robbie do such a thing, Prue? I loved him so much.'

'He probably thought he was going to live forever. How does anyone accept that they are going to die, especially at such a young age?'

'But for him to say nothing?'

'Would it have helped?'

Lily frowned.

'What do you mean?'

'There was nothing he could have done or presumably he would have done it, and how would you have felt when he told you? You loved him and you were having his child. He must have believed in the beginning that he would get better and he would clear the debt and everything would be all right.' Prue didn't say that if she had been able to get anywhere near him at this moment she would have broken a chair over his head.

'I don't know how you clear that amount of debt.'

'Neither do I, but men think differently. It would have spoiled the last few months of his life for both of you.'

Lily blew her nose and Isla started to scream. Lily got wearily to her feet. Prue listened to the brass stair rods clinking as Lily trod like an old woman up the stairs.

The next day, after morning surgery, Prue suggested they should put up the house for sale.

'Mr Bloody Connor will help us with it,' Lily said.

Prue had always thought that Lily had a foul mouth; it was a very useful thing and got rid of endless frustration.

'You should really go away from here, Prue.'

'Where to? And how? I don't have anything but a few pounds to my name.'

Things were not real any more. How Lily managed Prue was not quite sure but, luckily, the baby had taken to screaming for several hours a night so it was not a question of sleeplessness; they were both beginning to fall asleep at every opportunity. Once that week Ernie had come into Prue's surgery and said gently into her ear,

'Dr Stanhope, you still have patients to see,' and Prue found that she was asleep, hands cradling her head on the desk.

The bank manager was called Andrew Silverton. Most people were scared of him. He was important in the same way as the chemist, the doctor, the businessmen. He saw

Prue and Lily politely into his office, but when Lily enquired about borrowing money he shook his head.

'The practice will make money,' Lily said. 'Dr Stanhope here has kindly agreed to stay and help.'

'I can't lend you any money. You have nothing to put against the loan, no assets. I was going to come and see you. The house will be put up for sale to meet the debt. Indeed I must ask you to move out as soon as possible.'

When they left, walking back up the bank and then up the road towards the house, Prue said, 'I hope he gets something very nasty and I have to chop it off. Preferably between his legs.'

Lily choked, but it was half laughter, half tears.

There were other things they could do, such as going to the pit and asking Rory Gallagher if he would fund the workmen's treatment up front.

Prue had no idea how Mr Gallagher's business worked. He had pits both up on the fell and further across in various other villages. She heard how prosperous the big pit owners were and how many of them had pits that employed thousands of men over on the coast. Some of them employed agents and managers, and it was rumoured they had never been north of London and never seen a pit but they took the money from it. People were bitter that it was not spent here in the north-east.

Mr Gallagher's pits were tiny by comparison. He employed a lot of men but over what seemed to her like half a dozen pits, so he was a busy man, overseeing it all himself as far as she could tell from what she had heard.

Lily assured Prue that Mr Gallagher had his office just outside the village, so she took her courage and Mabel and followed the road across the fell.

Mabel, who had decided she was too good and too big for the foot well of the little car, sat on the other front seat, upright, gazing from the window like another person. Prue had found the fells daunting at first – nothing but sheep and the odd farmhouse – but she was used to it now and had grown to love the empty skies. When cloudless, the stars glittered down on her.

The pit was about a mile away and was the largest of them, so Lily had said. It was called Anne after his wife. Prue liked that. Pits were like people: difficult, unpredictable.

Prue was taking no chances and had put a note through Mr Gallagher's door three days ago, saying that she would like an appointment at this pit this afternoon at about two o'clock. He had not replied so she assumed he would be there. She took the unmade road off to the left and bumped the car slowly towards the buildings. She spied his car, big and grubby, parked in the nearest yard, so she left her car alongside and went into the building just beyond, Mabel loping beside her.

It was ramshackle, as though it had been hastily erected some long time ago when it was thought that it would not need to last. It had a rusting corrugated roof and rubble walls.

In the office there was a desk covered in papers and there were various filing cabinets and shelves. From the next room along she could already hear voices, one of them distinctly Mr Gallagher's. Two others she didn't recognize. They were poring over some paperwork, but turned around when they heard her in the doorway.

'Dr Stanhope, do come in,' Mr Gallagher said. The other two men gazed at Mabel. He introduced them as Mr Boleyn and Mr Farebairn, assistant managers. Prue shook their hands and then they went out, closing the door behind them. Mr Gallagher asked Prue to sit down. Mabel prowled the office, sniffing here and there before settling as ever by Prue's feet.

'I heard what happened with the solicitor,' he said.

'I didn't think anybody knew.'

'A great many people have had some idea of what was going on. They don't have a lot to do or talk about and the older Dr Fleming, though a very good man, had no notion of what to do about money. How bad is it?'

Prue was grateful to be taken seriously.

'About as bad as it can be.' She hesitated. 'The thing is, I'm trying to raise some money and I understand that the pit pays for the men's treatment.'

'The union pays, but I don't think they could pay up front. The money is taken from the miners' wages.'

Prue felt deflated. She felt small for the first time and she could feel the fire in her face.

'I didn't know that,' she said.

'There's no reason why you should. Money goes into the bank every month, as far as I know, and the ironworkers pay for themselves, but I would be willing to loan it to you.'

'That's very kind of you. We thought about a loan; we went to the bank and it was decided that we couldn't take on any more debt. We don't know what's going to happen now.'

'If it comes to the point where we have no doctor, that's a worse problem,' he said.

'We're going to try and sort it out ourselves, but there's another reason I came to see you. There is something you might do for me; it's about one of your miners.'

Mr Gallagher changed instantly, he thought it was bad news. His face closed. Prue shook her head in reassurance. 'I presume that Erik Watson works for you?'

Mr Gallagher considered. 'He's a bright lad. If he were a bit more confident I would try and get him some schooling.'

'If you help me here that could be the long-term result,' Prue said. 'I would like you to ask him to come to the surgery.'

Mr Gallagher frowned in thought but didn't ask anything – he would know he couldn't.

'I'll certainly speak to him.'

*

Prue and Lily went looking at empty houses in the village, including one in Back Railway Street.

'Near me mam? Have you gone mad?'

'It has a garden.'

'It has nowt of the sort, Prue. It's a yard with a bit of grass at the end of it. Nowhere for the bairn to play or Mabel to do her business.'

Lily wouldn't go and look at it, so Prue backed the car until she reached the main road and then she turned left.

'Where now?'

'Thornley Road.'

'Too far for people to get to, especially if they're really poorly.'

'Dan's Castle.'

'Whereabouts?'

'Next to the pub on the corner beside the fell.'

Lily looked impatiently at her.

'I'm not having my bairn brought up next to a pub.'

'It's all that's left. It has a view at the back. At least let's go and look at it. Mr Gallagher owns it,' Prue said as though that might help.

It was a terraced house and indeed next to the pub.

'Just right for you going out to rescue the drunks from falling into the road,' Lily said, but it did have a long garden behind it. The cold wind was screaming out there so they didn't linger, apart from Mabel who obviously smelled something interesting and had to be shouted at before she lumbered back inside.

The house had two good downstairs rooms and a decent-sized kitchen. They could live in the kitchen, Prue thought, and use the other two rooms as the waiting room and for surgery. The dispensing room was the cupboard under the stairs. Upstairs were three bedrooms. The biggest at the back had the view. This would do nicely for Lily and Isla and would be quieter than the others, she thought, though Lily would make up her own mind. These days, Lily varied between bad temper, and silence. Prue was not sure which she preferred. The other two bedrooms were on the front street, tiny and had the noise.

When Lily came inside the first thing she said was, 'My God, it's filthy!'

Prue didn't think it was as bad as that, but Lily was a true pitman's daughter in spite – or perhaps because – of her mother, and wouldn't have dirt anywhere.

Nobody had lived in the house for a good while, Prue thought, judging by the empty rooms, the thick dust and cracked windowpanes.

'The last people in here were pit sinkers, believe me,' Lily said. These were the men who had looked for coal, years since.

'Dan of the Castle,' Prue said.

'Aye, likely.'

'It's the best of the bunch and won't cost much,' Prue said.

'Well then,' Lily stuck out her chin, 'we'll have it, but I'm not moving in here until I've scrubbed it from top to bottom.'

Lily was so brittle, so organized, energetic and very angry; Prue thought that it was not surprising. She could not endure anyone's company. Prue kept the surgery going; she had put a plaque on the wall outside with her name and surgery hours, which Ernie had supplied with a hot poker and a piece of wood.

Lily scrubbed the house. She did not scruple to sell anything and had disposed of a good many pieces of what had been lovely furniture.

'At least it won't be need polishing,' she said, and sold an oak desk and a dining table with two generous leaves and six chairs.

'What are we going to eat off?' Prue protested.

'Our knees if necessary,' Lily said. There was, however, a long pine kitchen table with benches, like being back at school.

She got rid of standing lamps, a number of small tables and all the books, including a good many medical books; sold to a special dealer who came up from Crook to see what was on offer.

'I might need those,' Prue objected.

'I thought medicine was supposed to go forward,' Lily said, and Prue could not help reflecting that if Robbie could have seen her now, he would never have married her. She had changed so much since he had died. There was nothing gentle about her any more. Perhaps her mother had started off like her and then after her husband drank himself to death and left her with three children, she turned bitter and inward too.

Lily lost herself in activity. She stayed up all night with her child, she laboured all day. She spent the afternoons chopping up cheap furniture for firewood in their new home.

Isla went on and on crying. Predictably, Lily's milk had dried up.

'She's hungry,' Prue said.

'She can't be. I've spent all day feeding her.'

'She's not getting enough milk; you know it.'

Lily looked ashamed.

'Let's try something else, eh?' Prue said.

There was at the edge of the village a man who kept goats. He lived alone and it was not surprising, Prue thought, as she neared the place. The smell was awful. She had heard that billy goats pissed in their own mouths. She almost believed it and yet when she got there and saw the goats' huts, she knew that she had seen many dirtier houses. Each little hut was sweet with hay. In them the goats munched contentedly, their almond eyes watching her. They were black and white with neat hair and there was no billy goat in sight. She smelled the man, rather than saw him, as he came around the side of the building, but he smiled so cheerily at her that she forgave him. He was middle-aged and dressed almost in rags.

'Dr Stanhope,' he greeted her. 'I've heard many good things about you. What brings you here?'

He had an educated accent, and his face was full of confidence.

'I'm wanting some goats' milk,' Prue said.

He went over and caressed the heads of each of the nanny goats.

'These are British Alpines. Aren't they beautiful?'

Outside the huts dried willowherb hung, twined about with string and the goats' put their heads out of their huts and grabbed at the purple flowers.

'Their favourite,' he said. 'Mind you, they are partial to a garden rose.' And he laughed. 'How much would you like?'

'We have a baby girl who isn't getting enough breast milk.'

He frowned. 'How old is she?'

Prue told him.

'Just as a supplement,' she said, 'so that we might all sleep at night.'

'Dr Fleming was a good man and so was his uncle. He helped me over the years. You can have as much as you like, but be careful and water it and try just a little at a time in case it doesn't suit the baby. It's better than cow's milk, of course, not as rich but full of good things.'

Prue thanked him and offered to pay, but he said that no doubt he would need her in the future and she could take it as payment for when he was ill.

'You haven't been to the surgery in the time I've been there.'

'I haven't needed a doctor in ten years,' he said, smiling. 'I make a great deal of very good elderberry wine – you must stop by, doctor, when you have time.'

The baby took to watered-down goats' milk immediately. Lily was so thankful and at that point the child began to sleep the night through.

Prue was surprised a couple of weeks after she had talked to Mr Gallagher – he had not got back to her and she was worried – at late-afternoon surgery when a young man halted just inside the door. He was open-faced and said politely, cap in hand,

'I'm Erik Watson, Dr Stanhope.'

'Do come in.'

Prue was heartened. Mr Gallagher had kept his promise. Mr Watson hesitated and then he closed the door. He came across and saw Mabel, who for once had not retreated under the desk but was lying down to the side of it. Now that they were moved, there was not a lot of room in Prue's surgery and Mabel seemed intent on taking up as much of it as she could.

'It's a German Shepherd, isn't it?' he said.

'That's right. Did you have one?'

'When I was a little bairn, aye,' he said, bending down to stroke Mabel's ears. Mabel looked rather taken aback at this affectionate assault and then sat up and licked his hand.

'She never does that,' Prue couldn't help saying.

Mr Watson grinned.

'She's bonny,' he said, and then he sat down across from the desk and Mabel, since he had stopped stroking her ears, put her head in his lap so that he was obliged to go on, whether he liked it or not, but he spoke softly to her. He looked so young, Prue thought.

'Mr Gallagher said I should come. I think I know what it's about.' He blushed the colour of peonies and concentrated on the dog. 'I nearly didn't come,' he said, 'except that I had to or the boss wouldn't have stood for it. There's nowt nebody can do and I dinna want to be here.'

It was only then that Prue realized Mr Watson was not sober.

'Aye.' He read her face, 'I've had a few pints. I couldn't have come no other way. My Ada's that upset and she's a right to be. We'll never have no bairn, not with me like this. I should've been that riled she came to see you, but I can't be.'

'That's all right,' Prue said soothingly as Mabel banged her nose at him when he stopped caressing her ears. 'I'm just so glad you got here. It's not an easy thing to do. Can you tell me about yourself?'

'Nowt much to tell really.' Mr Watson shifted on his seat and glanced at the door as though he might run out.

'Do you have parents, brothers and sisters?'

'Nebody.' His voice was flat.

'Do you remember your parents?'

'Me dad died down the pit when I was little.' Mr Watson looked down at his hands. 'I was the only one. Me mam died when I was seven.'

'And then what happened?'

There was a long pause and he didn't look up. She waited but he went on saying nothing. Prue gave him more time. At that moment Mabel, perhaps bored with having her ears rubbed, began to lick his hands. Mr Watson's face went white and then crimson and he choked and pulled an arm swiftly across his eyes as though to deny any kind of emotion and he looked down at Mabel before stroking her head.

'I went into a – a home.'

Prue suddenly understood. 'Did somebody hurt you there?'

He said nothing, his face was shining crimson with sweat and embarrassment but Mabel would not let him stop stroking her. He nodded.

'Can you tell me about it?'

He shook his head.

'Can you talk to Ada about it?'

'She'd not want me no more if she knew what they made me do.'

'She cares about you,' Prue said. 'She loves you very much or she would never have come here. I know that you find it hard to talk about these things but she loves you. Coming to me hasn't been easy for either of you, I know that, but you should try to talk to her for both your sakes.'

'I cannot.'

'Just say what you told me. That will be enough. Try it.'

'I don't know how to touch her.'

'It doesn't matter as long as you do. Start very slowly. Sit and talk to her. Don't go off to the pub and hide there. Just try for once staying at home. Sit down by the fire after tea, just for half an hour. It'll be worth it, I promise you. It's not going to happen quickly but just talk, eh? Isn't anything better than what you're going through now? And the thing is that you and Ada love one another. Some people never have that. And you have to remember that you were a child and it was not your fault.'

He didn't answer. He didn't move.

'It wasn't your fault, Erik, you were just a small child and somebody should have been there to look after you and they weren't. You shouldn't have had to experience such awful things. You were just a little boy. Remember, it wasn't your fault.'

He nodded. Mabel gave Mr Watson's hands a good wash before he left. Prue just hoped that Mabel's care would show results.

Fifteen

Prue was coming back in the car from a farmhouse on the road to Wolsingham. It hadn't been a difficult diagnosis and she was thinking about dinner. It was still light, it being as close to summer as this place ever got. She was astonished at how undefined the seasons were. It could be bitterly cold in July and picnicking weather in December, but hardest of all were those days when it didn't clear; the sun didn't shine, there wasn't much rain and no wind and everything was grey.

Few people were on the street; they were at home finishing their tea or sitting over their fires reading the newspaper, so it wasn't difficult as she drove past a side street to spot what she thought was some kind of scuffle.

The local lads were always fighting, they did it outside the pub almost every night, but this looked different though she couldn't think why. She stopped, almost went on again and then began to reverse the car as softly as she could. She had been right, there a man had hold of a woman. He was not exactly assaulting her, but she could not have got away from him either. He had his hands at either side of the wall so that she couldn't move. Prue took the car forward just a little and killed the engine, then she walked back as quietly as she could.

It was infuriating that there was nobody on the street, but perhaps people would not have noticed. This was just a side street that divided the housing, an end wall. She could hear their voices.

'Just a kiss,' he said.

'I wouldn't kiss you if you were the last man on earth,' she said, glaring at him.

She was not frightened, Prue thought, but neither was she happy, her body sagging just a little as though unsure what to do, and Prue could sympathize: shout and he might put his hand across her mouth, struggle and he might treat her worse.

'Little Miss Gallagher, don't you think you're the best?'

She tried to break free then and the young man took hold of her wrists to stop her and that was when Prue said, 'Let her go.'

He didn't, but he was astonished and looked at her. He was Lily's brother, Tom, and the girl was the pit owner's daughter, Helen Gallagher. Tall, bonny and a long way above him socially.

The girl looked relieved. Tom looked worried, but recovered himself quickly.

'It's the lady doctor. My and isn't she a fine figure of a woman. Gan on, missus, or you'll be next.'

'I don't think so,' Prue said, but when she started down the side street toward them, he didn't move.

Prue sighed and then she took from her small bag the tiny silver pistol that she always carried. The lad stared and then he laughed again.

'What's that, a pea shooter?'

'Let her go right now or you'll find out.'

In answer he grabbed the girl by the shoulders, pulled her to him, then he put one hand on her neck and the other hard against her breast and squeezed so that she cried out and tried to move her face and body from him.

Prue was careful and aimed at the hand at the far side so that there was no possibility that the girl would be hit and then she shot him, just catching him. There were several split seconds before anything happened. At first he didn't seem to notice and then he registered the impact, screamed and released the girl, gazing at the blood. Helen was motionless for a few seconds. She sobbed briefly, pushed past him and ran towards Prue.

Tom stared at his hand.

'She's killed us!'

The blood was streaming down his arm as he held it up. He glared briefly at Prue.

'You fucking bitch,' he said, 'I'll get you for this,' and then he ran. By the time Prue turned around, Helen Gallagher had gone as well but in the opposite direction. Prue wanted to see her home, but she had disappeared among the back-to-back houses.

Prue had so much to do that she didn't think any more about the incident. Two days later when evening surgery was over and she was glad of it, she heard the door to her room. She didn't look up immediately, it couldn't be anything important; she was hoping it might be Lily with a cup of tea. She had no more notes and Ernie had not indicated that there were any more people to see. She was tired as the door opened and somebody came in, but not as far as the desk. When she looked up, Rory Gallagher stood in the doorway. It wasn't that he was hesitating, he was looking at her with a vexed expression, not the way most people looked when they came to the surgery.

'Mr Gallagher, do come in. How can I help you?'

'Dr Stanhope,' Mr Gallagher acknowledged. He didn't quite slam the door but he looked as if he wanted to. 'I think you have something to tell me.'

She wished he would sit down. He looked threatening, standing in front of her desk, gazing down a long way at her.

'Would you like a seat?'

'Not especially.'

Prue stood up. She was beginning to feel victimized.

When she stood up he was still taller than she was, but at least it made her feel better.

'Don't pretend you don't know what I'm talking about,' he said.

'Mr Gallagher, you're offensive.'

'And you, Dr Stanhope, did not tell me that my daughter had been attacked.'

'If she didn't tell you then why should I?'

This, she thought, was a new argument to Rory Gallagher. He said nothing.

'She's not a child,' Prue said, 'and I would be betraying her confidence.'

He said nothing for a moment or two and then since she sat down so did he, but with a sigh.

'You carry a gun?' He sounded surprised and so English. 'You shot young Bradley.'

'He wouldn't let her go,' Prue said. When their eyes were on a level she felt able to continue. 'Although she didn't seem to think at first that he was going to hurt her, I couldn't count on it and then he went beyond respectability and she was afraid, so I didn't hesitate. It was just a nick in the hand.'

'You could've killed him.'

Prue considered for a second.

'I'm a very good shot. It was slightly hazardous of course. A little lower, had I chosen, I could have got him square in the backside. If he had gone further with his assault and I could have got the angle right I might even have shot him straight between the legs.'

Mr Gallagher winced.

'Miss Gallagher was never endangered because of my pistol. I wouldn't like you to think that.'

'Tom Bradley has disappeared,' Rory Gallagher said.

Sixteen

Prue tried to go to church on Sundays. It was not that her patients came from a particular church, she was the only doctor in the village, but she knew that her being seen about the town meant a great deal to these people and even Mr Edwards thawed when he saw her in his congregation two weeks running. Mrs Edwards, nervous and running between husband, children and the various clubs and committees of the town, always looked so worn down.

Helen Gallagher ignored Prue, as though ashamed of what had happened. Prue watched her as she drank coffee after the service. The vicarage children slid down the bannisters and invaded the room, which was filled with parishioners as it was every Sunday.

Their mother was in the kitchen making tea with the ladies of the parish and their father merely pressed his lips together. The sun shone through the lovely floor-to-ceiling windows and Helen went over and opened the double doors which led into the garden. Immediately the children streamed out, Helen after them, shouting,

'Teddy! Teddy! Over here!'

Mrs Edwards appeared at Prue's elbow with a cup and saucer. Prue was dying to say to Mrs Edwards that she could do with more help. She knew that the women of the church baked for these mornings, but if just one of them had helped to clean or take a child it would have been easier, but she was not the sort of person to unload her responsibilities onto another. Mrs Piper had told Prue that many parishioners had offered more help but Mrs Edwards was too proud to accept and Mr Edwards, while Prue felt annoyed at his behaviour, was no worse than most men at not being there to give a hand.

The children were shouting and laughing and Helen was rolling down the lawn which sloped away from the house. They rolled down too, shrieking in excitement and Helen reminded Prue of some kindly Pied Piper. They fell on her and the five of them rolled over and over on the lawn in the sunlight, like puppies, giggling.

Prue had just fallen asleep when she heard the sounds of fighting below her window. She got up automatically as she did most Saturday nights, dressed and picked up her bag. By the time she was downstairs, Paddy, the landlord, was at her door.

'How many tonight then?' she said.

'Just four so far.'

'Can you just not refuse to serve them? It's always the same lot,' she said.

Paddy looked at her as if she were mad.

'They're Irish,' he said, as though that explained everything, and since he was Irish she thought he probably meant it as a compliment. She followed him into the pub. The wounded were sitting down and, to be fair, there wasn't a great amount of blood. She was grateful. She didn't want to spend the rest of the night in Bishop Auckland hospital. She patched them up as best she could and Paddy paid her as he did on most nights, with fish, butter, fresh vegetables, eggs or even flowers, which she appreciated, and Lily did not.

'You can't eat flowers,' Lily said.

They all had back gardens and or allotments. Prue was hoping that in the season they would have game. Lily was partial to such things, so she said. Also, and Prue had no idea which farm it came from, often there was a particularly lovely cheese which they all liked, so white and salty.

Prue fell in the door after Mabel, let go of her bag and made sure she put the food into the pantry and closed the door before they both stepped up the stairs to bed. She couldn't be sure the row would be completely over now but she hoped so.

*

Going through the books as she did Prue noticed payments which went out every month, quite a lot of money but there was no reference so, as soon as she could, she made an appointment to see Mr Sutcliffe, the accountant, and ventured into Bishop Auckland. She came here often to the hospital and the accountant's office, like many, was at the top of the town, in Cabin Gate before the road went on to West Auckland. These were Victorian terraced houses.

Mr Sutcliffe was a particularly sweaty man, no matter what the temperature in his office. He looked to Prue like somebody who had high blood pressure. He was overweight, obviously took no exercise and his stomach stuck out as though he could be six months pregnant. He smoked one cigarette after another and his nerves were bad, she could tell from his fingers drumming on the desk, and she could smell alcohol on his breath though it was only mid-morning.

Had he been a patient she would have advised him that he risked stroke or heart failure for such excesses. She questioned him, showed him the figures with regard to their outgoings, but all he did was frown and say that he knew nothing about it.

'Is it a business expense that I ought to know about?'

'I don't know what it is, just that Dr Fleming told me it must be paid every month without fail and so it has been.'

'Who is the payment to?'

'I can't say.'

Prue was getting tired of Mr Sutcliffe's attitude.

'You have an address presumably?' she said, 'and have been making the payments?'

'Aye, of course, but it's . . .' He got up and went over to a filing cabinet and spent so long in finding the relevant document that Prue's left foot went to sleep. He emerged, flourishing a paper. 'Here it is. I knew I had it somewhere. J. Featherall.'

'Is that Miss, Mrs, Mr?'

'No idea,' he said. 'Address is . . .' He paused here and moved back and Prue thought he really should have had spectacles – was it vanity or lack of care? But for an accountant not to be able to see close work – she was glad that she was not totally reliant on him any more. He had let Robbie get the business into this mess, or rather he had let Robbie's uncle. She did the accounts now before he got to them and knew where every penny went except this.

'I can't read the address. Miss Henderson does all this. She isn't here today. She only comes in on Mondays and Fridays.'

'May I see?' Prue put out her hand.

He passed her the paper. She scrutinized it. It wasn't easy.

'Is that Boulmer? Where is it?'

He looked at it and narrowed his eyes.

'It's a fishing village in Northumberland.'

Prue stared.

'Why would he send money there?'

'All I have is the address.'

'Mr Sutcliffe, this is a lot of money and we're still paying it.'

'The bank does these things.'

'I want to know about it.'

He looked coldly at her.

'With respect, Dr Stanhope, Mrs Fleming pays, not you.'

Prue felt like slapping him. She also felt like saying to him that the bank should stop paying into something Lily presumably didn't know about, except that she might. Her instincts were to go back and question Lily about this, but Lily was so open about everything that Prue felt she would have mentioned it, so instead she made an appointment to see Mr Silverton, the bank manager.

'I think you could have mentioned this,' she said, showing him the figures.

'Mrs Fleming would have said if she had wanted it stopping. It's none of your business. You are making the money but officially, until it's sorted out here, the practice is not yours.'

Prue couldn't say that Lily had a baby and her husband had just died, why would she think of such things?

'If it is to be stopped, I need her say-so,' Mr Silverton said.

Prue got out before she said something impolite, but she went back home unable to decide whether to tell Lily or not. This lasted until they had tea before bed when Lily looked frankly at her across the kitchen table and said, 'So, when are you going to tell me what's bothering you?'

Prue, who thought she had hid her worry convincingly, looked straight at her and told her what the accountant had said.

'I never liked that man,' Lily said, 'the only thing to do be done is to go up there and find out what's happening. It must be something important or Robbie wouldn't have given money. Maybe it's some old people who need it and are distant relatives. We'll go on Sunday. Besides, if that money isn't doing anything essential, we need to get it back,' and she poured more tea.

Prue hadn't seen Ada Watson for some weeks. She did not know how the Watsons were getting on, but she sat Mrs Watson down and then she said, 'How are things?'

Mrs Watson smiled at her. 'Better than they were, at least sort of. We do – I mean we have – it's just that . . .' She looked directly at Prue. 'I don't think it's the kind of thing which sorts easily.'

'No.' Prue wanted to add, 'if ever,' but she couldn't.

'The thing is, Dr Stanhope, that lately I've felt so ill.'

'How do you mean?'

'I don't know. I think it's just that I'm that sick of him

not being there and not being near and you know and it's makin' me ill.'

'What kind of ill?'

'Where I don't want to see him and I don't want to do anything and . . . you know.'

Prue didn't know. 'Are there physical symptoms?'

The woman shook her head.

'Nothing much, just odd, it's tender here.' Mrs Watson touched her breasts.

'Do you feel sick?'

'Often.'

'And are you bleeding?'

Ada couldn't remember.

'Why don't you get up on the couch over there and let me have a look at you?'

Mrs Watson frowned and then took off her coat and climbed up. Prue went over and tried her chest and got her to stick out her tongue and put a hand on her brow and then ranged her hands over Mrs Watson's body. Then Mrs Watson got up and ambled back to her chair.

Once she had sat down again, Prue looked at her. 'So you have had relations, you and Mr Watson?'

Mrs Watson raised her eyes to the ceiling.

'If you can call it that. It lasted all of two minutes.'

'Well, it may not have lasted long but I think it has had a long-term effect. I would say that you were pregnant, Mrs Watson.'

Ada Watson stared. 'From that?'

It was possibly, Prue thought, what some women had been wondering for years, but she could see Mrs Watson's face alter.

Mrs Watson sat there, trying to take it in, and suddenly her face cleared and an expression sat on her countenance that Prue could only have described as sunny.

'Am I really?'

'Really.'

Mrs Watson laughed.

'Oh,' she said, 'my mam will be so pleased. She's taken to asking. She won't ask no more and wait until he finds out.'

She left the surgery happier than most people did.

Tom Bradley turned up at the surgery. As far as Prue was aware, nobody had seen him for weeks and she was relieved, grateful even. She knew she had not hurt him badly but if the wound had become infected he could have lain in a ditch and died. Unable to sleep because of this fear at four in the morning, she felt guilty. His mother had even come to the house, crying over Lily. The rumours in the village varied, but none of them was good.

'Crocodile tears,' Lily scoffed and she looked hard at Prue, but she didn't ask. Helen Gallagher had said nothing it seemed, but Mr Dilston, who owned the works, had said that Tom needn't come back to the foundry; there were plenty of men who wanted his job if he didn't, he was only a labourer and labourers were two a penny.

On the Wednesday evening when surgery was over and she was tired and about to turn off the lamps and go into the back for a welcome meal over the fire, she saw in the shadows a slight young man and guessed.

'Is that you, Tom Bradley?'

There was an enormous sniff and then he came into the light. He was ragged, dirty, his cap had been lost somewhere and his hair gave evidence that he had just come in from the wind and rain. Mabel, under the desk, went on snoring and she would not have done had Tom Bradley been a threatening presence; Mabel could smell danger at half a mile.

He certainly didn't look threatening; his shoulders were slumped and he was exhausted, Prue could see. He must be in a bad way, she knew, to come to her now. She felt so sorry, he was just a badly brought up boy who had learned no respect for women and thought his world was only about what he wanted and in a way it was all he could handle.

'Is the wound infected?' she said.

'Don't think so, I just . . .' Tom's voice wavered.

Come in, then and I'll see what I can do.'

He shuffled toward her.

'You winna give me up to the constable?'

'It's over,' she said, not sure of her ground, but certain by now that he had suffered enough.

He held one hand over the other, though there seemed to her to be no redness.

'Sit down.'

He did. She poured warm water into a bowl and cleaned the wound, and it was not nearly as bad as she had thought it might be.

'It's going to be all right,' she said, and Tom sobbed.

'I meant nowt,' he said. 'She wanted me to. Lasses like that, church lasses, they're always gagging for it.'

'You shouldn't have run away,' Prue said.

'I knowed Mr Gallagher would be after me.'

Yes, Prue thought, an excellent reason for leaving.

She finished what she was doing and bound it, though it really wasn't necessary.

'Have you been to see your mother? She's frantic about you.'

He shook his head.

And then, as she never did, Lily appeared in the doorway.

'What are you doin' here?' she demanded.

'He's a patient.'

'He's a bloody clown,' Lily said. 'Me Mam's been here every day, crying over you, wondering where the hell you went to and no wage coming into the house,' and she fetched him a nasty clip round the ear. It echoed. Tom tried to duck but wasn't fast enough.

Prue looked over his head.

'He needs a bath,' she said.

'He's got a home to go to,' Lily said, and she fairly stormed out of the room.

'Sit there a minute,' Prue told him and she went into the back. Lily was stirring the dinner on the stove, brisker than she might have.

'He's your brother . . .'

'He's ne brother of mine,' Lily said.

'For God's sake, Lily, have a little compassion.'

Lily turned. 'Folk here know he's me brother, interfering with lasses. I hardly know how to lift me head in this town.'

'He's got nowhere to go.'

Lily didn't answer, she went back to her very well-stirred stew and her back told Prue everything she needed to know.

'Mr Dilston winna have him back neither,' Lily said, in case Prue had thought further, which of course she had.

Prue waited and the stirring slowed and then Lily's voice began to sound as wobbly as Tom's, and she said, 'You cannot think what he was like when we were little: he was such a nice lad, nearly the same age as me and we were close and now he's just like me dad. This place, it finishes everybody off, it's got no heart and no bloody soul. It's the end of the world, no matter what Mr Edwards says.'

'As a good Catholic—'

'I'm not a good Catholic. I'm not a good wife or a good mother or anything else that's heading in that direction.'

'It's only for one night,' Prue said.

The stirring stopped. Prue went into the surgery and

drew Tom into the kitchen. Lily put him in the pantry with a bath of hot water, some soap and a towel and told him not to come out until he was clean, hair and all, and then she went upstairs and found some of Robbie's clothes, the only things of his which she had kept.

When Tom was clean and dry and clothed, she banged plates down on the table and then she began to ladle stew on to the plates. There were dumplings, they would be light and airy; Prue had had them before, steam rising from them, glistening carrots slick with butter and a hearty brown bread that Lily had made that morning. Tom ate two bowlfuls and then Lily made him up a bed on the settee under the window and he lay there silent and watched the fire until finally he fell asleep.

Lily went into the pantry and washed up. They didn't talk about Tom any more, but the following morning, advised by Lily, he went home. Prue determined that afternoon to talk to Mr Dilston and she made her way into the foundry. The place was covered in sand and men went backward and forward with barrows and beyond she could smell the heat of the furnace. Mr Dilston's office was just as you went in and was a cut above Mr Gallagher's office, she thought. It was neat and clean, the whole place gave off an air of prosperity.

There was what looked to her like a laboratory to one side and then the main office with Mr Dilston's secretary. Prue was ushered down a short dark corridor which opened into a room which looked out over the entrance to the works and there he sat, a tall, tired-looking man with a pinched face. He did not look pleased to see her and when she explained that Tom Bradley had come back, Mr Dilston's face closed and he said, 'That's lad not coming back here.'

'What is he supposed to do?'

'I don't know and I don't care. Now, if you don't mind, I have work to do.'

'He has a mother to take care of. She has had no money since he left here.'

'Are you suggesting I should have paid her?'

'I'm suggesting that you could be more caring.'

Mr Dilston stared at her.

'I have sixty men working for me. If I cared for each of them like that I would never get anywhere,' he said.

'Yes, but they don't all behave like that. Most of them cause no trouble and this one needs your help.'

'From what I hear, he needs nothing of the kind. Please, don't bother me any further.'

Prue left, taking the car back to the house and wondering what she could do next. If Tom didn't work, how would he and his mother live? Mrs Bradley was not the sort of woman who could be useful as far as Prue could judge and when she told Lily, she seemed unconcerned at first, but then her face changed.

'I'm not having them living here,' Lily said.

'How are they to pay their rent or for their coals or for their food?'

Lily didn't listen. The baby began to scream and that was reason enough for the conversation to be left there.

It was quite a long way to Boulmer: they had to go through the middle of Newcastle and then follow the road beyond Morpeth before it wound toward the coast. They drove on and on and Prue began to despair of reaching the place. Lily read the map accurately but, even so, it took them well over two hours before the signpost actually mentioned the little village. The road had become smaller and smaller and the sand dunes on the right were tall with spiky grass and on the left were farmers' fields and right up almost to the beach itself, the fields were green and prosperous-looking.

It was no more than a dozen houses, most of them set well back as though they feared the full tides, but there was a row of five right at the front, defying the spray of water which crashed hard up the beach, almost as far as the little blue, white and black hulled boats which were hauled up there.

Prue was glad to get out and to let Mabel out. Mabel saw the beach and ran joyfully toward it and then Lily got out, took Isla into her arms and they followed Mabel. The beach looked as though it went on forever. There was a cool wind which blew Lily's hair about. Prue's hair was tamed with grips but even so she felt and smelled the sea, she loved the sound of the gulls calling.

The tide was coming in slowly and the sea birds rode it as if they were having a party. Lily and Prue stood while Mabel chased seagulls. It was a thankless task, the gulls waited for her to get near as though they were happy with the game and then lifted themselves effortlessly just out of her reach. She came back as Prue and Lily moved toward the cottages. The houses crouched low, one-storeyed, as though cowed by the North Sea and its harsh winds and long winters. Number three was easy to find.

Prue banged hard on the door, while Lily stood back with Isla and Mabel. Nothing happened. She banged hard again and after that she peered through the windows. No curtains, no furniture. It was empty. Prue knocked on the next door and eventually it was answered, though the door was opened so slightly that Prue couldn't see the person inside.

'I'm sorry to disturb you,' she said, 'but I'm trying to get in touch with the family next door, the Featheralls.'

The door opened further and a small middle-aged woman smiled at her.

'They've gone,' she said.

'Recently?'

'Aye, days since.'

'Do you know where to?'

'No idea.'

'Are they a large family?'

The woman's eyes turned suspicious.

'Why?'

'Because my friend here is trying to get in touch; they are long-lost and she knows nothing about them.'

Lily tried not to look at her, but nodded.

'Cousins,' she said.

'I don't know anything more,' the woman said. 'They were never much for talking.'

'A big family?'

'I can't say.' And she shut the door.

Prue and Lily walked away and Lily said, 'What do we do now?'

They knocked on doors. At three of them there was no reply. At the fourth, the woman said that the Featheralls were a woman and a daughter and at some time she thought there had been a young 'un but they kept themselves to themselves, there was no fisherman in the house, and this was the best that Prue and Lily could do.

Nobody else knew anything, which Prue thought was strange in a small village, but Lily didn't think it was strange. Folk in a place this small might not be that friendly to strangers such as they were and it seemed the Featheralls were incomers and since there was no man to work, they would be ignored, so what they had been doing there in the first place was a mystery.

Seventeen

Prue went to Mr Gallagher's office on the fell and he looked surprised and not very pleased to see her. When she told him what she wanted, he laughed in amazement.

'You want me to give Tom Bradley a job, after what he did to my daughter? You've lost your mind.'

He wasn't as rude as Mr Dilston, but then he couldn't be since she was the one who had effectively stopped Tom from hurting Helen any further.

'He's just a stupid boy,' she said. 'Is he to be condemned for his first mistake?'

'Mistake?'

'Oh, surely you understand. Helen is like a fairy tale to him.'

'So having a fairy tale you assault it?'

'He doesn't know what else to do. He hasn't had any upbringing, any affection—'

'Neither have a great many lads here, but they don't go putting their hands on young women. Can you think what people would say if I gave him a job? "Rory Gallagher's soft," that's what they'd say.'

'I didn't think you cared what people said,' Prue said scornfully.

'You just don't want more Bradleys on your doorstep.'

'You owe me,' Prue said, holding his gaze.

'That is low, Dr Stanhope,' he said.

'But?'

He hesitated. Prue wasn't having that.

'People are not born knowing how to behave, they are not born loved, they have to be taught such things and all Tom had was a bad time. You know what his mother's like and I'm sure you remember his father.'

'Lily isn't like that.'

'Lily learned because she met the right man and he loved her, but Tom hasn't had anybody to help. Are you going to let him go to waste because of that?'

He let go of his breath in resignation and then he said, reluctantly,

'All right, but if he so much as breathes when he shouldn't, he's finished.'

Mrs Edwards was not well. Prue would have known nothing about it but that Helen Gallagher called in and left a message at the surgery, saying that if it were possible she would like Dr Stanhope to call at the vicarage.

It was mid-afternoon and raining hard by the time Prue drove there. She told Mabel to stay in the car and then found the front door open. Helen must have seen her turn in at the gates. Helen thanked her for coming and then showed her into the kitchen where Mrs Edwards sat over the fire and Prue could see why. She had lost a lot of weight and she had been skinny to start with. She was pale and the dark shadows under her eyes were bigger than ever. She was barely conscious.

Prue would have insisted that Mrs Edwards be in bed but Helen said, 'There are no fires upstairs. Mr Edwards doesn't allow it.'

'Is he here?'

'He's in his study.'

Prue went along to the closed door, banged on it and went in. He looked up, irritated.

'Your wife is ill. She needs to go to a warm bed in a warm room.'

'Nonsense,' he said, 'she's as strong as a horse.'

'She's nothing of the sort. I've examined her. Her heartbeat is irregular, her breathing is ragged. Does she eat properly?'

'I know nothing about such things. The kitchen is not my domain.'

Prue wanted to ask him rudely what precisely his domain was, but she said,

'If you can't look after her here, then I will have her

taken into hospital and Miss Gallagher with her and you will have the children to see to.'

'That's woman's work. There are plenty of women in the parish to see to the children.'

Prue gave up. She and Helen hauled buckets of coal up the stairs and warmed the room and they warmed the bed too and Helen put her into a big flannelette nightgown. The woman closed her eyes and fell asleep immediately.

'Is there anyone to get the children from school or to see to Wilf?' Prue asked.

'No.'

'Then try to divide yourself between Mrs Edwards and the boy and I will collect the children and bring them back here.'

She didn't really want to take Mrs Edwards into hospital, mostly because the woman cried and fretted over her children and her husband and how much was not being done, so Prue didn't think it would help for her to be away from them, but she wasn't sure it was the correct decision.

Before she left, the children running about, she said to Helen, 'You need more help.'

'I can manage.'

'Perhaps you can, but Mrs Edwards and these children cannot.'

Helen flushed, but didn't reply.

'This is a huge house, there are meals to make and washing to do and Mrs Edwards is not coming down those stairs until I say so, so I suggest you ask for help because you certainly aren't to get it from her husband.'

Helen looked up and it wasn't a friendly look.

'He's a man of God.'

'I have no quarrel with God but Mr Edwards is also married with a brood of children. Now, shall I send someone to help?'

'I'll ask Mrs Piper. That's what I usually do, she'll know.'

'What a good idea,' Prue said.

Almost a week passed and then she had another note from Helen to say that Mrs Edwards was worse and when she went to the house she found Mrs Edwards fighting for breath, Wilf in tears and Helen walking up and down with him in her arms.

She tried to make Mrs Edwards easier, but she didn't wait for an ambulance. They carried Mrs Edwards out to the car and laid her on the back seat and since Helen was so upset and the child howled to see his mother taken away, she let them go too and she sat them in the front.

Mabel was obliged to sit on the floor but Wilf was so taken with the dog that he spent the entire journey patting her and saying all kinds of soft things to her, while Prue drove so fast that she worried for the car and corners.

When she got there, she carried Mrs Edwards inside and was glad when the woman was taken straight from her, though she called herself names for not having insisted that Mrs Edwards should be taken into hospital the week before. She tried the old mantra, that she was not a magician, that she had used her judgement but her judgement had been at fault and influenced by the woman's stupid husband. No, that was not fair to him, it was her own decision and it was nothing to do with him or Helen or the children. She had failed Mrs Edwards and now the poor woman was paying for it. She remembered reading somewhere that when you reached a certain place in your profession you didn't make progress, you didn't have wonderful times when you succeeded; you spent your life putting out fires.

Prue took Wilf and Helen back to the vicarage so that she could pick up the children from school. When she got back with them, Mr Edwards was standing in the hall.

'Where is my wife?'

'She's in hospital. I am going back after evening surgery. Will you come with me?'

He stared at her, uncomprehending.

'I have two meetings tonight.'

'Mr Edwards, your wife is very ill. I'm sure she would like to see you.'

'Is Helen seeing to the children?' he said and then he went into his study and closed the door.

Evening surgery was long, it always was when there were problems, so it was almost eight o'clock when Prue reached the hospital and the doctor she had seen earlier came to her, shaking his head. She stared.

'Mrs Edwards died?'

'She did. There will be an inquest, of course, but I think there was something seriously wrong with her heart which couldn't be detected until it was too late.'

'I should have brought her in sooner.'

'I don't think it would have made the difference,' the young man said, and she was grateful to him if not for his knowledge then at least for his empathy.

It was late when Prue got back to the village. She went straight to the vicarage. Helen came to the door.

'How is Mrs Edwards?' she said.

'I think I had better talk to her husband first,' Prue said and she went into the study where the vicar was sitting at his desk as usual.

He obviously expected to hear that his wife was better. He smiled, although it took him a minute or so.

'Ah, Dr Stanhope. How is my wife? When is she coming home to us? The children miss her and so do I.'

'Your wife died earlier this evening,' Prue said.

He gazed uncomprehendingly at her for several moments and then he said,

'You let her die?'

'She had a heart condition which could not have been foreseen.'

'But you knew she was ill and you didn't take her into

hospital. If you had done so, surely she could have been saved. I have prayed.'

'There will be an inquest,' Prue said, 'and if you aren't satisfied, then by all means go ahead and do what you will. I am going to take Miss Gallagher home now,' and she turned and walked out into the hall.

Helen was hovering there, tears in her eyes.

'She died?'

'Shall I take you home?'

Helen stood, shocked.

'The children are in bed and their father is here. Let me take you home now.'

'I can't leave . . .'

'You cannot stay here. There is nothing more you can do. If you choose, you can come back in the morning.'

While she hesitated, Prue found her outdoor things and helped her on with them. Then she drove back to Rory Gallagher's house. He opened the door almost immediately, saying as Helen got out of the car, 'Where on earth have you been? It's so late.'

She rushed past him and through the hall and up the stairs.

'Dr Stanhope? Will you come in for a few moments?'

Prue said she would.

'What is going on?'

So she explained, and he sighed and said, 'I'm so sorry. The poor woman.' He looked sharply at Prue. 'You aren't blaming yourself for this?'

Prue said nothing.

'You're a doctor. You have hundreds of people to see to. You can't be responsible for each one of them, that's absolutely ridiculous.'

'That's how it feels.'

'Oh, for God's sake,' he said, and she was comforted by the words; they made her smile. 'Come in by the fire.'

'I should go.'

'Why?'

'My dog is in the car.'

'Well, bring her in.'

Prue did. Mabel wagged her tail at him and went for the caress of his hand. She had no taste, Prue thought. She wanted to call the dog back, but it would have seemed so petty.

'You're just tired,' he said. 'I can make you some tea.'

'Have you anything stronger?'

He smiled.

'I assumed that you didn't drink.'

'I used to drink whisky with Robbie.'

'He was a good man and a fine doctor. Why do people have to die so soon? No, don't answer that, you've had a bad enough day.' He went over to the cupboard and scrutinized it. 'I've got some Armagnac in here that hasn't been touched for years. It should be all right, don't you think?'

'I don't care, pour it,' Prue said.

'It's supposed to be very good stuff,' he said, finding

glasses which looked like small balloons with short stems on them. He didn't pour much. Prue thought he was being mean and then he handed her one and he said, 'You're supposed to swirl it round, I think, and then sniff and swallow it. I had it given to me so I don't know what it's like.'

Prue sniffed the liquid after swirling it around in her glass and choked over the fumes, but she was not dissuaded from drinking it. It smelled of foreign countries, of leisure and water and little bridges and food being cooked over charcoal outside. It smelled of possibilities and the future. She took a very careful sip and when it caressed her mouth and went down her throat, she felt so much better that she couldn't think. Now she saw why you didn't pour huge quantities, because it warmed as it sat in your hand. What wonderful stuff.

He was watching her. He drank and then he closed his eyes and he said,

'Yes, it hits the spot.'

Prue relaxed; she could feel herself do so.

'I shouldn't drink.'

'Why not?'

'It isn't good for you and it puts things out of balance.'

He started to laugh. He had a very good laugh.

'Why would you want to keep things in balance when life is mostly hell?'

'So that you can make it better, I suppose.'

'Is that the puritan in you?' he said.

She sat back even further and took another sip of brandy, and she regarded the big fire and its flames and she said, 'I'll subdue it for now.'

She was aware all the time that he was not Robbie, that he was not married, but the photographs around him proclaimed otherwise.

'Your wife looks lovely,' she said.

'She put up with me,' he said, and then went on, 'I loved her very much. Difficult to get beyond such things, isn't it?'

He looked so directly at her that Prue was confused, but she was tired.

'I suppose so,' she said.

'You must have been in love, surely?'

'Very much, but I'm a doctor.'

'Hard to reconcile the two.'

He got up and poured more brandy and Prue was pleased about that. She watched the dark, thick liquid as it filled the outer reaches of her balloon glass and was grateful. They sat in silence for a long while and listened to the sounds of the fire as it hissed and burned.

'I shall never love anyone again,' she said, feeling the liquid ignite her throat and then her body. It soothed every ache and obviously made her more loose-tongued that she was used to.

'Nor me,' he said. 'I couldn't better it so it would always come second and that's not fair to another woman. What about you? You could have married?'

And that was when Prue remembered Silas and her marriage, and she sat up and said, 'I should go. It's late.'

'You haven't finished your brandy.'

'I will probably run Mabel and me off the road if I have any more, but thank you so much for making me feel that there will be another day. I hope Helen will not be too distressed or spend too much time at the vicarage.'

'I know what you mean, he said. 'Thank you, Dr Stanhope, for bringing her home.'

When Prue got home, the house was silent but Lily slept little and she came downstairs.

'Oh, Prue,' she said, when she saw Prue's expression, 'I've put a hot bottle in your bed. You look worn out.'

'I am,' Prue said, and she went up to her bed as best she could and somehow she peeled off her clothes and found her bed, but she could not forget that she had failed Mrs Edwards and now the four children had no mother.

Nurse Falcon lived in Stonelea village, which was a hamlet a couple of miles away from the town. It was a place Prue had been to only for patient visits. The houses were mostly detached and the people who lived there tended to be professionals like teachers or older people in small houses who had a little money and had retired there to the peace in the valley. The milder climate meant that flowers flourished long after they had died on higher land.

Nurse Falcon travelled by bicycle, which Prue worried about. The weather here was not conducive to such transport and very often Prue would take the nurse with her or make sure she got to out-the-way places if it was anything but dry. Often Ernie would go and pick the nurse up in the car in bad weather, or Prue would say she should not come that day if the roads were thick with ice or snow. If she wasn't told not to come she would, no matter what it took, and while Prue admired that she didn't think it was practical.

She talked to Lily and they decided that they should have another car. Ernie was very excited about the whole thing but he did not say immediately that they should spend a lot of money on such a venture. So he went to see a friend in Crook which was only a few miles away, and the man had a car which he would sell and Ernie seemed to think it might do for them, and so they arranged to go and look at it. It was cheap and though they knew nothing about cars, they had a drive in it and then bought it, with the proviso that if it didn't run well they would take it back.

Ernie was now in charge and he was very proud of the car. He ran Nurse Falcon everywhere she wanted to go as long as it was not in surgery time, and since he picked her up at home and deposited her there after work and she was always at the surgery during the time when people were seen, it worked well and Prue was pleased with it. So Prue had no reason to go to Nurse Falcon's house.

It was a small detached house with a little garden all the way round it. Ted Butterworth, the local auctioneer, lived next door which was to say that he had a huge house and gardens nearby, but when Prue went to call on Mr Butterworth, whose wife had reported that he was not well and since they had never called her out before and would have come to the surgery if they had been able, Prue made this one of her first calls that day.

As she passed Nurse Falcon's house, something attracted her attention. She was not sure what as she was concentrating on turning in at the gates of Mr Butterworth's house, and since his gates did not seem wide it took all her attention.

Mrs Butterworth had obviously been expecting her, however long it took Prue to get there, and the look on her face told Prue that she was worried. She was right to do so for even though Mr Butterworth, who was in bed, joked with the doctor, Prue thought he had pneumonia and tried to send him off to hospital, except that he wouldn't go.

Pneumonia was called 'the easy way out for the elderly', and Mr Butterworth was at least seventy, but when Prue tried to insist he ignored her. It made it worse somehow that she liked him. Mr Butterworth was a large man, had he been shorter he would have been called portly but he was six feet tall – unusual in such places.

Prue listened to his shallow breathing and looked at his anxious wife and she said,

'I can ask Nurse Falcon to call since she lives next door, but really he should be in hospital and she has a great many other duties to fulfil. After that you must pay for a nurse.'

'I will happily do so,' Mrs Butterworth said.

'I am not leaving this bed. People go into hospital and die.'

'They also die if they don't,' Prue pointed out, 'and you cannot expect your wife to look after you as if she were a nurse.'

He threw a dreamy look at his wife, which Prue envied, and then he said, 'I don't.'

Mrs Butterworth, much the more practical of the two, sent Prue a glance of what on earth can I do? They went downstairs, and in the hall Mrs Butterworth apologized for her husband's behaviour.

'He hasn't forgotten that his father went into hospital and died there. I hope you don't think too badly of us, Dr Stanhope.'

Prue said that she understood and would ask Nurse Falcon to look in on him and she would send Ernie to the house with medication. She would also look in tomorrow and Mrs Butterworth was not to worry. The poor woman, with tears in her eyes, nodded and went back into the house. Prue could not bring herself to curse Mr Butterworth, he was too amiable, but she did not want to lose him to the churchyard at this point.

Since it was mid-afternoon and she judged that the nurse might be at home, and if she wasn't Prue would leave her a note, she stopped the car outside the pretty cottage and banged on the door. Nobody answered so she thought that the nurse had found more patients to attend to and then she heard a shuffling from inside and she waited and then the door opened and on the other side of it she saw a man. Most of a man. His face was damaged badly on one side as though he had been burned and it was grotesque to look at, but Prue held his gaze. He was tall and very thin and his movements were so obviously restricted that she waited and then reacted as calmly as she could.

'I'm the doctor, Prudence Stanhope. I was hoping that Nurse Falcon might be at home.'

'Oh,' he said, 'she will be later. Would you like to come in?'

'That's most kind, but I think she is probably back at the surgery. I don't think we've met.'

'I am her brother. I was a flyer in the war. Felix.'

He held out his hand and the half of his mouth which could smile did and the eye which could gleam did also and he shook her hand and then he thanked her and told her that he would alert Nurse Falcon to her visit.

She told him she was delighted to meet him, what he should say to the nurse and then got back into her car and drove away.

*

The following day, Nurse Falcon came in before morning surgery and said, 'I gather you met my brother yesterday.'

'He was most helpful.'

'I didn't think you would go to the house.'

'I'm sorry, I didn't mean to intrude,' Prue said.

'He was badly hurt in the war and doesn't like visitors.'

'I wouldn't for the world upset him or you.'

'You haven't said anything to anybody.'

'I wouldn't do such a thing,' Prue said.

Eighteen

The general dread was the pit siren. The morning that it went off a week after Mrs Edwards died, Prue's heart contracted in such a way that it was painful. She had heard a strange sound a little earlier and had not recognized it, but she knew the pit siren and she remembered having been down there and severing a man's leg. Could it be any worse?

She was in the middle of morning surgery and she got through another half hour before Ernie came and told her, his face bloodless, that there had been an explosion at the Anne. She told the waiting people that she must go to the pit; most of them had left anyway, only three lingered, and she reassured them that she would be back that afternoon to see to their problems, and then she took her bag and rushed out.

It was unsurprising that she had not heard the explosion loudly, it was the pit up on the fell, the one where she had gone to talk to Mr Gallagher; the biggest pit of all.

She left the car and hurried over to the scene. The men knew her by then, but they wouldn't let her go down. There could be more explosions, they said, so she stood by and watched as the cage came up and injured men were helped out. There were cheers at first. None of them was badly hurt and she could bind their wounds and talk to them and tell them to go home and rest. Each time the cage came up, she was more pleased because it was cuts and bruises and they went off thanking her. But, after that, as the day went on and she waited, she understood that there might be more serious injuries.

She was so relieved when the men were relatively unscathed. She tried not to feel too good, she dreaded what more might happen, but as the women came forward to claim their men, it looked as though the day could turn out better than she had imagined.

When she saw Rory Gallagher in the last cage with the men she could have cried out with relief, he would not have come up if anyone had been left, but they carried one man out and he was not moving. It was Tom Bradley. She went over as they put him down gently as if he could still feel something but she knew he could not. She began to shake. She felt as though God were playing games with her. She was responsible for Tom being taken on at the pit. In a sense she was responsible that he was hurt in the first place and ran away and though she had done her best, there was nothing to hold back the guilt now. She couldn't get up, even after Mrs Bradley had come forward with a terrible cry.

Rory Gallagher helped Prue to her feet.

'There was nothing to be done. We think somebody took a light down there, a cigarette or . . .' He stopped there. Prue thought she had never seen anyone look so weary.

Mrs Bradley thrust herself upon Tom's body and howled. Another woman tried to comfort her, but Mrs Bradley held her off, pushed her away. Prue did not know how long it was before they took Tom's body away and Mrs Bradley came over. She looked like an old woman.

'You did this. I swore to myself I wouldn't have my lad down that pit after my man died. That pit drove him to drink. I was proud of our Tom when he got a job in the foundry and now look.'

Prue held the woman's gaze and then she saw Lily with the baby in her arms, just beyond. Lily came over.

'Howay, Mam,' she said, 'come away now.'

That night, when Mrs Bradley had been persuaded upstairs and had cried herself to sleep, Prue and Lily sat down and drank tea over the fire.

'The thing is that I remember being little with him. My dad used to hit my mam and our Tom and Tom sheltered me. I couldn't believe it when Robbie came along. I thought I was like Cinderella, you know, and I didn't bother no more with Tom. By then he was hanging about with other lads from the works, drinking his pay when it should have been for me mam and our May and me. I was ashamed of him. He was turning out just like me dad and I couldn't stand it. I was so glad when Robbie asked me to marry him. At least I got out, but I always felt as though I had left him when I shouldn't have and that if I had been there he might not have turned into such a bad lad.'

Prue hadn't known she would hate the idea of Lily's mother being at the house, but she fiercely resented the woman because she had not supported or looked after Lily when she married Robbie or when he died. She could understand that Lily would not let her mother go back to her own house. Mrs Bradley sat over their kitchen fire day after day. She ate nothing, Lily had to drag the clothes off her to wash and, worst of all, she didn't cry any more.

Having been a large woman, Mrs Bradley shrank. She wouldn't eat and all she drank was endless cups of tea. At night Lily would help her mother up the stairs to the third small bedroom and then there was silence. Whether Mrs Bradley slept or just lay looking up into the darkness, Prue didn't know, but then she could not imagine having her son die in such circumstances.

Prue began to wish that Mrs Bradley would cry or speak or do something other than stare endlessly in front of her. About six weeks after the death of her son, Mrs Bradley seemed to notice Lily and the child and she held out her arms for the baby. Lily hesitated because her mother had not offered to take the child from her before and she was worried that her mother would not understand how fragile children were, but she carefully gave the sleeping child into her mother's arms. Mrs Bradley looked down at the child and then began to sing some song which Prue didn't recognize. It was set in local jargon. She sang it over and over to the sleeping child.

Nineteen

Prue had called in at the vicarage not long after Mrs Edwards died. She just wanted to see how Mr Edwards was coping, but was not very surprised when Helen answered the door and said good morning to her as though everything were normal. She had Wilf in her arms and she said, 'I'm busy in the kitchen. Will you come through?'

'Where are the other children?'

'At school.' She glanced at Prue, worried. 'Do you think I should have kept them at home?'

'No, no, I think you did the right thing. They won't understand. What has Mr Edwards told them?'

Helen raised her eyes.

'That she's in heaven.'

'What else could he say?'

'I do hope so. She might get a sit-down there.'

Prue gazed around the kitchen. It had changed. It was warm and from the big stove which dominated the room came the smell of something savoury.

'I'm making broth for when he comes in and then he'll have something to give the children when they come home. You don't think I'm getting in the way?'

'I think it's very good of you to help, but you know, Helen, this is a very small town and you are . . .'

'The mine owner's daughter. It hadn't escaped my notice.'

'Don't you want to get away from here?'

No.' Helen raised her chin a little at that.

'Is that because of your father?'

'Do you think I could have left him? I'm all he has.'

'I'm sure he wouldn't like to think you'd stayed here because of him.'

'What else would I do since my mother died? I love him.'

Prue hadn't heard such words in a very long time, if ever.

'The world is big and wide.'

'Then how is it that a woman as clever as you ended up in a little pit village on the Durham fells?'

That made Prue smile. She looked around her and thought this young woman had spent several hours cleaning the place and, even though the door to the hall was open, the place smelled warm.

'I got my father to deliver a load of coal and I borrowed a pit lad to sort out the fires,' Helen said.

Prue had half expected that when the money no longer went to Boulmer, there would be some kind of reaction;

that somebody would write or somebody might arrive. When nothing happened, she lay awake for a couple of hours one night, wondering if some person had died and it wasn't recognized; if nobody cared, something had definitely gone wrong, but she didn't like to bother Lily. There was enough to do and since Lily had apparently forgotten about it and they badly needed the money, she tried to ignore it but it niggled at the back of her mind.

She was more immediately aware of John Edwards' problems and tried to send several suitable women to be housekeeper at the vicarage, but when she went to enquire Helen was still answering the door. She looked even more confused than she had done the first time, and when Prue asked she said offhandedly that none of them would do.

'Was that Mr Edwards' decision?'

'I assume so. It's difficult to give your children over to the care of someone else.'

The vicarage had never been so welcoming, Prue thought. The hall smelled of lavender polish. At that moment the back door opened and John Edwards called,

'I'm back. Is the soup ready, Helen? I'm starving!' and he came into the kitchen and then stood still, cheeks flushing when he saw Prue. 'Oh, Dr Stanhope, I didn't know you were here.'

Prue's first reaction was that John Edwards did not act like a widower. She had never seen him look better. And when she looked at Helen, she thought the girl had blossomed into a woman and then she realized what she saw and was torn between bewilderment and disgust. She stuttered and left.

That evening, when Mrs Bradley had gone to bed, Lily was crooning to her baby over the fire and Prue still sat at the kitchen table, Lily said, 'I didn't realize that children helped you through things. If I hadn't had Isla, I wouldn't have wanted to go on.'

'Oh, Lily,' Prue said.

'Look at her, Prue, she means the world to me.' She gave the child into Prue's arms and it occurred to Prue again that she had lost the child that had been hers and Silas's, and if she had not she would be living in New York. She felt that, despite his mother, they would have found a way through and they might be happy. They could have had another child by now, a girl and a boy; how wonderful and how much better her position would have been as a mother than as his wife or as a doctor.

'My mother had a letter from Mr Dilston, saying that if she was not going to live in the house any longer he would like to give it to another worker. He could have done it when Tom left so it's only to be expected now.'

Prue felt trapped then and she thought that so did Lily. If they could not get her mother to go back to the house, she would always be with them. She would not always be in shock and when not in shock Prue thought she was a horrendous person, but what could she say?

'We can't let her go back there,' Lily said. 'She doesn't know what day it is and I think she's getting worse.'

Why wouldn't she? Prue thought, having endured so much with nothing to look forward to but old age and poverty unless her daughter helped, and her daughter had so little money that this was unlikely. How frightening. Easier to retreat into age and confusion and stay there.

Prue was not prepared that evening after surgery to find Rory Gallagher at her door.

'Are you ill?' she said, at a loss.

'Will you come to my house for a few minutes?' He spoke gruffly as though he had rehearsed his request. He didn't look at her and she thought how strange that he had asked her.

Prue was glad to get out. She had been taking Mabel for walks recently. Mabel was not keen on walks and kept looking at her as though she had lost her mind. Prue needed the air.

Sometimes she drove up into the dale and strode across the hills, Mabel sulking behind her, unused to the country-side. She would not chase a rabbit, she merely watched them as they bounced away across the fields, and when she saw a pheasant she gazed at it in awe and Prue could not blame her; pheasants were unlikely exotic birds for such places. Partridges only made Mabel stand back so that they could reach the safety of the opposite side of the road. Prue thought perhaps Mabel wanted puppies, so she went to the man who owned another German Shepherd and they left them together. Mabel went to sleep.

'I think he's the wrong man for her,' Mr Backhouse said, and he laughed.

Prue went to another man who shot and asked him to take Mabel with him and his Labradors and springer spaniels, who were all very handsome, but he reported that Mabel had been bored all afternoon.

'What are you waiting for, Mabel?' Prue said. 'A good dog is hard to find.'

Mabel snored.

Mr Gallagher sat her down and didn't look at her. Then he took a couple of turns around the room and then he sat down and looked straight at her. Prue found that rather disconcerting so she made herself hold his gaze.

'I'm sorry about this but I don't know who else to talk to,' he said.

'Talk to me then. So far, I've cut off someone's leg and he died and I've advised you to take on the Bradley boy and he died, so really I don't see why you would hold back now.'

He looked sceptically at her.

'It's Helen,' he said.

'Is she ill?' Prue cursed herself for cutting in here, but

she liked Helen, wanted her to have a decent life, away from here if possible. She was so lively, so in tune with life. Her father slumped further back in his chair and shrugged.

'She is spending all her days at the vicarage.'

'Mr Edwards needs help.'

'He does not need my daughter's help.'

Prue looked at Rory Gallagher. The parenting of his grown-up child was defeating him, she could see.

'I think she likes being there,' Prue said, and she could not have said anything worse.

He glared at her.

'I had noticed. Goddamn him, what is he doing?'

Prue didn't know what to say. She kept recollecting that John Edwards looked better now than he had looked when his wife was alive.

'She was always here,' Rory Gallagher said. 'Now she's always there. I don't want her to be always here, obviously. If there are things she wants to do with her life, that's fine and I have always told her so and tried to help her, but now, when I come home, she's at the vicarage.'

Prue said nothing, but she remembered Helen running down the garden with the vicarage children, screaming in delight. She didn't like to say any of this to Mr Gallagher because he saw his daughter as independent and forward-thinking and he had gloried in it, she thought, but had Helen?

'I think he is trying to get his hands on my daughter,'

Mr Gallagher said. 'His wife has been dead no time at all. Will you talk to her?'

She stared at him.

'Me?'

'She speaks of you with respect.'

'Mr Gallagher, I am not going to tell Helen what to do with her life. How rude would that be?'

'I don't want her to make a mistake.'

'Everybody makes them, that's how life is.'

'But it would be such a huge error.'

'Would it?'

'What do you mean?'

'She has had opportunities, you have said so and so has she and yet she didn't want them, it's not as if she had no way out of here. She doesn't want to leave.'

'He has four children and no money.' Rory Gallagher got up and went to the dead fire, came back and then went back to it. 'And he's a vicar.'

Prue thought that in different circumstances Mr Gallagher would have laughed at this, but he was too involved and she knew what he meant. John Edwards was not a kind man, a sensitive person or even very intelligent. No sensible woman would have taken him on with his four children, his freezing house and the way that he never asserted himself to be of any assistance to anyone unless it suited him.

He was lazy, self-indulgent and stupid. What was it about him that attracted Helen? Prue could not imagine, but then he was tall, slender and handsome in a wishy-washy, cricket field, blond and blue-eyed sort of way, which Prue had no doubt a lot of women admired.

'Nothing I can say will make any difference if she wants him, but you don't know that.'

'Oh, come on, Prue,' he said. It was the first time he had used her name and it sounded almost musical on his lips and that didn't help; she liked it and felt her face warming and cursed herself for it when all this man wanted was her help.

'Please, just try, I can't bear to think of that – that idiot with his hands on my daughter.'

She heard herself saying she would, but it was not for Helen, it was for the way that he said her name, it was for the way that she looked at his hips; she was upset to think that she wanted this man, she had sworn not to do so again. That was foolish too, but she had thought after the way Silas had behaved that she would never again want a man and now she did. She was disgusted with herself and yet she heard herself saying that she would talk to Helen, but the problem might be that Helen did not want John Edwards and how foolish would they both look then.

'Will you speak to my father?' Helen looked appealingly at Prue.

It was several days later and Prue was thinking that she

might manage an hour off to find Helen and talk to her. Prue had finished surgery and was not looking forward to the evening. It was Saturday and she had not had a Saturday night in bed since they had moved. Always there were drunks, always there was blood and shouting and fighting and even on the odd occasion where this didn't happen, there was always a crisis on Saturdays. It was as though the Lord, knowing she was having a bad time, gave her a worse one because it was the weekend.

Prue took her uninvited guest through the hall and into the back room and it was thankfully empty. Lily was upstairs with Isla and her mother went to bed very early each night, thank the Lord.

She sat Helen down and didn't even offer her tea. The girl was so agitated that there seemed no point.

'What's wrong?' Prue asked.

'I want to marry John Edwards and my father is furious.'

Prue stared. She hadn't realized things had escalated so quickly.

'Marry him?'

Helen looked at her as if she were mad.

'Obviously,' she said.

'What did your father say?'

'He told me I'd taken leave of my senses.'

Prue agreed, but she didn't think it would help to say so.

'Will you talk to him for me?' Helen said.

'Not in a hundred years. I'm a doctor, not a magician.'

'Oh please, Prue, I need somebody on my side. I love John.'

'You're very young.'

'Oh Lord, don't do that to me. I love him, I love his children, I love his wretched freezing house and I want him like no woman ever wanted any man before. With me, he could become a bishop so easily. I could get him there, I know I could.'

Prue wondered whether John Edwards knew that.

'Does he have ambition?'

Helen looked at her as though she were simple-minded.

'Of course he doesn't, but I have no intention of staying here. He's young and he could do anything. He could be Bishop of Durham, we could live at the palace.'

'Has he asked you to marry him?

Helen looked at her as if she was mad.

'His wife is not long dead, but look at me, how could any man resist this?'

'He is in love with you then?'

The girl blushed, but looked steadily at Prue.

'He adores me,' she said.

'Helen, have you not thought about how he treated his first wife?'

'What do you mean? Oh, that he didn't help. What man does? When I was a child I barely saw my father and he didn't notice me, the only person he had any time for was my mother.'

'There are rumours that John Edwards drinks and that he sees other women.'

Helen raised her eyes in derision. She made Prue feel very old.

'I have heard them. Mrs Edwards was a lot older than him and she wasn't the right woman for him but I've never seen him take a drink and there are a lot of women in this village who would be jealous of his wife. He comes from a very good Gloucestershire family. He is – he's fair and handsome and tall and he is educated and knowledgeable and his voice is pure music. Where else can I get that?'

'I thought you didn't want that.'

'Of course I want it. And besides, how could I give his children into another woman's keeping? I love them. I know that my father is concerned, but this is what I want; it's the only way I want to live. Everything else is so boring. I want the vicar and the vicarage for mine and then everything will be wonderful.'

After Helen waltzed away to do Prue couldn't remember what, but doubtless back to the vicarage, she found herself in the street even though it was late, banging on Rory Gallagher's door. She half thought he wasn't going to answer, had almost gone away when the door opened sharply and then he saw it was her and collected himself and so did she. She knew the way into the sitting room, or the dining room or whatever it was. The room was always covered in papers, but not now. The house was clean and smelled of polish and everything was tidied away. He saw Prue looking around.

'Mrs Saxony,' he said, 'she doesn't know the meaning of "please don't touch that". I can't find anything, my collars are so starched they hurt my neck and her cooking is vile. You should taste her fruitcake. It was so heavy that even the sparrows wouldn't eat it.'

Prue smiled. He waved a hand as though to discount what he said.

'Oh, I'm sorry. Obviously I don't care about these things if Helen wants to be away someplace else, but every instinct tells me this is a mistake. I daren't contradict her for fear she stops coming home all together.'

'The only thing you can do is to let her go,' Prue said.

He looked helplessly at her.

'To him?'

'That's what she wants.'

He said nothing for what felt to Prue like a long time but was probably only a minute or two.

'My God,' he said, 'after all I've done.'

'You did it for yourself, as a decent parent, surely.'

He looked at her and he reminded her of Helen then, they both had a disconcertingly clear gaze.

'Did she say anything about marriage?'

'I don't suppose he's going to ask her without coming here to you.'

'People said he was unkind to his wife.'

'People's views of such things vary.'

'If he even raises his voice to her . . .'

'He has four small children and you are about to become a step-grandfather.'

Rory Gallagher glared at her. Prue couldn't help smiling.

'I'm glad you think this is funny,' he said.

'I'm sorry but you aren't very old yourself; it seems so incongruous.'

'I feel a hundred. Isn't there anything I can do?'

'Yes, you can pay for a lavish wedding I would think, and I'd be happy to help.'

He looked seriously at her.

'What if he really wasn't kind to his wife?'

'I know,' she said, 'that's what worries me, but I don't know what to say to her and it looks as if neither do you. And she's a girl in love so none of it will make any difference unless you can think of something?'

He shook his head.

'I would have married Anne if the whole world had been after us,' he said.

Lily's mother began to recover and as she did so she became less amenable. She complained about the house, she complained that her bed was too small and that the meals were inadequate. She talked incessantly about Tom. She had now the son that she had desired all along. He was dead and could do nothing wrong and from his mother's lips it sounded as though he had been a paragon. He had been precious to her, he had been her child and Prue tried to understand, but it was difficult. The house seemed full of Mrs Bradley and the sound of her voice, complaining.

She didn't seem to like Mabel. There came a day when she aimed a kick at Mabel and Prue walked into the kitchen, saw it and shouted at her. 'Don't you dare!' she said.

'That dog is under my feet.'

'She's nothing of the sort. She spends her whole time with me. She came in here because she thought I was here.'

'If she couldn't smell you, then how come she did?'

Prue could hate this woman, she knew.

'Don't you ever touch my dog,' she said.

Lily appeared in the doorway.

'What is going on?'

'This lass who got my Tom killed thinks this is her place.'

Prue had to stop herself from arguing. She went back into the surgery and made sure that Mabel was following. Lily went after her.

'Prue, I'm sorry.'

'I wish I had a place of my own.'

'Oh no,' Lily begged, 'don't go and leave me with all

this. I couldn't manage.' She started to cry. She turned away and pretended it wasn't so and Prue felt awful, but it had become so difficult with Lily's mother taking every available minute and both of them trying so hard to make things work.

Twenty

Helen was married to John Edwards in the spring. She wore a plain white satin dress, which many of the matrons in the congregation thought clung too much to her figure and white was so showy. The bridegroom looked triumphant, the bride was radiant, everybody said, and the children stood in the pew and beamed at their new mother. She waved at them and scandalized everybody with her enthusiasm and lack of rectitude.

The reception was at the bride's home, as it should be, spilling out on to the street at both sides. The weather was fine and the ladies of the church put tables and chairs outside, and all that afternoon and well into evening her father talked to people and smiled at everybody. It was the whole village and everyone was fed; one thing about it which Prue approved of. Since the village was big, there were plates heaped with sausage rolls and sandwiches and cakes so pretty with pink icing and chocolate that a good many children were running around with brown moustaches before long. They ran up and down the street and laughed and screamed and nobody stopped them, and later there was beer and sherry and whisky so that the men said there had never been such a good wedding in the village.

After that there was dancing. Rory Gallagher had paid a band to play all the old favourites and some new songs and people sat at chairs and tables outside and drank and ate. The evening went on into the night so that it was very late indeed when people returned to their homes with many thanks to Rory Gallagher for having put on such a spread for everybody he knew and even those he didn't.

Lily took her mother and Isla back to the house at about eleven o'clock, but Prue thought she must stay and she spoke to everyone and was glad that they were so well fed and so pleased at the mine owner's daughter's wedding.

It was well after two when the last of the guests left and Prue would have done so except that, the front door shut, he said to her, 'Don't go, not just yet.'

'It's very late.'

'Are you tired? Will you not stay a little?'

Prue went with him back into the house. It seemed so empty, though it should not have been more so than it had been in months and she knew that to him it had been empty all that time and he was trying to grow accustomed to the idea that his daughter was not his any longer. She was a wife now and he had lost her.

'Are you sad?'

'Aye.' And then he smiled at himself for the way that he should have been and was not. 'She's happy.'

'She will sort him out in no time,' Prue said, and he laughed.

'She always did that with me. God, I miss her. Do you think it was all right, the do?'

'Oh, absolutely. It was for everybody. It must have cost you a fortune.'

'They deserved it. I want to do that twice a year, you know, summer and then Christmas to thank them. Do you think it's a good idea?'

She nodded, and then he said, 'I want to do more.'

'Like what?'

'Pay them better wages, give them more help without seeming patronizing.'

'I don't think they see you as patronising.' They saw Mr Dilston like that, but she didn't like to say so. Dilston did nothing for them which he thought they could do without.

'I was one of them, you see. Early on. I was brought up in Sunniside, my Dad was a foundryman, but when I left school there were no jobs and I went down the pit.'

'Prue.' He stopped and looked at her.

Afterwards, Prue was not sure who had moved first, but within seconds he had her in his arms in a good, decisive way, as though he had been thinking about doing this for a very long time. She had thought that because of the way Silas had behaved, she would never want to be close to a man again. She had deceived herself. She very much wanted to be near Rory and it dated back to the accident down the mine and the way that he had picked her up and helped her back to the surface.

Such a small incident and yet she knew that she had been not been drawn to another man more than any time since she had met Silas. No memories came to her rescue. It didn't matter now that Silas had betrayed her in every possible way. She didn't know that she had longed for someone's arms around her, but that was no excuse either. It wasn't that Rory was pushy, it wasn't the kind of situation she might have had to fight her way out of, and yet when she did think about it afterwards, she had forgotten how a man could compel you just by the feel of his body.

She had thought doctoring would be enough. Now, apparently, that was not so.

They didn't even leave the room, it was a question of hunger and closeness. Prue had never had a man down on a hearthrug, Silas was not the man for impromptu sex. It had always been in the dark, in a bed and at his mother's house not at all most of the time. Even that, she thought, at its best was not like this, but perhaps she felt like that because she had been alone for so long and possibly because she had few illusions left. She thought she had never wanted anything in her life as she wanted Rory Gallagher now. It didn't even occur to her that she would regret this in the morning.

They did go to bed eventually. Obviously he kept fires in all the main rooms, and although this one had almost died, the warmth in the room was cosy, the bed was big and there were lots of pillows. Prue had not thought she could be so happy.

It was fun too. Silas had regarded this as something sober and dutiful. He was wrong, but she hadn't known any differently. There was no seriousness about this, it all flowed and was easy but, best of all, was the lovely animal passion that her body had not lost. She loved the way that she was taken to a great height and satisfied. It made her feel very smug. She was better at this than she had thought. Silas had not made her feel this good in all their married life.

Sometime in the late dawn she found herself waking. The room was thick with shadows, the curtains were closed. She didn't even want to run away at first; she was happy to lie there and watch him sleep, but he didn't sleep for long and when he opened his eyes and smiled at her, Prue smiled back.

'I must go before somebody finds out.'

He agreed to this, he even offered to go with her but she knew that she must walk back to the surgery alone. People meeting her so early would probably just think she had been out at a call, though there was no black bag. She dressed quickly and without any noise, went back to the bed and kissed him and let herself out.

She didn't meet anybody on the way back up the hill towards Dan's Castle. Thank God it was Sunday! She slipped into the house and her bed, and all was quiet. Mabel didn't even wake up, as though she knew what was going on and didn't mind.

Prue slept until it felt like very late, mid-morning. Lily was up and singing by the time Prue came round and when she went downstairs Lily gave her tea and a jug of hot water. Prue took the tea and the jug back upstairs and had an all-over wash, trying not to think about what she had done.

Twenty-one

Mr Dilston wasn't well and Prue was called to his big house outside the village to attend him. The place was huge; she hadn't known he was quite so prosperous, which made him seem all the meaner. His house stood well back from the road and in grounds. She left the car at the back door and walked around to the front. From there the view was clear down into Weardale and back up again to the distant skies.

She had to climb several steps to reach the front door and after she banged on it, May came to answer. She was in a proper maid's outfit and Prue couldn't help thinking how silly it looked in the country and that the Dilstons really did think they were important.

May didn't even acknowledge that they knew one another. She saw Prue formally into a huge drawing room. It had the view also and it was difficult to think of anything else as she walked into the room.

Mrs Dilston got up. She was a young woman of about

thirty, very pretty and not at all as Prue had thought she might be. She didn't look the kind of middle-aged woman who would be married to a man like him. She offered Prue tea and was friendly. She said, 'I wouldn't have called you out but I'm worried about his cough. It's been going on for weeks and he wouldn't have you come here so I've insisted as best I might. You know what he's like, I'm sorry.'

Her apology for her husband was not unfounded. When Prue got into his bedroom he said, 'What the hell are you doing here? I didn't ask for a doctor.'

'Your wife did.'

'Go away.'

'Mr Dilston, I have come here especially to see you.'

'Doctors cost money and I don't have any,' he said, and then he started to cough and couldn't stop. He was red in the face and gasping when Prue sat down on the bed and demanded to hear his breathing. He didn't speak but neither did he try to stop her.

'You have a chest infection, Mr Dilston.'

'Nothing of the kind.'

'I'm afraid you have,' Prue said. 'You must keep in an even, warm temperature and have plenty of water so that you don't dehydrate and you must have pillows so that you can breathe at night. I will send you some pills—'

'I won't take anything.'

Prue didn't argue. She went back downstairs and gave his

wife instructions and just hoped she didn't have to come again.

May came to visit shortly after this. Prue was convinced she only came to show off the finery which Mrs Dilston had given her. The hat with the feather fell halfway down her brow, the coat was too big for her and she could not walk well in the boots. Prue thought she would have blisters before she got back as it was a long way, but May paraded around the house pleased with herself and boasting that Mrs Dilston had said they would spend most of the summer in Whitley Bay at a nice hotel.

The following day, after morning surgery, Lily came racing through. 'Have you seen my mother?'

'Not since breakfast.'

'She's not in the house, she isn't in the garden and I've searched the streets around us and I can't find her.'

'What about her old house?'

Lily looked confused and then they both rushed out together, Lily with Isla in her arms and Prue with Mabel at her heels. They took the car because it was quicker. Prue parked it abruptly outside the house. A new family lived there. Fresh net curtains hung at the windows and outside it was swept clean and all was tidy. Lily hammered on the door. The new family was called Parkinson. Mrs Parkinson smiled when she opened the door and saw them.

'I was just going to send one of the lads. Your ma is here, Mrs Fleming.'

They trooped into the kitchen and there Mrs Bradley sat. Her eyes lit up.

'Lily,' she said, 'I was wondering when you would come home.'

'Here I am,' Lily said softly. 'Are you all right?'

'Where is our Tom and your dad?'

'We've moved,' Lily said. 'Come back with me.'

Her mother sat still and gazed at her in confusion.

'I have to wait here. They'll be coming home at the end of their shifts and I have to get the water ready and a meal and they'll want their beds.'

'Not just yet,' Lily said, 'come on now.'

'Where to?'

'To my house.'

'Where is May?'

'She is living at Mr Dilston's, don't you remember? She's doing very well there.'

'I worry about her.'

'I know you do.'

Mrs Bradley stared at Prue.

'Who's that great big woman?'

'That's Doctor Stanhope.'

'A lass like that? She looks like a carthorse.'

They urged her out, Lily apologizing to Mrs Parkinson, who said that she understood, her mam had gone the same way and in the end she had had to go to the loony bin.

When they got Mrs Bradley back to the house, she began to cry. She didn't know where she was, she didn't know who they were, she wanted to go home, back to her husband, her son and her two daughters. Isla screamed and Mrs Bradley backed away.

They persuaded her to bed, but it was a long night. Mrs Bradley kept waking up and wandering about the house, trying to find her family, and Isla, sensing that something was wrong, screamed so much that Mabel lay by the back door, well out of the way, in the darkness. Prue began to wish she could do the same.

The night finished at about four when there was a knocking on the door which meant that Prue had to leave everything and go to see a patient. A young man at the farm just beyond the village was screaming in pain and had to go to hospital. Prue went with him.

When she got back, several hours later, the house was silent. Lily was coming wearily down the stairs.

'What was it?' she said.

'Peritonitis. We almost lost him,' Prue said. 'Here?'

Lily's eyes filled with tears.

'My mother doesn't know me,' she said.

*

Prue had managed to avoid Rory Gallagher during the time since they had been together. She seemed to be whisking herself around corners, absenting herself from places she should have been until Lily noticed and asked her if something was wrong. Prue said vaguely that everything was fine.

Eventually he came to the house and waited for her on the Saturday afternoon, and when Prue came back from making several calls, there he was sitting drinking tea and Lily looked very confused. As soon as Prue came in, Lily got up, made an excuse and left the room.

'I feel as if I've done this the wrong way round,' he said when she had gone, getting to his feet and looking apologetic and eager all the same time.

'Rory . . .'

'I do intend to put it right, I wouldn't want you to think that I was playing some daft kind of game with you. I didn't plan anything, but you see, since you got here, I've thought about you very often and I like being where you are and – and I don't like being without you. I – I want you to marry me.'

Prue stared.

'Marry you?'

'It's what people usually do before they do much of anything else. I would never have spent the night like that for any other reason. I think I took advantage.'

'No, you didn't,' Prue said.

He smiled. She didn't smile back at him; she didn't know how to react or what to say. He looked hard at her.

'I don't sense you're pleased to see me. I'll apologize till the cows come home if you like. There's something very special about you and – I love you, Prue.'

'No.'

She hadn't known she was going to say that or anything like it. She had been denying that she had been brushing off the whole idea of him, but the truth was that she wanted nothing more to do with him. She wanted to pretend that none of it had happened.

'Oh God,' he said, 'you're disgusted with me.'

'I'm nothing of the sort. Spending the night with you was the best thing I've done since I came here, but . . .'

'But there's somebody else?' He stopped, waited and then smiled just a little. 'You couldn't resist my lovely body?' He went on smiling, but it was a faint show. 'What is it then?'

'I don't want to get married. Not you and not to anybody.'

'Is that because you think it would harm your professional status or something like that?'

'Not exactly.'

'I wasn't going to expect you to dust the house, you know.'

'I'm sure,' Prue said.

'You think I might start telling you what to do. I am not that brave or so misguided.'

'I don't think marriage is to women's benefit,' Prue said.

He looked at her as though she were speaking in a language he didn't understand, and it was probably true.

'I don't need you to keep me so why would I want to marry you?'

That was when he winced.

'Ow. It wouldn't be because you liked me?'

'I don't have to marry you for that.'

'No, you could keep on using my body and rushing out when daylight arrives, but it's not much of an arrangement.'

'You wouldn't like being married to me. I have thought about these things and being a doctor was all I ever wanted.' It was almost true.

'What about having children?'

'No,' she said.

'You don't want children?'

'Not everybody does.'

'No, of course not.'

There was an enormous silence. You could have covered the fell with it, Prue thought, and she felt sick. He wasn't looking at her any more, he looked like a boy being turned down at a dance for the first time. His face was all blank as if he needed to make sure it didn't say anything and then she could feel the disappointment, sharp on him.

He turned around and looked at the door as though it would take everything he had to get through it.

'Well, I – I had better go,' he said, and then he went.

When he had gone, Prue let go of her breath and shortly after that Lily came downstairs, eyeing her carefully.

Prue said she had work to do and went off into the surgery and stayed there until it was time to eat.

Twenty-two

Three months after the wedding, Prue called at the vicarage. She hadn't had time to go to church for weeks and she hadn't seen Helen. She didn't quite know why but nobody answered. It was midday on Tuesday, the morning surgery was over and she thought that Helen would have been there to answer the door. She was just about to leave when she thought she saw a shadow in the hall and then she lifted the letter box and called out Helen's name. Shortly after that the door was answered.

Helen didn't look up and she stood back. Prue could soon see why. She had a big mark on her face.

'What happened?'

'I fell.'

'Into what?'

'Does it matter?'

'It would if it was a man's hand.'

'Don't be silly, Prue, it was nothing of the sort.'

'May I come in?'

Helen held the door wide and when Prue walked in, it was just as it had been when John Edwards' first wife was alive. The place was cold, it was dusty, there was no cheer, no light and when Helen moved back Prue could see that she was pregnant, not a long way on but enough for a doctor to notice and see other things; the tired way that she held herself, the shape of her was already so different.

'You didn't come to the surgery.'

'Why would I? There's nothing wrong with me. This is a natural state, surely.'

Prue followed her into the kitchen. There was no smell of cooking, no pot on the stove. Everywhere, children's clothes hung drying and it had been a week of sunshine so they could have been outside in the back, blowing in the wind like coloured sails.

'How do you feel?'

'I'm fine.' Helen turned away even as she spoke. 'Would you like tea?'

'I just hadn't seen you in so long.'

'The children are well and so is John. You haven't been to church.'

'I've been busy.' Prue said. 'If you want to talk . . .'

'I don't.'

'I meant about the baby.'

'I don't need a doctor.'

*

Prue made certain she went to church that Sunday and it was odd, so like the first times when she had been there, the ladies of the parish eager to help and Helen, who seemed to have shrunk, saying little and moving around a lot and the children, lined up on the sofa as they were before, only worse, their eyes downcast and they were still. Prue remembered them with Helen, rolling down the lawns at the back, shrieking and yelling and laughing.

John Edwards held forth as always, fair and handsome and his eyes sparkled. He came to Prue, smiling.

'Dr Stanhope, we haven't seen you for weeks. How good of you to give up your time.'

'Helen needs taking care of, you know.'

He merely gazed at her.

Prue hadn't been as inclined to lecture anybody as she was to lecture John Edwards now. She knew that it was not common for anyone to discuss such things, for a doctor and a vicar to talk about such matters was unsuitable, and yet she wanted to tell him what it was like to lose a child, how much it hurt and went on hurting, how it was something you always remembered and she had the feeling that if he hurt his wife she would miscarry his children. He didn't look as if he had any cares. He went off, smiling at his other parishioners.

Two nights later there was a hammering on the door and when Prue got herself downstairs, it was a man from the row of houses in the town which were the nearest the vicarage, at the end of the lane. He said, 'The vicar sent me. His wife is ill.' So Prue made haste and drove the short distance since it was the quickest way along the bumpy road and when the door was opened by a woman she knew from church, she ventured up the stairs and the door to the bedroom was open and Helen was sitting up, holding her stomach. The bed was soon covered in blood and all Helen could say was,

'My baby. My baby.' And crying out for the pain.

Prue soothed her and initially decided she didn't need a hospital; the child, such as it was, was stillborn. Then Prue thought Helen might die; her breathing was so shallow and she lost so much blood. Prue panicked and wished she had sent the girl to hospital, but gradually it got better and by the time the dawn had come in Helen was quiet and her breathing was free. Prue reminded herself that blood was like that, it always made you feel as if there were lakes of it.

John Edwards was pacing outside the door. Prue didn't want to face him. She thought he might react as Silas had and hate his wife for what had happened except that he was white-faced and as she came out he said, 'Is she going to be all right? Is the baby?'

'The baby has died and she needs care.'

'May I see her?'

'She's asleep.'

'The children want to see her.'

'I want you to go and tell Ernie to get Nurse Falcon.'

He hesitated.

'Now?' Prue said, and he left hastily, running down the stairs so fast that she thought he might trip and fall.

The children came out on to the landing and she took them back to bed and reassured them that their stepmother was going to be just fine and so would they be, but she was asleep and they must let her rest. They went obediently back to bed.

It was a long hour before Mr Edwards came back in with Nurse Falcon. Prue dismissed Ernie, thanking him. The nurse clucked her tongue over Helen and she said, in a very low voice, 'I never liked that man.'

'She needs someone here. Do you know another nurse who might help? I can't ask you, I know you have too much to do already.'

'She would have to be paid.'

'Then she will have to be. The practice will pick up the bill,' Prue said. She went downstairs and found him sitting in his study at his desk with a pen in his hand. He did not look up, so Prue walked out and left him to his sermon.

Helen was better almost immediately, Prue thought, two Sundays later. She was rosy-cheeked and running about after the children and the vicarage was clean again.

Prue followed her into the kitchen, the only place where they might be alone, but various women kept coming in with cakes and wanting more tea and the children ran in and out so that Prue had to say to her in the end, 'Should you be doing so much?'

Helen ignored her, making her way out of the kitchen into the hall and beyond that into the sitting room where her husband was even now holding forth about the gospels.

'Matthew, Mark and Luke, the synoptic gospels, have much in common, but John stands alone,' he said.

Two weeks later, Prue found John Edwards in her surgery. She was amazed. It was morning surgery and it was early. He was the first patient and he held a cloth covered in blood to his face.

'What's this?' she asked.

He sat down, clearly glad to do so.

'Last night I was coming from the house of a parishioner and two men set on me.'

It was not just his mouth and not just his face – he was covered in bruises as far as she could see though she didn't want him to explain any further. Four of his teeth were missing, his mouth was bloodied and swollen and both his eyes were blacked and like slits.

'Who would do such a thing to the local vicar?' was all he managed.

She gave him painkillers and sent him home. That evening she banged on the door of the house on the corner and when it opened she barely recognized the man she had thought she knew. He looked so keenly at her that she almost took a step backwards. Anger was coming off him and impatience, as though he would like to shut the door on her.

'What do you want?' he said.

'You had John Edwards beaten.'

He wasn't looking at her now.

'Why don't you mind your own business?' he said and went back inside, but he didn't shut the door so she followed him down the hall.

'It is my business.'

'Really? Then why didn't you tell me what he was doing to my daughter?'

When he turned around from the fire in the back room she saw a look on his face that she wouldn't have credited him with, it was hatred and not for her.

'I have no idea what he is doing or is not doing and I don't think you do either,' Prue said.

'You didn't even tell me she was expecting a child,' he accused her, glaring.

'If she wants to tell you she will. I'm a doctor. There is such a thing as patient confidentiality.'

'You think I'm going to stand around while that bastard ruins my daughter's life?'

'What is this "my daughter"? She is not your possession,' Prue said. 'Do you think you have a right to interfere?' Prue could feel her temper slipping and she never gave it space; it was unprofessional, but she was riled.

'I was not interfering.'

'Well, what the hell do you call it then? She is a fully grown woman and what she does with her life has nothing to do with you. You are supposed to act like an intelligent adult, not a hooligan.'

He didn't move, wasn't threatening, but he glared at her and his voice was loud. 'She lost her child because of him.'

Privately Prue was convinced that Helen had, but she couldn't say that now.

'You don't know.'

'As a woman, surely you understand what such a loss is like?'

'And is this a "Rory Gallagher, that was my grandchild" speech?'

'It could be,' he said, reluctantly, 'or it could be that if he knocks my daughter about again I will make sure he doesn't do it to another woman.'

'Oh, wonderful,' Prue said, 'and what about his children? What will happen to them? Or are you quite happy to have them put in the nearest orphanage?'

'It couldn't be much worse than watching their father beating the shit out of his wife.'

'What did you do, get other men to beat him or did you do it yourself?'

'Oh, shut up, Prue!'

She was trembling. She was amazed that he said such a thing to her and called her by her first name while he was doing it. She wanted to throw something at him. He stopped looking at her and turned and went to the fire to gaze into it, perhaps because he too was finding his temper hard to control.

'Helen could have died losing that child,' he said.

'Nothing of the sort. I was there. If she had been worse I would have sent her to hospital. She is capable of making her own decisions. Don't get in the way, she won't thank you for it and if you lose her to John Edwards it will be a disaster. She doesn't have to stay with him and you know that.'

'Then why does she?'

'I don't know. You cannot control her. Men have tried to control women for centuries and it's the most awful thing you can do to anyone, and it isn't love, so don't give me that.'

'Control?' He frowned at her and it turned into a glare. 'Was that what that was all about with you and me? You thought I was going to try and control you?'

'That had nothing to do with it.'

'I think it did. I think you hate men.'

'Rubbish, Rory. Nothing of the sort.'

'No? Do you know I've been thinking about what happened with us and you were not a virgin, you had been to bed with somebody lots of times. You knew exactly what you were doing.'

'That is none of your goddamned business.'

'It would be if he had hurt you so much that you don't want anybody else.'

'I did want you, I thought you knew that.'

'Yes, like I was some kind of male whore.'

'That's not right, it's not fair and that's an awful way to describe that night. I told you before, it was the best—'

'You didn't want to repeat it so it couldn't have been that good.'

'I have wanted to repeat it every night since then,' she said softly. 'But I can't.'

'Because? If you're worried about getting pregnant—'

'I'm a doctor. I know all those things. It's not something I worry about, I have control of my life.'

'You certainly do. You've bloody well got control of mine too. I want you so much I can't sleep or work or—' He stopped short and turned away.

'Rory, I'm sorry.'

He turned back, looking at her as though for the first time.

'Sorry? You know what? The awful thing about it is that you behaved like a selfish man.'

'I did not.'

'Yes you did. You went to bed with me knowing you didn't want to marry me, that you didn't even want a decent relationship with me of any kind.'

'You were to blame for that.'

'So I seduced you and you were so innocent? Who was it, Prue, who did it?'

'Nobody did anything.'

'You are a bloody liar,' he said.

'Don't you call me names!'

'What then? Go on, tell me. If you don't want me you could at least tell me why. Who was it, who did this to you? I'm just a decent ordinary man, I'm not a threat, I'm not going to . . .' He ran out of words at that point. 'I love you, Prue. You could at least tell me why you won't marry me, and honestly.'

She had intended never to tell anybody, but she looked straight at him and she said, 'I was married. It was a very bad marriage and I swore that once I had my freedom I would never do it again.'

'You were married? What happened?'

'I left him.'

'So you're married?'

'No, I'm divorced.'

He didn't believe it, she could see, but neither did he say anything and that was hardly surprising. He stood like somebody who would never move again.

'So you see,' Prue said softly, 'I can't marry you and you

certainly can't marry me. I'm a scarlet woman. I would rather you didn't tell anybody; I don't want the whole village knowing my background. I think I had better go now.' And she smiled very slightly at him and walked out.

Twenty-three

Every day Mrs Bradley tried to get back to her husband and children, and every day Prue or Lily, or both of them, had to persuade her into the house and then she would sit over the kitchen fire and cry and tell them that she wanted to go home.

Prue was so tired. She crawled into bed and willed sleep, but every time she almost got there she saw Helen's bruised face and the way that she had lost her baby.

Ernie was a big help at this time. He was good at running after Mrs Bradley and one day, several weeks later, he took her to see his mother, who lived just down Ironworks Road out toward Wolsingham and Thornley. Mrs Bradley seemed happy there. She and Ernie's mother had known one another when they were small and they talked for hours about their families. Ernie would go and get her at the end of the day. Prue could have kissed him for easing the burden, instead of which she paid Ernie more money so that his face warmed and he thanked her.

After a day there, Mrs Bradley was content to come back and eat with them and talk about her father and mother and her school and her school friends and then she would go to bed and sleep ten hours.

Isla too began to sleep and suddenly Lily and Prue had the evenings. It was strange, but from seven onward they had nothing to do other than the bookkeeping and that was easy because Prue paid the accountant to do most of it. Over the summer they became restless and had taken to sitting in the back garden not knowing how to fill their free time.

On those nights when Prue did not get called out, and there were several of those, sometimes she would wake and listen to the silence and she loved it. They were coping. She and Lily now went to church on Sundays and took Isla with them if Lily's mother was at Ernie's house. Ernie went out with his friends; Prue thought he spent most of Sunday in one of the local pubs and nobody deserved it more, so everybody was happy.

She didn't see Rory Gallagher, but Helen looked a lot better and there were no bruises on her and somehow, Prue thought, John Edwards had learned his lesson. She didn't know whether it was because he was afraid of his father-in-law or just that he had thought he might lose his second wife rapidly and the shock had got to him.

The vicarage was a happy place that autumn and they were all looking forward to Christmas. Prue wanted to be able to enjoy it, hoped that everybody would be well and went about her duties joyfully.

The weather was warm well into the autumn. It rained when it should and everything grew and the crops were good. Apples and plums littered the vicarage orchard and people were encouraged to come and pick fruit. Prue would go past the open doorways of people's houses and smell the jam-making. The harvest was good and when they sang in the church 'all is safely gathered in', Prue lifted up her voice with every other person and was pleased.

The holly had a lot of berries on it when the bad weather came and everybody told her that that meant it would be a hard winter, but Prue had not envisioned that it would be hard in other ways. This started in November when she went to the vicarage – she sometimes called uninvited just to make sure that things were all right – and Helen was bubbling with news.

'My father has found somebody he likes,' she said. 'It might put him into a better frame of mind. I haven't spoken to him since John was hurt by those men. He said he had nothing to do with it and I'm convinced he lied, but I've heard the gossip and now he has something else to think about besides me.'

Prue stared. And somewhere inside she was jealous. How strange.

'Who is it?'

'Mrs Dilston's sister. Her family comes from Consett and she has been staying at the house. He was invited to drinks in the evening. I'm so glad he's found somebody. I felt guilty leaving him alone and neglecting him. If he gets married I will be so pleased.'

'What is she like?'

'I haven't met her, but apparently she is young and beautiful and even has money, so what on earth she sees in my father I have no idea.'

Helen went back to her baking. The kitchen was full of the smell of bread; she made several loaves all on one day and Prue liked to drop in at the right time, when they were out of the oven and she could sample a slice of warm brown bread, butter and honey from the man who had several beehives as well as the goats. Today she didn't want it.

Rory was tired of living alone. He had not thought that silence had its own sound. These things had become so much clearer since Prue had refused to marry him. She had somehow changed the way that he thought. He had had to get used to the loss of his wife but he could not get used to the loss of Prue, even after one night. Helen had blamed him for what had happened with her husband and would not see him. She was right, of course, but he thought of her and her battered face and he sat there in the evenings and devised various nasty ends for the vicar.

He had no connection with Helen any more. She must have known he had ordered men to beat her husband. He half expected she would come to him as Prue had done and shout at him and relieve him in some ways of the responsibility and she would know that he cared for her so much that he would let no man hurt her, but he had not realized that marriage was somehow different and indeed sacred, at least to those people who believed in God and the Church.

He believed in nothing any more. He knew that once a man had bedded a woman, she was his in the most basic way possible. He had seen Helen's shiny face after her wedding and known how much she was in love and admitted to himself that she had loved John Edwards possibly from the very day that she had met him.

He didn't understand a man like the vicar was. He must have been very badly treated by somebody somewhere and he took it out on his first wife and now on his second, but it did not stop Helen from loving him.

Rory didn't pretend to himself that she was afraid. If she had been she could have come home and he would have taken her in and been glad that she had got away from the monster that her husband was. He could see what was happening; she was moving further and further back as her husband and his temper advanced on her and she was shifting ground to keep the illusion of her marriage going, hoping, praying perhaps that it would survive, maybe even blaming herself that she was not the wife she should be, not the person who suited John.

Rory could not help regretting that his bright and beautiful daughter had ruined her life. What could she do after such a marriage that would satisfy her, that would be some kind of a future? The children mattered to her almost as much as if they had been her own. He understood that. Anne had been like that. She would not have turned a cat or a dog from her door and each child must be cherished.

But Helen was not staying with John Edwards because of the children. She loved him. Rory wished he could understand that.

He was tired of worrying about things he could do nothing about, so when Mr and Mrs Dilston invited him for a gathering at the house, cocktails for goodness sake, he was inclined to go. He never went out, but Mr Dilston had a lovely house only a couple of miles away and he thought just for once wouldn't it be nice to talk to people who were in business like himself.

So he put on his only decent suit and drove across. He was welcomed by the Dilstons, and right from the beginning he enjoyed it. The other guests were a shipyard owner from the Tyne who was staying the night, a man from Wakefield who was in wool, and another from

Manchester who was in cotton. They had with them their respective wives, but the final guest was Mrs Dilston's sister, and this was why he had been invited and he could not but be flattered. She was older than Helen, but not much, and she was lovely.

They had champagne. It was Mrs Dilston's birthday and they stood about in the lovely room which in daylight had the view down across the valley and up to the dale, all little square fields and stone walls, and Mrs Dilston's sister, whom he thought was called Molly, came to him at the window from which he could see nothing but the shadows of small farms and dim lights from their windows.

She said, 'Isn't it bonny?'

'I love it.'

'I understand you have pits.'

'Very small ones.'

'But several of them.'

'Half a dozen. Are you interested in pits?'

She smiled and shook her head.

'Not really, I just wanted to start the conversation and you are the only single man here.'

Rory hadn't heard himself described like that and wasn't sure he liked it, but perhaps it was better than widower which always made him shudder.

'Do you like the theatre?'

He was surprised at the question.

'I like any form of entertainment.'

'We have a very good theatre in Consett, the Empire. Perhaps I could entice you there.'

'Why?'

She looked hard at him.

'What you do mean?'

'Well, I'm a lot older than you so it can't be anything to do with me. You're very beautiful, young and I understand have plenty of money. Are you bored?'

'Not at the moment. As a matter of fact, my sister asked me to come because she thought I might like you.'

'There are men in Consett, surely, some of them more your age?'

'Yes, I have already met most of them. They go to university and talk about themselves all the time or they go into business with their fathers and are told what to do. You don't seem to have such problems.'

'I have a daughter as old as you.'

'Oh dear, is that supposed to quench me? I don't think you are more than seven or eight years older than me, so you're wrong there.'

'Miss – you see, I don't even know your name.'

'We were introduced. I'm Molly Donaghy. How could you possibly have forgotten such a name? My family comes from Derry. My grandfather came here to the ironworks and prospered. They tell me you have done something similar without crossing the sea.'

After the second glass of champagne he was quite happy sitting with her, talking. Her conversation was so light, as though she felt obliged to be no weight to a man and by the evening's end he was ready to be entranced. He had felt so neglected for so long.

When he was invited to dinner he was happy enough to go and he talked to the men about business, something he rarely got the chance to do, and they welcomed him as one of them. He was sitting next to Miss Donaghy at dinner and had not forgotten how beautiful she was, how taking, how light-hearted and he could see now that he was desperate for company and also possibly for a pretty woman to want to be with him. He tried not to think about Prue, he had loved her very much, but this girl was glamorous and he was flattered that she liked him.

Mrs Dilston came to him when the evening was almost over and she said,

'We are getting up a party to go to the theatre in Consett next week. We wondered if you would come with us.'

He couldn't think how to say no.

His glance caught the smile on her sister's face and she was so taking and he wanted her and he began to think that he had been mistaken and she could be his. He could not stop thinking about what she would be like in his bed or anywhere else at all. He found himself nodding and saying that he would be pleased to go. All the way home he cursed himself, but when he got back to the silence and the cold house he saw that he had nothing here. He thought of Mrs Dilston's sister and her sweet young body and it was a very long time before he fell asleep.

That December, two weeks before Christmas, Mr Dilston held the winter party at his house and they were all invited. Lily had heard that Rory Gallagher would be there with this woman and was desperate to go. She waved their invitation at Prue.

'What about Isla?' Prue said.

'Ernie will look after her.'

'Ernie can't do that.'

'He is very good with her, Prue.'

This, Prue thought, was true. Ernie spent as much time as he could with the little girl.

'We never go to parties. We could have new dresses and everybody's going. May says there's to be champagne. Have you any idea what champagne tastes like?'

Prue shook her head. She couldn't remember.

'Won't it be wonderful? There are to be musicians and dancing. Will you teach me to dance?'

'I don't know anything about it.'

'You haven't danced?'

Lily looked so dismayed, but it was true. Prue hadn't danced in years, but she had learned as a small child. Lily's face sobered.

'You think nobody will ask me to dance because I'm a widow,' Lily said.

'I don't think they are so nice about such things in a place like this. Why would they be?'

'Helen and John have been invited.'

Prue had noticed that they were on first-name terms, yet why shouldn't they be? She and Lily went to church regularly now.

Prue said that she couldn't possibly go, what if there was a call out?

'You're not that far away,' Lily said, 'why shouldn't Ernie deal with things? Why are you making excuses? Don't you want to go?'

'He can't look after Isla and deal with calls,' Prue said.

'Well then, I'm sure Mrs Saxony would come or one of the other ladies from the church – it's only once.'

'It just isn't me,' Prue said, having run out of excuses.

Lily grew sober before her eyes and Prue was sorry to see it, she had spoiled the whole thing for Lily and all Lily had had since her husband had died was financial problems, a screaming baby, the loss of her home and her mother losing her sanity.

'I remember how to waltz,' Prue said suddenly, finding that she did and although they had no music she hummed as they danced and Lily laughed and said that there must be a lovely man out there for both of them. So she taught Lily the waltz and after that she remembered other dances from when she had been young and she and Silas had been in love.

Nurse Falcon came in and announced that she too had been invited. She confided that she was never asked anywhere and that she knew someone who made clothes. Lily fell upon her and there followed a discussion about the dresses they should have made, and for once Lily and Prue did not think about expense.

Ernie, to Lily's obvious surprise, didn't seem to like being asked to look after Isla.

'You're going to the party?' He was staring at her.

Lily stared back.

'So, because I'm widowed and have a bairn, you think I shouldn't go out for a bit of fun?'

Ernie shook his head.

'No, but – I just didn't think you'd want to leave the bairn.'

'Won't you watch her?'

'I see. I'm not good enough to be asked to a party but I can stop at home like some grandma and watch your bairn?'

'No I just . . .' Lily looked nonplussed.

'My dad was a workman like yours. We went to school together and now you're too good for the rest of the village because you married the doctor.'

Lily was speechless, Prue could see.

'So you get invited to posh parties, but me, I don't get invited nowhere.'

Ernie charged out of the room. They could hear the outside door slamming. Lily stood as though she couldn't believe the argument and then turned beseechingly to Prue.

'Did I do something wrong?'

Prue shook her head.

Ernie came back for evening surgery, but he didn't speak unless spoken to, and afterwards Prue called him into the surgery, closing the door as he turned and said, 'I'm sorry, all right? I didn't mean it.'

'You could do better.'

He looked defensively at her.

'I never should have yelled like that.'

'No, I mean you could study.'

This had obviously never occurred to him.

'You're clever, Ernie,' she said.

Ernie blushed until his face resembled the kitchen fire.

'You could be a chemist.'

He shook his head and disclaimed and talked about his mother.

'The way that you reacted showed that you wanted more. I know a professor at Edinburgh University. He might recommend you for classes at Durham and I could help you.'

Ernie shook his head.

'Think about it,' she said. 'You could go up in the world and do all sorts of things. You could get out of here.'

'Don't be soft, Dr Stanhope, I've got nobody to help with me mother. I've got no money and I know these things cost money, they don't take lads like me. I'm never going to get out of here and I know it. And I thank you for caring, but it won't make no difference.'

Lily put dinner on plates after Ernie had gone and her mother was sleeping.

'I don't know who Ernie Smith thinks he is. Too good for the rest of us,' she said.

'He couldn't look after Isla. All his friends would laugh,' Prue said. 'You know what lads are like.'

'He's good with her.'

'That's not the same thing,' Prue said.

'He's got ideas above his station,' Lily said.

'So he should have. So everybody should. I've suggested to him he should study chemistry.'

Lily started to laugh. 'What, him?'

'Why not?'

'That's right, Prue, give him ideas and then he'll be up and gone and we'll have no lad to help you.'

'And is this to be the height of his ambition?' Prue said.

Lily ignored her, but afterwards she asked Mrs Saxony, who had no children, to look after Isla for the evening.

Prue dreaded the party. She couldn't imagine being in the same room with Rory Gallagher and his beautiful new woman. She prayed for the flu. She felt awful doing it, but if she could be in bed – but no, the doctor could not do such a thing. She was the only one; she must be ready for people being ill. She couldn't think of why she wouldn't go, but she knew better than to wish bad things on them. Just for one night surely she could bear it.

Lily's dress was blue and Helen's dress was claret-coloured. Lily had insisted on paying for it and then apologized to Prue, but they agreed that she needed something new and someone to look after John's children, and they spent time persuading one of the older ladies of the parish to see to the vicarage children.

Prue's dress was black and white and she had not paid much attention to it, but when she saw herself in it in front of her bedroom mirror she saw herself as a woman and not just as a doctor, and wanted to cry. She didn't understand it. She had given up everything for medicine and now it was her lot.

She and Lily went out looking for mistletoe that week and they took Isla and Mabel with them. It snowed before Christmas and they took mistletoe and holly, bright with berries, back to the house and decorated the kitchen, and they made paper chains while they sat at the kitchen table.

Isla fell asleep as they did so, but it was such an easy thing to do, so mindless and yet the different coloured paper, glued into circles and plaited one into another and then strung across the room, corner to corner, made such a difference, and Prue missed New York then and her mother.

Lily had made a Christmas cake and the smell from the kitchen was of sweet wine and spices. She had also made Christmas puddings and they had stirred the pudding and made wishes. Paddy had given Prue brandy for the cake and rum for the puddings and there were mince pies. The first lot Lily made were eaten the same day, but she made a second batch the following day and took them to the pub, and she was the toast of the pub that day, the place ringing with drunken cries of her beauty.

New Year would be worse, Lily said. In Scotland Christmas was for the children, New Year for the grown-ups and it was the same here, really. New Year was sacred and the workmen were given both days off because there was no point in asking them to go in since they were drunk from the night before.

The evening of the party, they dressed carefully, but Lily was worried that Isla would cry. However, when they left, Prue driving, Nurse Falcon in the back, in her finery, Isla was happily asleep. Mrs Bradley was dozing by the fire and Mrs Saxony had arrived and the baby seemed to take to her.

Prue drove so slowly that Lily complained, but it seemed the shortest journey she had ever done. The house was lit and all around it people were arriving and chattering and the cars were being parked or some of them, presumably richer, had people to drive them and were going away.

Lily was eager to be inside, so Prue followed her. Mr and Mrs Dilston were perched as they would be at the entrance in the hall ready to greet their guests.

Prue had never seen the local people all done up for a party. The music had already started up and the musicians sounded good. It was not many minutes later that Prue spied Rory Gallagher across the room. She didn't recognize him at first, clean-shaven, neatly barbered and wearing a good suit, but when she did and saw the woman he was with she felt the size of a house.

The young woman was tiny beside him. She wore glittering white ornaments in her hair and a pale blue and grey stole around her creamy shoulders. It was obvious to Prue that she had not gone to some local dressmaker, her silver dress was so lovely that Prue took in her breath and she had plenty of time to admire it because when they danced the silver dress shimmered as they moved beneath the lamps and the candles.

The music went on and on. Prue wished she had been able to find an excuse to leave. Nobody asked her to dance and why would they? She was taller than most of the men and, besides, she was the doctor so she was different, out of place here. They came to her with their physical problems; why would they want to see her like this or make conversation?

There was supper and Lily giggled at how good the champagne was, but Prue couldn't eat and she couldn't drink much either. She had been standing with the older people all the evening but nobody talked to her. They avoided her eyes.

In the dining room May was helping people load their plates with food, but Prue could see how unhappy she was and it was hardly surprising. She had no one to help, she was close enough to watch the other women go by, some of them in gorgeous dresses such as she might never wear and here she was in a maid's uniform, listening to the music, the talk and the laughter. Prue thought probably May had never been to such a party and now she was at one she could not join in, she was captured, handing people plates and helping them to sandwiches cut like triangles and tiny sausage rolls.

May, Prue thought, was like a pale version of Lily, but where Lily was slender May was skinny, where Lily was blonde May's hair under the cap was dull brown. Her face was white and her eyes were pale. No wonder she had not liked to help in Lily's house.

As Prue stood there, however, a man came toward her, smiling, arm outstretched. 'Dr Stanhope? I am Maurice Allen, a Weardale doctor. I've been hoping to meet you for some time. How are you, how are you getting on here?'

Prue was so relieved to find someone interesting to talk to that she rather resented the way Lily turned up after a few minutes. Dr Allen looked at Lily and asked her to dance. Prue was cross, she couldn't even have a few moments' conversation with a nice man without someone butting in, but then she watched them dancing, Lily was smiling and he was talking to her and Prue didn't resent Lily from that moment on.

She did remember how she had met Silas, but she did not miss the complications of their life together, how he did not want her to compete as a doctor, and she remembered how his mother had behaved. She shuddered and was pleased to watch other people dancing except for Rory Gallagher, and that was ridiculous. She didn't want him, but apparently she didn't want anybody else to have him either.

It was the first time that Lily had looked animated since Robbie had died and Prue became happy for her as they danced three times in succession and other people were watching and she thought that many an ambitious woman was seething that a pitman's daughter like Lily Bradley could ensnare first one doctor and then possibly another. It made Prue want to laugh.

She didn't notice the man who stopped in front of her, asking politely,

'Will you dance with me, Doctor Stanhope?'

Prue turned, she had been pretending she was not interested.

'I'm not dancing.'

'Why not? Everybody else is.'

Prue wanted to make a rude remark about the lovely girl he had apparently fallen in love with, but she didn't.

'Oh, come on, Prue, just once.'

So they waltzed and all the way through the dance, which seemed to last forever, Prue was trying not to cry. The last time she had danced was with Silas before they were married and she had been so happy and he had been hers. She remembered to be polite. What was the girl called?

'Miss Donaghy is very beautiful.'

'Isn't she?' he said, as though surprised that somebody so lovely could like him.

'Helen looks happy.'

'I don't think you're very happy tonight.'

Prue was now surprised.

'That's not your concern.'

'Of course not.'

When the music ended, they were right beside the double doors which led into the hall. Prue would have pulled away, but he clasped her to him just sufficiently so that she would have had to be obvious to break free.

'You're holding me,' she pointed out.

'I thought you might like to dance with me again. It's the first time I've had the chance to hold you since you ran out on me.'

'Rory, have you been drinking?'

'Not yet. I haven't had opportunity. Oh go on, Prue, just once more and then you can run home before the clock strikes twelve.'

'Now you're being silly,' Prue said, but the music started up and he danced very well. She hadn't thought he would, and she liked being in his arms, but the ghost of Silas haunted her every moment that Rory Gallagher held her close and, besides, she was aware that another woman waited for him. She was nowhere in evidence but she could have been standing on the sidelines somewhere, watching.

Prue was determined that she would not ask Lily to go before she was ready, but midnight came and she thought they should leave. Ernie had sullenly offered to stay after ten, when Mrs Saxony who was looking after Isla had said she must go home, but Prue didn't think it was fair to make him wait any longer.

When she ventured across to them, however, Dr Allen looked disappointed and Lily, for the first time, put herself before her child when Dr Allen said he would see her home. Prue could not help being glad for them both. Dr Allen might be able to solve one or two problems if he became keen on Lily.

*

Prue drove home and found Ernie glowering, though Mrs Bradley had gone to bed and Isla too by the sound of things.

'Where's Lily?' he said, searching the doorway for her.

'Some friends said they would drop her off. You wouldn't begrudge her a little pleasure?'

Ernie went home without another word. Prue went to bed and lived and relived the two dances she had had with Rory and she remembered so very clearly what being in bed with him was like. She turned over and over, but sleep wouldn't come to her. She told herself that she should have accepted him. She told herself that she was right to have nothing more to do with him, and she heard the church clock strike the quarter, the half hour and the three-quarters and then chime the hour until her pillows and her bed were so hot and uncomfortable that she got out of bed and went to the window and threw back the curtains.

It was snowing. She thought of what it might have been like in New York now had she and Silas had children, but she couldn't envisage it. She had done the right thing, she knew she had, and afterwards she had taken it out on a man she loved. She did love him, she acknowledged it to herself for the first time. He was a good man and would make Molly Donaghy a good husband, as no doubt he had been to Anne. She wanted to hope that he would be happy, but there was a very selfish part of her that wouldn't agree.

*

Helen came to visit the next day to talk over the evening. The children had gone to school, the ladies of the parish, aware that she had suffered a miscarriage, were even now cleaning her house and the church, and Helen said that John had insisted a woman came in to do the washing and ironing.

She was therefore involved in all kinds of things at the church, the Mother's Union and the Sunday school classes; she helped John with the Young Men's Christian Association meetings and the Bible classes which were a new idea she had started up herself. She sounded so merry that Prue was glad for her, only to find that when Prue excused herself because she had paperwork to sort that Helen followed her into the hall so that Prue turned around.

'I think I'm expecting a baby, Prue. I want to get it right this time.'

Prue looked at her and thought that John Edwards had given his wife no time to recover from her miscarriage, he had had relations with her almost immediately. Privately she thought it couldn't be good for Helen, but she could hardly say so.

'Have you told John?' Prue had long since been thinking that John Edwards did not want his new wife to be pregnant. Stupidly, he made her pregnant, of course, but he wanted to come first with her as perhaps he had not done before. It was illogical, Prue thought, but understandable perhaps.

'I've said nothing, I want to be sure.'

'Go ahead, but be careful.'

'Do you mean I shouldn't let him near me?'

'That's up to you, but don't upset him and he must be gentle with you.'

'He's not a monster, Prue.'

Monsters came in varying forms, Prue thought. When she got home Lily was singing in the kitchen.

Two days later, Dr Allen turned up and Lily had him all to herself; Prue kept out of the way.

Prue heard conversation and then mirth and she was convinced that they were getting on very well so it was a shame that since she had to go out and see to various patients, she missed the rest.

When she got home again he had gone and Lily was in the kitchen, rather red-faced, busily taking loaves from the oven. Lily was too practical these days to burn the bread. Prue was sorry for that, in one way.

'So, what did he say?'

Lily turned round, her face alight with excitement.

'He wants to take me out to dinner.'

'Oh my,' Prue said.

Lily's face fell. 'Do you think I'm being stupid?'

'Absolutely not,' Prue said. 'Where are you going?'

'The Bay Horse in Wolsingham. What will I wear?' Lily said.

*

Evening surgery was over and Ernie should have been clearing up before going home, but he came into Prue's room, saying, 'Is that the doctor from Wolsingham?'

'Is he here?'

'In a nice motor. Has he come to see you?'

Prue wasn't looking at him. It was none of Ernie's business, but she couldn't very well say that.

'Why, where is he?'

'In the kitchen.' Ernie's look altered and he understood and looked suspiciously at her. 'Lily's all done up.'

'Then I expect he's come to see her.'

'Has he?' And then Ernie said in altered tones, 'He's middle-aged.'

Prue didn't say anything to that.

'Does she like him?' Ernie asked. 'Where did she meet him?'

'Why don't you ask her?'

'How can I?' The anger showed in Ernie's eyes and the exasperation in his voice. 'I thought . . .'

'What?'

'Nowt,' Ernie said, and he walked back to the dispensing room.

Lily was home by half past ten. Isla was sleeping, Mrs Bradley was in bed and the house was quiet. She came alone into the kitchen but her face was glowing. Prue had never seen such a look on Lily's face. It was pure joy. She began to laugh with glee, put her hands over her mouth to stop herself, but her eyes were lit and she was so beautiful that Prue was not surprised the modest doctor was entranced.

'I think he likes me,' Lily said. 'We had such a lovely time.' She did a little twirl, like a child in her first party dress. 'We had a meal and then he took me back to his house on the road to the reservoir, just outside of the village. So pretty it is up there with the river at the bottom and fields on every side. It's a world away from this place. He introduced me to his housekeeper, such a nice woman, Prue, and oh, his house. It's lovely. He told me about his family, his father was a greengrocer in Westgate and his grandfather was a lead miner. He's done so well.'

'And when are you seeing him again?'

'Tuesday, though I don't know that I should go. I can't keep asking you to look after Isla and my mother, you already have too much to do.'

'Mrs Saxony would do it.'

'I know, but I feel guilty asking her.'

'Why on earth should you? You've been through a lot and we are paying her. I think you should see him as often as you both want and see what comes of it. What have you to lose?'

The following morning, Prue was about to leave to make house calls, when she heard raised voices in the kitchen.

'I take your mother all the time. I don't see why you shouldn't take mine when she needs company,' Ernie was saying.

'I didn't say I wouldn't take her, just that I'm not here that evening and Prue has so much to do.'

'Not here? Where are you going?'

'I don't see what that has to do with you.'

'I've had your mother at my house nearly every day for months,' Ernie said. 'I don't see why you can't return the favour.'

'I can, any day or any evening except Tuesday,' Lily said. 'If you wanted to go away, Ernie, she'd be welcome to come and stay with us for days, you've never been away from here and it might do you good. She would have to share Mother's room, but—'

Ernie cursed almost under his breath and as Prue came in, he pushed past her and slammed the outside door. Lily was staring after him.

'What's the matter with him?' she said.

May had made a rag doll for Isla and came to the house with it, and Lily was so pleased that Prue thought May must be happy living with the Dilstons. Lily dutifully asked May to come to them for Christmas Day, but May proudly said that the Dilstons had asked her to stay with them. Lily gathered her sister to her and said how pleased she was that May had done so well May nodded and gulped and then spent a little time with her mother since Mrs Bradley recognized her and they sat by the fire.

Christmas Eve arrived and Prue had finished evening surgery. Although she thought somebody might need her that evening, she was hoping they would not. Lily had asked Ernie and his mother there to spend the evening with them and her mother was pleased and so was Ernie's mother, and although the pub was riotous as usual, they had grown used to it.

Isla stayed up, and they had ginger wine and a piece of boiled bacon with potatoes and red cabbage and various sweets to follow and they played silly games and laughed a great deal. Then Ernie took his mother home and Lily and Prue said goodbye on the doorstep and went to bed, very tired.

Prue could not help looking out of her window, even though it was hours since they had pulled the thick curtains across all the windows to keep out the keen wind which screamed across the fell but all was silent now and it was snowing.

The flakes, big and square, stole down softly. Prue was mesmerized, watching their varied patterns and the comforting cloak they formed. She left the curtains open; the fire was dying in the grate and tiny sparks tried for more and then gave up, blackened. She lay there in her bed for a few moments amidst the cold and the warmth, and she was so glad for the way that things were going.

Everything was fine as long as she left Rory Gallagher out of it. He would be married soon, and she would be safe from him and he from her, and Molly Donaghy was a lovely young woman and would give him children and they would have a good time together. She could see that Miss Donaghy was the right sort of person for him. She was not reliant on him for his money or his position; she was marrying him because she wanted to, and that was the best reason of all.

Prue thought of Lily and Doctor Allen and of Lily's mother and Ernie's mother and how Ernie was more valuable to them day by day, and of Mabel, snoring by the bed, yet keeping an ear open just in case.

Twenty-four

Prue felt as though she had only just gone to sleep when she heard a banging on the door. No, she thought, it could not happen. It was Christmas morning, very early, not yet light. She opened one eye slightly and was reassured; no, she was dreaming. She turned over and heard Mabel snuffling and reassured herself that all was well.

Then she heard the banging again and this time she opened both eyes and Mabel heard it too, as though she had been ignoring it, and Mabel sat up, ears erect, and that was when Prue admitted to herself that somebody was at the door and most likely somebody was ill in an out-of-the-way place that she would struggle to get to because there was snow which, by the feel of the air, had frozen stiff overnight and it would need hospital admittance for certain. What a start to her Christmas Day, but only to be expected.

She got out of bed in the semi-light and put on sufficient clothes so that she could make her way downstairs without freezing to death. Mabel followed, just in case somebody was going to rob and kill Prue, which seemed unlikely, Prue thought, but she was glad of Mabel's presence.

She undid the bolts, turned the key and hauled back the door, and the whiteness of last night's snowfall made her blink. When she had opened her eyes again, a woman stood on her doorstep. Prue waited for the woman to say that someone needed help, they were ill. Prue didn't recognize her and that was unusual. She knew almost everyone now.

The woman was about her own age, badly dressed, small, skinny and Prue thought she was very poor, her dress, pale face and sunken cheeks said so. She must have been beautiful when she was younger, but her blue eyes were bright no longer and her yellow hair had faded.

Prue stared.

'Who is ill?' she said.

The woman stood back.

'This is where Dr Fleming lives, isn't it? They said so when I called in at a house further over. That he had moved recently.'

Prue was alert now and rather worried. If this woman did not know that Robbie had died, then she was not a close friend of any kind, so what was she doing here and on Christmas Day unless it was a crisis?

'I'm Dr Stanhope. Can I help?'

'Is this where he lives? I need to see him.'

'What is it about?'

'I'd rather talk to him myself.'

'Who are you?' Prue asked.

'I'm his wife,' the woman said.

Prue felt as if it were a hundred years or even a bit more since the young woman had spoken, and she thought, this could only be a dream, it couldn't be happening to her on Christmas morning. Then she heard the church bells, and though she expected to wake up nothing happened; the young woman went on staring at her.

Prue gradually became aware of how cold the woman must be, of the fact that she wore a thin old coat, of the desperation in her eyes. She was on the point of collapse and as a doctor Prue would have seen this sooner if she had not been thinking otherwise.

She drew the young woman into the comparative warmth of the kitchen where the fire had long since died, but it was obviously a lot warmer than outdoors and the woman began to shiver.

Prue went upstairs and took a blanket from the bed, and then she got down, lighting the kitchen fire amidst the ashes, reassured by the way that the dry newspaper and sticks caught. Somehow the coming of warmth helped them both. The woman held hands up and her face was better already, Prue thought.

She badly wanted to talk to the young woman, but, as she sat there, the woman's eyes began to close; she was what Ernie called 'done in' and she went to sleep sitting there.

Prue woke her and guided her to the settle across from the fire. She took off the woman's worn boots and made her comfortable there, considering how hard the settle was though it was padded. She fastened the blanket around her and gave her a cushion for her head and then she went back to the fire and watched until the kettle boiled.

By the time Lily had come downstairs with the wailing Isla in her arms, Prue was about to make tea. Lily stared at the intruder.

'Who is this?'

'She was on the doorstep. What would you have me do, turn her away in such weather?'

Hearing their voices, no doubt, the woman turned in her sleep, awoke and then stared at them. She got up from her cramped sleeping position and sat up and gazed at them.

'Would you like tea?' Prue said hastily, and when she nodded, Prue went off to the pantry for the big brown teapot and brought with her the tea caddy. When she took the kettle off the boil she made tea.

They sat around while she poured out the tea and put in sugar and milk and they cradled the teacups in their hands and Prue put more coal on the fire.

'Who are you?' Lily said, 'and what are you doing here?'

'I have no money and he promised me he would always take care of me so I had to come.'

'Who promised you money?'

'Robbie. He said I was to have the money until he could come for me, but he never came and the money was all I had and now that's gone too and there's nothing left. I need it.'

Lily stared. Prue tried not to.

'I knew he was here, from his letters: he said he had found a good place, his uncle's, and he would make money there and things would be easier and then he would come for me, but he didn't and I have waited and waited. I cannot manage. I have had to leave Rob with my mother in order to come here. We cannot go on like this.'

Lily's face was as white as it had been on the day that her husband had died.

'Who is Rob?' Lily said.

'He's our son. Where's Robbie?' the young woman asked.

'What?'

'Where is Robbie? Why has the money stopped?'

Prue got up and took Isla from Lily. Lily was staring at the young woman.

'Who are you?' she said.

'I did say. I'm Robbie's wife.'

From outside Prue could still hear the church bells. The snow had started up again and was hurling itself at the window.

'We were married in Edinburgh six years since and his parents resented me so much that he hid me away. Me and Rob. I was up in Edinburgh, in service at the house where he lived while he studied at the university and the hospital, and there we fell in love. It was such a good time and I was so happy, but they would never accept me.

'In the end he kept coming and going while he tried to make us a living and when he had done at the hospital nearby he said he had found this place down here and he would make good and come back for us.'

The silence in the kitchen of the little house took on its own sound, Prue thought.

She was only glad when Mabel padded through and wanted to go out so she unlatched the back door and let the dog into the garden, but Mabel was not impervious to atmosphere, did what she had to do and then dashed back indoors and made straight for the kitchen, thinking no doubt that she might have missed something. Nothing had altered, nobody had moved, but to Prue's relief, Mrs Bradley was calling from upstairs.

Prue went up there and found the woman needing to get out of bed, wanting the pot, for about the sixth time in ten hours. After that Prue helped her downstairs.

Neither Lily nor the other woman had moved and Prue thought she must try to go on as though nothing had happened, and since it was Christmas Day she made the big breakfast she had planned with bacon and eggs, black pudding and bread and lots of tea and they all sat around the table and ate and drank and nobody said anything. The young woman ate so quickly that she was almost rude, but Prue gave her more and the woman looked gratefully at her. Eventually Lily said, 'Robbie died some months ago.'

The young woman looked hard at her.

'Aye, I gathered something must have happened. He would never have seen me and our bairn without. I wasn't hoping for much, but I need to keep us.'

'The money had to stop,' Prue said. 'He left nothing but debts and we are still paying them off. There is nothing.'

'But he was a doctor.'

'The practice was in debt when he inherited it and it has been so ever since.'

'What am I meant to do, me and Rob?'

'Don't you have family to look after you?'

'Nobody. I want my money and I want it now.'

'You can't have what we haven't got.'

'It looks like you're doing all right.'

'That's because Dr Stanhope works. If she didn't I'd be homeless.'

'That's where I am. And who are you, anyroad?'

Lily got up and went upstairs with her child. Prue didn't know whether to follow her or to stay with the young woman. The woman fell asleep almost instantly after she had eaten, so the decision was made. Lily was in her bedroom but the door was open. She was standing at the window with her child in her arms, something of Christmas about her, like a Madonna.

'I don't understand this, Prue.'

'Neither do I and I don't think she does either.'

'She must be lying. He wouldn't do such a thing.'

Prue didn't know what to say.

Lily turned on her.

'You don't think she's lying then?'

'We have to find out who she is and why she thinks we're going to give her money, unless you think we can just put her out.'

'Of course I don't think we should, she's poor as I've never seen,' Lily said. 'She's lying obviously, spoiling our Christmas Day so that we will listen to her at such a time.'

Prue said nothing. Lily looked helplessly at her.

'You think he did it? You think my Robbie went with a lass like that? You think he lied to me and that he – he did such a thing. He would never have. Never. He wouldn't, he wouldn't, he wouldn't.'

She collapsed on to the bed, sobbing. Prue didn't know what to do, but was surprised when Mrs Bradley came into the bedroom.

'Why, what's the matter with my bairn?' she said. And for the first time that Prue had seen, she came over and put her arms around Lily, and Lily hid her face against her mother's shoulder.

Prue went back downstairs. She had to start the dinner. Ernie and his mother were due at twelve. Luckily Lily had made soup the day before. Prue put the Christmas pudding to steam on the stove.

Lily followed her downstairs, where Prue was trying to be busy; she only wished they had not spent the evening before sitting at the kitchen table together, scraping vegetables and putting them in water, talking about how good the day would be. Lily went over to where the young woman was sleeping the sleep of the exhausted on the kitchen settle.

Prue prepared the dinner, put the chicken into the oven having stuffed it with sage and onion, this had meant many tears and she was sure she shredded parts of her fingers in with the breadcrumbs. Later she put pre-boiled potatoes and carrots and parsnips in the oven and other potatoes to be steamed and later mashed with butter, and she even made Yorkshire puddings. Lily had insisted on this and Prue remembered that Lily had said it all depended on eggs, so she put five of them into the mixture, beat it all with a fork and then slid it into the big oblong tin in the oven. She could hear the sound of the mixture spluttering against the fat in the heat and she kept the oven closed so that it would rise.

There was a hammering at the outside door, and she found Ernie and his mother there, as had been arranged.

He had come with presents for them all and she told him how grateful she was. His mother had knitted and stuffed with old rags a felt donkey for Isla, and Isla loved this. His mother had embroidered handkerchiefs for Prue: they were exquisite and Prue said so. He gave Lily a dressing table set: a tray, two candlesticks and various little pots with lids in white with tiny pink roses around them that Prue thought must have cost him a lot of money.

Prue found the young woman a shawl, badly knitted but a Christmas gift and some soap which smelled of lavender. She took these without a word of thanks.

Ernie watched the woman all through the meal and when they had eaten Christmas pudding and Prue judged he had had a little too much parsnip wine which one of Paddy's regulars had donated he asked, 'Who are you?'

She stared but replied, 'I was Jeannie Featherall, but now I'm Jeannie Fleming. I'm Robbie Fleming's wife.'

Ernie gawped.

'His wife?'

'Well, his widow now.'

'You were married to him?'

'Aye, in Edinburgh. We have a bairn, a lad.'

Ernie turned to Lily who was sitting next to him.

'Is this right?' he said.

'How should I know?'

'So this is Mrs Fleming?'

Lily turned on him a look of hatred.

'What would you know?' she said, 'what would a daft lad like you know about owt?'

'I know that a lad can only be wed to one lass at a time,' Ernie said with a hard look.

Lily got up, holding him with her gaze.

'Why don't you shut up?' she said.

'I'm not the only one that's daft then, am I?'

The young woman gazed at them both.

'You thought you were wed to my Robbie?' she said to Lily, and then she threw back her head and laughed.

Prue lay awake all that night, turning the day over and over in her mind, trying to think of a good outcome and failing. In the morning she hid under the covers until Mabel, wanting to be out, began whining, and then she was obliged to get up, but when she went downstairs she found the young woman going through the coats on the hallstand at the bottom of the stairs, presumably for money or anything she could sell. Prue had had enough. She gave her what money she could spare beyond the bills and turned her from the door.

Twenty-five

Rory hoped that his daughter might have forgiven him, wasn't that what religion was basically all about? He was hoping that she would ask him if he would like to come and spend Christmas Day with them, but she didn't, and when he ventured across to the vicarage the day before he was told by the woman who answered the door that the vicar was out and that Mrs Edwards had gone out and she didn't know where and she didn't know when she would be back and they were busy the following day. He asked her just to tell Helen that he had called and would like to see her, but nothing happened.

It was as though everything in his life was sending him to the arms of the sweet Irish girl and though he was resisting as best he could, she was so pretty, so attentive and she had nothing to gain from him so he didn't understand why she bothered. He liked the society which the Dilstons were providing for him. He liked the company of other men to talk on subjects which they all knew about, and their wives were so kind to him, they reminded him of Anne. That made things worse. He didn't think about Prue, he couldn't bear to.

He was asked and therefore went to Consett for Christmas Day to be greeted by Molly's parents as though he was a saviour. He didn't understand that. What was it about him that they liked, that he was older than she was? What kind of reason was that for asking a man to their Christmas table?

They lived in a big house on the winding bank between Consett and Blackhill where a good many prosperous people lived in big detached houses in their own grounds. There was a park nearby and that Christmas Day he walked there with Molly. She put her hand through his arm and chatted about nothing in particular. It was cold and foggy and he wished he could be back with Anne on their last Christmas together when it seemed as though he owned the world and everything had been all right.

He thought of how hurt and disappointed she would be at Helen and tried to brush the thought aside. He tried to think of what a lovely day he had had. He had friends here now, they accepted him. The Christmas dinner around the huge table with lots of other people had been as good as it could be where there was no one but Molly he loved. He was lucky to be there. He halted halfway up the bank.

'Shall we go back?'

She let go of his arm and turned and looked at him.

'Do you know how many men have tried to get me to themselves like this?'

'Miss Donaghy—'

'Have you any idea how many men have called me softly by my first name and tried to kiss me?'

He didn't answer and she went on looking at him until he said, 'You must know that my wife died.'

'It's been quite a long time, hasn't it? Most men remarry almost immediately. 'Men aren't like women who grieve for years and years; they replace their wives.'

'You make men sound very cold.'

'It's just the nature of the being, isn't it? An empty bed for a man is not to be borne.'

'What do you really want, Molly?'

She looked surprised, not very pleased.

'Do you know, no one has ever asked me.'

'You could have married a dozen times I would think. On the other hand, you don't need to, you have money of your own, so I understand. If you had wanted to marry there are men much more prosperous than I am, more intelligent, more in tune with culture and well read and I really am not so vain as to think I am so very fascinating.'

She stood for a few moments and then she laughed.

'I do find you quite interesting,' she said.

He laughed too at the look on her face.

'Then what is it you want?' he said.

She leaned forward and kissed him. He wasn't just

astonished, he couldn't move for several seconds. Then he remembered what being kissed was like, what having a woman was like and he couldn't understand why he had denied himself for so long, but his restraint was such that he took hold of her arms and drew away from her. She looked puzzled.

'Don't you want to kiss me?'

'Of course I do, but this is not the way.'

'Then whatever way you wish.'

He kissed her and drew her into his arms and it was as if he had Anne again all to himself. She would never leave him and everything would be right again, just as he had longed for all this time.

He was aware of the sound of the dripping trees and of the thick winter fog creeping down the bank toward them and with the beautiful girl in his arms he drew away just a little and he said, 'Will you marry me?'

And she said, with a little smile, that she would.

They went back to the house and talked to her parents and he apologized for not having asked her father and Mr Donaghy said that he didn't blame him, it was women who had their way in marriage, not men.

When Rory went home, happier for himself than he had been in years, he wanted Helen to know. On the Monday when he thought she might be alone, he called at the vicarage. He wanted Prue to know as well, but he didn't have to say anything; gossip got round the village in no time.

Helen didn't slam the door in his face, she just left it open and went back to the kitchen.

'Helen, I'm sorry for what I did. I couldn't stand the idea of him being like that with you.'

'It's none of your business.'

She had turned to the stove and was busy pouring carrots into a stew or a soup.

'I just wanted to tell you before somebody else does that I've decided to get married.'

She stopped stirring. She turned. He told her about the young Irish woman.

'Molly Donaghy?' she said. 'She's far too young for you.'

'I know.'

'She's not that much older than I am.'

'I know that as well.'

'She could do a lot better. What on earth does she want to marry you for?'

'That I don't know,' he said.

There was a slight glimpse of forgiveness in Helen's eyes.

'She's educated, intelligent, cultured, beautiful and rich,' she said.

'So, might you come to the wedding?'

'I shall have to think about it,' Helen said.

Twenty-six

Mr Allen came to see Lily two days after Boxing Day. Prue was grateful for any distraction because May was visiting her mother and they were trying to keep from her that a woman claiming to be Robbie's wife had spent Christmas Day there. Prue answered the back door, before she went into morning surgery. He was only there for half an hour before he left the house. Prue watched from her window as he wrenched his car away from the side of the road and made it roar away from the village, but she was busy with patients by then and had to wait until late afternoon before she asked about him. Even then the house was so busy with people now that there was no privacy. Mrs Bradley was sitting over the fire with Ernie's mother and May while Ernie was in the dispensary.

'How was Mr Allen?' Prue asked later when the kitchen was empty of anyone but Lily.

'I'm sure he's very well,' Lily said, not looking at anybody or anything as she toiled over the stove.

'Was he talking about New Year's Eve?'

'We're no longer going out on New Year's Eve,' Lily said.

'I thought he was introducing you to his family.'

'So did he,' Lily said and with a tone which did not invite Prue to question her further, so Prue went off early to evening surgery and stayed there for as a long as she could, sorry for once that so few people were ill.

She was not even tired. She took Mabel for a long walk in the dark; it was easier than staying inside. Nobody bothered her. She still carried a pistol and it seemed the village lads knew because they melted away as she came near and she was sorry. She had not meant to be a gruesome witch to them. When she got back to the house, Lily was sitting over the fire with Isla almost asleep in her arms.

Mabel lay down thankfully by the fire and Prue, having hung up her coat, hat, scarf and gloves and taking off her wet boots said, 'Why aren't you going out with Mr Allen?'

'How could I trust him?'

'Whatever do you mean? This is not about that young woman, is it?'

'I just don't want any other man around me after Robbie. I can't do that again.'

'Mr Allen is . . .'

Lily glared at her.

'Mr Allen is what? He's not Robbie? Well, he certainly isn't that.'

'He's a very nice man and he likes you.'

'Robbie has let me down and in doing that he has let down his child and he has let you down too. So he did it over financial matters and family matters. I get so frightened. I don't want to put any man in charge of my future and especially not Isla's future. Do you understand?'

'I think I would feel like that but it's a terrible shame when he is obviously so nice and so taken with you and it would give you and Isla a second chance.'

'I've run all that through my head but I still don't feel right about it and it's not fair to see him when I think such things and especially if any of it turned out to be true.' Lily's face rivalled beetroot by now and she didn't look at Prue. 'If I really was never married to Robbie, then I have a child out of marriage and we all know what that means. People will find out. I'll bet our May can't wait to tell the village and even if that lass was never married to him, people won't care; they will like the idea so much that I won't ever be able to hold up my head here again.'

May came to visit again the next day and she was scarlet-faced with suppressed fury. They weren't expecting her, it was mid-afternoon.

'I got half a day off to come back here and tell you that everybody's talking about you, our Lily.'

They were sitting in the kitchen, Isla was asleep in Lily's arms. Lily stared.

'You told somebody?'

'Of course I didn't. How do you think it looks up at the house now that they know my sister had a bairn without a husband.'

'He was my husband!'

'He was nowt of the sort. He was married to that bitch who came on Christmas Day.'

'She says he was.'

'Aye, well, folk believe it. It's all over the village. How do you think that makes me feel? I come back for one day to see me family and that's what I get.'

'Do you ever think about anybody but yourself?' Lily said.

'Aye, that's what me mam said about you when you were that full of pride. You wanted the doctor and now look where it's got you. A bairn that doesn't even deserve her name and folk looking on you like a loose woman.'

'I was nowt of the sort,' Lily retorted. 'I married him in all good faith.'

'And what did he marry you in? You, thinking you were so clever,' May said. 'He took you for gormless.'

Come evening surgery, Prue went straight through to see Ernie when he arrived early as usual to set everything up.

'So you couldn't wait to tell people about the Christmas Day we had?' she said.

He turned innocently.

'What?'

'You told people about Lily, didn't you? There's no other way they could have got to know.'

'May came to visit.'

'May said nothing because she knew nothing then.'

'What about Lily's mam? She talks all the time.'

'Her mam doesn't talk much sense any more and you know it.'

'Well, there you are then,' Ernie said, and he went back to his shelves and his bottles.

Prue went after him.

'You're finished here. Get out,' she said.

For a few moments he said nothing and then he stopped what he was doing and turned to her.

'I said I didn't. Why would you not believe me?'

'Because I haven't got this far in life without knowing a lie when I hear one. Get out and don't come back.'

Ernie stood for a few moments and then he hung his head.

'I didn't mean to.'

'Yes, you did. Leave.'

'I cannot. I won't get another job—'

'No, you won't and I don't care. You can go and labour in the foundry. Mind you, when Mr Dilston finds out you did such a thing he won't employ you and I shall tell Mr Gallagher not to.'

There was panic in Ernie's eyes.

'Please,' he said, 'I didn't think. I didn't know it would make such a mess, I didn't—'

'That was what you intended. The truth of the matter is that you don't want Lily to marry Dr Allen and do you know what, he has heard as far as I know and he was still willing to have her and she told him that she couldn't trust a man now, not after what had happened to her.'

Ernie stared.

'She didn't!'

'Wasn't that what you wanted?'

'No.'

'Did you think she would marry you?'

He shook his head and his head went lower and his voice shook when he said,

'Not in a million years. I never thought it, even though I – I always cared about her, always wanted her. It was bad enough seeing her with Fleming and then seeing the way that he treated her. How could he do that to her, when she's so lovely and so bonny?'

'So you treated her worse?'

'I didn't!'

'You have. The whole area knows and she has to live with that now and she has done nothing wrong and she has the shame of it because you couldn't keep your mouth shut. Get out!'

'But—'

'Out!'

It was hard running the dispensary without him. Prue had known it would be, but it took so much longer and she didn't know of anyone who would do it as well as he did, nobody with his skill and knowledge, but she was determined not to have him back. In the night she was called out three times and the following morning she was so tired that she could hardly work.

After dinner there was, thankfully, nobody to go and visit, so she started on the books and it was not long afterwards that Ernie appeared in the doorway, cap in hand and a look on his face which she had never seen before. Even Mabel came out from under the desk and sympathetically licked his hands.

'Please, give me my job back. I'm sorry. I need the job and I want it so badly. I'll do anything. You haven't told her, have you?'

'She'd be disgusted with you.'

'You don't know what it's like wishing for somebody for year after year and knowing you'll never have them—'

'How do you know what I wish for?' Prue couldn't help saying. She didn't give him time to reply. 'You should have known that everything that happens under this roof is not to be discussed with anyone outside of this practice or this house.'

'I did know.'

'It didn't stop the spitefulness.'

'I couldn't bear to lose her twice.'

'She was never yours in the first place.'

'That's the trouble,' he said. 'I wanted to rise in the world, to make summat of meself and I cannot, you know I cannot. I'm just the lad who sorts the drugs out. Please, Dr Stanhope, give me another chance. I know I don't deserve it but it's all I've got and I'll never ever let you down again, I swear it and I'll never even look at her. Please.'

'You should remember one thing,' Prue said, 'if you really love her then you won't ever hurt her badly like that again. There's no chance that she'll marry Dr Allen now and she really liked him. She was lit, like never before. She wasn't like that when I got here because Robbie was dying and you took that opportunity from her in a selfish way because it wasn't as if she even cared for you.'

He flinched.

'That isn't love,' Prue said. 'You don't love Lily, you want to possess her, to own her, and that's not right.'

He said nothing.

'You can go back to the dispensary,' Prue said, 'but don't think I will forget about this. I won't.'

He scuttled away.

Twenty-seven

Fine days in Consett were rare and this was definitely not one of them, Rory decided. He was bored, he admitted to himself, he felt as if he were wasting time here and that was ridiculous because he and Molly were looking at houses and she was excited about the idea of them setting up home.

There were a good many lovely big houses in Consett, but for him the huge ironworks conquered all and cast its shadow there. Everything was covered in red dust; the streets were grimy with it. He thought of his modest terraced house where the air was untainted and stopped outside the third house which Molly had insisted on going to see.

She turned to him.

'You aren't enjoying this, are you?'

He didn't like to say such a thing to her. He had asked her to marry him, she had said yes and this was how things went forward. They should choose the house together, he felt certain, but he could not bring himself to be enthusiastic.

'Have you liked any of them?' Molly said patiently.

'It isn't that.'

'What is it then?'

'They're a long way from my work.'

'You have a perfectly decent though rather grubby car, so as an excuse that won't do.'

He suddenly realized that he didn't want to leave the house that had been his home with Anne. He could hardly tell Molly that, it would have sounded and was ridiculous. He denied to himself that any of it was to do with the way that he had felt for Prue. It had been a passing fancy. She was a gorgeous woman, he had wanted her in his bed and that was all it had been. He could not understand why he missed Anne more in the middle of the wedding preparations. It wasn't fair, it wasn't right. Molly read him not quite well but she was there.

'You cannot expect me to live in the house where you were so happy for so many years with another woman.'

'Of course I don't.'

'You tell me that, but I think you don't want to move, even for me. These are beautiful houses and not far from my parents. Is it them? You don't want to be near them?'

Her parents were not much older than him, not something he was very happy about.

'They've been very good.'

'You have nothing back at that house. Your daughter is married and I couldn't live in a little village where everybody would talk about me and where people think a night at the church hall singing hymns is the height of society. Your house is very small and I don't like it. I don't want to live in the country; I like being near my family and friends and you haven't much to leave.'

He knew all this. He nodded and then he followed up the steps and into the house and it was what people called grand. It was even grander than her parents' house and her parents had offered to buy them whichever house they chose.

Molly had been particularly difficult to marry off. She had turned down a dozen suitors better than he was, her father had told him in jest when rather drunk and though they might have despised him for who he was they seemed pleased, relieved to have their final child leave their house. They might even wish she had gone further away so that they could have some peace.

He listened to his footsteps echoing in the hall. The staircase went up on two sides so that it created a huge bowl. He went after her into half a dozen lovely rooms and then upstairs where she stood by the window and talked of the view and it was clear beyond the town, turned so far away from the iron works that they might not have existed.

Outside it stood in half an acre at least. He just couldn't see himself there, being polite to the neighbours, when all his life his neighbours had been the workmen and their families. He had always liked living among them, he didn't want them to think that he, a workman's son, imagined himself so much better than they were. He didn't think so, he was of them and they were of him and he didn't want it to end as it would if he moved here. He was not cut out for this kind of society, but how could he ever tell her that?

He had not thought that he would regret his decision and yet from the very first night when he went back happily to his home he awoke in the darkness and knew that he did. He wanted her, he had not known that what he wanted was her body, not her life. How typical of a man, he thought grimly. He was starving, had kept away from women he did not love, but now, faced with a beautiful girl, he had wanted her so much that it had clouded his judgement. Prudence Stanhope haunted him as well as any ghost and night after night he put her from his mind as best he could.

He called himself names. It wasn't love, it wasn't anything like the feeling he had had for Anne. He told himself that he had wanted Anne and the love had grown, but he was young then. He had stopped feeling anything much at all after she died and now he had mistaken want for something better and he must go through with it.

She said that she liked this house best of all so he summoned the required enthusiasm and said that he thought it was the right one for them and they went back and talked to her parents and the look on her face was so joyful that he pushed his misgivings to the back of his mind.

Twenty-eight

Prue had not quite understood what New Year meant here and in some ways it was a good deal more than Christmas. For a start you could not go to bed before midnight because someone could knock upon your door and bring in the new year after twelve. He had to be a tall dark man. Prue would have killed by then for a tall dark man, but she did not like the idea of having to wait up for him.

He was meant to bring coal for warmth and bread for food for the year ahead and you were meant to ply him with whisky, but New Year next to the pub was a succession of singing and people throwing up outside and Paddy shouting for her since he knew that she slept at the front. Prue, dashing out to deal with those who had fought on the street, found wounded soldiers everywhere.

Downstairs, in Paddy's front bar, the floor was bloody, smashed bottles and glasses cracked under her feet and tables and chairs were overturned.

'For God's sake, Paddy,' Prue said, 'do they have to get like this?'

Paddy looked at her in amazement.

'Why, it's New Year's Eve, doctor, Scottish Christmas.'

'You're Irish, Paddy. What the hell would you know?' Prue said.

Even as they spoke, a bottle sailed across the room and Prue ducked so that it didn't hit her. She was glad she had made Mabel stay at home even though she knew that she would be whining at being left out and was even now rousing the household, scrabbling at the front door.

'In such a lovely place as Ireland you cannot possibly go on like this.'

Paddy looked lovingly at her.

'Ah,' he said, 'I was born in Consett. My family was from Derry.'

That was Paddy, a complete mix, like so many people, Prue thought.

Nobody was seriously hurt, Prue was glad of that, but she bandaged a lot of limbs that night and watched men throw up, or lie down and sleep, and some of them were still singing when she finally made her way out of the pub towards her bed and it must have been nearly four by then; she was certain that she heard the church clock.

Even Mabel had gone to bed and didn't budge when Prue fell onto the bed without even undressing. She could hear the singing in the street as men rolled their lovely way home.

'Abide with me, fast falls the eventide.'

Such a beautiful hymn, sweeter still on the voices of sinners.

That January Prue went to the vicarage. Helen was not at home, the woman who opened the door told her, to Prue's surprise, and she found her at the church, running something. Prue could hear her voice before she got inside and then Helen saw her and she said, 'Oh, Prue, how lovely. I haven't seen you since before Christmas,' and she came and hugged her. 'You didn't come to the Christmas carol service.'

'We had other things to deal with. How are you?'

'I'm very well. We all are.' And she was, Prue thought, as Helen went about the church directing people to this and that; the baby was so in evidence but all in one place, she was so tall and slender and her baby was nothing more than a bump. She looked good.

Prue no longer worried about her. She seemed happy in her marriage, glad of his children and she had got the women of the parish on her side. They cleaned the house and the church and they made cakes for stalls, raising money for different good causes. Prue thought she had rarely seen a woman as happy, and she was glad.

Mr Kitson, a regular at the surgery, came back to Prue after taking his pills home the day before saying, 'You've changed them, Dr Stanhope, these aren't the ones I had before but you didn't say anything about changing them so I don't understand. Are these going to be better for me?'

Prue took the pills from him, consulted his notes and then she sighed and said, 'Wait there, Mr Kitson, I won't be a minute,' and she went to the dispensary and told Ernie that the pills were wrong. He said he was sorry but when the surgery was finished, she went in to see him and she said, 'You could kill somebody, going on like this. I don't care how bad things are, you have to concentrate . . .'

'I'm sorry.'

'Sorry won't do it,' Prue said.

'But—'

'No.' She looked at him. Ernie bowed his head. 'If you want this job you had better sort yourself out. I don't care what you feel or what you think, you are responsible for the people in this town getting the right medication. Are you listening to me?'

He nodded.

'Are you?' Prue shouted. 'Forget about Lily. Forget you made such a mess of it all. It's finished, right? You are my dispensing chemist. You are very good at what you do. Now try to remember who you are and put everything else out of your head. Right?'

'Yes, Dr Stanhope.'

*

People talked about Helen's father and his coming marriage with the lovely girl from Consett. Prue tried not to think about it. She knew that she was not entitled to and she knew that she could never measure up to Molly Donaghy. She didn't know of any woman who could, so she tried to ignore the talk, and Helen, thank goodness, did not talk about her father and his bride-to-be.

As Helen's pregnancy progressed, Prue increased her visits, but they were casual. Helen seemed fine.

The vicarage children were well, their faces shiny with health. Prue saw John Edwards each Sunday at church and he was just the same, though some of his teeth were false and a slightly different colour than the rest. But as time went on and Prue called in one fine day, Helen's face told the story. She was six months pregnant. Her eyes had great shadows beneath them and her cheeks were sunken. She was so different, quiet and avoiding Prue's eyes.

'You look worn out.'

'Aren't you proud of me for having got this far?' She sounded brittle.

'I think you need to rest.'

Helen laughed and it seemed to Prue that it echoed all the way around the house.

'When would I have time to do that?'

'You must make time. You have plenty of help. Lie down in the afternoons. Everything else will get by.'

*

Prue was always tired now. She got used to it, she slept when she could and during the cold weather which followed during January, February and March. There were coughs and colds and worse things where some folk couldn't breathe and panicked and several old people died of pneumonia. She was on the go late and early, so that the night a man crept into her bedroom she didn't hear him and Mabel had not alerted her so she awoke with a start and a cry.

'It's only me, Ernie, Doctor Stanhope. I let meself in.'

Prue remembered to try and breathe.

'What the hell are you doing?'

'I was out with me mates from the farm and we went along Church Lane where they live and there was this screaming going on at the vicarage and it just didn't seem right. Will you come and see?'

He went outside. Prue pulled on some clothes and she and Ernie and Mabel got into the car and drove the short distance to the vicarage. There was no sound. The other boys had retreated into the shadows and came out now, murmuring among themselves, and one of them came to Prue, saying, 'I divvent think yer should gan in there on your own, missus.'

Prue, understanding the local dialect well by then, said, 'I'll be fine.'

'You winnat,' he said, 'howay, lads.' He indicated with his head and they trooped in with him.

Prue would have said more, but the lads insisted on going ahead and she was glad of them. She didn't like the silence. When they reached the outside door she told the lads to wait, and they did, but she was aware of them at her back and grateful for it. Then she took Mabel and her bag forward.

The front door was closed and when she tried it, it was locked so she went around to find the back door ajar. The lads followed her in there and hovered.

She went in, making as little sound as possible and all four of them crept in with her. The only light was coming from the kitchen. She thought that up above she discerned small children in the shadows as though they did not dare to come and look through the staircase at her and she reassured them in a very low voice that it was just the doctor, they knew her and everything would be all right.

The lads hung back, not wanting to frighten the children. She thought that the children knew Ernie and she could hear his soft reassuring voice. He was talking to them and the other lads followed him and they were the same, and Prue thought she had never heard a more welcome sound than men's low pitmatic voices. It was like music.

From the kitchen there came the sound of sobbing as though the person could not breathe well. Prue gestured Mabel to sit, and although Mabel did not look convinced she sat down to wait, gazing up at the lads around her as they took the staircase, chatting all the time so that the children came forward to greet them.

Tom, a farmer's son who lived at the end of the lane, picked up the smallest.

'Why man, Wilf, are yer's all reet?'

And one of the others saying, 'Hey, Teddy, how's it gannin', marrer?'

Another said, 'Why Lizzie, what's thee doing, lass? And Mary, howay ower here. Divven't greet, hinny, thoo's all reet.'

Prue made her way toward the kitchen.

Ernie followed her. When she would have remonstrated with him, he said in a low voice, 'You aren't going in there on your own, I don't care if you are the doctor.'

'Thanks,' Prue said and she smiled even though she knew he couldn't see it.

She pushed open the door and there in a pool of light she saw Helen on the floor and also John Edwards. He was lying still and his wife was sitting over him. Ernie stood still behind her in the doorway.

'Helen?' Prue said her name softly.

Helen looked up and Prue had never seen a look like it, blank. She had a huge kitchen knife clutched in both hands. There was blood on her face. Her hair had come down and hung in long locks and she was crying as though she might not stop. There was blood on her clothes and on her hands and arms. Her mouth was bleeding and there were huge red marks on her face where he had hit her. She was bleeding from her left ear, her dress was torn at the neck and there was the start of bruises.

There was crockery broken all over the floor and kitchen chairs overturned in the struggle. Cupboard doors were open, and the contents strewn on the floor; flour and sugar and broken glass made white glistening molehills and cutlery shone silver in the lamplight, in sharp and grotesque heaps, stuck in the flour and twisted in the sugar and even wooden spoons which had fallen in fine array like a fan.

Helen sobbed, while her breath was all horrified gasps and moans of pain. Around man and wife was a lake of blood. As he saw it, Ernie would have come forward, but Prue put up one palm facing him and he stopped.

Prue spoke softly in case Helen was so caught up in what was happening that she didn't see or didn't recognize her. Prue gradually eased herself down, putting her doctor's bag well beyond her.

'It's all right, Helen, it's only me.'

She sat there as Helen's eyes gradually accustomed themselves to someone new who was not trying to hurt her and Prue could see recognition there among the shock and fear.

'There's nothing to be afraid of now, nothing to harm you. It's just me and Ernie. We came to see what we could do. Do you think we might help?'

She waited for what seemed like a very long time and Helen looked at her and then at Ernie and back at her and then at the man on the floor and Prue could see that she did not understand what had happened. And then Helen saw the hands that held the knife and gazed at it and very slowly she made her fingers move and gradually she let the knife down to the floor and she went on looking at it as though she might never be able to see beyond it.

Helen's body was placed unnaturally, almost twisted away from her husband, as it would be because her baby was a large bump and also because he had hit her in other places, Prue thought, by the way that she moved so carefully. None of it was easy for her or without pain and her first instinct had been to protect her child.

Prue had not realized that Helen was so skinny, the baby took up so much of her that she had just about disappeared, Prue thought, it seemed almost like an insult to what was happening around her. Helen's breath was ragged and went on like that and Prue waited until it had some kind of steadiness before she reached down very slowly, making sure that Helen saw what she was doing, feeling for John Edwards' pulse in his arm and in his neck. There was nothing.

Helen sat up straight and gazed at him. More confident now, Prue looked down and then she began to examine him for any sign of life, though there could not have been, she felt. He was dead. Prue became aware of Ernie at the door and without moving she said very softly, 'Will you ask one of the lads to get Nurse Falcon?'

He disappeared without a word. Prue prayed that the children would not come in, but, she thought, the lads between them would sort it. She started talking to Helen.

She couldn't think of anything else to do, but her voice sounded ridiculous. It didn't matter what she said, she told herself, it was only the rhythm of her voice which might bring some normality to the room and after a while Helen seemed to relax. She looked at her husband and there was no comprehension.

It seemed years and years before Ernie came back. Prue was almost hoarse with speaking and pushing back emotion.

'Dinna fret,' he said, 'Matt has gone for the nurse and Tom and Jake are with the bairns. I'll stay about.'

It couldn't have been more than half an hour, but felt like forever before anything else happened. Prue didn't move or even look up, but she had never been so glad to hear the arrival of anyone as she was when Nurse Falcon sank to her knees beside Prue, just as though it were an ordinary situation. When Prue could see the nurse properly it made her want to cry in gratitude.

Helen began to sob afresh. At first Prue thought it was reaction, but she was clutching at her stomach.

The baby was nowhere near full term and Prue was objective enough to see that this could be regarded as a good thing. If the baby had lived, then all Helen would see was that she had murdered her child's father and then she would have five children to look after.

It was awful, trying to help a woman who was miscarrying and almost deranged. Helen was in shock, she didn't clutch at herself any more. Prue wanted to sit down and cry.

Throughout, all she could hear was Nurse Falcon's re-assuring voice which sounded as if it was for Helen, soothing her, encouraging her as the pain grew and the sweat mixed with blood on the girl's face and Prue thought she had never been as glad of anything, as she was of the nurse's flat and confident Durham tones, so practical and kind.

When the morning arrived, grey and cloudy, Prue could hear the rain banging hard against the window after Helen stopped crying out. The baby arrived dead and neither Prue nor the nurse was surprised.

Twenty-nine

Prue did not know who told Rory Gallagher what had happened, only that he burst through the back door before the day was properly light, ran to the kitchen and stood in the entrance, staring. The scene was carnage, Prue thought, like a battleground, blood and bodies, and ridiculously she longed to tell him that it was not as bad as it looked.

He saw his daughter, the body of his son-in-law and when he could tear his glance away he looked at Prue and the anger in his eyes made her go cold. He came over and lifted his child out of the mess. Prue longed to say something to him, but she couldn't think of anything which was relevant or helpful. She just watched him carry Helen off.

After that Prue cleaned herself up as best she could, she didn't want to frighten the children, and then she went upstairs. They were all in one bed and Ernie stood by the window, watching day assert itself over night. He turned, hearing her and it seemed to Prue that he had aged ten years at least.

'Is he dead?' he asked, very softly in case the children might awaken.

Prue nodded.

'I think you had better go for Sergeant Tweddle if you will,' she said.

He nodded and looked glad that there was something for him to do, and when he had gone Prue sat down wearily in the armchair by the window, so grateful for the light. The children slept on.

When Sergeant Tweddle came into the hall with two constables, Prue went downstairs, and after she had told him that John Edwards was dead he said they could clear up the rest of the room, and so they did.

Nurse Falcon went upstairs and Prue went outside with Sergeant Tweddle. The day was blinding with sunshine just as though everything was normal.

'What now?'

'As little as possible, I think,' he said gruffly. 'I'll send Ernie for the undertaker. What do you think?'

'I think Mrs Edwards will not be able to give you any answers, possibly for a long time.'

Sergeant Tweddle looked at her and Prue thought how capable and reliable he was and she was so glad of it. So few people managed such things. He was all reassurance, his body and his voice.

'This will never go to court, the law is not that vindictive, at least not on my patch,' Sergeant Tweddle said, and then he lowered his head and said very softly, 'I never liked him, he was a devious evil bastard, but I'm sorry about the bairn.'

When the undertaker had taken John Edwards' body away, Prue and Ernie did more clearing up while Nurse Falcon stayed with the children. The day was well advanced by then. When she could think of nothing more to do, Prue stood, blinking through the sunshine in the kitchen and then Ernie said, 'What can we do with the children?'

In a fit of what could only pass for sensible, Ernie got the children's clothes and as many of their belongings as he could fit into the car and they went back to the doctor's house. Lily sat them all down to breakfast, only Teddy came to Prue.

'Where is Auntie Helen?' Not 'Where is daddy?' – the other sentence she had been dreading.

'She's gone to her father's house. She's tired and not very well.'

'My father – he shouted and shouted at her and he kept hitting her and hitting her and she cried and I tried to stop him knocking her around, and because of the baby too and she pushed me out of the kitchen and I had to look after the others,' Teddy said, what was left of colour in his face completely draining. 'He was always doing it. He did it with our mother and when I tried to get between them he . . .' Teddy ran out of speech then. They stood in silence for what felt like a long time but could only have been a few moments. And then Teddy shot her a look so adult on his young face that Prue flinched.

'Is he dead?'

'Yes.'

'Good,' Teddy said, and he went back to the breakfast table and sat down and ate toast so calmly that Prue shook. The youngest child, Wilfrid, got down from the table and came over and tugged at her sleeve.

'Can I go over and stroke Mabel?'

Mabel was snoring by the door. Prue nodded.

She went to take Nurse Falcon home. The nurse had said she didn't need that, but she let Prue drive her, and when they reached Nurse Falcon's house and the car stopped, Prue began to cry. She didn't understand this, she was always so capable, always in charge, but now she gave way and Nurse Falcon took Prue into her arms and she said, 'Let it out, lass, it's too much to bear.'

Prue had had nobody to lean on for so long that she howled into Nurse Falcon's shoulder, moving back when she could and saying, 'I have never ever been as glad to see anybody as I was to see you. Thank you so much.'

'Don't you worry, you're doing grand,' Nurse Falcon said before she got out of the car and went up her garden path, just as though everything was as it should be.

*

That evening Prue went to see Helen at her father's house opposite what had been the old surgery and was now a private house. The memories rushed her, how she had arrived there, Isla's birth, Robbie's death. She swept these from her mind as she banged on the door. The door was almost torn off its hinges when Rory Gallagher answered it.

'What?' he said.

'I've come to see Helen. She is my patient.'

He stood for a few moments and Prue could see the fury in his face, even though he tried to hold it back. And then he said abruptly, 'You should have sent for me when that happened.'

At any other time Prue might have stood this but she was angry too about what John Edwards had done and how dearly it had cost his wives, his children and his two dead infants. She glared at Rory's dark and angry face and she said, 'Don't tell me what I should have done. I had a dead man, a woman half out of her mind miscarrying and four children on the upstairs landing who were terrified. Strangely, I did not think of you first. Now, do you mind?'

He stood back but accompanied it with, 'She's asleep.'

'Good.'

'Come in then.'

Prue no longer wanted to go inside, but she went.

He took her into the same room as he always did but he was not working. There he gazed into the fire, back turned to her, not deliberately she thought, just because he couldn't think how to act and that was hardly surprising, this problem was new to all of them.

'Sergeant Tweddle came,' she said.

He swung round, eyes dark and narrowed and lit.

'You sent for the law?'

'What did you expect me to do, throw John Edwards over some convenient hedge, leave him to rot in his kitchen?'

'I neither know nor care, but I will not have my daughter go through any more so you can tell Tweddle—'

'He's Sergeant Tweddle to you and I will not tell him anything. He is a good man and he understands much more than you think.'

'If Helen has to go on trial for this . . .'

'He has reported it as an accident and the undertaker, Mr Lewis, is a fine, upstanding man and he too knows what John Edwards was capable of and the dreadful things that he did. This is a small town where people are loyal to one another and that includes you and Helen. They are not stupid and it is low of you to think otherwise.'

To her surprise all he said was, 'I thought the baby might have lived,' and his voice quivered.

'It was far too small.'

He shook his head and said nothing, and since he was turned away as though the fire needed his attention, she couldn't see his expression.

'It's still a huge loss,' he said, and Prue was glad to hear the regret in his voice, despite the fact that the child would have been John Edwards' son and she suddenly saw that this would have been his first grandchild. People thought nothing of a child who died in childbirth. Prue practically wanted to cheer for his apparent sensitivity over his fury. She liked him a good deal for it and wished she didn't.

'There was nothing you could have done,' she said gently.

'I should never have let her marry him.'

'Oh, Rory, you know very well it wasn't your decision to make. No decent man who loves and respects his child does such a thing, and she is far too intelligent to let you rule her, thank God, as though you would have.'

He shook his head.

'How will she live with the fact that it was her decision?' And when he turned and looked at her, his eyes were wet. 'If I had played the heavy father this would never have happened.'

'It still wouldn't have been the right thing to do because that isn't how you brought her up. There was no way in which she could have known what he was really like. We have to learn to take people on trust.'

'She'll not do it again,' he said. 'It's such a hard lesson.'

'I hope she does at some time in the future. She's very young.'

At that moment she heard Helen's voice from upstairs. She waited and glanced at him, and when he nodded she left him there, though what she would say she could not think.

Helen, clean and out of danger, looked even worse somehow, like an old woman with shrunken, skinny hands and white face, her hair thin and lank with great oblongs of black beneath her eyes and terror still in them.

When she saw Prue, Helen started to cry. Prue talked softly to her and told her that everything would be all right. For how many thousands of years had people told one another such bloody lies? All Helen said was,

'My baby. My baby.'

Prue said nothing, she just waited until Helen drew back and asked in an almost sensible voice, 'Where are the children?'

'At my house.'

'Thank you so much for taking them in. I was worried about them. What have you told them?'

'That you will be fine.'

'Teddy knew what was happening. I worry most about him, he tried to help me, I thought John might kill him. I tried to stop him and to get him out of the kitchen but he wouldn't go, he went on fighting with John to keep him from me and shouting and swearing and screaming at him and John was past all reason by then. It was only when I pushed Teddy out of the way and he saw how bad John was that he had sense enough to be afraid.' She stopped here and breathed carefully. 'Teddy is so clever and has been through so much. I want to go back to the vicarage and take them with me.'

'You can't,' Prue said more flatly that she wished she had to.

'Why, what will happen now? Will I be hanged? Will I go to gaol?'

'None of that,' Prue said, looking into her face so that Helen would know she was telling the truth. 'You aren't to blame for what happened.'

'And is he to blame?'

Prue thought it best not to answer that.

'I killed him,' Helen managed.

'He tried to kill you and your unborn child and he would have killed Teddy too. You had to stop him. You didn't have any choice. You had to.'

'I want my children. And I want to go back to the vicarage.'

'That's not possible. When the fuss dies down there will be a new vicar.'

'Then where can we go?'

'We'll work something out. Don't worry.'

'I want to see them. They must have some reassurance that things go on.'

Prue was convinced that the vicarage children already knew things didn't go on, but she couldn't say that.

'Besides,' Helen said, 'you haven't room for them.'

'We're managing.'

'They must come here. We have four bedrooms, lots of space.'

'I think you should concentrate on getting better and in a few days we will sort things out. You must sleep and heal. Lily and Ernie are perfectly capable of helping with the children and you know how much they love Mabel. She is having such a good time with them.'

Helen nodded, but her head was down. She was soon exhausted and as Prue got up she lay down with a sigh and closed her eyes. Prue sat there until she could see that Helen was sleeping, her breathing was so even. Prue's heart ached for her.

Downstairs, Rory was hovering over the fire.

'How does she seem?'

'She's a lot better already.' She didn't tell him that as far as she knew, and that wasn't very far, women rarely got over having killed their husbands. That wouldn't help.

'I'm not having his children here.'

There he went being impossible again, but why would he want such a man's offspring? Also he knew Helen too well; he knew that she would want the children here.

'Of course not,' she said, 'I'm sure we can find some convenient orphanage and of course Helen won't mind.'

He didn't answer that, he didn't say anything at all and Prue thought this was hard on him too, thinking he might have done differently, that he could have protected his daughter, though how he could have done so she could not imagine.

'I'm sorry, that was a stupid thing to say,' he said, looking straight at her, and Prue was astonished again at how he realized she was right and he was grieving for what his child had been through and needed somebody to blame and John Edwards dead was not much help.

She thought as a man and as a father, Rory Gallagher would have liked to beat the shit out of him over and over again and she would almost have applauded the brutality. Experience taught you not to wish for such things.

Experience also taught you that you would have tried to help a decent person you cared for beat to the ground a man like that, so big and apparently unstoppable, who cared nothing for the woman who had married him when people were opposed to it and then not cared for any child she bore him or for his eldest son. Even some of the most inadequate men could not have tried to hurt their eldest sons. How would their genes carry on?

'It's a natural way to feel though. Why would you want his children in your house?'

'Because Helen cares for them?'

'That wouldn't move some people.'

'She's my whole life,' he said.

So much for Molly Donaghy, Prue thought. Blood was so much more important than love, however it showed itself. She wanted to tell him that his daughter would be all right, but it would have been a lie and he was too intelligent to try and fool.

If he had met Molly before this and married her and maybe she was even now having his child, it would have changed everything. Timing suited no one.

'She will get a lot better you know,' Prue said. 'She's strong and capable.'

He smiled as though he didn't believe her and she was not even sure she believed herself.

When she reached the house, Lily and Ernie were putting the children to bed. It was not easy. They wanted to go home, and the two middle children, Mary and Elisabeth, were crying loudly, while Teddy and Wilfrid were trying to ignore them. In among all this Isla was crying too, possibly brought on by the others, and Lily looked so tired that Prue immediately told her to go to bed with Isla because Isla would soon calm down, but Lily was not easy to convince.

'These bairns have lost so much,' she said.

'So have you and God knows how many times in the night your mother will get up.'

In the end the four children piled into bed with her and though she was short of space, she was glad as they dropped off to sleep, exhausted by what had happened. She lay listening to them breathing and Mabel snoring and eventually she fell into the bliss of sleep with arms and legs and hands and faces warm and in her way.

There was something Rory had to do. It was something he didn't want to do and he understood his own reluctance, but if it had not been for certain men that night, things, bad as they were, could have been so much worse. First of all he went across the village to see Ernie as Ernie arrived for work. He had his mother with him so all Rory said was, 'Can I have a word?'

Ernie eyed him suspiciously but nodded, led his mother inside and came back, looking cautiously at the pit owner.

'I want to thank you for what you did for my daughter.'

Ernie squirmed.

'It was nowt, Mr Gallagher. All I did was get the doctor.'

'If it hadn't been for you Helen might have died.'

Ernie shook his head.

'That's not true. The doctor did all the important things.'

'From now on your house is rent free. I understand that you are clever and if you want to go on with your studies I will help you.'

Ernie coloured.

'But—'

'No. You've had nobody to help and a lot to contend with. And if there's ever anything else, you have to let me know.'

'Mr Gallagher—'

'That's the way it is. Thank you for what you did.'

Ernie was so embarrassed he couldn't look at the pit owner.

Two of the other lads worked for Rory so he called them into the office. They were both about to get married, so he made a generous contribution towards their weddings, and the farm lad he offered to send to the agricultural college at Durham, and since it was what both he and his father wanted, everybody was satisfied.

Sergeant Tweddle was another matter. He couldn't offer the man money or anything else that might be seen as a bribe but he went into the sergeant's office, and Sergeant Tweddle listened to him for a few minutes and then he said, 'I was just doing my job, Mr Gallagher.'

'It was more than your job.'

'This is my patch, my area. I like to think I look after everybody within it, not just you and Mr Dilston because you have money and such; I would have done the same for anybody.'

'I know, and that's what makes it so wonderful. If it hadn't been for you things could have been so much worse for us. I know you can't accept anything from members of the public, but if I can ever do anything for you and your family personally, I will be glad to do it.'

The undertaker was another matter. He had been one of Rory's father's friends and all Rory had to do was to send him a dozen bottles of malt whisky and put in a note which told him the order was to be repeated as necessary. He got a lovely note back, saying, 'Oh, Rory, what a grand lad you have turned out to be.'

Thirty

A few days later, Helen turned up at the back door of the surgery. The minute they saw her the listlessness went from the children. They shrieked with joy and flung themselves at her. It was some time before they quietened down, though it was good to see them happy, even if just for a short time. Helen sat down and had tea with Prue and Lily. It was Sunday and Prue could see that Helen was remembering how things had been and how as the vicar's wife she should be at the church now, her children neat on the front row and her husband preaching a sermon in the pulpit, and she with her new baby to come. Such awful things could not have happened, she was not ready to accept it and yet Prue could see a hardness in Helen's face which had not been there before.

'Could we trouble you for your car? I want to take the children and all their belongings back to my father's house. I'm going to take the children to evensong this afternoon, Prue,' Helen said, 'will you come with me?'

Prue hesitated. She didn't like to say that it was too soon and the wrong time, but she didn't need to. Teddy had overheard, and he stood up like somebody much older and came over and he said quite clearly, 'I'm not going back there now and neither are the others.'

Helen stared at him.

'But, Teddy?'

'We're not doing it,' he said flatly, and he didn't even wait for Helen's response. He simply turned and walked away.

Helen had more sense than to insist or perhaps she saw what he was trying to do. Whatever, she gave in. They packed the car and Prue drove them to Rory Gallagher's house and when Helen opened the front door the children spilled into the hall. Prue had not thought that he would be there, it being Sunday, or that a slight pretty figure would be there with him. Molly Donaghy looked bewildered.

Prue stood there with two bags of children's clothing and couldn't think of a thing to say. Helen didn't say anything, she let the children run into the house.

When she ventured through into the sitting room she saw Molly Donaghy, large-eyed and unhappy.

Prue introduced herself, but Helen didn't speak, and Molly Donaghy was faced with the problem of what you say to a woman whose husband has recently died.

'They can't stay with Dr Stanhope and Mrs Fleming any longer,' Helen explained eventually, ignoring Molly.

Rory Gallagher stared at the way that the children were running up and downstairs and round the rooms and back out into the hall and screaming and laughing and crying all at once.

'Which bedrooms can we have?' asked Mary, who was almost eight and had already been upstairs and explored. 'I'd like the one for Beth and me to have the view across the fields. It's very pretty and Teddy and Wilf don't care for such things.'

Molly Donaghy watched in horror as though she had never seen children before, Prue thought, but it was not more than a few minutes before Wilf came in and threw himself at Helen, knowing that she would lift him into her arms. He put his arms around Helen's neck and hid his face against her.

Rory Gallagher had not told his intended bride that Helen had killed her husband. He had no intention of telling anyone what had happened. It was a secret which nobody outside the village, as far as he was aware, understood. No one had said anything and he was convinced that only Prue, Sergeant Tweddle, his most trusted men, the undertaker, Helen herself, Nurse Falcon and probably Lily knew exactly what had happened. Ernie Smith and the farm lads were close-mouthed, as people were around here when serious things went wrong, and he hoped to keep it like that.

There was speculation in the village, but no suggestion that anything had been Helen's fault. It was widely rumoured that Mr Edwards had been done in by burglars at the vicarage and Mrs Edwards had lost her baby because of the shock. People were very sorry.

Molly wanted to go home. She didn't have to say anything. Watching the four vicarage children running around his house was sufficient, and the two women with them finished her off. She barely had to ask him. They motored back across the tops to Consett and neither of them spoke.

When they reached her house she said, 'I didn't know that your daughter and her four stepchildren would be coming to live there. I know that her husband died but he must have family who will take her and the children in, surely. They can't expect you to do it, especially when you're coming to live in Consett.'

'Things being as they are, I think Helen must have the house.'

'How is she to live there alone with four children? You will be forever running back and forth.'

'She is my daughter.'

'I didn't mean to sound unsympathetic but you must look at it from my viewpoint. My future step-daughter is not much younger than me and she has four children. That makes me some kind of grandmother.' And she shivered before she got out of the car.

'I will make it up to you,' he said, after he had tasted the sweetness of her lips when they reached the door. 'I will not always be there fussing about them.'

'I know. I'm sorry I doubted you,' she said, and went inside. He imagined himself going in there with her, going to bed with her, taking off her clothes and feeling her body against him.

When Prue and Lily sat down to eat after evening surgery, Prue managed to make Lily laugh with her description of Rory Gallagher's face when his step-grandchildren arrived to take over the house. Although they knew it wasn't funny, it was such a pleasure, finding humour in something.

Lily's mother was asleep by the fire. She was sleeping more and more and was less and less trouble. Prue wasn't happy about that as it was not a good sign. Lily was also relieved to have the Edwards children out of her house. She didn't say so, but Prue could read it in her face.

'So do you think Molly Donaghy will marry him now?' Lily asked.

'She was horrified.'

Lily thought about it.

'Inheriting four step-grandchildren at the age of twenty-five? Not something to look forward to. He's far too old for her, of course, but he is quite nice. He has lovely hips.'

Prue could remember thinking the same thing herself.

'Lily!'

'He moves well. I would have married him if he'd asked me.'

Prue didn't comment.

'What about you, have you thought about marriage?' Lily said.

Prue was disconcerted.

'I wouldn't marry anybody.'

'What for?'

Prue wasn't terribly happy about the way the conversation was heading, but anything was better than thinking about what had happened at the vicarage and they were tired of it all and also their crisis seemed over so a little levity was welcome.

'Because you can't be a wife and a doctor.'

'I'm sure some folk do and it's a waste. I've seen you around Isla and you love bairns. Or is it that you think there's nobody here fit to marry you?'

'No, of course not,' Prue said quickly.

'Maybe you think they're all scared of you.'

'Hell, I hope not but it's a difficult one. It would take a rare man to marry a woman doctor. Besides, you got rid of Mr Allen.'

That silenced Lily for a few moments.

'It was too close to what had happened. If it had been another five years on, maybe I would have said yes but things are too complicated. I worry about Robbie and that woman. I don't think I'll be happy about it until we know for certain that there is no child.'

They promised one another that they would go and sort this out the first Sunday they had the opportunity.

When the washing-up was done and nobody had banged on the door needing the doctor, Prue was inclined to relax and they sat over the fire in the rare silence. Even the pub was quiet on a Sunday. Prue had come to rely on that.

'I did think he liked you, you know,' Lily said.

'What?'

'Rory Gallagher. He kept asking you over.'

'For my advice.'

'He's never done that before with any woman as far as I know.'

'He admires me as a doctor.'

'So do most people in the village, but they don't have that look about them.'

'He's safe from me now that he's marrying another,' Prue said, pulling a face, and they giggled. Prue didn't feel like that at all, but she couldn't explain herself to Lily. Apparently she didn't want to marry Rory Gallagher but she didn't want him to marry anybody else, which was not love whichever way you looked at it.

It was such luxury to go to bed early and sleep all night. It happened so rarely that they slept in. Even Mrs Bradley and Isla didn't awaken, and Mabel was still snoring when Prue finally found her way to the kitchen about twenty minutes before surgery was due to start and Ernie was banging on the door.

Rory Gallagher and his bride-to-be had, according to gossip, bought a huge detached house in Consett and planned to move there once they were married. Prue had been to Consett a couple of times for shopping and she knew that there were a great many big detached houses next to the park which linked Consett and Blackhill; and she had no doubt that Miss Donaghy's family lived there and would be pleased when their newly married daughter moved in just down the road.

Prue went to see Helen on the Thursday afternoon when she was sure that Rory would not be there, but even so she was surprised to find Helen opening the door herself, Wilf hanging onto her skirts.

'Where are the others?'

'I took them to school.'

Prue considered that very brave of her. Mrs Saxony was still doing the cleaning, but Helen somehow made the house warmer just with her presence. Wilf left Helen and came to Prue so she picked him up and cuddled him. When she saw Wilf she wished she had had a child, it made her ache for a baby of her own; he was a lovely little boy and his hair smelled like warm apricots.

Cheerfully Helen made tea and gave Prue shortbread biscuits. She said, 'My father is furious.'

'What did he say?'

'Nothing, that's how I know. Molly Donaghy is unnatural you know, Prue.'

'What's the matter with her?'

'She hates children. She didn't even speak to them, knowing they had nowhere to go and some of what they'd been through. She stood there and glared and then he took her home.'

Prue thought this was hardly surprising since John Edwards' family had intruded on Molly Donaghy's love affair, and rudely. Any woman would have reacted the same way.

'He drove her home very soon afterwards and he has been at work ever since. Mind you, when he comes back here he does have a lot to face.'

'Has your father talked to you about this?'

Helen looked at her as though she were mad.

'He isn't going to let me leave. Where could I go and be respectable when I am widowed with four small children?'

'Does he like them?'

'He loathes them,' Helen said roundly. 'He stays at work until he's sure they are in bed so I feed him at half past nine at night. He's gone in the morning before they get up.'

'When is the wedding?'

'It hasn't been mentioned,' Helen said.

Wilf had gone to sleep in Prue's arms and Prue had not known she was looking down fondly while holding the little boy, but when she looked up she blushed and Helen smiled in acknowledgement.

'Don't you just want to eat him up, he's so lovely,' she said, and Prue was thankful that Helen was not openly mourning her lost child, but she felt that there were deep problems which at present Helen was denying and in time they would be costly.

There was soon a new vicar at St John and St James, but Prue thought that the church might have looked on Helen with something better than total neglect. She thought that at the very least the Bishop of Durham or somebody representing him might have come to her to offer help, but nothing happened. It was as though John Edwards had not existed. He seemed to have no family. Prue knew nothing of that, but worse was that there was no help at all for his four children or his second wife who had suffered so badly at his hands.

Prue and Lily didn't go to church any more after that. They kept making excuses to one another, but they just let the weeks go by and though Helen professed to wanting to take the children there, she didn't, and the three older ones were seen playing in the streets on Sunday afternoons which was generally not approved of.

Helen so clearly didn't care. Some people said she had lost her mind. If there was anything that guaranteed you losing your sanity, what Helen had been through would do it. However, Prue thought Helen fully in command of her mind and senses.

Prue and Lily saw Helen often and on Sundays they would take the children up the dale to Bollihope Common, beyond Stanhope on the way to Eggleston in Teesdale. Prue liked the village which was her namesake and pretended that her ancestors came from there. You turned off and wound your way up to the tops with glorious views of small square fields and tiny stone farms all the way. It was a huge squeeze in Prue's car for them, but they didn't care.

They loved the outing. The children shrieked and shouted all the way. Mary liked holding Isla and the children adored Mabel. She was patted and cuddled and loved. It was mayhem.

When they reached the common there was a stream in the bottom and other families loved to come there and picnic. They took their children and their dogs. There was lots of room to park their motors or their cycles and they sat down and had sandwiches and pies and cakes. The children plodged in the stream and ran in and out, yelling at the cold water and loving it. It was shallow and Mary even introduced little Isla to the water and guided her amongst the flat stones under her bare feet, crossing to the other side.

It was, Prue thought, the perfect way to spend a Sunday, and much better than church with its sermons and shadows. Mabel loved it. She ran in and out and back and forth like a nanny, watching the children, barking with excitement and ignoring the other dogs, who would have played with her. Mabel was too high and mighty for that. She had a family to look after.

The summer was warm and the days were long. Out there, Prue thought, Helen could forget what had happened.

When the children went back to school, Helen, with Wilf in her arms, came to visit just as morning surgery ended. Prue followed her into the kitchen where Lily was offering her something to eat and Wilf was running about the floor with Mabel. Prue didn't ask if she was all right, she could see by Helen's pale face and downcast demeanour that she was not.

Prue sat down beside her.

'Are you sleeping?'

Helen shook her head.

'Are you eating?'

Helen shook her head again.

There was no point in telling her that she should sleep,

that she should eat. If you couldn't then you couldn't and somebody telling you to was of no benefit.

'I feel so awful for what I did.'

Prue was about to say something she thought would help when Lily banged the teapot down on the table, glared and said, 'To that bugger? Are you mad?'

Helen looked first at Wilf to see if he was listening, which he wasn't, he was talking loudly to Mabel and patting her, and then at Lily. Prue looked at her too, it was not something a doctor could ever have said to someone who had to be her patient first and her friend second.

'He was my husband,' Helen said.

Lily snorted.

'You didn't know what he was like and presumably neither did his first wife. What were you going to do, let him do you and the baby in?'

'Maybe it wasn't like that.'

'Rubbish, of course it was like that. Prue said you were covered in blood and bruises, not for the first time, the bastard, and you with a bairn inside you and your second, my God. It's my belief he cost you your first with his fists, and his bloody loud voice and his women and his drink.

'If I hadn't married Robbie, I'd have gone for him with his airs and graces, God saving I'm a Catholic. Half the lasses in the village thought he would do. None of us knew what the bastard was like, except his first wife and he practically killed her, but we didn't see it like that at the time.

You were unlucky because the bastard was so good-looking and if he had done for you, then what? What about the bairns, 'cos nobody would have taken them on? They would have ended in an orphanage, whichever way you look at it. You have given them a mother. What more could you have done? Don't you waste a minute because of that bugger. He wasn't worth it.

'You did the bloody world a favour by standing up to him and thank God you did. It was either your funeral or his, and thank God it was his or some other poor lass would have had to go through it all again. Sit there and I'll get you some cake.'

Prue watched Helen demolish an enormous piece of fruitcake and a huge piece of Wensleydale cheese and two cups of tea. The colour came back into her face.

By the time she took Helen to collect the children from school Lily was busy in the kitchen, but Prue came back and said, 'Lily, you were so good with her.'

Lily waved her away with one hand.

'I daresay we've all learned a few home truths these past couple of years,' she said.

Thirty-one

Rory Gallagher and Molly Donaghy were supposed to be married in July or August, as far as Prue could gather, and Prue and Lily half-expected an invitation, but it didn't happen. Prue thought she must have got the date wrong and waited, but by the end of July it was obvious that the wedding had been delayed.

They talked about it over the kitchen table, but not to Helen, who was looking better. Prue thought part of that was due to Lily and part to the fact that she had four children to look after and loved them all, and so had little time to dwell on what had happened.

They didn't go to Rory Gallagher's house because Helen came to them with the children more and more. Isla was their pet and Lily said to Prue that it was easier when the other children were there, and it was true. They could sit around the table and talk, and Mary and Elisabeth liked to take Isla between them. Wilf wasn't interested and Teddy was too old; he would often sit at the table with them until he slumped with his head on his arms and slept. Children, Prue had discovered, slept when you least expected and Teddy was so concerned about being the head of the tribe that he often went to sleep, worn out.

The wedding had actually been planned for the middle of August, but it did not go ahead. Even Molly understood that priorities had changed, but they went on with other plans. The house had been bought by her parents and every time Rory went to see Molly she was surrounded by rolls of wallpaper and snippets of curtains. She had catalogues for him to look at and they would go into Newcastle to choose furniture, none of which he wanted to do.

Every time he left Helen alone he worried. He knew it was stupid – John Edwards was dead, he should not have been able to hurt her from the grave, and yet he did every day. His influence was endless. She had lost all confidence, she had the tradesmen come to her, she did not go out and even answering the door was a trial. The children were on holiday in the summer. She surrounded herself with them and spent a lot of time at the house where Prue and Lily had set up the surgery. She did not ask him to go on any outings and the friendship which once they had had was gone. Nobody said anything and he was grateful to Prue and Lily, but he missed the girl who had been his daughter and did not recognize this silent, sad woman, thin, pale and apparently lost to him.

Less and less did he want to go to Consett and he found that he would make excuses if he could; he had to stop himself. Equally, Molly did not want to come to see Helen and the children so he went between the two like a ping-pong ball, which was very tiring. He felt like apologizing, when he was with each of them for the circumstances which had not been of his wanting, but in his more truthful moments he knew that his engagement to Molly was a mistake. But then would it have been such a mistake if Helen had been happily married and not in his house with four children?

He thought that had he been left alone to sort this out, he would have seen that Anne's spirit was no longer in the house, that he was lonely, that he was in love, that he wished dearly to move on, to have new experiences and new friends, a different life, but somehow he couldn't manage it. John Edwards had cost him his happiness too and the happiness of a young woman who deserved better.

Rory drove to Consett for dinner one Saturday night that autumn. He had left the office late, had to go back to bath and change, and by the time he reached Molly's parents' house it was half past eight.

Dinner had already begun, they were about to embark on the second course when he was announced, apologies on his lips. Molly didn't even look up. She didn't speak. He couldn't tell her that he hadn't wanted to leave Helen alone.

There was no let up from children, day after day. Endlessly they wanted food and drink and attention and Helen was so pale, so tired. He felt like a traitor as he walked out of the door. He had tried to tell her that he would find someone to help her with the children but she was stubborn and said no to everything. He couldn't blame her for that.

She didn't want people staring or talking about what went on in the house. She didn't want company. She was silent and he understood why. In a way she went over and over that dreadful night and it did not mean that she needed conversation. Sometimes she cried in the night, but he had learned not to go to her. He thought that even her father coming into her bedroom might send her beyond reason. Her hands sometimes shook and her eyes were so dulled that they were almost colourless. She had been beautiful. Now it was gone. She was lifeless but for the children.

After dinner he tried to explain that he did not like to leave Helen by herself in the evenings. There wasn't much he could say. How could a girl like Molly, so carefully protected, understand any of it, especially when he could not tell her what had happened? It was not his story to tell and he did not want anyone to know, for Helen's sake. Molly said, 'You are her father, not her husband.'

'She doesn't have a husband any longer.'

'And by all accounts he wasn't much good to her when she did have him. That is not your fault or mine. Are we supposed to give up our future because your daughter married the wrong man?'

'It wasn't that—'

'What was it then?' Molly said. 'He was widowed, he was older than her and he had four children. What woman in her right mind would marry such a man? The whole thing was ridiculous right from the beginning. Surely you could see that.'

'That I could see it didn't make the difference.'

'You are her father, you could have stopped her.'

'I couldn't do that.'

'No? Most fathers would have insisted that she not marry him. Wouldn't it have been more sensible?'

'I'm not sure it would, but I brought my daughter up to have free will, which I think everybody is entitled to.'

Molly stood in silence for some time and when she replied her voice was unsteady. 'I'm sorry, I know how I sound but I want so much for us to be happy and I don't see how it can work and I don't think you do either. I have no child so I can't tell, but it looks to me as if your love for Helen is greater than your feeling for me and that there is also a reluctance because of your first wife. You seem weighed down with other people.

'I want you for yourself, not for your dead wife or your difficult daughter. I don't want her – her children wailing around me. I don't understand children yet. I wanted it just to be me and you. I know it sounds selfish but it's how most people start out. In time we could have had our own children and our own lives. That will serve me right for falling in love with a widower.'

She tried to smile but was almost in tears, and he didn't know what to say to her. She was right, of course, and he was sorry for it and he very much resented the complicated life which he was obliged to lead but he could not live in Consett and leave Helen, not even for such a lovely girl as Molly.

Rory said nothing. He had never wanted her more. He watched her tug furiously at the pretty ring he had bought for her at a shop in Consett. He remembered the happy day when they had bought it. He had wanted to take her to a big jeweller's in Newcastle and for her to choose diamonds which would be set especially for her, but she had said that all she wanted was a token of his love. It was pretty, tiny diamonds and opals flashing in the light. She held it out. He took it from her.

'And don't worry about the house,' she said, 'my father bought it at a very reasonable rate and no doubt it will make a profit when he sells.'

Her tears would not be contained and as they began to spill she rushed from the room and he left. All the way home, with the ring in his pocket, he blamed himself. Was he never to stop blaming himself for what happened, or was he really responsible for all this grief?

*

It was all over the village that Molly Donaghy had decided she didn't want to marry Rory Gallagher and Prue was certain that it was because of the children in his house, but she couldn't quite see why he didn't buy a separate house for himself and his wife other than that he couldn't leave his daughter to herself and her circumstances and the four children. Prue was ready to be admiring, but he was not there to be admired. He spent more time at the pits than he had ever done, his daughter said.

Sometimes when Prue went to bed at night she thought about him and how much he had apparently given up for his daughter and her mistakes. Was that parenting? What was it like to be Rory Gallagher, with four children beneath his roof, none of them related to him by blood and to find that the woman he had chosen, presumably so very carefully, did not want to shoulder the burden which his daughter had cast on him? Who could blame her for that? Prue wouldn't have liked it and she was older and more experienced than Molly. She felt sorry for the girl, she just hoped her parents were looking after her as well as Rory Gallagher was looking after his daughter.

So he was lying alone, as he had done for so long, none of it of his own choosing, nobody caring. And he could not even blame fate because he had decided that this was more important than his own happiness.

She decided its best was also its worst for the person concerned and if you put your child first, and some mothers did, but not to her knowledge any fathers before now, this was what was entailed and the hardest thing about it was that Helen so far did not count the cost to her father; she would not think of him as anything beyond her parent, and he had paid a high price for having had a child, as he lay alone in his bed.

The October holidays, when Prue was not too busy, were mostly spent with the children and they ventured to the seaside. Prue even went and asked Dr Allen if he would cover her practice for a couple of days. He had recently taken on a partner and said he would.

Prue had a letter from America. The handwriting was Silas's and inside was a stilted note telling her that he had decided to get married again. He hoped she wished him well, he presumed she had the life she had wanted. He was very happy to be marrying a woman who wanted no more than to be his wife and have his children. That stung, and though Prue took the letter away as soon as it came, she endured several meaningful glances from Lily, but she avoided them, saying nothing.

Thirty-two

Coming back from a visit to a lonely farm that autumn in the early afternoon, Prue thought she saw a figure she recognized, but she wasn't sure until Mabel barked just once, as she did when she knew the person outside. It was Teddy. He had grown so much and looked older than he was. He didn't run away when Prue stopped the car or make any reference to the fact that he should have been at school. He had changed, Prue thought: in some ways he was like an old man. It was his eyes, full of experience he should not have had, as so many children did.

'Want a lift?' was all she said.

He hesitated and then got in, and he sat with an arm around Mabel.

'How's Auntie Helen?'

He gazed from the car window.

'She cries a lot late at night when she thinks we're asleep,' he said.

'And what about Mr Gallagher?'

'Huh,' was all Teddy said, and he gazed further out of the window.

'He doesn't speak to us,' Teddy said, after a few minutes.

Prue could hardly point out that Rory Gallagher was keeping them all in the kind of luxury which was rare for a pit village. Teddy no longer looked like a shabby vicarage child. His clothes were expensive, his shoes were new and he had put on weight from the good food which Helen gave them, all of which her father paid for. Teddy was glowing with health and the doctor in her was glad of that.

'Wilf doesn't even like being left on his own in a room with him,' Teddy said. 'Mr Gallagher pretends we aren't there. Doesn't he understand how frightened Wilf is of men after what our bloody father did?'

Prue, wisely, she thought, said nothing to the swearing. Teddy had to get it out of his head somehow.

'Does he shout at you?'

Teddy threw her a scathing look.

'Hell, no, he's never there and when he is he goes into that room he uses as an office which we aren't allowed into and only comes out of it to go to bed, hours after us. He doesn't even eat with us. I hate him.'

How useful Rory Gallagher was being, Prue thought. Teddy needed a safe man to hate right now.

'And the girls?'

Teddy looked at her again and then raised his eyes to the car roof.

'He bought them new dresses. Girls are so stupid.'

'So how is school?'

'I took the day off.'

'Did you let the teacher know or Auntie Helen?'

'Obviously not,' Teddy said. 'Will you tell on me?'

It was Prue's opportunity to look scathingly at him.

'I shall tell them I had a stomachache,' he said. 'When your stepmother kills your father you can get away with almost anything, I find, even when people don't know what happened.'

Prue was horrified. She didn't speak until they stopped in front of Rory Gallagher's house. Teddy would have got out but she delayed him just by speaking his name softly. He looked down as though if he hadn't been thinking he was old enough never to cry again he would have done so.

'Teddy, look . . .'

'No, don't say anything. You have to remember that this is the best that things have ever been,' he said, and then he got out of the car before she could think of something sensible in reply.

Teddy was supposed to go to the grammar school in Wolsingham that autumn. His uniform had been bought, but according to Helen he was refusing, saying that he would stay on at school here with the other lads he knew.

Prue thought it was a bad system, choosing the most academic students and condemning the rest to woodwork and football in a back street, but there was nothing to be done, as though society had no further use for anyone who did not conform to its narrow ideas of education. It was obvious to her, seeing him, that Teddy rarely bothered to go to any school, here or in Wolsingham.

There was a great clashing of doors one night after evening surgery and Prue found Teddy, heaving from having run up the bank too fast and almost in tears, banging on the door. He burst into the kitchen as though he were being chased by wolves, and not stopping to greet them he cried out,

'He threatened me if I wouldn't go to school.'

They stared at him.

'If you mean Mr Gallagher you should call him that,' Lily said. Prue thought it was not the time.

'With what?' she said.

'With threats,' Teddy said vaguely.

'You should think yourself lucky he doesn't wallop you,' Lily pointed out. 'Isn't it hard enough him having to pay to keep you all when you aren't his bairns? Have you thought about that? A lot of men would have sent you off to the nearest orphanage.'

Prue tried to frown at her, but she knew Lily wouldn't have taken any notice.

'Couldn't you try school, just for a week?' Prue said.

No!' Teddy said, still breathing hard.

They were just about to sit down and eat. Teddy refused food, but then when Lily ignored what he said and filled his plate, wolfed two helpings of minced beef, carrots and dumplings. Prue offered to take him home.

'I'm not going back there. I told him I wouldn't go to school and I won't.'

'The law says you have to.'

'Then I'll stay here with you,' Teddy said, and he ran upstairs.

Half an hour later, Prue went up and he was asleep on the floor of Lily's room, Isla in the bed. Prue not unsurprised to find Rory Gallagher at her door shortly afterwards. She didn't even wait for him to ask.

'Yes, he's here and he's asleep.'

Rory slumped in the doorway.

'You look tired,' Prue said.

'I can't think why.'

Prue said nothing but she asked him in and since Isla had begun to grizzle, Lily went upstairs.

Prue took him into the kitchen and took down glasses and whisky. Rory eyed it and said, 'No wonder you're such a good doctor, you know exactly what people need.'

'I know this stuff rots your guts, but slowly.' She poured generously and handed him a glass.

He looked down into the golden pool and then he sniffed

it as all good northern men do and downed a mouthful, sighed and sat back.

'What am I going to do? I don't know anything about boys.'

'Didn't you used to be one?'

He smiled.

'It was about three thousand years ago,' he said.

'Why don't you take him to the pit with you?'

'He'd hate it.'

'He needs to be among men,' Prue said slowly. 'The only person he knew was his father and he beat both his wives and possibly even his children.'

'You think he hit the children?' Rory looked as if he really didn't want to believe such things.

'I don't think we'll ever know, but I do know that Teddy tried to rescue Helen and maybe even his mother. Why don't you give him time off school and take him to the pit, show him around, introduce him to Mr Boylen and the other men, make him feel grown up?'

'And this is going to make him go to school?'

'No, it's going to make him aware of what he wants. If he doesn't want to go to school there's no point in you wasting time, energy and breath getting him there. Keep him close, he may surprise you.'

'Helen wouldn't think so.'

'Oh, do the male thing, ignore her.'

He laughed. Prue was glad, it had taken her so long to get him to laughter she had almost despaired.

'Can I take him home?' Rory said.

'Not at this time of night, you'll just frighten him. You can come and get him in the morning, but not early.'

'In that case you can give me some more whisky,' was all he said.

Lily had found Teddy some of Robbie's old pyjamas. They were too big but it didn't matter and she squeezed him into Mrs Bradley's room where there was a single bed and there he slept until eight. Lily roused him, fed him porridge and let him linger at the table and at half past eight Rory Gallagher came to pick him up.

Teddy got up abruptly from the table.

'I'm not going to school,' he said.

'I have a better idea. Would you like to come and see what I do?'

Teddy hesitated.

'You go down horrible dirty pits, don't you?'

'Just for today?'

Teddy hesitated again and then relaxed, Prue could see him.

'All right but I'm not going for long,' Teddy said. Then he remembered his manners, said thank you, and was covered in blushes by the time Isla had screamed because he wasn't staying, Mabel had licked his hands and Lily had said he could come and stay any time that he liked because he was such a grand lad and it would be good for him to get away from the rest of them. Prue said nothing.

At the end of the week Prue saw Rory in the main street.

'Did he like the pits?'

'It terrified the hell out of him. He practically begged to go to school,' Rory said with a grin. 'I said if he went to the grammar school for a month to see if he liked it I would buy him a bike.'

'Ah, bribery,' Prue said, 'the way forward.'

Thirty-three

It seemed to Prue that autumn that Lily had something on her mind. She became quiet and contemplative and Prue couldn't see the reason for it until one day in October Lily came to her and she said, 'The woman that came here on Christmas Day. I'm still thinking about her and we never have time to go anywhere. Shall we just go? I know it's awful to ask Dr Allen to take over, but will you?'

Prue had almost forgotten about this, only reminding herself sometimes uncomfortably that Lily might have been turning this round and round in her mind. It was best not thought of, but she could hardly say so. She didn't ask why, she didn't want to dwell on it any more. Prue hovered in the surgery. It was midday and cold, wet and windy and Prue had several calls to make but Lily would know that. They hadn't yet eaten their midday meal and Prue needed to get on, but she couldn't say anything.

'I think that if we went to Fife, Robbie's parents would know about it.'

Every nerve in Prue's body screamed at her at this point. How on earth had Lily got to there? And why bring it up again when they had so much to cope with? She didn't understand.

'Lily, that's a day's drive away at least and with our car probably further and I don't see the point.'

'They would know.'

'And where would that get us?'

Lily stared at her.

'You do believe she knew Robbie?'

Prue could have cursed herself. Had she given that impression?

'I don't see what we would gain from such an expedition.'

'Let's try it,' Lily said.

When Prue's afternoon calls were finished, she had time to go to Wolsingham. She was only about a mile away up at a farm on the top. She motored down the two banks and turned right up the lane and beyond the village just a little way and nowhere near the reservoir; it would have been foolish for a doctor to live so far from the village. His house had been an old farmhouse, complete with orchard, surrounding wall and pretty gardens. It was stone-built like all the old houses in the dale.

A small maid answered the door with a smile and a word and ushered her inside. Dr Allen came to her, not quite smiling, rather shy, but he greeted her in a friendly manner and sat her down in a comfortable armchair. Prue could not help thinking that this was how successful doctors lived. A good fire, hot tea and coffee cake.

She told him only that they would like just a little time away to take Isla to see her grandparents. She was certain this would sound reasonable to him and it was almost true. He said that if they went over the weekend and came back on Monday, he was sure he would manage and Prue said that Ernie would be there to help. Dr Allen agreed readily. Prue was so pleased. She went back and reported to Lily that he had been glad to help and would she prefer to go by train.

It was, she thought, a long way however they went.

'All right,' Ernie said when asked if he would take care of things.

'You and your mother must stay here and if you let Mabel out of your sight or Lily's mother either, you will not be forgiven.'

He looked resentfully at her and then sighed.

'She'll whinge the whole time you're away.'

'You can stroke her ears.'

'I'm talking about Mrs Fleming's mother.'

'So am I,' Prue said.

The train journey was not at all as Prue had imagined. She remembered coming here and how hard it had been, how cold and dark. The autumn leaves bedecked the trees in lime, ochre and gold and the train went up beside the sea throughout Northumberland so that the sea reflected silver off the sky and the dazzling low sun. They ate on the train, something Prue had never done before. Even Lily liked it though her face was closed and they didn't talk much.

They reached Edinburgh and Prue thought of Professor Mick and felt guilty that she had not been in touch. She hadn't wanted to let him think that his venture had failed. She had wanted to succeed, both for him and for herself. Until that time she would not contact him.

They stayed overnight in Edinburgh. It had seemed a good idea. Lily had not been there before, but Prue could see as soon as they got there that she thought of Robbie, how he had been here at university, how he had qualified here and that his parents were not that far away. But possibly also that Jeannie Featherall had been here.

They had dinner brought to their room since they could not possibly take Isla into the dining room and had no one to leave her with. It was quite comforting to sit at a small table by the fire.

'If Robbie's parents have never heard of this woman I will be content,' Lily said.

Neither of them slept. Isla was fretful and Prue lay and watched the dawn reach toward the edge of the curtains. She was glad to get up and go down to breakfast and set off again.

Fife was nothing like she had thought it would be. It was industrial, with dark grimy streets and great gashes in the hillside, black hills where pits and quarries spewed out their coal and ore.

When the train stopped and Lily and Prue got out Lily said, 'Why, it's almost like home,' as though the place Robbie came from held some magic within it.

His parents lived on a modest street of terraced houses, though bigger than Prue had seen in Durham, and Mrs Fleming opened the door herself, saying, 'Oh my goodness,' when she saw who it was. 'Oh.' She put both hands up to her cheeks which flushed with confusion. Then she saw Isla and the ice in her manner melted and she stared at her granddaughter.

She ushered them into a dark hall and then through into the sitting room, saying, 'Look who has come to see us.'

Robbie's father got up from his armchair and stared at Isla who was alert and gazing, and then he said, 'She's just like Robbie.' He came forward and Lily handed her daughter to him and he laughed.

This was worth coming north for, Prue thought. His wife took the baby from him when he would allow, saying what a bonny bairn she was and how she was growing and how lovely it was that they were able to see her.

'We have come for a purpose,' Lily said, and she explained about the woman who had turned up on Christmas morning.

The way that they looked at one another and their faces told Prue that Lily had been right.

'We prayed that this would not happen,' Mr Fleming said. He said nothing more and his wife gave Isla back to Lily and turned her face away.

'Were they married?' Lily said.

'We don't know anything about it.' His wife began to catch at her breath with emotion and he put a reassuring hand on her shoulder.

'But there was a connection?' Lily said. 'Tell me what you know, please. I feel betrayed, as though he never loved me.'

'Oh, he did.' Mrs Fleming turned her wet face, her red eyes and distressed expression toward Lily and Prue. 'He talked so much about you, told us in his letters.'

'But you didn't come to the wedding?'

'We – we worried.'

'About his connection with this woman?'

Mr Fleming looked frankly at Lily.

'We weren't sure what had happened and had nothing against you but it was all so confused and he told us nothing. We wanted him to marry someone we knew, someone we understood, and to stay here so that we could take part in his life.'

'So,' Lily said, relentless as a terrier down a foxhole, 'did he marry this woman?'

'Oh no, he couldn't have,' his mother said, and Prue thought mothers were all the same: when you gave birth to someone you fell in love with them. It was as bad as Helen with the vicar. When you fell in love with a child or a person, you could never believe they would stumble, fail, betray others, betray their parents and themselves and finally you, and yet people did it over and over again.

'What do you know of her?'

'Virtually nothing,' Robbie's father said.

'Was there a child?' Lily plunged back in. 'If you know anything of the child tell us.'

'We thought there could have been.'

'But you didn't look?'

'When we tried to help he told us that it was none of our business. He was difficult and abrupt and we felt stupid and old and – and unwanted.' Robbie's father stopped. 'He could have been married to her, there might have been a child, we were never invited to anything again. Much later we heard that he had married – and that was you and there was nothing more between us, it was as if we had died as far as he was concerned.'

Robbie's mother was crying openly now. Her husband touched her arm and she moved toward him as though for shelter.

When Prue and Lily left, they went back to Edinburgh, to the hotel, and there Lily broke down and wept.

'It's as if they are talking about somebody else, but I think they know about her and I think there was a bairn and we have to find her, Prue.'

'Let's be careful. We still don't know if there was a marriage or a child.'

'Why would he send her money, even if they were not
married? It meant that he felt some responsibility, it means
there was a child,' Lily said.

That night they slept from sheer exhaustion. Not
knowing what to do any further they went home and Prue
thought while they might have failed on one level, they had
brought Lily much closer to Robbie's parents.

Thirty-four

Having put the children to bed, Helen ventured into her father's study. She realized that she was afraid. She had never been afraid of him before, John had done that to her. She half-expected, when she opened the door, to find John sitting at the desk and she back at the vicarage. She held her breath.

When she went to bed at night his bloody ghost stood beside her pillow and she could not sleep. She was even pleased when Teddy awoke from nightmares, which he regularly did. She would go in to him, soothe him, leave the lamp lit. Wilf never woke up, he was too little to worry over such matters. She thought he was happier now than he had ever been. The spectre of his father did not hang over him at night, she thought he must have heard and seen many hard things, but she was convinced that as far as Wilf was concerned she had slain the dragon of darkness, and Wilf adored her.

During the day he barely left her side, so afraid, she thought, that John Edwards would come back to them, shouting and using his hands and voice and physical presence to scare and hurt them but he was so big and he was their father and they were aware that they must love him, whatever he was like. That was how it worked.

The girls were different, they had accepted Rory in place of their father and she thought that he responded better to them because he had had a daughter.

As soon as she opened the study door, her father looked up and he was not John, he was not angry, he was not about to get up and shout and she did not have to beware of his fists. The relief was so huge that she felt breathless and sick and then the sickness passed and her breath returned. She had been brought up in this house and there was nothing to fear. She couldn't even close the door and stood there in a mist of tears. All she could manage was, 'I'm so sorry.'

He got up and came over and the stone in her throat melted and she cried.

'It's all right,' he said.

'It will never be all right. Look at what I did.'

'You didn't have any choice. In time you'll see that. There you were like an avenging angel, for God's sake. It's my belief he knocked those bairns around.'

'Not while I was there, I made sure of it.'

'Wasn't that part of the reason you went there while his first wife was alive, you may not have known it but your instincts were good?'

She drew back, finding a handkerchief in her skirt pocket,

sniffing into it and then blowing her nose and trying to pretend that the tears, which drenched her cheeks and ran down her neck, did not exist.

'To begin with I didn't believe what people said. I was so taken by him I wanted him for mine. I don't remember being afraid for the children. And now look,' she said. 'I'm so sorry. This wasn't the way I intended to make you a grandfather.'

He smiled just a little.

'I could move out, find a little house somewhere . . .' she said.

He shook his head.

'But what about Miss Donaghy?' she said. 'You didn't marry her. I couldn't understand it at the time or believe it, but . . .'

'We thought better of it.'

Helen choked and put her hand over her mouth.

'But that's not right, it isn't fair. This is my fault. She's the only woman you've cared for since my mother died. Please marry her. I will always blame myself if you don't.'

'That would be silly and she wasn't the only woman I cared about anyway.'

'I thought you were going to live in Consett. I can manage perfectly well here, I have Lily and Prue and the children will be fine. They will be.'

'No,' he said.

'But they're not yours. Oh my God, what have I done?'

'It was a mistake on both our parts, Molly's and mine. We weren't a pair, it's just that she couldn't find anybody she liked enough to marry and I think her parents approved of me and I was taken in by the way that she looks. They expected her to marry and she'd turned down everyone else.'

'But she's young and beautiful and . . .'

'That's the point really. She ought to marry somebody a lot better and much younger than me. I don't want to go and live in Consett and ignore my family and live like a young man. It would be foolish and I would tire of it. I like being here, this is my home. I wouldn't in fit there, no matter how hard I tried, and I don't want to try.

'I'm tied to this place, not just because of you or your mother but because of the men and their families. How would it look if I went and lived over there in a great big house? I don't like people thinking they're better than the men who work for them. It's not right, we're all in it together, especially when it's dangerous work like ours. I'm not going to put myself beyond limits like that, I'm not moving away. Not ever.'

It was after three and a half weeks of school, on the Wednesday, when Teddy ventured into the study after tea. He hovered. It was irritating. Rory wished people wouldn't do that. He was making himself go home earlier these days, but it wasn't easy.

He was inclined to say 'either come in or go out' but he didn't because he could see the look in the boy's eyes and it was not promising. So he tried a vague smile and said, 'Come in, shut the door. Are you all right?'

Teddy closed the door but did not venture further into the room. Rory remembered himself as a child, with a request he was convinced his father wouldn't grant, though he had never been afraid of his father as Teddy seemed to be of him, but then he knew it really hadn't much to do with him. Teddy was afraid of all men because of his father.

The boy's movements were slow. It made Rory think that this child had a great deal to remember, and to forget, if he ever could, even though Rory hoped he had not seen all of what had happened on the night that Helen had killed her husband. There must have been quarrelling, shouting, perhaps even attempted blows, when Teddy attempted to shield his stepmother and Rory liked and admired the boy for that.

Fancy having to try to shield a woman who was not your mother, having known that your mother was dead, and possibly because of neglect at least by your father and probably even worse? And now a strange house for him to get used to, a whole new set of rules, somebody in charge he had not yet learned to trust and maybe never would, and to have been rescued by a bloody, dreadful act, how could any child of that age accept it and go forward?

Teddy stayed by the door, ready for flight.

'I just thought I should say that I don't want the bicycle. I don't deserve it,' he managed, looking down.

Rory surveyed him for a few seconds.

'You really don't like that school, do you?' he said.

The boy's face lightened just a little at Rory's quick understanding, at least he didn't have to explain any further and no doubt he had rehearsed quite a lot of other things to say if Rory should argue the case.

'I didn't . . .' Teddy said and then stopped and pre-empted Rory, 'I know it hasn't been four weeks but I didn't want to leave it any longer in case you should buy the bicycle and then it would be wasted because I can't accept it. It would be – morally wrong.'

Dear God, Rory thought, an understanding of morals at that age.

The bicycle had for some reason come to represent what was amiss with Teddy's life, Rory thought. He didn't know how but he was beginning to understand why.

'Don't worry about it,' Rory said, 'you don't have to go.'

'Don't I?' Teddy's face was perplexed. 'But you don't like the other school.'

Rory waved a magical hand to make the school disappear.

'Do you want to go there?'

'No.'

'Well then, don't.'

Teddy gazed at him with the look of a prisoner suddenly set free.

'What will I do?' And his eyes filled.

'What would you like to do?'

'I hadn't got that far.'

'Helen and I could teach you lots of things.'

'Do you know anything?'

It wasn't what the boy had meant to say, Rory could see by the way that he coloured up and even more so when Rory laughed.

'I must have gleaned something useful along the way,' Rory said.

'And Auntie Helen, won't she mind?'

'She'll be delighted,' Rory said. 'She went to school a lot, you know. She's good at all sorts of things that other people don't understand. She did Latin,' he pulled a face.

'She is very clever,' Teddy said gravely.

'Well then, we'll sort something out. You could work in the pit offices and learn arithmetic and such like. Mr Boylen is an engineer and Mr Farebairn was a pit sinker in his young days and they know all sorts of things. Auntie Helen has read hundreds of books and knows French and geography and history so it wouldn't be too bad.'

He had never seen such a look of release on anyone's face as though Teddy could not believe that a grown-up was letting him out of yet another hell.

'Must I call you "uncle"?' he managed.

'You can call me anything you like as long as within my hearing it isn't "that bugger". Lots of people call me "Rory". Do that if you want.'

Teddy rushed from the room so that his new-found deliverer would not see him break down.

The trouble was, Rory thought, that the bicycle had been ordered. Would Teddy think he was a soft touch if he gave him it anyway? And then he decided that perhaps Teddy need a soft touch in his life so on the Friday, two days later, when Rory came back from work, he wheeled a beautiful new red bicycle in from the car and shouted in at the back door, 'Teddy, are you there?'

When the child ran breathlessly toward the doorway, Rory saw his first reaction. It was pure delight.

'I can have it?' he said, hardly daring.

'I think you should,' Rory said. 'It is yours.'

In the late autumn the weather was icy and snow fell. Dr Allen's partner became ill and he called on Prue to help him. She hated the hills between her practice and his. She always said a quick prayer when it was icy as she skidded and slid from side to side down the steep slopes. Mabel up on the seat and obviously worried for her life in case they should slip over the edge of the road, which was sheer on the left side, drive into the air and turn again and again until they reached the bottom, very far below. It was not a comforting thought and Mabel knew it.

The practice reached the whole of the dale, way beyond Stanhope and Eastgate, and though it was pretty country, Prue could not appreciate it, she was so concerned with finding different farms and tiny villages and humpbacked bridges and often there were few street lights to guide her. She talked to Mabel a lot then; she needed someone to complain to.

Dr Allen's partner was a man called Finch Adams, which she thought a splendid name. He was fat and forty and had succumbed to flu so badly that Dr Allen was concerned for his health and Prue came down those slippery hills so often that she forgot to say her prayers.

She was grateful when she had to visit Frosterley or Stanhope or anywhere she recognized that she could ask directions and, thankfully, towards the end of the month, Dr Adams recovered. Dr Allen invited her into his house for tea when it was dark in the late afternoon and Prue was so tired that she accepted.

He petted Mabel. Mabel was a big fan of Dr Allen. She liked being where he was; she had decided that he was a very good man. Prue thought this had a lot to do with the fact that Dr Allen thought German shepherds enjoyed cake. Mabel did, though Prue was not convinced that it was good for her and never gave her cake, so no wonder she liked being there. In his presence, before the cake, Mabel would swish her tail in endless arcs before the fire; after the cake, which was often chocolate with coffee icing, or coffee with chocolate icing, she would settle down and snore on his hearthrug.

'How is Mrs Fleming?' he ventured.

Prue was surprised at this, she was certain he would know what people said.

'She is humiliated and upset at what she thinks her husband did,' Prue said. She was not sure he would appreciate her frankness, but he nodded and said, 'She did not deserve what life gave her.'

'Does anybody?'

'I suppose not. I wish I could have been of more help. I did like her company very much.'

Prue was astonished. This man must love Lily or he would not have spoken.

'I think she thought that what had happened to her would matter to you.'

He looked straight at her.

'Dr Stanhope, I made my way through four years of unmitigated hell in France. I consider myself lucky to be here. I am not in the habit of concerning myself with trivialities, or is it that you think she was so sorry he let her down so badly that she wants nothing more to do with me?' He softened this with a smile.

Prue beamed at him.

'Perhaps you would like to come for tea – not if you are busy, of course, but on Sunday?'

He said that he would be delighted.

'You didn't,' Lily said.

'Why should I not? We are spending lot of time together, we have many things to discuss.'

'You have bloody nothing to discuss and you are trying to outmanoeuvre me.'

'Why would I do that?'

Lily looked confused.

'Because you love me,' she said, and they both laughed.

'Prue, this is not going to work, and you are so kind and he is a very nice man . . .'

'All he is doing is coming for tea. If you don't want to be there you can spend half an hour with us and then retreat upstairs.'

'I don't feel that I can trust any man again.'

'You should if you are going to go forward.'

'What if he betrays me as Robbie did?'

'Would you rather live like this? He can give you a good life. All you have to do is try for half an hour.'

Lily said nothing for so long that Prue was tempted to speak, but she didn't.

'I'm so surprised after what has happened that he can even entertain the idea,' Lily said.

'Well you will have to forgive him for being more intelligent than the rest of us.'

Lily said nothing to that.

On Sunday, therefore, Dr Allen drove up to the surgery and Lily greeted him at the door. Ernie and his mother had not been invited for tea; they never were on a Sunday because it was thought they might like a rest, but on the Monday Prue could see that Ernie knew the doctor had been there. Something about the set of his shoulders told her that he was aware of it.

Prue called him into her room after morning surgery and said to him,

'I have written to Professor Mick in Edinburgh, my old teacher, and he has said that if you go to Edinburgh he will do everything he can to help you.'

'That's lovely, Dr Stanhope . . .'

'No, hear me out. The practice will fund you.'

'How can it do that, when you owe so much money?'

'It will.' Prue said. 'And we will take in your mother. All you have to do is say that you will come back here and help for a year or two when you are qualified before you go out into the big wide world and make your mark.'

He shook his head. He didn't look at her. He gazed at the floor.

'There's nothing to stop you,' Prue said. 'Why don't you try? Edinburgh is a wonderful place for learning. You would love it and Professor Mick is a lovely man and he would help you, place you, see that there were people who cared about your education.'

'How can I leave my mother and – and all of you?'

'You have to,' she said, 'it's the only way you can go forward. I will drive you there myself.'

He waved a hand at her.

'There is a train.'

'I haven't seen Professor Mick in years. We'll go together,' she said. 'You will need books and clothes and money, and the practice will see to it.'

He nodded wordlessly. Dr Allen's car was outside for the second day running when Ernie left after evening surgery. He did not look at it as he walked away.

'You said that we would take his mother in?'

Prue could have pointed out that if things went well, Lily and her mother and Isla would be moving to Wolsingham, to Dr Allen's splendid house where he had a housekeeper and Lily would have nothing to do but look after Isla and be nice to her new husband, but she didn't.

The prospect of living alone with Ernie's mother and Mabel was not something which appealed, but she had no choice. In mitigation she said, 'Your mother is easier when Mrs Smith is there.'

'Yes, but to have her all the time . . .'

'They can sleep in the same room.'

'When is Ernie going?'

'As soon as I can arrange it.'

'So who will do the dispensing?'

'I don't know yet.'

Prue went off into the dispensary and clashed things about until after five minutes Lily came in.

'I'm sorry,' she said. 'I really am, Prue. Why don't I help with the dispensing?'

Prue stared at her.

'You want to?'

'We can have more help in the house and I would like to learn something and it would be nice to get a break from Isla. Besides, I think Dr Allen would be pleased.'

Prue tried not to smile.

Thirty-five

It was cold and wet and dark and windy, day after day. Prue hated getting up and going to bed with barely any light. Lily kept the fires burning and made broth and other hot soups.

Prue was glad when it was not long until Christmas, when people would leave their houses to sing carols and scour the hedges for holly. She could see why from way back long before Christianity, people had a mid-winter festival. It was the only bright spot in the darkness and how sensible!

Prue found a stranger at her door one cold afternoon. Lily was upstairs with Isla and her mother. Evening surgery was only an hour ahead. It was not four o'clock but darkness had long since set in. He was tall and that was all she could tell about him.

'The surgery's not open yet,' she said.

'I don't want the surgery.'

He had a Scottish accent and he sounded so like Robbie that Prue was astonished.

'I want to see Mrs Fleming. I'm Robbie's uncle, on his mother's side. Keith McKinnon.'

'Come in, then,' Prue offered. 'She's busy at the moment but I can take you into the back room and she won't be long.'

Mabel came in and watched him, dark fur rising along the ridge of her back because she didn't recognize him and sensibly, Prue thought, remained unconvinced of people before they had shown their hand.

'My God,' he said, 'what's that?'

'Oh, she's perfectly harmless unless you mean no good in which case I wouldn't count on getting out alive.'

He sat down, gazing at Mabel.

Prue called up the stairs and Lily said she was busy but wouldn't be long so. Prue had to leave him there, she had patients to attend to. Mabel stayed with him on guard as she did to potential threats so Prue was not worried about who he might be or what he might do.

At the end of surgery Prue went into the back room and found Lily downstairs, free of Isla, who must be sleeping, and Lily was looking very white-faced and most relieved to see her.

'Mr McKinnon has evidence of Robbie's marriage before he met me,' she said.

'Oh,' Prue said, as though it happened every day.

'I was at the wedding,' Mr KcKinnon said, 'when he married Jeannie Featherall.'

'You were actually at the service?' Prue asked.

'It wasn't a happy occasion; people wept. She had

claimed him because she was having a bairn. Folk weren't convinced it was his, he was such a fool, a lovely lad and he had made a mistake. By God, it cost him dearly.'

'Have you seen the child since?' Prue said.

'I went to the baptism.'

Lily had turned into a waxwork. Prue wished she had never let him in, she felt that if she had bolted the doors and stood behind them this would not have occurred.

'A boy?' Lily said.

'Yes, a little lad.'

'So, what happened to him?'

'That I can't tell you but there were plenty who thought the bairn was not his. Lassies like that, who can tell?'

'Then why did you come here?' Lily cried out and he looked at her stupidly, and Prue wanted to hit him around the head. All he thought was that he could provide information and perhaps he would be paid for it; this was true, she thought when he smiled and said, 'It has cost me dearly. I needn't have. You should recompense me.'

'For what?' Prue said.

'Well, it is the truth and I heard from his parents that truth was what you needed, that you had searched both Scotland and the north of England for it and since I knew so much—'

'You don't know where the boy is,' Lily said. 'You don't know that he lives or even if he's Robbie's own.'

'I don't know that he died. He seemed healthy enough at the time.'

'We have met the mother and she had nothing,' Lily said.

Prue gave him money to get rid of him. She paid his train fare back to Scotland; she didn't care how much he lied. She closed the door and only hoped that the Black Bull still wasn't doing rooms, though according to gossip it was by now. She hoped the dinner he would eat was awful, the room had fleas, the train broke down and he had to walk back.

Lily cried. Prue was not surprised. Why did he have to come here and make things worse?

'There is a child, a little boy,' Lily said, as though it wasn't obvious. 'That woman was telling the truth.'

'She wanted money, just as he did.'

'But if there is a child and he is Robbie's—'

'We don't know that, Lily.'

'His parents were so unnatural, I think they knew that Robbie had married that woman because she was having his child and I was no more married to him than I was to the man in the moon; they just didn't like to say.'

'That's not fair to him or to you,' Prue said. 'He married you because he loved you.'

'He married me when he was already married to another woman.'

Prue couldn't think of what to say to that.

'How could he do that, to her or to me?' Lily said and her voice shook. 'We have to find her.'

'What good would it do?'

Lily's face was so white that Prue thought she was going to faint.

'If the child is Robbie's, then where is he?'

'She went back to him.'

'Did she? And where to?'

'How on earth are we to find out?'

'There has to be a way. Let's go back to Boulmer.'

'She lied to us about it. Why should she be there?'

'It would be a start.'

Prue hesitated and then agreed. Lily would not rest before she knew but the trouble was that if they found the child and it was his, what effect would that have on Lily and the memories of her marriage?

The following Sunday they went back to Boulmer and this time they knocked at every door, asked for Jeannie Featherall at each one, but there were shaken heads and closed doors. They came to the end of the village and Prue looked both out to sea and in at the land – it was good farming land.

They followed the road almost to Alnwick and came back and drove through the village again and beyond it to the north side. After two miles there was a set of farm cottages. They looked derelict, as though no one had lived in them for a long time. The roof was off the first one and the other two were falling down, but they all had front doors and Prue and Lily got out of the car and banged on all of them.

At the third one Prue recognized the woman who opened the door. She had visualized this, dreaded it, told herself it could not be, but she was aware that if this woman had been truthful she might have had Robbie's child in there somewhere. Her heart didn't want to believe it, but her head thought it was a possibility.

The young woman recognized her too, half shut the door and then saw that it would not do. She did not say, 'I didn't think you'd find me,' but her face said it, her eyes, her whole demeanour. She lowered her head.

Lily was by Prue's side by then.

'Can we come in?' she said.

They did. Most people's idea of a cottage was nothing like this, Prue thought. Those people who said, 'a cottage, how charming', had never lived in so few dark damp rooms with tiny windows because the snow and ice had to be kept beyond and here, almost on the coast, the winds swept the streets and sent people huddling inside. It reeked of poverty, was Prue's first thought. There had been no decent food in many days, you couldn't smell anything other than want, and clothes and bodies which were seldom washed.

There were several people in the dim light: a man, not tall but skinny so that his cheekbones stood out almost obscenely and in the back children, she could see their eyes, dull, without hope. She didn't like to go further in: it seemed intrusive. Lily too hesitated. Her instincts were good, though Prue was aware of how much depended on her finding nothing to do with Robbie here and her heart said that something was amiss and Lily had known it.

Lily, Isla in her arms, moved further into the gloom, looking for a boy of five or six, but the children were younger than that. One of them was three at most. The other was not walking.

'So, where is your other child?' Lily said.

'What child?'

'The one you claimed you had with Robbie.'

The woman laughed.

'There was no child. I needed money.'

'You are a liar,' Lily said, 'we know there was a child.'

The woman stood for a few moments trying to think of an answer.

'Where is the child?'

'I don't know.'

The woman moved back.

'You must know,' Lily persisted, moving forward. Prue stayed where she was, in a sense guarding the door. She missed Mabel's presence and wished she hadn't left her in the car.

The woman stood for a long time, so long that Prue wanted to move but didn't.

'Aye,' she said, lifting her chin, 'we were wed. I have the certificate to prove it so you should be glad that I didn't come on to you for more.'

'We have nothing.'

'You call that nothing?'

She was right, Prue thought, it was a long way from nothing compared to this.

'Where is the child?' Lily would not be stopped, Prue thought.

'He died.'

'Rubbish!' Lily said loudly, and while Prue was proud of her she wanted to whisk Lily out of there before she became more hurt and Isla might be damaged by her mother's reaction.

'Where is he?'

'I don't know. I gave him up so that Jack here would marry me.'

Lily was staring.

'You gave up Robbie's child because this man wouldn't marry you unless you did?'

'He didn't want other men's bairns, you can't blame him for that. Robbie wasn't paying us enough for me to keep the bairn. I had nothing. He didn't care about us even though he had a son. What I gained from you was that Robbie was dead and there was no more money so I could marry again, because I already had Jack's bairns.'

'Who took the child?'

'My mother.'

'Where does she live?'

'Newbiggin.'

*

Newbiggin was a mix of a place, was Prue's first thought; it was a fishing and pit village, with cobles drawn up on the beach and evidence of pits behind. Its houses crouched low, some of them single-storeyed, as though they had been buffeted by wind and tide for many years. Lily put it perfectly.

'But for the sea it's just like home,' she said.

It was a lot bigger than Boulmer and although they had managed to extract the address of her mother from Jeannie by means of money, Prue was in no way confident of what they would find. The street was called Percy Avenue and they went up and down the roads until their feet ached while Prue, beneath her breath, called the woman all the names she could think of. There was no Percy Avenue so, in the end, they called at what looked like an important building which turned out to be the library and asked if anyone knew of a Mrs Featherall living in the place. One of the librarians knew of the woman, though looked darkly at them and their enquiries, and it turned out that the house was outside the village, up a road in the country.

They took the car to a street of houses in the middle of nowhere and as far as Prue could see when she parked the motor, nobody lived there. Lily got out of the car reluctantly and Prue followed her.

'There are no roofs,' Lily said, and she sounded despairing. On most of the houses there were no windows and the doors were ajar. There was only one house which seemed occupied and that was just because the door was closed and there was glass in the windows.

Prue banged on the door. There was no answer but after she banged again she heard a voice from inside but nobody came to the door so, after waiting a little longer, she pushed it open.

It was dark inside and cold and although she had thought the last house where they went seeking the child had been bad, this was worse. An old woman sat over a dead fire and gazed almost unseeing at them. They peered at her through the gloom.

'Who is it?'

'I'm Prudence Stanhope and I have with me Lily Fleming. We have come to enquire after Robbie Fleming's child.'

The woman appeared to be listening and then she said, 'Who are you?'

'I'm a relative of his,' Lily said, 'we are anxious to find the child.'

'Ah, he's gone.'

'He was here then.'

The old woman muttered a curse which Prue didn't catch and then she said,

'Aye, but I couldn't manage with him. She came and left him here with no money to clothe or feed him.'

'He was Robbie Fleming's bairn?' Lily said.

'I've no notion of whose he was. I can't see much.

All bairns look alike to me. She wed him because he had money at the time, as far as I could tell. Could have been anybody's, seems to me. I brought her up decent and when my eyes failed me she walked out. She never came back but to leave him. He didn't even cry when she went. I thought any bairn would have cried, its mother leaving it. I couldn't stop her. I did what I could but all I have is what other folk give me and there isn't much of that so one morning when I got up I couldn't find him. I don't know where he's gone.'

'But he's just a little lad,' Lily said.

'Not a taking bairn though, nowt but curses and spit. I wasn't sorry. I can hardly look after meself, never mind a bairn.'

'Can you think of any place he might have gone?'

'How would I know? I've hardly been out of this room in five years and out of the house in ten. I've nowhere to go and nothing to go for.'

They left soon afterwards and although they made a search of all the other houses; these were uninhabited so they went back to the library and made enquiries, and from there to the town hall.

The man behind the desk looked suspiciously at them, and why would he not? Prue thought.

'What can I do for you?' he said, even after Prue had tried to explain in her best English accent, which she had a feeling would get her further.

'We are trying to find a little boy of about five or six. Do you have children's homes, an orphanage?'

The man looked scathingly at her.

'We just want to find this child,' she said. 'He was staying with his grandmother who is almost blind; his mother was ill and could no longer look after him. He has run away, he was so distressed, but he hasn't gone home and we are worried about him; we want to know where he could possibly have reached from here. He can't be far, he's no age.'

'Are you related to him?'

'Yes,' Lily said, 'I am his aunt by marriage on his father's side. He was called Fleming. My name is Mrs Lilian Fleming, from County Durham.' She used as much dignity as she could, but Prue had a feeling that it was her beauty which swayed the man. She didn't care what the hell did it as long as they got out of him what they wanted.

There was a children's home in Morpeth, several miles away, he told them. Prue didn't think the boy would be there. What child would run so far to a home like that? She thought they would gain nothing more but Lily was still questioning the man as to where he thought any child might go, but he shook his head and they left. She could feel the despair come off Lily and then Lily discerned her mood as she did so often now, they knew one another so well.

'You think he can't be there?'

'I don't know where he could be.'

'And you think that maybe he isn't Robbie's and does it matter?'

'I think it doesn't matter whether he is Robbie's, he's a child.'

'Somebody might have taken him in, but it isn't very likely. Folk here have nothing, they can hardly feed their own. Why would they take in another?'

'Do you want to go to Morpeth?'

Lily looked helplessly at her. They should be at home by now and if a visit to Morpeth was lengthy, that would be another night's lodging.

Morpeth was a pretty substantial Northumberland town. The children's home, after they enquired, was set down a side street, a big shabby building with a wall around it and heavy gates. They banged hard on the door within the gates but they had to shout for several minutes before anyone came and a thin middle-aged woman listened to their enquiry and then said, 'You can't just take a bairn from here, you know. There are rules.'

Prue suspected that meant money must change hands.

Eventually they were allowed inside. Prue had never been to a prison but she thought it must be very like this. The air seemed narrow and breathless and there was a hush over the place and it stank of unhappiness, of despair.

There wasn't a child to be seen. The woman led them

into the gloom of the building. Its windows were so narrow that they let in little light or sunshine and Prue blinked to make out the woman behind the desk, but she did smile and give them a seat and listen to their story.

'I could offer you many a child of that age, any of them to a decent home, but some of them don't give their own names, some of them don't know them.'

She led them through a widening corridor to a large room where three dozen children or more were sitting down to a meal. It smelled decent was Prue's relieved thought and they were tucking in as though they needed it but although Lily was there a long time and scrutinized each child from a slight distance, she shook her head and Prue could see the frustration on her face. She turned to Prue and said softly, 'He may be here but none of these children has any look of Robbie.'

'There is the workhouse,' the woman said.

They left with directions for the workhouse. Prue did not think anything could have been worse than the orphanage, but it was. There was nothing open or light about it. The sun would never have dared venture here. The gate was locked, they had to ask for entrance and even then Prue wanted to run away. Keys grated in locks. The woman who let them in was wearing a dress so filthy that Prue and Lily moved back from the stench. Her hair was lank and had not been washed possibly in her lifetime. Prue could not have said her age because she did not look straight at them and poverty made her look old.

All Prue asked was the boy's name. The woman took them into a room, opened a book and looked down the lists and she said, 'Nobody of that name here.'

Lily held her gaze.

'Are you sure?'

'I don't make mistakes. Mind you, if there was a bairn you took a fancy to we could come to some arrangement, I feel sure.'

Lily was pale but she insisted on seeing the inmates. Prue wished she hadn't. The children were seated on long narrow benches because they were having a meal. They were ill-dressed, skinny, and Prue thought a lot of them would not live long. They did not look up, even when they were told to, and Lily scanned the lines and kept shaking her head. Prue wished she could have carried all of them out of such a place. What kind of society which ruled an empire and was rich, left its poor and children to starve and lead hopeless lives?

She was glad not to be English in that moment, she was grateful that she could not be held responsible and then she thought of all the poor people in New York, of the black people, held so cheaply, of the slaves who had been imprisoned and badly treated for so long and she was ashamed for the whole world that cared nothing for its poor, its young or its animals.

Lily did not speak and did not cry, and they walked back to the car. They got inside and Prue drove home.

Thirty-six

Two days after they reached home, Helen came to see them.

'I want to take the children to church,' she said. 'I haven't done it since – since John died and now it's not far off Christmas and they are asking, at least the little ones are, because they miss the carols and the fuss and – I don't know what to do. The new vicar hasn't come to me, and I can see why not, but I really think I should go.'

'Does your father say he'll go?' Lily asked.

'I don't think he will ever go into a church again. He hated John so much. I can't go alone. Will one of you at least go with me?'

'I'll go,' Prue said.

Helen looked hard at her.

'I want my father there. I think I need a man to hide behind. Will you talk to him? He listens to you.'

'He does nothing of the kind.'

'He won't come then.'

*

Prue had calls to make after evening surgery and made sure she went past the Anne on the way home. It was late for him still to be at the pit but she could see the lights and although she had told Helen that she would not go she still turned, parked the car and walked in with Mabel at her heels.

Nobody said anything, he just looked up and put down his pen.

Prue sat down across the desk from him. His office was almost comfortable, which was possibly one of the reasons he was still there. The fire burned brightly in its black grate and the wind was howling outside.

'Don't tell me, Helen asked you to come and see me so that I would agree to go to church with her.'

'She can't go on her own with four children.'

'I have the feeling that she's going to get there any way that she can and it will be weird for her with the new vicar, and all the memories will come back and – she's so fragile, Prue. She's taken to pretending that everything is all right, the children distract her.'

'I noticed that she has lost a lot of weight and although we don't want her to feel guilt, I don't think she is getting past that.'

'She has horrible dreams and sometimes wakes up screaming. I have to get up and go to her in case the children wake up and sometimes they don't sleep. Teddy in particular has problems.'

'He's at a difficult age. He wants to behave like a man but part of him is still a child.'

'And the best thing would have been for the new vicar to come and see her, but whether he's been told not to or whether he doesn't want to, I'm not sure.'

'Perhaps if we all went with her it would be better.'

He looked gratefully at her.

'And Mrs Fleming?'

'I don't know. I could ask. She was married in the church.'

'I was there.'

Prue went into the dispensary the following morning before surgery started and she said to Ernie, 'Were you and your mother intending to go to the carol service on the Sunday before Christmas?'

Ernie looked so intelligently at her then that Prue could have hugged him.

'Of course we'll come,' he said.

When Prue asked Lily, Lily looked carefully at her too and then she agreed.

So the Sunday before Christmas they took both cars and drove up the muddy lane to the church. Mabel had been left to guard the house. Prue thought the good thing about living next to the pub was that nobody would care if Mabel howled. Nobody would even notice.

They were not early or late to the carol service and people tried not to stare. Rory Gallagher went into church with his daughter on his arm and her stepchildren all neatly dressed behind them, and Lily holding Isla, taking her mother's arm to guide her. Prue went in with Ernie and his mother. They didn't sit at the front or the back but in the middle where there was a gap and they all sat together.

Prue had not seen the new vicar, but was shocked to see how frail he was.

'He's old,' Lily whispered.

He was tiny, white-haired with a gleaming rosy pate on top and he hunched over the lectern, but his voice carried well enough. After the morning service Prue had thought they would go home, but Helen insisted on going to the vicarage. Rory shot Prue a look but Helen had seen them.

'I have to go there sometime, don't I, and you are all here with me,' she said and so they followed her. Wilf had his hand in hers as always and her father was on the other side. Teddy was pretending he had something better to do but didn't like to say so and the girls clung to Prue at either side.

Their feet dragged the nearer they got to the place which had been their home but as they walked the short distance between the church and the vicarage, it began to snow thick, square flakes.

By the time they reached the vicarage, the children were ready to go inside and though they stayed close to one another and to their stepmother, they were surprised and delighted because the vicarage was warm with fires, there was the smell of punch as far as Prue could tell and a large round woman came from the kitchen.

'Come in, come in, I'm the Reverend Roland's sister and his housekeeper.'

She ushered them through into the sitting room and another fire greeted them and had obviously been on a long time because the room was full of warmth. Two long-eared spaniels burst into the room and Prue was only sorry that Mabel was not there; she would have enjoyed their company. Miss Roland came straight to Helen and she said, 'I'm so sorry, we did want to come and see you but we are so old that everything we thought of was clumsy. Forgive us. We have had such a time trying to settle in.'

Helen smiled and introduced the children and Miss Roland took them to the table and gave them gingerbread men, except for Teddy, who would not have appreciated it. She also came to Lily and said, 'What a beautiful child. My dear, she is lovely and so are you,' and she touched Lily's cheeks with her pudgy fingers.

Prue went to the window. Rory followed her.

'I could do with some whisky,' he said.

'Me too.'

Prue tried not to think about the last time she had been here but it was not easy. Even though she was not in the kitchen she could smell and see blood and she could hear the children's voices from upstairs. In the end she went outside and thankfully it was snowing; Rory went out with her.

'Why don't you come to us for Christmas Day tea?' she said. 'We'll love having the children with us and Isla would miss them if you didn't.'

The snow was coming down faster than ever and Prue could remember when she was a child, putting out her tongue to taste the snowflakes and how in the mornings the windows were iced in exquisite ways. The frost patterns were so beautiful.

As they stood there, Wilf came running out of the house.

'Grandpa! Grandpa!' he shouted and Rory Gallagher lifted him up in his arms and the child squealed with joy. 'Can we make a snowman when we get home?'

'Of course we can,' Rory said.

Prue was surprised to see that Rory now had a relationship at least with one of the children if they were waking in the night, afraid, and he was there for them it would make up for a lot.

The snow fell faster and faster so Prue was glad they had not a long way to go before they reached home. She parked the car and let Mabel out. Mabel had not realized that it was snowing and so she darted hither and thither through the whiteness, pushing her nose into the snow so that it made tracks and tracing them and after that rolling in the stuff and then, quite calmly, she came into the house and settled before the fire, keeping the heat of it from everybody else so that they complained.

Since they had all come back to the surgery house, the children piled into the garden. They insisted on having a snowman, so barring Lily, who eventually took Isla back inside to watch from the window, the rest of them built a huge snowman in the garden.

The children came inside and Rory gathered them and his daughter up to drive them home and for once Prue was sorry to see them go. When he had driven them away she felt a big sense of loss.

Christmas Day was difficult, why wouldn't it be? Prue could never get past the spectre of Robbie's wife turning up and the idea that somewhere out there was a child. She had not said so to Lily, what was the point, but perhaps that was the difference between a man and a woman. Many men abandoned their children, few women did. Had he done it for Lily or had he just unloaded his wife and child because they were no longer deemed by him to be an essential part of his life?

She was so tense that she spent the entire morning waiting for a knock on the door and when nothing happened she didn't even feel glad. Ernie and his mother were there and, since Ernie was going off to Edinburgh after Christmas to study, with Prue's blessing and as much money as was needed, thanks to Rory and the practice, he thanked her again and again, but she thought it was owed. The world was owed a decent intellect like his and she was glad to furnish it as long as he didn't disappear along with the practice's money. Ernie insisted on going by himself and since Prue was very busy she was glad of that.

They were almost out of debt, but she had impressed upon Mr Silverton, the bank manager, that she was the only doctor in the village so he had not made them pay anything beyond a tiny bit of interest and in that time she had made sure the money went to other places. It helped that Mr Silverton had to come to the surgery one night after work with a bad back. She urged him to take more exercise and although he grimaced she said, 'Go walking each evening when it's fine and at weekends. I promise you it will make all the difference.' And it had, at least so far.

Rory, Helen and the children came to tea and they sat down and ate lots of chicken and stuffing sandwiches and great wedges of fruitcake. Prue could eat nothing.

When the meal was in progress and Prue had gone back to the stove for more tea, Rory came to her and said softly, 'Have you any whisky?'

She nodded like a child and said, 'My surgery in five minutes.'

Somehow they managed to sneak out. The fire was still going in there and he sank into a chair while Prue built up the fire further with coal from his own collieries which they had cheap, as everybody did in the village.

'Oh, God, the peace. Thank you, Prue. I have never felt quite so old.'

Prue took the short, stout glasses which Robbie had introduced her to and handed him one of them and she took the chair opposite.

They didn't talk while they sank the first lot of whisky. She refilled the glasses generously as Robbie would have and even then knowing what she knew, she was sorry he was not there.

'You seem to be getting on well with the children?' she said.

'What?'

'Wilf ran to you that day at church.'

'Oh, right. I think they've just got used to me.' He looked sheepishly down into his drink. 'And I did a deal over ponies with the local scrap man. The children were very impressed. I own the fields around the back of the houses and he keeps his horses there, much cheaper than bicycles. Teddy won't ride a horse and Wilf is too little, but Elisabeth loves it, Mary can be persuaded and I sort of supervise.'

'What a good grandfather you make.'

'Don't I? I thought that perhaps Dr Allen would be here today. The poor man's here and gone so much he must wonder what on earth he's doing.'

'I think she feels that she can't marry him because of the way that Robbie acted and she can't trust anybody.'

'That's a shame, he seems a good man.'

'There is more to it,' and she went on to explain about their search for the child. He listened intently and didn't interrupt, frowning in thought, and she knew that was one of the things she liked about him; he was a problem solver and that was the best kind of man. All some men seemed to do was create problems.

'Can you think of anything more we might have done?'

'Not really. How hard.'

'There are thousands of children out there. The workhouse — it was awful, and the children's home too. People need to be offered better contraception.' She stopped there. 'Sorry, I forgot who I was talking to.'

'No, no, I've got nothing against limiting families. If people keep on bringing into the world children they can't afford to feed, things will only get worse. Why have a child that will starve?'

He understood, of course he did, having had John Edwards' children foisted on to him.

'I don't think Lily will marry Dr Allen if the boy isn't found and I know, I've given her all the arguments and it isn't logical or sensible but she won't. Somewhere out there is a child that looks like Robbie. He was her first love and even though he was imperfect, he was a lovely man.'

*

It was January when Dr Allen turned up in the middle of a snowy afternoon. Prue had been out visiting patients and when she walked into the kitchen he and Lily were drinking tea. He greeted Prue with a smile and she said, 'I'm sorry we have nowhere to sit. One of these days we should move to somewhere bigger.'

'That's what I came to talk to you about. Dr Adams and I were very grateful for your help when he was ill. You made such a difference to us and – well, we think we would be the better for a woman in the practice. Sometimes it's very difficult for women to talk to a man about their problems but not just that, you've proved yourself so very capable. The people like you and you have a good, fresh mind. We wondered if you would be interested in joining up our practice and yours.'

He paused there but only for seconds. 'I want to have special clinics for women who are expecting children; we have started but we need to do more and we need to talk about how families and their special problems are to be handled. I have heard you are something of an expert in these matters.' He smiled just a little. 'And also we need you there for the children and for – oh, the delicate things which people care about. You have done so much and we admire it.'

Prue was surprised when Lily said almost instantly, 'It all sounds very exciting.'

He smiled at her.

'What do you think, Dr Stanhope? You don't need to move house, we could find another building nearby for this surgery and we could all even have holidays and take it in turns doing weekends.'

'That would be wonderful,' Prue said gratefully.

Lily smiled ruefully at her.

'You haven't had much of that since you got here,' she said.

'We could take a hotel at the seaside and all of us go,' Prue said, and she and Lily beamed at one another.

Thirty-seven

Rory thought a lot about Prue. He didn't come to any conclusions, he didn't want to – he had had enough of women and he had Helen and the four children to take care of – but, as the winter began to loosen its hold and first the snowdrops and then the crocuses began to burst through the soil, he thought about how the practice was moving on.

Helen, spending a lot of time with Prue and Lily, knew that the two practices were to merge. Rory thought it a very good idea. Prue would have a proper wage and although Nurse Falcon was a good nurse, Dr Allen had two more nurses and they would make a difference. He slept better at night knowing that he had so many people belonging to the medical profession around him. You never knew when things would be bad and he had had two disasters at the pits within recent months so he was not about to become complacent.

He watched Lily when he did see her and he thought that Prue was correct. Lily was haunted by her husband's first relationship and why wouldn't she be? It was a horrible thing to do and yet he had done much the same thing but he was able to marry the woman. He had been lucky because she had been the right person but it was no better than what Robbie Fleming had done, he knew.

Robbie had married the wrong woman and it was purely chance. Rory could not imagine what it was like when you found the right person and you were already married with a child, and while he could not condone what Robbie had done, it was true that his second relationship had borne fruit. When Rory went to bed at night he thought about the child.

He cursed Prue for it in a way and yet she had been so frank with him. The idea of her marriage and divorce had been a shock at first. He didn't know anybody who was divorced, but those who could afford it did so, and why shouldn't other people admit that at eighteen or nineteen they might make mistakes and why should they spend the rest of their lives paying for it?

It made a mess, of course, but life was a mess. It seemed to him that the only way to avoid it was a convent or a monastery and even then you had to make huge efforts. He didn't understand why all the bad things that happened to you fell down on your head and all the good things you had to strive endlessly to accomplish.

Besides, it was only the Church that wouldn't allow divorcees to remarry; the law as far as he knew simply required that both parties be free.

He wished that he could conjure up this boy; he had the feeling it would solve so many problems and then he dreamed that he found the child and it was Robbie's and that he took it back to Lily and she rejected it. He dreamed that he found the boy and it was not Robbie's and rather like a stray dog he had to leave it there in some dreadful place with hundreds of other starving children.

He became so grateful for his step-grandchildren. He could afford to keep them and they had accepted him. Teddy didn't go to school, but Helen kept him at his books and when Rory had time he walked long distances over the fells with Teddy. Teddy loved being out there and liked being with Rory to such an extent that he asked to go down the pits with him.

'I thought you didn't like the idea,' Rory said.

'I haven't decided yet,' Teddy said loftily, but when they went down the pit together the boy was not afraid. Rory grew to count on him day after day so that Helen complained Teddy was not there for his lessons.

The pit managers became used to him and Teddy grew tall and he cared about the pitmen and the pits and Rory thought that in time he would be a very good manager and, if he cared, he could take over, or he could go on and do other things.

At home the little girls were a pleasure; he read to them in the evenings and he encouraged Helen to go out. Mary was a shy, confiding child, whereas Elisabeth was bolder and would go out with Helen to various things at the church and to her friends' birthday parties and such like. Mary was quiet and would sit over the fire for hours and read. Helen thought Mary did not take enough exercise, whereas Elisabeth was fond of horses and loved the fresh air. Wilf became Rory's shadow. Rory had not thought you could care for such an awful man's children and yet children were not their parents.

Wilf didn't speak very much for a long time and Helen went around with him on her hip but, for some reason, after a while, when Rory came home, Wilf would run to him shrieking greetings, the like of which Rory had never known. It had to be something to do with the way that John Edwards had not treated his children but Rory had no idea what it was. It was not long before he would work in his office at the house with Wilf on his lap, falling asleep. He thought it a small sacrifice. He loved Wilf as he had loved Helen when she was that age.

Elisabeth had also become a problem but in a positive way. She was causing disruption in class because she was bored. Helen went to the school, dismayed, thinking that Elisabeth's troubles had been caused by what had happened to her.

'But I don't think it is,' she reported to her father that evening when the children had gone to bed and they were sitting over the table, drinking tea.

'Miss Michael,' Elisabeth's class teacher, 'says she's

just so bright that she gets bored quickly and the classes are so big that I think the teachers find it difficult seeing to everybody. She can't go to the grammar school yet.'

Rory said, 'She could go to the convent.'

The Sisters of Mercy ran a convent school in Wolsingham.

Helen's face changed; she hadn't considered that, he thought, and then it clouded again.

'We aren't Catholics,' she said.

'I don't think we have to be. Mr Boylen's girls go there and are very happy.'

'It costs money.'

'I'd rather we tried something new. Why don't you ask her what she wants to do?'

Helen shrugged, but the following afternoon when Elisabeth came home she put the question to her. Elisabeth frowned and then she said, 'Could we go and look at it?'

So Helen arranged with the headmistress that they would look around the school. Helen hadn't yet learned to drive so Rory took a couple of hours off work and drove them down the hills into Wolsingham.

It was, he thought, a very impressive place, set just back from the pavement in pale stone. The gardens at the front were neat and when they went in, greeted by Sister Luke, the headmistress, he liked the atmosphere. She took them into various classrooms and the children wore uniform in brown and gold and looked fine to him. There were not just nuns, a lot of the teachers were just that, smiling and polite. The girls rose to their feet as the visitors walked in. They were small classes, which he thought encouraging. There were bright paintings all over the walls and nature tables in the younger children's classrooms. There was a library with hundreds of books and one of the things which Rory liked best was that they took children from four upwards; it brought about some kind of neat cohesion which he thought worked well.

It was a fine day and there were extensive gardens at the back and tennis courts and big trees. There was a chapel and there were quarters where the nuns lived. Elisabeth's face shone as they looked around. There was a big hall where concerts and gatherings were held and where the children played sport when the weather was bad.

They went back to Sister Luke's office and had tea and biscuits. She talked directly to Elisabeth, and afterwards one of the other nuns took her off to find out what her reading and spelling and arithmetic were like and Sister Luke got down to the business of how much it would cost and what would be expected.

When Elisabeth came back and the other nun nodded at Sister Luke and left the room, Sister Luke said that she would be happy to offer Elisabeth a place in her school but they should go home and talk about it. Elisabeth skipped towards the car and Rory felt good that they had been able to give her a different chance.

Helen went with her to buy the uniform, but on her first day Rory took her there in his grubby car and her face was lit with anticipation. He didn't have to say to her, 'If you don't like it you don't have to go,' because he thought it might discourage her in her first few days, but he was touched when she gazed out at the front of the building and the children pouring inside and she turned swiftly to him and said, 'Thank you so much, Rory. I do like my uniform.'

He was astonished, he had not known that the children other than Teddy called him by his first name but this child turned gleaming eyes upon him before she smiled and leapt from the car like a salmon reaching up and landing on top of the waterfall.

Mary was good at playing the piano and had a fine voice, so they encouraged this and Rory sometimes did not think about Anne for days. When he first realized this he was astonished and ashamed and then he thought that Anne would have wanted him to do these things for Helen, no matter what the circumstances. He also felt rather guilty that once he had ceased to see Molly Donaghy he didn't think about her and he knew now that she had been a substitute because Prue had made her feelings clear. He was done with women, he decided, it was too much like hard work.

The children mattered so much and were a joy he looked forward to at the end of his day and it was nothing like it had been at first. He came home at teatime now, looking forward to seeing them, and the two youngest ran down the hall to him, shrieking, 'Grandpa! Grandpa!' as though they hadn't seen him in weeks. They would vie for who should be lifted up first in his arms and thrown toward the ceiling and they would shriek and yell in delight, and he was captivated.

The two elder children he listened to over supper – Elisabeth full of her new school and Teddy always ready with talk about the pits. Being with him all day, Rory had discovered, meant there was even more to talk about when they got home. Helen looked better now and had put on weight. She was not happy – how could she be? – but she was helped in a lot of ways by the children and so was he.

His days and evenings were full, but when he went to bed Prue's voice invaded the space and he remembered the possibility of Robbie's child. He attempted to dismiss it, but it wouldn't go away and during the night he would awaken and wonder what on earth he could do that they had not and no answer came to him.

He was so pleased when the winter gave way to the spring and the nights began to lighten. It was hard to get up in the dark and go to bed in the dark as his colliers did, but he would not have asked them to do anything he could not meet.

Thirty-eight

Prue and Lily were looking for a bigger house. Neither of them was happy about it. They had decided that they wanted to live at the surgery, otherwise it would be too complicated, but there was no big house in the village other than those which were occupied, and it was not the kind of place where anybody moved. There was the odd property outside the village, but that was no good; it had to be somewhere people could get to easily. Prue didn't see how they would solve the problem and it was becoming more and more important.

Prue came back one late afternoon to find Lily saying, 'I think I've got the solution to the moving problem.'

'What is it?' Prue was not enthusiastic.

Lily looked smug and she so rarely did that Prue thought positively about it.

'The people next door are moving away,' Lily said.

They went outside.

'They rent.'

'Ah, yes, but the lovely Mr Gallagher owns the house, as he does this one and I daresay if you asked him nicely he would rent it to us or even eventually let the practice buy them both. It's much bigger than this house and would be perfect to go alongside it and the back garden is huge, big enough to add on to again if we needed the space. The Wolsingham doctors will be really pleased. It's such a good idea, don't you think?'

Prue did. It meant they could have private quarters, sufficient room for all of them easily and though she had given up thinking that Lily might marry Dr Allen and she would spend the rest of her existence with Lily's mother and Ernie's mother, she was glad of all that extra room. It meant some privacy for them.

Prue had come to Rory about the house next to the surgery. He didn't like to sell houses; he said he would rent it to them and, in typical Prue fashion, she came back at him. 'We want to alter it,' she said. 'We can't do that if you still own it.'

'What do you mean, alter it?'

'Build on at the back. It's on a great big plot and Lily thinks the house could be as big again if we could build out from the back of ours. We could buy them both if the bank helped, so it needs to be a really big building. We need three separate surgeries and the dispensary and then extra bedrooms.'

'What for?'

'In case people are so ill that they can't go home.'

'That's a hospital, Prue.'

'No, just a kind of stopping-off place. To give them the chance to go back or forward or whatever they need. Obviously if they're really ill, we'll take them to hospital, but sometimes people need just a little time. We would have to employ extra staff, but the women in this village, a great many of them, want work, need it. One of us would be there to supervise always.'

A little time. He liked that. Maybe what everybody in the whole world needed was a little time and decent food and water, and a friend of course. And some books and the sky.

'I'm not selling it to you, but I will pay to have it altered,' he said.

A few days later, Rory went to see Sergeant Tweddle.

He told him exactly what Prue had said about Robbie's child. He had thought that the sergeant would say nothing, as he kept the village's secrets, but at the end of it the sergeant was frowning.

'Now that's a tough one,' he said.

'The thing is,' Rory said, 'that Dr Allen—'

'Ah yes, I know,' the sergeant grinned. 'He hankers after the lovely Mrs Fleming.'

'It isn't going to get him anywhere unless the boy is found.'

Sergeant Tweddle shook his head.

'Women,' he said, 'they always feel responsible for everything, whereas men, saving your presence, feel responsible for nowt.'

Rory had long since taken the sergeant for a great philosopher and shook his head in agreement and sighed.

'I could ask about,' Sergeant Tweddle offered.

Rory had no idea what Sergeant Tweddle's 'about' could be, it might be the village, the countryside, the county or even the entire north-east of England, as far as Rory knew. He left it with the sergeant and went home.

It was a week later that Sergeant Tweddle came to Rory's office. Rory was surprised and not very pleased about it. He thought that the sergeant would only come to see him here if he had something bad to report. Also, it was the middle of the day and Sergeant Tweddle would know that Rory was working.

He stood in the open doorway, looking anything but sorry. The look on his face was grim.

'What is it?'

Sergeant Tweddle came inside and closed the door but he didn't sit down. Rory watched him.

'The bairn disappeared,' Sergeant Tweddle said.

'What kind of disappeared?'

'Exactly.'

The sergeant sighed and that was when he sat down, heavily even for his short stout frame.

'The lads think he was taken. Some bairns were, apparently, at the time we think Dr Fleming's bairn went missing, according to what you told me.'

'Who would take a child? The bloody orphanages are full of them.'

'Aye well, that would depend on the child.'

'What do you mean?'

'It would depend on how bonny he was.'

Rory shot out of his seat.

'Oh Jesus,' he said, going to the fire and then hovering over it like he was cold.

'From what I've learned, Jeannie Featherall was a real looker before life got the better of her; like a Viking, you know, that bright-yellow hair and blue eyes and those pink cheeks and that skin.'

'Dr Fleming didn't look owt like that.'

'No, but he was a grand-looking lad and a combination might mean the bairn was worth something to somebody.'

'Is there any chance of finding him?'

'Jeannie says she sent him to her ma and didn't see him again and her ma says he ran off. Mebbe it's true and he got caught by people who like bairns too much. I always worry about those who don't think children are little divils. It's not natural.'

'Oh God,' Rory said.

'I'm not saying it's so, he could be anywhere, but it was a thought and we've turned up nowt else. If owt else happens, I'll let you know.' And Sergeant Tweddle went back to the village.

It seemed to Rory that Prue had extra instincts. But for that why would she have turned up two hours later?

'You've been busy,' she accused him.

He glared at her across the desk.

'I am working, you know. Do I bother you when you're working?'

She eyed him cynically.

'Don't try to hide. What have you been doing?'

He stopped, threw down his pen.

'What are you, a mind-reader?'

She smiled.

'I just heard from one of the policemen's wives that you and Sergeant Tweddle were making enquiries of a certain kind.'

'Can nowt be left alone?' he said.

'It's a village, what do you expect? Have you really been looking for Robbie's child?'

'I did what I could.'

She stood for a moment and then she came over and when he turned to look at her, she kissed him on the mouth. It was brief, but it happened. She went back to where she had been. He stared.

'What was that for?'

'You're a good man,' she said.

'Hell,' Rory said and shifted uncomfortably.

'So what did you discover?'

'Nothing.'

'You're also a bloody liar,' she said smoothly.

'They don't know anything yet.'

'But they suspect something?'

He didn't answer that.

'We could go and see what we can do.'

'I don't think there's anything to be done.'

'What you mean is, you'd rather go by yourself?'

Rory didn't answer that either.

'You think something horrible might have happened to him?'

He pretended she was not there.

'When are you going?'

'First thing in the morning.'

'Right, well, I had better come and pick you up very early or you will leave me behind.'

'Don't you have surgery?'

'The Wolsingham doctors will cover for me. I have already asked them,' she said.

Thirty-nine

Rory had never been in a car with a woman driver before, but it was not that that worried him, it was the way that Mabel so obviously resented him sitting in the front seat. She was obliged to sit in the foot well and glowered at him from glinting black eyes, thrusting her nose between his legs from time to time so that Rory feared for what she might do next.

'Don't fret. If she'd been going to bite you she would have done it months ago, but you have her seat.'

'Why did you bring her?'

'She goes everywhere with me.'

'Good God,' he said. 'Can't she sit in the back?'

Prue gave him such a look that he shut up.

Prue's idea of driving was to move as fast as she could. He put it down to her profession but he couldn't help closing his eyes from time to time, thinking they would never get round a certain corner or that, passing another vehicle while one was coming the opposite way, there was bound to be a collision. She glanced at him after the first hour or so, saying, 'Are you all right? You look a bit peaky.'

'I'm grand,' he said, looking straight out in front of him.

They stopped up on the moors and called in at a pub there. They sat in the back garden and drank coffee and looked out over the heather.

'Is this the quickest way to the coast?' he ventured.

'You know it isn't. I want you to talk to me. Tell me what you know.'

So he told her what Sergeant Tweddle had said and had the dubious pleasure of watching her face turn as pale as he thought his own was. When he couldn't think of anything else to say, she was looking down at the ground.

'I didn't think it would be that bad,' she said.

'It may not be.'

'But the sergeant thinks so, as do his men. He tends to be right, you know.'

'There could be a reasonable explanation,' Rory said.

'Or we could never know?'

'Maybe not.'

'Who would do such a thing?' she said.

'You have to remember that people always think they are right, no matter how other people view it. Otherwise none of this would happen.'

'You think so?'

'People don't do things they think are wrong.'

'That's true,' she said. She looked out at the view. 'Isn't it beautiful? Why does man spoil everything?'

'We try hard.'

'Don't we?' she said.

She hesitated when she got to the car.

'Would you like me to drive?' he offered.

Prue looked astonished.

'Would you?' she said, obviously unused to the idea.

'I would do anything to get away from Mabel.'

That made her giggle, just a little. He was glad of that.

He didn't know where to drive to. He didn't think she did either, he just wanted to be out there, trying to help, trying to make things better for so many children who were having a bad time. Just to help one of them would be something.

He changed direction and went east and he liked the driving, he liked having something to do as they moved away from County Durham. Once they got beyond Newcastle it was another world and yet still theirs, he felt.

He always thought that Cumbria and Northumberland and the borders was all his somehow. Daft really and yet comforting, driving there, knowing that your ancestors had been around the same place trying to pull some kind of decent living from the land.

They ended up in Boulmer and, of course, she knew where Jeannie and her family had lived, but when they walked up to the house the door was open. She went inside as though they could be hiding and he stood in the doorway. When she had searched the two rooms and found nothing, she came to him with a look of despair on her face.

'Do you think the police frightened them?'

'Possibly.'

'Let's go to Newbiggin.'

She directed him, he didn't know the place and why would he? she thought when they got there. It was so poor, so downtrodden, as though the sea and the pits had never been enough and when they walked up to the cottage, which was the only one that had retained its roof, it was the same story. The door was open and the house was empty. While they stood about an old man came past and he said, 'She died, two weeks Thursday.'

Prue and Rory walked slowly back to the car.

'What kind of institution wants orphaned children?'

'I don't think anybody really wants them,' he said.

She gazed up at the bright-blue sky. It was a cold sunny day.

'Somebody must. Or do you think someone took him in from the goodness of their heart?'

He looked at her.

'No,' Prue said, 'I didn't think so either. Isn't it awful, how many children there are who have no means of survival?'

'It's what happens.'

'No. We can take control of such things, science enables

us. We don't have to be ruled, we can say what we want and when we want it. In the future they will laugh at us for how little medically we knew and how stupidly we clung to old ways which made us poor and helpless.'

'That's what I like best about you,' he said. 'You never give up.'

They were tired. Neither suggested going back. At the end of the day they were at the coast, having gone to various villages and found nothing and nobody who could help. There was a pub and it had candles in the windows and for that reason alone they stopped there.

Prue's first concern was Mabel. They walked her along the wide beautiful Northumbrian beach. Mabel was not terribly bothered, he thought. She humoured them, she didn't run up and down but then, Prue said, she rarely had, having realized that the seagulls wouldn't go far in spite of her efforts. Also, she was so very aware of who she was and who her family were but, in the end, she made a dash for the waves in the darkness and quite enjoyed having her paws soaked. They stayed out until it was late and cold and dark and there was a wind blowing off the sea. Rory was glad to go back to the pub.

Before they had gone in Prue said, 'Don't go asking for two rooms.'

He stopped and stared at her.

'What?'

'We can't stay here if we aren't married. It's going to look awful. They'll think we're having an affair.'

'All right, please yourself,' was all he said.

They decided to eat upstairs. Prue sorted this out and Mabel had sausage and chips, how very odd, he thought, but Prue said it was her favourite. After eating, Mabel settled down there by the fire with a happy sigh.

After that, the landlord brought red wine and dinner and they sat at the tiny table and ate.

'How did you get him to bring all this?' Rory asked.

'Well, he makes his own wine, I think it's elderberry—'

'It's very good,' Rory said.

'And since it's the coast they had fish and lamb and some cheese, which is local, and then brandy which obviously isn't local. I think they smuggle it, so I thought we'd have that.'

He had nothing to complain about.

Prue said, 'I'm rather glad we didn't find anything, but I'm so frustrated by it.'

'We can try again tomorrow.'

They kept the fire burning long into the night. He let Mabel outside and went with her. He hadn't known that Prue had followed him down. The waves broke so gently upon the shore again and again, so reassuring. She came and put her hand through his arm.

'Don't you love the sea?'

'Are you sure you don't mind the arrangements?'

'I trust you.'

'I'm not sure that's much of a compliment.'

He could hear the waves and he could somehow almost see the stars and Mabel came and sat at their feet and waited.

In the night it was just the two of them and that was good, no matter how hard their quest. They needed to be together to try to work out what was happening and to try and face that they might not find Robbie's child. Why would they do so? Why would fate grant them such a boon and yet it was suspect. A child brought back from such an existence would be damaged, perhaps beyond repair. And yet he hoped. While Prue slept, he still thought about the boy and about the idea that everyone would be saved. It was rubbish, he knew; life was so cruel, but being there with the fire dying and the woman breathing so smoothly against the white pillows, everything seemed possible.

He wished the dawn would not arrive. He tried staying awake to hold it back. He wanted to be there always, with Mabel sighing and sleeping on the floor and Prue close against him. At some time in the night he had turned and put an arm around her. He and Anne had always slept like that. He was happy. If you could halt life and hold it, this would be his perfect moment. He felt guilty then because he had loved Anne and Helen had been so very precious, so perhaps his view was at fault, but he was happy in the moments before Prue awoke and moved away.

Then it was all activity. The night was forgotten. He was sad about that. He wished she had lingered, if only for a few minutes, but no, she was so energetic, wanting to go on. How could he keep her there? She moved so fast that he was slow and that was a new idea to him. He had always been so much quicker than everyone else. He kept up with her, except that she would have gone without breakfast and he was not having that. They sat down and ate and afterwards she said, 'Shall I drive?' in such a way that he didn't argue. It was easier to let her. He knew that she was worried about what they would turn up that day or that they would not turn up anything.

He didn't want to go home. He would have done almost anything to prevent her from saying, 'Do you think we ought to go back?'

He had the feeling that if they did they would never sleep together again, that this would be just another passing time and he would end up by himself as he had been on so many nights that he couldn't bear to think about it. He wished he didn't ever have to spend another night alone. He wished he could have back those few hours when they had been together in bed. He had never known such bliss and now it was gone, evaporated like morning mist and she was at her most practical, in charge, as she liked to be. He had begun to enjoy sitting there, watching her guide the car along the roads, concentrating. He felt so much for her that he was glad she was not looking at him.

'Well, what are we going to do then?'

'I don't know,' he admitted. 'Why don't we go up to Alnwick? Sergeant Tweddle said the police there had been very good.'

She accepted this and they set off. The road was straight between the coast and Alnwick and there was a bridge with lions on it, presumably something to do with the Percy family, as many things were, not far from the castle.

Prue drove the car up what looked a main street; it was always easy to find the police station. They parked outside, left Mabel guarding the car, though that seemed unnecessary to him outside a police station, and went in. Prue explained who they were and they were directed into a small office at the back where Sergeant Cooper greeted them, offered them seats and said he knew what it was all about.

'I was just going to contact Sergeant Tweddle. We had some information from Alnmouth and we went to a house where several children had been left alone and the neighbours eventually became suspicious and let us know. The thing is,' he said, 'that all we found was the children and we have had such varying accounts from them that we can't be sure of anything. None of them is above four years old, three of them only just walking. We think from what they have said that there was another child but we can't find him and we think this child might have been Robbie Fleming's. The children talk about him. He had Fleming's name. We couldn't even get a decent description of the men who took them.'

Rory couldn't think of anything to say to that, it seemed so obvious. Prue was looking at her feet and for the first time was reacting like a woman rather than a doctor. He was glad of it in one way but pitied her in another.

'So where did you find them?'

'It seems the two men who were holding them just walked out one day. After that we talked to people. These children did not exist outside of the house and yet the village went on around it. You wouldn't think it possible, would you, and yet it happens. It was a big house in Alnmouth on the seafront.'

'And have these children been returned to their families?'

'Those who would have them back. Some people don't want tarnished bodies, so they went to the nearest orphanage. Of Robbie Fleming's child, we have no idea.'

In the afternoon, when they left the police station, Prue faltered. They were in the middle of the town so all he said was, 'Let me drive,' and she did.

He drove back to the coast, to Boulmer, because it was

the first place you hit down the road from Alnwick. He stopped the car on the front there and she sat in silence and he said, 'Let's take Mabel for a run.' They got out and walked down to the windy beach and Mabel loped about because they seemed to require it. Prue cried into the wind so that her tears were not seen.

They stood there while cold waves assaulted the beach and Mabel did her best to make the seagulls feel that she really wanted to catch them. Prue turned to Rory and he put his arms around her and she cried into his shoulder with such force that he thought she might never stop and her tears would soak through to his skin and beyond.

'Let's go to Alnmouth,' he said, and that stopped her. Action, he thought, was everything.

Mabel was quite worn out with pretending she cared about the gulls. She settled on the floor beside Prue and snored. How reassuring her snoring was.

The road between Boulmer and Alnmouth is so beautiful that you want to stop at every turn in the road because of the view of the sea and the sand and thank God for such benevolence and even on that awful day they were grateful for it. God made such land for those who suffer, balm to every wound.

Alnmouth has an estuary which reaches well into the village and it was a smugglers' haunt for a great many years. It is a fine old village. They drove down the main street and followed the road on the right towards the beach. They halted outside the house which Sergeant Cooper had described. It was one of the large villas which looked out over the estuary and a big detached building it was with bay windows and balconies leading out from upstairs rooms. Rory could imagine sailors, if they had enough money, retiring there and sitting upstairs by the windows in their old age, looking out and having to do nothing and the tide coming and going at will as they dreamed of the things they had done and thought they might have done.

'Well,' Prue said, 'this is the house. Now what do we do? There's nobody in it presumably.'

'Let's go and take a look.'

Mabel was not going to be left. She followed them across the sandy road toward the house. The house did look empty, he thought, and it was nothing to do with the curtains at the windows. What was it that distinguished empty houses from others? It was as if once empty the house itself had stilled. It was so different from the other houses there. As though the lives of the people, the coming and going, the laughter and conversation were all completely gone in a big way and the house was no longer whole, no longer used, redundant.

They went up the garden path and he was not surprised to find that the door yielded, it had not been locked. Who would care to be inside, in such a place where children should never have been? It would frighten off the most eager of buyers, there was something about it which was repellent. Rory didn't want to go inside but he made himself do it.

The hall was dark and even Mabel drew back and cowered behind him. Prue went into each downstairs room. He followed her, waited until she had investigated the kitchen, the other two big rooms downstairs and then she went up. His instincts told him that he should have gone first but she wouldn't have listened and he didn't want to do that to her anyway so he followed behind, safe in the knowledge that a large German Shepherd was there at his heels, so obedient as Mabel never was and yet so reassuring as she was always.

Upstairs were four rooms. Prue swept into each of them and yet they were empty and up the final flight of stairs were another two rooms, smaller and darker as the roof closed toward the summit of the house and in these it was different. He could feel that children had been kept in such places, away from the light, away from the day, away from help and in despair and in pain.

The feeling was so oppressive that he wanted to run away, but Prue went over every inch of the rooms and he followed her and when he couldn't think of anything else to do there he waited and she went round and round, like Mabel trying to find a bed and he knew that she was searching for some clue of Robbie Fleming's child and the whole reason why they were there.

Mabel followed Prue and sniffed at the floorboards and

the walls and even at the fireplaces, following to the windows and on but nothing gave itself up as he had feared it would not. He did not want to go back and have to tell Lily that Robbie's child had been taken but not discovered and after that, Rory feared, the child was dead.

He knew that Prue would not accept it, at least not yet and that she would go on as Lily might go on and that it was not the way to do it; it would help neither of them because it could have an endless trail and they had their lives to lead but neither of them would listen.

Indeed, he began to despair of ever getting Prue beyond the house. Even Mabel was tiring and had taken to wandering the upstairs hall, back and forth she went, like a soldier on guard and after that she lay down and then he thought he should tell Prue that there was nothing here. He was not sure she would believe it.

Forty

Prue saw the house and it was as if she had seen it before in a dream, it was so known to her. It was her nightmares come true. She hated each corner, she dreaded the shadows, she could feel evil here. Did evil exist? Rory had said that people always thought they were right. Of course they did, how could they go forward but for that? And yet some of it was evil, it depended on subduing another person's will and body to yours, how could that be right for anyone? The truth was that some men regarded women and children as less than human and so it did not matter what they did to them or they felt that their traditional way of life inspired them to take all for themselves.

She could feel the house moaning. Why had it been chosen for such awful acts? Why should any house be used in such a way? The rooms would haunt her, she knew, even the kitchen because the back door led out to a wall. Beyond it was the garden but there was no evidence of any kind and she feared that the house had a hundred secrets and she worried that one of its secrets was Robbie Fleming's child.

She wanted to run away, but she had to go into each room and stay there and try to decipher what had happened and, however awful it might be, she had to find out.

She could not stop herself from thinking of what a lovely man he had been, despite everything. He had made mistakes but everyone did that. He had tried to right them, every decent man did that, and he had failed and he had died so very early and she wanted to help, she wanted to be there so that Robbie could see even from heaven that what he had been and done on earth had not been in vain and that the good hugely outweighed the bad.

The wind was howling off the sea. The tiny back garden was deep in shadow. She had not expected to find anything there, the local police were not stupid, but listening to the waves crashing hard upon the shore and feeling the wind biting into her face even beyond the buildings, she despaired and yet was glad that the weather regarded no one. She had seen children dead before but from disease, from things which could not be mended or prevented but would be in time as medicine progressed. She could see the way forward, but she had not seen a child dead because of neglect or abuse and she hoped never to.

She was aware of Rory hovering at a distance. He was so comforting to be with, automatically somehow doing the right thing. She hadn't seen that in action before like this and was so grateful that she wanted to give up and go home and try to forget about the boy, but she knew that it would haunt her.

When they went around to the front an old man was passing by and he stared at her for a few moments and then he said, 'They're going to pull it down, you know. Best thing for it if you ask me. Goings on like that in a place like ours. It doesn't bear thinking about. And for nobody to know. How can it happen? Nobody even heard a bairn crying before they managed to get out by themselves.' He shook his head and moved on.

How stupid, Prue thought, all they could think of was to blame the house. How misguided and trite. She had no idea what to do next. They wandered about at the top of the beach until finally she halted, not wanting to go on any further. Rory came to her and took her into his arms and she buried her face against him in a way that she thought she could begin to want and had never been able to do. To be able to trust a man not to hurt you, not to demand anything made her want to cling for hours. He didn't even suggest they should go home which was what she felt they should have done.

When she finally lifted her face he kissed her very gently in case she should decide to move away but she didn't. She didn't ever want to move.

Mabel, however, had other ideas and began banging her nose off the back of Prue's knees, but the kiss changed everything. She thought she might never feel lonely again, however bad things became.

They walked slowly back, leaving the car and went into the village. They went to the nearest pub and sat by the fire and Rory bought whisky and they nursed their drinks and didn't talk. Eventually the landlord came over.

'Not from round here then, eh?' he said, wiping the table and pausing to look carefully at Mabel but then she judged him a decent person and pushed her wet black nose into his hand so that the landlord proclaimed her a wonderful dog and got down and patted her head. Mabel didn't like people patting her head like that but she merely closed her eyes and endured the salutation, only looking gratefully at him when he ceased to pound her brains.

'Heard the talk then, have you? You will have done. I'm ashamed to live in a place where such things can happen. I'd stand them up against the wall and shoot them if it was me.'

'Did you hear there was a little lad they didn't find?' Rory said.

'Aye, and don't think we rested. We looked everywhere for that bairn. We even went over the churchyards and such, dreading what we might meet but it was no good. We started to think that there had been no bairn, that they were all accounted for, why would they kill one and not the others? I don't know, the more I think about it the worse it seems. It'll put folk off coming here. We'll be known as the village that hurt little lads, for ever and a day,' and he shook his head and went back to his bar.

Prue was beginning to think she wouldn't be hungry for the rest of her life, but just for something to do she went to the bar and asked if he would make some sandwiches.

'I can do better than that,' he said, 'my wife makes good broth and you can have ham and pease pudding sandwiches with that if you like.'

She said that would be fine and then she said, 'The men who abducted the children, they didn't come from round here?'

'By God no. There would have been lynchings. Funny accents they had, the two of them. Odd, you know. I did wonder why they never went out but for buying food, but then you get people everywhere that you can't explain.'

'What kind of accents?'

'I don't know. Not rough, like you might expect, people say.'

'Did you see what kind of men they were, what they looked like?'

'I didn't and even those who didn't are saying they did and we've had reports of wings and forked tails and all bloody sorts,' the landlord said. 'All I remember was that one of them was a lot smaller than the other and seemed strange to me somehow.'

Prue and Rory sat over their sandwiches. She managed the soup but couldn't face trying to get bread down. She gazed into the fire and didn't find any answers but somehow, mid-afternoon, while Mabel snored, having devoured Prue's sandwich, Prue suddenly thought of something different.

'What if they weren't men?' she said.

'What do you mean?'

'Well, if they weren't caught, how would anybody know?'

'Do women do things like that?'

'Why wouldn't they?'

'I don't know. It would be very unusual, wouldn't it? And in any case don't you think the children would know?'

'We are talking of small frightened children. If these people dressed as men and behaved as men in a lot of ways and spoke in strange accents, then why couldn't they be women?'

He stared at her.

'So if you were a woman in such circumstances you might get away with it. You wouldn't even have to leave the area. You might take what you wanted and go.'

'Are you suggesting that Jeannie Featherall knew?'

'Or here's a different idea, one of them might have been a woman so fascinated by a man that he was the one who abused the children and she aided him. A couple would not be discovered. And if the woman was in disguise and it was the man who spent time with the children, then that would be confusing, wouldn't it?'

'So where are they now?'

'They could be anywhere, they could have left. If they have left then there's nothing we can do but if they're still here . . .'

'Why wouldn't they go?'

'They like the danger of the situation, the excitement is in being only steps away from discovery.'

'Or maybe Jeannie does know. Maybe what she's been telling us was a lie all along and she gave the child or, more like, sold him to these people. And in the end they left the house because people were becoming suspicious and they took with them the child they wanted most.'

'They can't be local, they would be too recognizable.'

Prue and Rory motored back to Boulmer and wandered the village and after that they went back and forth over the roads, not knowing in which direction to turn or what to do next.

They turned off towards Alnwick, two or three miles in, and since Rory was driving Prue could see, away from the road, a group of children playing.

'Stop a minute!'

He did. Mabel was lying in the well of the passenger seat, but bumped her head off the bottom of the dashboard and even Prue gripped what was in front of her.

'What?'

'Those are Jeannie Featherall's children.'

He squinted.

'How the hell can you see from here, we're nearly two fields away?'

'They are.'

He pulled off on to the farm track which was full of holes. The house itself was almost hidden among a belt of trees. As the car drew nearer, the children disappeared into the building.

Prue got out, shutting the door behind her, but Mabel was too quick and as Rory climbed out of the driver's side, Mabel was out before him, nearly knocking him over as she went.

A man emerged in the fast fading light. It was Jeannie's husband and he had a shotgun in his hands. It looked like a very old gun so Prue was half-confident it would not fire. Where would he get a decent gun from, when he had no money? Probably he had found this in a scrapyard and was pretending, but she was not certain.

'You're not welcome here, I thought you knew the last time,' he said.

'I want to speak to Jeannie,' Prue said.

'She isn't here.'

'Of course she's here. I saw the children. Where else would she be? If you don't let me speak to her, I shall get the police.'

'On what grounds?'

'On the grounds that I believe she sold her child to other people.'

As she spoke, Jeannie came up behind him and said, 'I can do what I like with my own bairn. Robbie Fleming did nowt for us, even after I was wed to him and I came to you for help and you turned me out. What chance did I have of anything?'

'A child is not a pet. You cannot sell him.'

'I got good money for him. I never liked him. He looked too much like Robbie. Why should I put up with Robbie's leavings?'

'Where is the child?'

'I have no idea. Go away and leave us alone.'

'You told me you sent him to your mother.'

'Aye, I did but I got a better offer, you see, and she never knew what happened any road. She's dead.'

'Where have they taken him?'

'I don't know owt so you can just turn around and take your friend with you. It's nowt to do with you or nobody else.'

'They'll tell the police,' her husband complained.

She looked scornfully at him.

'You're going to shoot them then, are you? Don't be soft. The polis can't prove owt,' and she turned around and went back inside.

Prue and Rory retreated. Mabel would have lingered, but Prue called her immediately to heel and she obeyed. They walked to the car in silence and then took the track to the main road.

'Do you think we should go to the police?' Rory asked.

'You can't compel people to tell you things and I don't think she knows where the child is, do you?'

'They'll probably take off.'

'If we do find him I have a horrible feeling that he'll be dead and we'll have to go back and tell Lily,' Prue said.

They drove some way and waited in the car behind a deserted barn and, sure enough, it was not long before Jeannie and her husband and children fled across the fields, carrying with them what they could. Prue felt sorry for the children; she had caused them to have to move once again.

Prue and Rory watched until the family disappeared over the horizon. Then they went back to Alnwick and told the local police. Sergeant Cooper looked irritated.

'We had already spoken to her several times and she told us nothing. There is no evidence.' The sergeant sighed. 'We think that the people who did these things have left the area and, in any case, I have a great many other things to do and so have my men. To put some of them in charge of finding one child when the streets are full of homeless children is not useful. I know it sounds hard, but what can I do? We have already spent a great deal of time and money sorting this out and all of the victims, save one, have been rescued. You're welcome to carry on looking, of course, but I wouldn't think you could make any progress.'

Dismissed, they went back outside.

'Do you think we might find the answer back in Alnmouth?' Rory said.

'Why?'

'Because you thought if they weren't both men, they had the perfect disguise.'

'So we go back there and scrutinize all the married people we see?'

'It sounds stupid when you say that. Would you rather go home?'

'No. I feel as if this is the last shot at this problem and so much rides on it and I don't know where to turn but I have you here and Mabel so why not stay?'

He said nothing and when she had waited what seemed like a long time she went to him, close, and looked into his eyes and she said, 'I do love you.'

He still said nothing.

'I just didn't see myself caring for anybody after the disaster of my marriage and I'm sorry it has been so hard. Are you past caring?'

'Never past that,' he said.

He had a disconcerting gaze, straighter than she had ever seen before. She smiled into his eyes and saw the warmth there.

'What do you think we should do?'

'Let's stay around. Where would you like best to be?'

'Boulmer, in spite of the fact that I don't think it offers us anything which might help. It feels right.'

Forty-one

They drove to the little village just as the tide was coming in, and got out of the car and walked along a tiny lane which ran between the beach and the fertile farms. Beyond it was an inn. It had no name outside, but the empty sign swung in the breeze so that Prue thought perhaps they were having it repainted. That was odd but it was a stone building and so open that she could see into the rooms at the back. She liked that.

They walked in with Mabel and sometimes people didn't like the dog so they would soon know if it was right for them, she felt, but the man who came down the staircase, on hearing them, said, 'Oh, what a beautiful dog,' and he came forward and got down to Mabel and Prue thought he must have had dogs all his life, nobody else would be so confident, so easy, so smiling and accepting. He looked at Mabel as though she were the first dog he had ever seen and therefore a gift from God.

Rory said they would like a room and to their surprise

he said, 'Upstairs or down? We have a room here on the ground floor. The view is lovely but you can have a bedroom upstairs if you like.'

He showed them into the room on the ground floor. It was huge and had floor-to-ceiling windows with a door so that the whole room led out on to the beach. The tide was still coming in and the further in it came, the more seabirds arrived as though they had an invitation. Prue was entranced.

The landlord opened the door and they stepped outside and even Mabel was transfixed with how lovely the incoming tide was, with a myriad of sea birds riding it and the party it seemed to be.

The landlord sensed how they wanted things and offered to bring dinner to the room, and they both agreed. After that they stayed on the beach and at high tide they retreated to the garden and watched there as the waves broke white and grey and full and proud, and Mabel was not inclined to go any nearer as though she liked the floor show.

The dinner was Craster kippers with bread and butter and then local cod with chips and vinegar. To finish they had Northumbrian cheeses and apples. They sat with the door open until it was dark and cold and even then there was sweet wine from Lindisfarne. They walked Mabel up the beach and she wandered the wet shore now that the tide was going back. Her paws made prints in the sand and the moon rose over the water.

They went back to their bed and left the door open even though it was cold because the bed and their passion was warm. It was a great deal later when Rory stepped over Mabel to close the door.

Prue dreamed about the child, always slipping away from her, just around a corner on the street, his dark clothes shadowed so that there was no colour to help her. It was as if he didn't want to be found, perhaps he feared worse than he had already been through. The anguish when she awoke didn't abate, but dawn was breaking so she put on some clothes and went outside. It was cool but the sun was rising. Mabel sauntered along behind her.

If the people who took him wanted to keep him they could have been many miles away by now. What was the point in looking any further, she thought: there had been nothing but dead ends. Why would anything change?

When she got back Rory was sitting outside. She went and sat down and put her arms around him. He kissed her.

'I think we ought to go back,' she said.

'Maybe when we get old we could buy a house here.'

'Isn't it perfect?' she said. Nobody spoke about the child, nobody said anything more, but Prue was reluctant to leave. She couldn't see herself coming back here again if the child was not found.

As they sat, not wanting to go in for breakfast, she could see two people walking on the beach. They were men; that was all she could see from so far away. There was nobody else about. Prue watched carefully. She didn't think Rory had noticed, he was talking to Mabel who was obviously thinking about breakfast because her tail was wagging.

As Prue watched, the two men stopped and, to her surprise, they came close together, touching, and that was when she thought that the movement of one of them was not like a man's gait at all.

'Rory, can you see those two people?'

He squinted. 'You must have incredible eyesight.'

'They're kissing.'

'People do.'

'They look as if they're both men.'

Rory didn't answer immediately and when he did he had shifted his position as though he were uncomfortable.

'They probably don't even know we're here.'

'I think one of them is a woman.'

Rory looked at her and then back at the couple.

'Doesn't look like that,' he said. He got up. 'Will you stay here?'

'No.'

'I didn't think you would.' He set off walking, Prue and Mabel just a little way behind him.

The two people were apart by the time he reached them. Prue thought they might even have run away, but they didn't and it would have been such a giveaway if they had, as though they had something to fear.

They were both wearing suits and hats, but one of them was small, almost dainty by comparison.

'Good morning,' Rory said.

They nodded warily.

'Are you from round here?'

The bigger one shook his head.

'Just passing,' he said. He spoke in an educated southern way.

'Strange place to be just passing.'

'Spending the night. Such a lovely beach, we thought we'd explore it.'

'The two of you?'

The man looked around him in mock gesture.

'I don't see anybody else, do you?'

'I don't know, I might,' Rory said, and he was taking up that stance. Prue had seen it before, both feet flat on the ground and some distance apart, as men did when they were about to start fighting. It didn't bode well, Prue thought. 'I might see a child or a number of children.'

'You need glasses then.'

'The perfect place to hide, of course, the most obvious where nobody ever thinks of.'

'Who's hiding?'

'I think you are.'

'Look, we know this kind of thing is frowned on, but

we are being very private about it and to be fair it isn't any of your business.'

'Where are you staying?'

The man jerked his head in the direction of the land. 'Not far.'

He moved as if he was going on and Rory blocked his path.

'You can't stop us.'

'Watch me.'

Prue wasn't at all happy with such things. When it came to confrontation, men handled it so differently. She wanted to barge in and offer to help and give advice, but she didn't.

'Where is the boy?'

'What boy?'

'Where is he?'

The younger person moved as though afraid now. Rory took a step forward and pulled the cap from the person's head and though the hair was short like a boy's, she had the features of a woman.

'You had better tell me or I will take you to the police,' Rory said.

'Take us? How many are you?'

'Try it.'

The man shifted.

'We don't want trouble.'

'You're already got it. Where is he?'

'I don't know what you're talking about.' And that was when Rory moved in and hit him.

'Where is he?'

'Rory, stop it,' Prue said.

He looked at her in apology.

'Please don't. That's not going to help,' she said.

'We don't know anything about what you are implying,' the man said, moving away.

'The little golden-haired boy that you took and wouldn't give up. That's what I'm talking about,' Rory said.

'It has nothing to do with us,' the woman said.

Prue was beginning to believe her. She wanted to grab Rory by the arm and move him away so that these people could get on with their lives. Maybe it was just the way that they chose to live, but it was such a rare thing in places like this. What could they be hiding that mattered?

She could see the movement of other people on the beach, a number of men, who had been dealing with the fishing boats pulled up on the dunes and were now approaching fast.

'Should you have done that, mister?' one of them said to Rory.

'We think they are the people who abducted several children from Alnmouth,' Rory said.

The men looked at one another. Then the same man spoke.

'Maybe you should let the police decide such things,' he said, and the other men helped the man from the beach, gazed at the woman who had put on the hat again and was looking down and then led her away.

Rory and Prue followed. The nearest police house was not far and covered a number of villages as far as Prue could tell, being between this one and the next with houses all around. She put Mabel into the car and she and Rory drove to this building, but waited so that everyone could go in together.

The policeman took the details and then he told everybody to wait. He took the two away, came back after about an hour, and said, 'There's no proof of this. I'll have to let them go, and you,' he pointed at Rory, 'leave them alone or I'll have you in a cell.'

'What about the police in Alnwick, they know all about it. If you contact them they'll tell you,' Rory said, but the constable didn't take any notice and, moments later, they were free.

Rory stood outside glowering at everybody and watching where they went. The fishermen went back to their boats.

The couple disappeared along the sands. Rory, not content, wanted to follow them.

'No.' Prue said.

'You think we shouldn't?'

'I think we should let them get almost out of sight,' Prue said.

He looked relieved.

'I'm sorry,' he said. 'I didn't mean to behave like that but . . .'

'You're right, I don't think what you did was right, but . . .' This time she let her words hang in the air. 'I think we should try and do something.'

They waited, even after the two people had gone and then they went to the sand dunes and began to follow, Mabel with them. It was so easy to keep out of sight and though the two hurried, Prue and Rory kept back among the tall grass and watched from a distance as they went around the corner. They began walking more rapidly, looking back to make certain that nobody was following them. Within ten minutes they reached a little beach house up among the dunes. It was quite alone, no other chalets with it, built of wood and didn't look as if it would last many more winters; it was battered. They made their way there.

Prue and Rory stopped and waited, but nothing extraordinary happened so after another ten minutes Rory said, 'Do you think we should go in?'

'Could it be that simple?'

'I think if a child was there or had been, somebody would have heard him or seen him, but it is a hell of a long way from anywhere.'

'It still looks as if it isn't going to last.'

'What if they're settled for the night? It's only midmorning.'

'I think we should wait.'

'What, here?'

'What else would you suggest?'

He shrugged.

'All right, I think that I should stay here and watch and you should go to Alnwick and talk to the sergeant. If anything happens, I'll leave a note here under a big stone.'

She went, Mabel keeping pace but not getting ahead. She tried not to think about what might happen. It seemed to take such a long time to get back to the car, though it couldn't have been more than about twenty minutes and then she and Mabel tore away up the road as if they were being chased.

Alnwick was only a few miles away, but every minute was endless and she screamed to a halt right outside the police station. People stared at the noise and, when she and Mabel got out, they went on staring.

She barged into the police station, hoping to God that the sergeant was about. The constable on the front desk tried to stop her but she insisted on seeing him and was ushered through. She sat down and the sergeant offered her tea and biscuits.

'I haven't got time for that,' she panted.

'Sit down, lassie, for goodness sake and explain, quietly and slowly so this old brain of mine can take it in.'

She did, watching his face. At least he didn't dismiss it.

'What made Mr Gallagher so sure?'

'I think it was something I said to him, that they needn't

be men just because they were dressed as men and sure enough one of them was a woman and I know that shouldn't matter and it seems as if they could be a hundred miles away . . .'

Sergeant Cooper shook his head.

'You wouldn't believe it but some people tend not to do that and if they have a struggling child how far would they get before somebody noticed? He could be right.'

'He could be wrong of course.'

'Well, it's worth a look.'

'What about the local police?'

'Let me worry about it. I have a couple of coppers to come with us and if you lead the way we can follow.'

So they did. The police car was in worse condition than hers, but it went and so she drove back and then they walked over the dunes. Rory was still lying there. As they reached him he looked up, apologetic.

'The longer it gets, the more I think I could be wrong.'

'Well, let's see, shall we?' the sergeant said and without speaking and without making any noise the two other policemen went round the back and the sergeant, Rory and Prue went round the front. The door was locked. The sergeant hammered on it.

In a minute or so the door was opened by the man.

'Not you again,' he said.

'Can we come in?' the sergeant said.

'Help yourselves. I don't understand why we are being

persecuted and do you know I could have this man,' he indicated Rory, 'for assault. He hit me and my wife was badly treated for no reason but that she is an American and is differently dressed.'

'American?' Prue said. 'Where are you from?'

'New York.'

'Right. Any particular area?'

'Upper Manhattan obviously.'

'Obviously,' Prue said. 'Your voice doesn't sound like Upper Manhattan to me.'

'How would you know?' the woman said.

The policemen who had been to the back door now came in the front and Sergeant Cooper directed them to search the house but it was tiny and to Prue it was already obvious that there was no child. It made her want to cry. To think that they had got it completely wrong. Had they been so desperate to take back a child to Lily? She was ashamed to think it.

There were three rooms, the first, the biggest, went the full width of the chalet and looked out over the sea. It was a beautiful prospect. The two rooms behind were a kitchen and a bedroom and they had views over the dunes and then the farmland behind to a certain extent, but the land rose and obscured the full horizon.

It was mid-afternoon now and she could see that the police had found nothing and that they were no longer interested. Sergeant Cooper went outside and came back and they went over the land around the chalet while the man smirked and the woman looked down, and Rory walked around like a caged cat and Mabel meandered from room to room, not stopping but going on again and again, sniffing at each corner, each floorboard, watching the people around her.

It was almost dark by the time the sergeant said that he thought they should go and leave these people in peace. They had all given up by then. The policemen hovered by the door. Rory sat still, not wanting to leave. He was stubborn, she thought. Mabel was still padding about. Prue was tired and wished to go home, but she felt so defeated that she wanted to howl. Then Mabel, who had been in the back, appeared now with a fragment of cloth. It was nothing much and nobody would have taken much notice but that Prue saw the reaction of the two people. They looked panicked.

She took the fragment of cloth from Mabel, it had been brightly coloured once and was patterned with diamonds. She took it and went into the back. There wasn't much to see. At first she thought she had overreacted. Mabel looked as bemused as she was but didn't budge when Prue said, 'Come on, we ought to go.'

Mabel began to whine by the back door.

'The police have been out there, Mabel, and found nothing. What do you think you could find that they could not?'

Mabel whined even more so Prue let her outside and after that Mabel scoured the dunes, she went up and down and up and down like a bloody wave, Prue thought, as though she would be ashamed to say she had found nothing. She came back eventually, tail down, but there was another scrap of cloth in her mouth.

Prue followed her a long way further than the policemen had gone but dogs had different ideas about smell and touch and distance and Mabel covered ground that they did not think of. Way out beyond the house, the sea and the sand dunes, over where the ducks were now flying in in the dusk, landing on the pond on the flat land, Mabel discovered something more and she sat there, ears erect and tail wagging.

It was a child's toy, a doll, naked but for a small piece of cloth which matched the others. It face was black and white and its expression sad with black tears. It was a clown.

The police station in Alnwick seemed bigger than before, perhaps puffed out by the sergeant's chest as he brought his two suspects inside. He put them in separate rooms and had them questioned. Rory and Prue sat in another room, Mabel under the table, and were given tea and biscuits. Prue thought that if she had to eat biscuits and drink tea again that day she might throw up. On the other hand, she couldn't have eaten anything else.

Eventually the sergeant, looking weary, came to them and he said, 'They have admitted that the child was there, but they say they didn't kill him and they don't know where he is, he ran away.'

'Not very likely,' Rory said. 'Give me ten minutes out in the backyard with him—'

'We don't do things like that.'

'This child is alone and frightened.'

'He may not be.'

'He may be dead,' Rory said, and he got up and paced the room. He swung round and looked accusingly at the sergeant. 'He could be dying right now.'

'We don't know and I don't know where to look. Do you?'

'No.' The word seemed dragged from Rory's mouth. Prue longed to go to him but there was no point. She was beginning to think she might spend the rest of her life in this wretched police station where people were telling lies. She felt like Rory did, she wanted to kill these people for what they had done. They had admitted that they had taken the child and it was enough to provoke savagery in her.

'Perhaps back at the house in Alnmouth,' she said.

'We went over and over it.' Sergeant Cooper said.

She looked at Rory.

'Shall we go there?'

'It would give us something to do,' he agreed.

*

She let him drive and did not criticize the savage way that he took the corners, the swinging of the car around the bends. When they got to the house it was dark and she remembered being here and the sense of failure.

The house was full of black shadows. She wanted to admit defeat and go home but she couldn't because of him and how eager he was and how angry, that somebody had hurt a child so badly. She was proud of him, proud of Mabel, proud of herself for staying with it in spite of opposition and even now, if there was nothing, they had tried hard and she felt that Robbie, if he was in heaven and where else would he be, would be looking down and thinking, my God, how my friends tried to help my child.

Prue felt that things could only go forward if Robbie's child prospered. That was stupid because it was so fragile and it should not affect anyone, but it stayed with her. Something good had to come from the union between Robbie and Jeannie Featherall. He must have loved her once. He had betrayed her or she had betrayed him and the child between them had been a tug of war. It was no way to go on and yet people did it every day. Their children were less important than they were. How could they think so? How could they do that?

Room by room, Prue and Rory went through the building and there was no sound and no movement and she despaired and longed to be anywhere but here. She was so afraid that if they did find the child he would be dead and everything that mattered would be over. If children could not be the future, if they were only the past, then there was nothing left.

Back and forth, up and down, and nothing but footsteps and Mabel's keen breath. Mabel had insisted on keeping the first piece of cloth nearby and now she carried it with her like a talisman and yet they got nowhere and they went over and over with it until even Prue was ready to give in, even she wanted to cry and she went to Rory and she said, 'I think they killed him.'

He held her close. Mabel had sat down. It was over.

They went downstairs and into the living room and there she stepped on a squeaky board and Mabel came to her and sniffed particularly around it. Prue paid no attention. She hadn't noticed Mabel doing that before so what did it matter now?

'Come on, Mabel,' she said, 'we're going.'

Mabel stilled and looked down at the floorboard and as she did so her head turned. It was one of the things Prue loved best about her that when she was unsure she paused, but when she heard even a tiny noise she turned her head and her ears somehow became bigger and she listened.

There was no noise and when Prue got down the floorboard was not even loose but Mabel would not move. Rory came to them and being Rory he insisted on finding some stupid crowbar type thing which Robbie had kept in the car. Rory took up the floorboard and even then they could hear or see nothing. It was pitch black when they peered down and even though Mabel sniffed, she didn't do it with any degree of certainty so that they thought they should go but Mabel was still not to be moved and then she whined and had let go of the piece of cloth long since so in the darkness they felt along and around under the floorboard and there they found a space. They couldn't tell how big it was or how far down it went even when they had taken up several floorboards. Rory went off back to the car and brought a rope. He said he would go down but he was too big. Prue, big as she thought she was, was much smaller than a man so she let him fasten the rope around her waist and lower her down and down until she thought her feet would not reach and then they found solid earth. There was no sound and she could see nothing but Mabel whined just a little more and Prue began to feel about her. It was a hard thing to do. She imagined rats and mice and insects crawling over her hands and then over the rest of her and she shuddered but she kept on feeling her way until she reached some kind of bundle and then she cried out.

'Oh God, Rory, I think it's dead whatever it is.'

'Can you get hold?' he called from above and she moved forward, aware of each breath, clutching what seemed to her like a large inanimate object. She gathered it to herself and found that it was warm and breathing. She moved back as best she could in the restricted space and then put the rope around its middle so that Rory could take it from her, then he lowered the rope which she refastened around her and he pulled her toward him until she found ledges which helped.

'My God,' she said as she reached the surface, 'it's alive.'

Rory put the child into her arms.

'This child is drugged,' Prue said, and Rory drove back to Alnwick police station as if all the devils in hell were following. Prue would have taken the child to hospital, but when he came out of whatever drug-enhanced sleep he was in, he merely looked at her. Not particularly afraid, perhaps still too drowsy for that, but she could not find anything physically wrong so they decided that they would take him home.

She had no idea what would happen then. All the way back to the Durham fells she held the child in her arms while he dozed and Rory drove. It was very late indeed when they got back there and Lily, who never slept that well, came down the stairs like a pale ghost in a white nightgown.

'You found him,' she said.

She tried to take him, but the child clung to Prue and in the end Prue and Rory and the boy went to Prue's room and there they lay down together. The boy slept. He was the only one. Rory and Prue lay wide awake until the morning and when the boy awoke Prue took him downstairs and Lily had made porridge and Prue spooned it into his ready mouth as if he were a baby bird because he did not respond but simply took the food.

All that week Prue did not leave the boy. She was careful with him, tried not to touch him when she didn't have to. She coaxed him to swallow food and she held him close in her arms. The other doctors covered her ground and she was grateful for it. He slept and slept and ate and ate and she held him near all that time until eventually, on the eighth day, Mabel came to him and he smiled and put a hand out and patted Mabel's black and tan head.

When Prue took up her doctoring duties the week after, she took him with her as she had done with Mabel. He sat on the passenger seat with Mabel and kept an arm around her and he would wait when she went inside and during surgery he curled under her desk with the dog.

He slept with her at night and did not cry out or complain, and though she worried about him, she was glad that they had found him and that the people who had hurt him would be severely dealt with by the law. At least she hoped so and if Rory had anything to do with it, they definitely would. He spent some time in Alnwick making sure that they did not go free and Sergeant Tweddle did the same.

Over time Prue took the boy to visit the other children in Rory's house and here he found a friend in Wilf. Wilf was younger than him but he seemed inclined to think Wilf was a god and followed him around and, in the end, Helen encouraged Rob to stay and sleep with Wilf.

Prue missed him, but it seemed that he did not miss her. He liked being with the other children. He was the most beautiful child that any of them had ever seen with white-blond hair, navy-blue eyes and a creamy skin.

He was so beautiful that Prue thought it a crime. They would not have taken him in any other case, she thought. How appalling beauty was. It was a cruel master and did nobody any good. Those who lived long enough discarded it gratefully. This child had suffered because of it. What a stupid way of regarding people, as if everyone who did not have a perfect body was less. It was not true, it was not right, and it had served this child so very badly.

People had lusted after his body for such.

Forty-two

Lily was busy organizing the alteration of the house so that there would be two consulting rooms with more waiting rooms and a large dispensary.

They were going to have big windows in the waiting rooms there so that the rooms would fill with light, encouraging people to feel better about being there than they would feel in dark little rooms with tiny windows. Lily was so enthusiastic that Prue let her get on with the planning. It gave her a new importance. She was enjoying the work too, she saw herself so differently than she had, reading chemistry books and becoming proud of her ability.

Prue expected daily that she would hear something from Lily about Dr Allen and hopefully their new relationship. And then she realized how stupid she was being. Things were never that simple, how could they be and in a way what Robbie's child had suffered made things worse, and she waited in vain for Lily to find some space in her life for the doctor.

Prue spent more and more time with the two Wolsingham doctors. When Dr Allen took a surgery, even though Lily was doing the dispensing full time and had become good at it – she said it was a bit like baking cakes – the talk was only of the patients.

Prue liked the merging of the two practices, she liked how she got to go to different places but, most of all, she liked the clinics which had been set up for mothers and children, for infants and their mothers and she set up a special clinic so that people for whom life had become too much might tell her how they felt. It was not well attended, but she kept it going, remembering the farmer, Jeremiah Miles.

They also had help looking after Lily's mother and Mrs Smith. Prue hired two nurses to come in at different times so that she and Lily were freer to get on with their work.

When Ernie came home he talked to Lily about dispensing but Prue could have told him that he was wasting his time. Her eyes were cool on him even though he stayed at the house, which was so much bigger that Lily could almost avoid him.

Lily snubbed him daily and Prue wanted to tell him to bother no further, but didn't feel that she could so she said to Lily, as they sat over the fire late, drinking tea, 'Don't you want to marry again?'

Lily sighed.

'No,' she said, 'I don't think I do. Do you think Ernie will come back and want my job?'

'He'll go on to other things.'

'Well then, I think I shall stay as I am. I am being paid and decently by the practice. I don't want to study further as he does. I'm content to bring up my daughter.'

The damage that Robbie Fleming had inflicted was huge, Prue thought.

'But you liked Dr Allen.'

'I do like him and I like Ernie and I know that if I put it off so that I begin to lose my looks no man may ask me again, but I don't think I care to put my future in a man's hands. My money is mine and my child is mine. I'm done sharing. I want my space and I have it here, the house is so big now. For the sake of a close relationship in bed, I'm not willing to sacrifice my independence.'

Prue said nothing.

'When I think of what happened to Robbie's son,' Lily said, 'it makes me worry that so many people care nothing for anybody but themselves, so I'm going to shield my child from men who may want her or me and when she's grown she can make up her own mind.'

Prue still said nothing.

'What about you?' Lily said.

Prue looked up.

'What about me?'

'You spent two nights with the delectable Mr Gallagher. Are you going to marry him?'

'I don't know yet.'

'Why not?'

Rory was not happy about it.

'What?' he said. 'You still don't want to marry me? What are you going to do, pay me?'

'That's not funny.'

'It bloody isn't. I'm expensive.'

Prue thumped him.

They were alone but it was difficult to be there, they had to move off, go for long walks so that there was nobody near.

'We can't keep coming out here, having it off in the gorse bushes, it's prickly.'

She laughed. 'I don't intend to do any such thing,' she said.

'Then what the hell do you intend? I want you in my bed.'

'I can't marry you.'

'You can marry me lawfully. Nobody will know, nobody would care anyway here.'

'What if people find out?'

'They're going to sack you as their doctor? It would be a nine-day wonder. We could be married and not invite anybody. We could be legally together.'

'So this is for practical reasons.'

'If you call sleeping with somebody at night practical reasons. Oh come on, Prue, for God's sake. What if you were pregnant?'

'I take precautions.'

'You do hell,' her lover said.

'I miscarried once, you know. It finished my marriage.'

He clutched her near.

'Nothing would finish our marriage, not while we had life.'

Prue thought about it.

'I suppose we could be married in Durham at the register office, but what would Lily think? And what about Helen and the children? And Ernie and his mother and Sergeant Tweddle and his wife and . . .'

'Oh, for God's sake. Why don't we tell them that we are getting married like that and they can come to the party at my house if they like. How would that be?'

'Not really respectable.'

'Well, it's the closest we're going to get so let's try it.'

The register office in Durham was a gloomy place and not many people were married there. Mostly the registrar went to the church and it was complicated but, on this day in June, when the notices had been put up and nobody had objected – how would they have seen it, Prue thought and hoped – they were married in a dark little room with two witnesses from the street, by a rather stuffy-voiced man who obviously didn't like such doings and couldn't say so because he was being paid.

They came out of the room into the brown corridor with its squeaky dark green linoleum and clutched hands like children who had had an ordeal and then he said, 'Let's get the hell to the County and have a drink.'

She agreed and together they stepped outside into the summer sunshine and a great roar of approval rose up from the pavement. Prue gazed at Lily and Helen and Ernie and both mothers and the children and Sergeant Tweddle and his wife and Mrs Piper and her husband and brood. And Dr Adams and Dr Allen.

They came forward and kissed the bride and shook the hand of the groom and congratulated them both and then they all went off to the County Hotel where, unbeknown to the married pair, their friends had set up a bridal lunch and so it was that the children played and they all sat outside on the river bank and they had champagne and cake and lots and lots of tea which Prue had become so used to that she needed it.

Mabel sat in the shade and the children, including Robbie's child, young Rob, played round and round. He still hadn't spoken, but she was hopeful that he would in time.

It was only one day, Prue thought, nothing lasted, nothing good ever went on for long but they had the day and their friends and one another and, most importantly of all, the children.

Prue didn't know whether she would have another child, but she secretly hoped so. For all she loved the ones they had around them she knew how special it was when you had a child of your own. It was the only thing that was missing from her day, it was what the future might offer her.

'We ought to buy a house, you know,' the bridegroom said, ever practical.

'You have your house and I have mine.'

'Exactly.'

'The house opposite Paddy's pub is empty,' Prue said.

'Oh, lovely. You out of bed every night ministering to the drunks.'

'It's part of what I do,' she said. 'It's a nice house, it has a lovely view of the dale and I think you already own it.'

'It's not very big.'

'It's big enough for you and me and Mabel.'

'You're bringing the Alsatian with you?'

'Don't call her that, she can hear you.'

'I need another drink. Would you like one and perhaps Mabel would like a pint?' Rory said, and he went off to the bar.

Acknowledgements

I would like to thank my lovely editor Kathryn Taussig and everyone at Quercus for all their work. For the first time ever one of my audiobooks, *Far from My Father's House*, came out read in a northern male voice. They are putting bold covers on my books and making sure that people out there see them.

Also, as always, my thanks to Judith Murdoch, who has been my agent for over twenty years.